OVER ON THE EAST SIDE

Rachel Gunn

Rachel Gunn

Published by
Chipmunkapublishing
PO Box 6872
Brentwood
Essex CM13 1ZT
United Kingdom

http://www.chipmunkapublishing.com

Chipmunkapublishing gratefully acknowledge the support of Arts Council England.

OVER ON THE EAST SIDE

Dedication

This book is written in memory of my Uncle Eddie who tragically died of leukemia at the age of 7, my Aunt Margie who died of breast cancer, my Aunt Goldie who also died of cancer and was a mother to all, Grandma Evelyn, Grandpa Sam, Grandma Sadie, and Grandpa Joe who tragically was murdered, all such wonderful people who had to undergo such traumatic events in their lives. May we meet again in a higher more peaceful place.

Rachel Gunn

Acknowledgements

Without question my daughters, Ivy and Madeline, my shining stars, my little angels. Thank you for giving me so much joy and love. I will love you forever.

My husband and soulmate, Michael Clark, who has taught me finally the meaning of real love.

My sister, Hannah, who listens to me always and accepts me unconditionally

My parents, Morris and Marge. Thank you for giving me life and teaching me so much.

My stepkids, Mikella & Tyler. Thank you for accepting me with open arms and hearts from the beginning.

My best friend, Kelly, who I have been through so much with. We met years ago and I'll love her forever.
Kelly's mom, Sara, who was like a mom to me and took me in when no one else would.
My dear friend, Sheri, for always helping me and helping me with her big heart.

My friend, Christa, who has always been like a mother to me.

My friends, Dan & Crystal, Linda, Kim & Mike, & Melynn who are always there to lend a ear.

My wonderful fans who always have a kind word when I am attacked for who I am and what I represent.

Finally, a special thank you to Jason Pegler, Mary Dow, and Chipmunka Publishing for making this book possible.

OVER ON THE EAST SIDE

CHAPTER 1

This is not a story about love. Instead it is a tale spun from heartache, inspired by a demented interpretation of humankind. It is a story about a woman, her sweetened illusions of mankind ravished. This story is about me, a pleasantly attractive, intelligent young woman who allows sin to feast upon her soul, until all hope and passion for life is lost. It is about impure visions that intrude upon my mind continually, nibbling away until my brain is a desolate wasteland. It is my rendition of how one's heart, though untainted, faithfully dwells in a world of immortality. My spirit longs to mingle in a realm of righteousness, to sample the delicacies which humanity offers, but instead is conquered by corruption. This is my chronicle of how I alienated every significant person in my life, whomever dabbled in evil, concluding in a lone existence.

My name is Tuesday, a name that is scarce but yet self explanatory in its significance, but to ease any confusion which one may confront, I will clarify. I was born on a Tuesday afternoon at approximately 2:20 p.m. in Cincinnati, Ohio to Jack and Helen Wiseman. My mother and father could not resolve their differences for one afternoon and decide on a name to best suit me. Therefore to identify me the nurse called me Tuesday, and the name has stuck with me ever since. I was born in the year 1975, a year when "Love Will Keep Us Together" by Captain & Tennille reigned number one on the charts. In entertainment, Jaws and the cult classic, the Rocky Horror Picture Show were number one at the box office, and All in the Family and Laveme & Shirley prevailed as the leading shows in prime time television. The Altair, the first home computer, was introduced, a simplified version of today's artificial intelligence. It had no screen, no printer, not one single luxury. The Altair was basically a kit computer you had to assemble for yourself, In the news, President Ford escaped two assassination attempts, the first attempt made by Lynette "Squaky" Fromme, a member of Charles Manson's cult, and the second attempt made by Sara Jane Moore.

An unsettling truth of why I was allowed to emerge from within my mother's womb has shadowed me from the first time my underdeveloped lungs wheezed in the disinfected hospital air. I was a child blessed to be breathing due to being conceived in the appropriate circumstances. Fortunately, I was created by two Jewish parents, married at the time, who were both ready to bring a child into the world. To my mother, these conditions were perfectly acceptable; therefore, she could not deny her offspring. If I would have been conceived in what my mother interpreted as morally wrong circumstances, I would have been aborted as soon as my mother was aware of my existence. Every day I express gratitude to a higher power that I was conceived by a married Jewish couple, or I would not be alive, able to express my story to others. My mother longed to live through me, to thrive through me, to breathe through me, to recapture the animated persona she once possessed. I was going to embody absolute perfection, be the centerpiece that all other parents aspired to bring into being. I would not only be physically flawless but would contain intellectual capabilities superior to all of my peers. My mother tried to mold me, to sculpt me into her version of a mastermind that all other parents would envy. I was to be beautiful, thin, a journalist, mathematician, scientist, inventor, actress, gymnast, dancer, musician, chef, Olympic swimmer, lawyer, doctor, a rabbi's wife cooking huge meals for my congregation, but I did not excel in any of these fields. I was a source of great disappointment for her. In my mother's eyes I was the black sheep of the family, a wicked witch drowning in a sea of filthy morals.

Every time she would look into my face, her scowl translated to me that I represented a painful reminder of what could have been. To her I was only a ghost, a ravaged memory, the nightmarish spawn which she so discreetly tried to tuck away under her pillow. My kind spirit, loving heart, and upstanding values were not of importance to her. I always acted honorably and showed sensitivity to others. I would not even sacrifice the life of an insect for my conscience would not let me inflict such suffering onto another, no matter how insignificant that life appeared to be. In a superficial respect I could be looked upon as a failure, but if one was to explore my center, cradle my spirit, embrace my soul, cuddle my heart, I would not be critiqued for such artificial frivolities. If my mother would cease to scrutinize only the surface and instead delve into my essence, she would be pleasantly surprised, for her firstborn would not have been the failure that she so hastily assumed. This is only a fantasy though. My mother's insides will always be frosted. They will never thaw, and this is a truth which I will someday be forced to accept.

OVER ON THE EAST SIDE

At first it will be quite painful, to realize that I was hatched from a detached heartless mother who never took a sincere interest in getting to know me. Eventually though I will be filled with peace, not having to desperately try to please a mother who will never be satisfied, for my imperfections complete me. These blemishes in my outward appearance and character churned out a unique individual, not conforming to the weaknesses that swirl around me. If only I could appreciate my individuality, celebrate my rare qualities, then I could finally be at peace, but I am blind to what is truly important. Therefore, I will exist as an empty shell, blindfolded and tiptoeing in a shadowy underworld, in search for my soul. If only I could stop criticizing myself and comparing myself to every other girl out there. If I could do that, then maybe my adult relationships could stand a chance to survive and flourish, but how do I even begin to live my life in such a healthy fashion?

I can remember when my eyesight began to worsen in the sixth grade. For months I remained in denial regarding my deteriorating vision. When teachers would call on me in class and ask for me to read something off of the blackboard I would squint my beady little eyes until the blurry chalkboard letters scrambled into something halfway legible. Of course my denial only exacerbated the problem, but I did not want to acknowledge to myself or my mother that I was less than perfect. Eventually I was taken to the school nurse for a vision test where it was confirmed that my need for eyeglasses was inevitable. That day I cried. I shed tears of shame for who I existed to be, tears of regret for who I was about to become, and tears of fear for how disappointed my mother would be in me. When I confessed that day to my mother that I would need eyeglasses, this small deal became a big production. My mother cried, just as I had predicted, regretful of the fact that her daughter would never have perfect vision as she did. Instead her daughter would be forced to wear a massive pair of goggles, be physically branded as a defective specimen. To cheer myself up concerning my new defect, I chose an appealing pearly pink frame, which attractively accented my features, but I still felt less than whole for I had once again saddened my mother.

My little sister, Sarah, had endured a similar crisis at the tender age of four. Until the age of five my sister had not uttered one word. For five years she remained perfectly silent, only expressing herself by crying, whining, or pointing. At times she would attempt to articulate a phrase, but only with a good deal of stammering. My sister lacked the refinement that most children learn from their parents. It was as if she was raised in the woods. She craved strange mixtures of food such as dipping cheese in ketchup. She wiped her feces on the wall creating smelly masterpieces. At the age of four my sister can remember being so excited about a movie that was previewed on a television commercial, "The Pink Panther." Breathlessly, my sister dashed down the long hallway and into the dining room, her sweet chocolate colored curls bouncing up and down as she ran. For at least five minutes my sister tried to tell my mother that a Pink Panther is coming to a theater near you, but it was useless. My mother, patience not being of her greatest virtue, began to frantically scream, frightening Sarah so badly that she climbed under the dining room table to try to find some solace, but my mother could not let it rest. She climbed under that table, remaining on all fours like an impatient dog, insulting my sister by screaming "Are you stupid?"

As a child my mother had also suffered from a speech problem, severely stammering. The children at school teased her mercilessly, which would make her nervous and aggravate the stuttering even further. She carried her speech problem into adulthood and to this day stammers which would cause me to think that she'd be more sympathetic to her own daughter's deficiency, but of course instead my mother was mortified. She marched right over to our family doctor, Dr. Stein, and demanded that he perform all sorts of speech and hearing tests on Sarah until the root of the problem was discovered. That day my little sister was incorrectly diagnosed as being part deaf. My family was torn apart. My mother and I cried for hours while my dad tried to console us. My sister stacked her multicolored wooden blocks, oblivious to our sorrow, and the obstacles she would have to encounter in the future. As time progressed though my sister became more comfortable speaking, and her improper diagnoses of being part deaf was recanted.

I do not understand how my mother developed such unreasonable standards for her daughters to aspire to. Her of all people, should realize how precious life is. Therefore, I would expect her to cherish her children, and be appreciative that we are alive and healthy. After seeing her beloved brother fade away, I cannot understand how she could become preoccupied with such trivial problems.

My Grandma Evelyn and Grandpa Sam gave birth to a baby boy, Eddie, in the year 1940. My grandparents and mother fondly recollect Eddie as being the perfect child, as courageous as any child could be at the age of seven. He was extremely handsome, the spitting image of my grandfather, always defending his little sister's honor in front of the neighborhood kids. I do not know if this deserved praise were exaggerations, since survivors of loved ones usually embellish the character of the dead, but I can imagine that Eddie was as wonderful as my family illustrated. My mother idolized Eddie just as many younger siblings idolize their older sister or brother. Nothing in this world could have prepared my three year old mother to tearfully watch Eddie's casket slowly descend into the ground. My mother could not grasp why her seven year old brother was so tragically snatched away from her. He was so young, fresh, and healthy; the one person in her life who always came to her rescue. What could possibly have justified his disappearance? Why did Eddie of all people have to be infected with Leukemia? My mother might have been a survivor physically but mentally she died that day with Eddie.

Any pleasure or compassion stirring in her soul was lowered into the earth along with his casket, left to be consumed by the worms and maggots. My mother could not make sense of something so unfair. Instead she buried her mourning and grief so deep within herself that it eventually materialized into a tight knot of deadened sensations. Life from that moment on would only present heartache and betrayal. She would never be able to develop a close meaningful relationship with another human being for the intense fear that they too would be taken from her. Every day I struggle to absolve my mother of her shortcomings. I try to forgive her for displaying such insensitivity and instilling such tremendous insecurities within me. To alleviate my rage I imagine her as a three year old girl. I can picture her dressed in black from head to toe, her shiny patent leather shoes twinkling, her glossy black curls pinned back in a felt pillbox hat.

Her ashen skin greatly contrasts her hair and outfit, but compliments her clouded gray almond shaped eyes. She resembles a porcelain china doll, her flawless skin so fragile and her cheeks painted with two pink smudges. Her little hand, adorned with perfectly manicured nails tightly grasps her mother's hand while the other hand firmly clutches her Raggedy Ann doll. The other adults standing amongst her appear passive, unaffected by the gloom among them, but my mother can not conceal her grief. She hysterically wails while her brother lowers into the ground, her tears and grieving the only way to console herself. At the age of three she has not developed faith; therefore her witnessing her beloved brother enter his new home terrifies her. To her he is not soaring into heaven, but tumbling into hell with no angels to protect him, only the cold earth surrounding his casket.

Over the past hundred or so years tragedy has continually prevailed as a leading theme in my family. My father, at the age of two, tragically lost his father. It was the year 1938. My grandmother, Sadie, and grandfather, Joe, lived in Indianapolis, Indiana. My grandfather, Joe, a junkyard dealer, frequently conducted business in Champaign, Illinois. On the evening of March 15, 1938 at approximately 11:00 p.m. Joe called Sadie on the phone. He was at a late night poker game with about five other business associates. Joe seemed unusually downhearted and emotional that evening even beginning to weep when his eldest daughter, Margie, got on the phone. My grandmother could barely understand him with the combined bawling and heavy Russian accent. Never before had he expressed emotion so openly.

I believe that my grandfather had an inkling that that night was going to be the final time that he spoke to his family. My grandfather in his tearful tone professed his love for my grandmother and their three children. Around four hours later, at 2:00 a.m., my grandfather, extremely inebriated, left the poker game, and began to drunkenly wander among the unlit city streets of Champaign. He staggered onto Bell Ave., a quiet residential street lined with several bland box shaped wooden houses squeezed closely together and stumbled upon the front porch of a small white house where he fell asleep on the porch swing. At around four a.m. he was rudely awakened by a blow to his skull by a metal pipe. Apparently two men stole his wallet and repeatedly bashed his skull, crushing it so severely that he became unconscious. For two hours he laid on that porch, dead to the world, his head bleeding profusely. At 6:00 a.m., the owner of the house, a Hungarian woman, opened the door, as she regularly did every morning to retrieve the newspaper and was shocked to find a man bleeding to death on her doorstep. She promptly called the paramedics, who upon arriving at the scene amazingly found that my grandfather was still alive, but their hope was short lived, for sadly he died in the ambulance on the way to the hospital. They never found the culprits that were responsible for my grandfather's murder. It was unfortunate that my grandfather lost his life for a couple of measly dollars.

Naturally, my grandmother was devastated when she learned of her husband's death. Sadie, a Polish immigrant, possessed no skills and had no resources to support herself, or more importantly her three small children. Her only family in town was her brother, Harry, and lately he had been so preoccupied with his new wife, Juanita. Her eldest daughter, Margie, was only four years old. Goldie, the middle child was three, and the baby, my father, Morris, was two.

My father didn't even have a chance to create a visual image of his father. For years he could only imagine what his father had looked like. My father could not find one photograph of Joe that recaptured his essence. When envisioning his father he could only fabricate a fictional character which most likely displayed no similarities to Joe. Growing up as a boy, my father had to compensate for having no father figure in his life. Morris would fantasize about his father being a mythical figure, a firefighter, a policeman, just about any daring man he could imagine. My father would always contain an emptiness within him, a decaying cavity which would never be filled. While the other boys played ball with their dads my father would press his face against the window, wistfully longing for a dad that he could toss a ball with. Looking into the mirror my father would gaze for hours examining his every feature and wondering if he could thank his father for these attributes. In every heroic tale my father contrived my grandfather, though elaborately dressed in colorful costumes, bore the same expressionless face, a doughy lump of skin, a blank canvas which could never be painted. There was not one known fact to quench my father's insatiable thirst for knowledge of his father. He was never made aware of or taken to the burial site to pay his respects, so he never had closure. As far as he was concerned, without witnessing concrete evidence, the murder never transpired. He did not know who or what was culpable for his father's supposed death. Was it the two mysterious men who clobbered him in the head with a steel pipe? Was the alcohol, which prompted him to dazedly wander the streets of Champaign the culprit? My father would never have closure or find an answer to the dream he was chasing. This caused my father to assume an antagonistic attitude, blaming and alienating anyone who assumed an authoritative role in his life.

My poor grandmother could not continue raising three small children with her limited income. Therefore, she was basically forced to put her children into an orphanage. She had no choice. Ironically, father described his years in the orphanage as the happiest in his life. At the orphanage he made many lasting friendships and was provided with some of life's little pleasures that he never had the good fortune to receive before. Just as every worthy thing in his life had been snatched from him this was too. If it was not for the constant disappoint in his life, my father would not have formed such a bitter outlook. Too many times my father had witnessed pleasant well-to-do couples visit the orphanage and express an interest in him only to be rejected in the end. Each time he was cast aside by these couples, memories of his mother having to abandon him would surge back, but at least he still had the orphanage. The orphanage was the only family he had ever known, but the imminent threat of abandonment by this surrogate family always loomed in the distance. While many boys indulged in frivolous fantasies, my father only dreamed of stability. Receiving a candy apple red fire engine or a shiny new bicycle were indulgences that my father found trivial. All he had wanted from the beginning was a family, but it seemed as if this dream would die as soon as it began.

My father's uncle, Harry, due to pressure from his sister, Sadie, had my father and Goldie and Margie live with him in his trailer in Indianapolis.. Harry was a wealthy man who owned a profitable trailer home business. He was married to Juanita and had a stepson, Lou. Juanita was a very domineering woman who was not happy unless she controlled everyone around her. She was very spiteful and extremely envious throwing juvenile temper tantrums if Lou was not put upon a royal throne. Time and time again my father recounted how terrible the summers at Uncle Harry's house had been. Throughout the sweltering summer months Juanita would have the three children pick weeds daily for hours at a time, but Lou would never have to pick weeds or perform the daily chores the other children did. Juanita made sure of this, and Harry was too passive a man in his personal life to do anything about it. As a businessman Harry was a leader, but at home Juanita's conniving ways overpowered his strong demeanor. You would not think that one person's actions could effect the destinies of everyone around them, but somehow everyone that Juanita crossed paths with was emotionally disfigured in some way.

Poor Aunt Margie, her destiny forever tarnished ever since the evening of her father's murder. That night she lost the only man who would ever place her on a pedestal high above any other female in his life. Joseph doted on his adorable doll like no other; not even Morris and Goldie were made a fuss over like Margie was. There was just something special about Joseph's first born, her full head of chocolate cuffs, her wide grin, those chubby crimson cheeks. Margie was his special little angel. That night he died the last person he spoke to was Margie. He cried and cried on the phone, longed so badly to rock his little angel to sleep, to kiss her warm forehead and pat her soft curls. Perhaps deep down inside he knew that Margie would share his fate, brief and heartbreaking, and he felt he needed to protect her.

Margie was a soft spoken gift, gentle and passive, but these were the traits which doomed her, sentenced her to a hell on earth she could not break away from. Her silence; this was her downfall; the beginning of the collapse of her spirit. Silence was not only the downfall of Margie but of woman since the beginning of time. Silence is what enables women to be treated as sex objects and permits men to profit off of womens' sexuality. Silence is what a stripper practices as she smiles for her customers, slaps her naked ass, spreads her legs. The stripper is silent, an otherworldly creature void of emotion and a voice. To men she is only here to gratify their sexual desires and to put man's needs before her own. She is empty, a quality evident in her soulless eyes, but no one cares. In their one-dimensional minds she is only a pussy.

Misfortune was a continual theme in my family. They had all of the necessary ingredients for a great tragedy; murder, drama, heartache, confinement, disease, and eventual death. After the death of my grandfather, Joe, my grandmother, Sadie was lost. She couldn't raise three children by herself, let alone bring them up during the depression. She also suffered from depression which paralyzed her, drained her of any little energy she contained, and unfortunately she passed her depression onto her daughter, Margie. When Morris, Margie, and Goldie were teenagers she decided that the best thing she could do for them would be to have them live with their wealthy uncle, Harry. She possessed great optimism for her children towards the future. Finally, her children, the victims of ill luck would be able to get anything they ever wanted. With her brother, Harry, owing a trailer park lot, she had no doubt in her mind that she was definitely doing the right thing. Harry even promised her that he would take good care of his nieces and nephew, treat them like they were his own children. He did not foresee his wife, Juanita, to resent the children so. She had one son, Lou, from another marriage, and Lou was to be spoiled by Harry or he'd suffer the consequences. Lou terrorized the three siblings, once even holding a gun up to Margie and threatening to shoot her. He had everything he'd ever want, including a promise from Harry that when he was old enough he would be a guaranteed partner in his trailer home business. While Lou loafed around wasting time Morris, Goldie, and Margie were expected to complete a long list of chores, including picking the weeds which surrounded their trailer in the sweltering heat of summer. They were essentially kept as slaves, expected to bow down to their every little whim.

Eventually, Juanita grew tired of housing Morris, Juanita, and Goldie. Therefore, they sent Morris to a military school in Louisville, Kentucky, pushed Goldie out of the house to get a job and live with a roommate, and sent Margie to the well known sanitarium, Central State Hospital, located in the outskirts of Indianapolis. Margie, destined to a hellish fate from the beginning, inherited depression from her mother, Sadie, and unlike now, there was no medicine for depression. Unfortunately, people could be confined to a mental hospital for such minor mental illnesses as depression or even for being handicapped.

Central State Hospital opened its doors in November of 1848. The exterior of Central State might have looked inviting with its elaborate steeples, ornate craftwork, and lush gardens, but inside Central State there was nothing but coldness and misery. Many say that Central State is haunted to this day. There were dark damp dungeons below the hospital grounds crammed with patients wailing for food, air, and daylight. Some of the patients were even restricted by shackles attached to the cold brick walls. The roof leaked, the floors were rotted, patients were forced to sleep on straw mattresses. There was a "dead house" attached to the main building where bodies were stored and prepared for autopsies. Patient abuse had been a recurrent rumor over the centuries, consisting of use of restraints, beatings, and neglect.

The patients' moans can still be heard, especially in one particular area on the grounds behind a cluster of trees where one patient was stoned to death by another. Silhouettes of long gone patients have been seen running into the streets and vanishing in the darkness of the night. Footsteps scuttling across hallway floors can be heard by maintenance workers in the still of the night. Understandingly, the rich history of the Central State Hospital has lingered for decades, but no one had ever delved into the personal history of each patient, such as my aunt and grandmother who were confined there for years.

If Margie would have stood up for herself then perhaps she would not have been confined to Central State during such a critical period of her life - adolescence. Juanita and Harry did not see her as her own father did; an irreplaceable angel. She was only a burden to self-centered Juanita and timid Harry. Yes, Margie did suffer from depression, but she did not deserve to be imprisoned in a sanitarium. Depression did not justify the many electric shock treatments she received. Electric Shock Treatment (EST) was a form of therapy widely used to treat certain psychiatric disorders, particularly major depression. EST did not cure depression though. Instead it only exacerbated it, in addition causing brain damage, memory loss, and diminished intelligence. Patients have burned their skin on the head where the electrodes were placed, broken bones during seizures, committed suicide due to anger brought on from the therapy. The most heartrending element of the electric shock treatment though was how she felt afterwards; those final few disoriented minutes she lay on those crisp white linen sheets in that chilled drab room, the electrodes still plugged into her forehead. She was powerless, likened to an unwanted puppy put to sleep at the pound.

Margie did not deserve to be sterilized, deprived of the gift to reproduce. Because of her sadness and silence they forever marred her, robbed her of the one thing which may have saved her; an angel of her own. Margie was beaten, force fed, basically treated as an animal, and this inhumane treatment would eventually be the cause of her death in her latter years. Margie was basically destroyed upon her release from Central State. The Electric Shock Treatment had slowed her reflexes and caused considerable memory loss. She would have trouble functioning as a self sufficient adult in society. She personified and gave life to the stereotype of the unmarried spinster, destined to a lonely life fulfilled only by her horde of precious cats. Sure, Margie dated a multitude of uniformed officers, got involved with cruel men and many meaningless relationships, but she'd ultimately live by herself in a trailer with eight kittens, her only companionship besides her younger sister Goldie. Out of the three of them Goldie was definitely the strongest. She was resilient, self sufficient, and empowered with strength only to be admired. There was no one like Goldie.

I loved any Aunt Goldie. I remember when I used to visit her as a small child. She doted on me only as an aunt could. I felt safe with her, this towering woman who stood over me at 5'11 ". She not only exuded strength but personified it in every state of the word. With her statuesque frame and strong features nobody crossed Goldie. Goldie had a strong roman nose, jet black hair, and gray beady eyes she'd use to her advantage when she was angry. Yes, Goldie went through her share of tragedy, but it was her faith in the lord and jesus that carried her through the rough times. Goldie had her share of personal failures, including her three futile attempts at marriage, but she didn't let these get her down. Instead she used these disappointments in her life to educate others. Goldie was never at amiss for words. How many times had she made me cry during one of her many lectures on the evils of men. "Men are bad! All they want to do is get down your pants! They'll drug you, kidnap you, take you down to Mexico and sell you for prostitution!" "Yes, Goldie," I'd obediently say as I turned around and rolled my eyes. As a sixteen year old nai've adolescent I did not take her seriously, but as I grew older I could see that she was trying to express her pain through her warnings. She was preaching from the heart.

Her first marriage had ended in divorce. She had married a very nice man. He was faithful, responsible, willing to support her, but he was sterile. Goldie was a very motherly person. She felt she had a purpose in this world; to have children. She liked this man, but she did not love him. She knew what she must do - divorce him.

Her second marriage was not to such a nice man. Jay Shepherd was handsome in a rugged sort of way. He was a country boy, raised on a farm by his grandparents about forty miles south of Indianapolis. Jay was not a tall man, only 5'6" and almost looked like a dwarf when standing next to his towering wife of 5' 1 1". The years had wreaked havoc on him prematurely aging his tan weathered skin. His most obvious flaw though was his missing index finger on his right hand. He'd go to great lengths of hiding it, either stuffing it in his pants pocket or burying it beneath his shirt sleeve. Other times though, such as when Goldie had to push him to look for a job, he'd use his supposed handicap as an excuse. He was nowhere near as supportive as her first husband, but he offered the kind of excitement Goldie had been craving for so long. Goldie did everything. She wholeheartedly raised her two children, Steve and Cindy, performed all the household chores, volunteered for school activities, and now she was going to have to look for a job and support her family also. She found a job at Wonderbread Bakery two miles away from their home. It was an honorable position, good benefits, a decent income, but the conditions were grueling, and the hours were demanding. Every week night she'd stand for twelve hours straight in that hot humid factory packing buns and loaves of bread. Her shift started at 8:00 p.m. and ended at 8:00 a.m. when she'd have to rush home, get the children ready for school, clean the house, prepare dinner for that evening and sneak in just enough time to sleep and get refreshed for the next work night.

Jay watched her slave every day and evening and did nothing. He found it amusing. Instead he only watched television, drank himself into a drunken stupor at the neighborhood bar, or womanized with his friends. Goldie had claimed that her husband had committed adultery many times, but this was never substantiated. I can almost guarantee though that Jay, a drunk who never took his wedding vows seriously, cheated on Goldie many times.

It was one evening though which would alter Goldie's perception of men forever. It started like any other average night in the Shepherd household, Jay cursing because he was out of cigarettes again.

Goldie would patiently listen to his slurred grumbling about how he needed a smoke even though his fingers and teeth were bright yellow. He'd then slam the door which would shake the entire house and cause little Steve and Cindy to run to their mother and hug her leg. Jay would disappear for hours either drinking at the bar or out with one of his girlfriends, and Goldie would finally have some peace, but this night was different. Goldie watched the hands on the wall clock, listened to the ticking as each hour passed by. She prayed to the lord, cupped her hands and pleaded to her savior that the same curse would not be passed onto her husband as her father. She pictured Jay, bloody and battered, his nose broken, his head smashed, strewn out on a neighbor's front porch. What would she tell her children? How would they cope after hearing that their father was murdered? She couldn't bear to have to visit her children in Central State like she did Margie every other Saturday afternoon. She kept the radio and television on to offset the silence and to listen in case there was any breaking news on her husband, but she heard nothing

The next morning she awoke to the Sunrise Centennial landing with a thump on her front porch, but there was no Jay. Many days passed like this, Goldie frantically looking for day care while she worked, taking the kids to school, finding transportation since Jay took the car, but still there was no Jay. Goldie was beside herself. Jay was a lazy no good womanizing drunk, but he was her husband and the father of her children. It was a different time with different values, and people loved to gossip. What would they say about a single mom raising two children after her husband left her?

Goldie faithfully watched the news, read the newspaper, and listened to the radio, but she never did hear or see the headlines JAY SHEPHERD FOUND DEAD ON FRONT PORCH! POLICE SPECULATE HOMICIDE! She was in denial, but in her heart she knew that Jay had left her. He never had the decency to even tell her he was leaving. He bought a pack of cigarettes and was gone, gone from all of their lives. It broke her heart, to have to look her children in the face and tell them where their father was. How would she persuade them that it wasn't their fault when they asked why daddy left them? Jay was not an extremely attentive father, but he had his moments. Little Steve feverishly giggled as Jay would let him swing off his arm, and Cindy would blush brightly whenever Jay called her his "little princess". Every night for two years after Jay left Cindy would stay up till odd hours of the night wailing for her dad. Goldie hated and distrusted men, but she didn't want her children to feel the same way, especially Cindy.

Cindy was only eleven years old, on the brink of adolescence. Amazingly, she had already begun menstruating at the tender age of nine. She was far more developed than her peers, and this bothered Goldie greatly. Goldie tried to keep a close eye on Cindy, but it was extremely difficult to watch her at nights when she worked at the factory. One year later her worst fears were confirmed when a tearful twelve year old Cindy confessed to her mother that she was three months pregnant. Goldie was livid! She cursed Jay until her ears were as pink as a tulip bud, and her forehead was drenched in sweat. Without a proper male role model, a father figure, Goldie knew this was destined to happen. She felt responsible for what had happened. Her daughter was unruly, sneaking out at all hours of the night to be with her boyfriend, Lee. The neighborhood was obsessed with their business, whispering as they walked by. There was nothing subtle about a twelve year old pregnant girl.

Goldie had believed that she had instilled the right values in her children, but premarital sex was not one of them. She was strongly against abortion, and these values transcended in her children. Cindy might still have been a child herself, but she couldn't quell the bulge in her stomach. It was a time of celebration in most women's lives, but Cindy was too young to enjoy it, and the circumstances made it difficult. Cindy loved to sneak into my room when I was an infant, tiptoe up to my crib, pick me up and cradle me in her arms. She loved to nuzzle her nose in my baby soft hair and smell my skin freshly sprinkled in baby powder. When the neighborhood busybodies whispered as she walked by she just tried to remember how much she enjoyed holding me and how much she'd enjoy holding her own baby. She'd shut out their whispers with her thoughts.

Nine months later Cindy gave birth to a healthy bouncing baby boy and named it Lee after the father. She tried to be the best mom she could, but Goldie wound up taking care of that baby. Cindy was just too young.

Goldie worked so hard for forty years, putting in grueling hours at the Wonderbread Factory, raising her two children and grandson alone, taking the children to church every Sunday, and what did she get in return. At the age of sixty-five she died of cervical cancer, lost one hundred pounds, evolved into an emaciated skeleton not even her family could recognize. This was the fate that so many in my family received. Was the cycle going to end?

OVER ON THE EAST SIDE

CHAPTER 2

As a small girl I always felt different from the other children. One could say that I was sexually aware. I am bewildered as to how my comprehension of sexual behavior formed at such a youthful age. My mother and father were both too conservative to sexually educate me. In fact they tried to bury any reference or symbol to sensual pleasures as deeply as they could. I cannot consciously recollect being a victim of sexual abuse. If I was then either I had repressed it, or I was too young to remember. In the late seventies, early eighties, the graphic sexual content on television was kept to a minimum. Therefore I cannot hold television culpable for my early experimentation. There is no rational explanation as to how my sexual wisdom and curiosity bloomed. My appetite for discovery pesters me, the hunger pangs severely interfering with my daily life. If I had a reasonable explanation, some tragic event to neutralize my premature fascination with sexual exploration then my years of feeling like a sinful person could have been avoided.

I cannot explain as to why as early as the age of five I developed such explicitly sexual fantasies. Could my creative imagination have conjured up such demonic visions? One evening, at the tender age office, before falling asleep for the night, I can remember slipping off my cable knit fights, and conjuring up a dirty romance with the devil. At age five, in my distorted mind, I was the devil's mistress. I laid naked on the fire breathing beast as he slithered beneath me, his foul smelling blistered membrane rubbing against my soft powder fresh scented skin. We then waltzed stark naked through a dirty dark dungeon, satan my companion in this sordid dance. I then began to envision muscular oiled men with well-built pectorals. Their bronzed skin glistened as they posed for me. Finally, Woody Woodpecker entered my fantasy. His long well formed beak began to chisel away at my intimate places, invoking pleasurable sensations. I do not know how I found a cartoon character and a feathered creature sexually attractive, but I did.

I could not have conceived of a more wicked symbol to quench my peculiar curiosity for evil. How could a five year old conjure up such adult fantasies? I was not daydreaming about boys my own age. No, my imagination was overflowing with images of muscular oiled men, sexually appealing fowls, and a black hearted figure, a symbolization of all things immoral in this world. I had to be taught about sexuality somewhere, presumably by an adult, but I cannot remember. When I travel to my past my exploration for answers leaves me stranded, searching for some sort of explanation to soothe the confusion within me. If, as a youth, a grown adult somehow took advantage of me, then this could explain my dirty and twisted perspective towards life. The molestation could justify my clouded attitude towards sex and men, could account for my ripened daydreams. I always assumed I was naturally infected by a touch of perversion, that somehow I created these poisonous visions all by myself. My parents avoided discussing sex with me. Their attitude towards sex was strange, going to great lengths to either avoid the subject or become furious and irrational when confronted with it. It was the year 1979. I was four years old, not yet a graduate of my preschool. A friend of mine, a year older than me, Jason Burger, lived a couple of houses away from my apartment building. After using his bathroom and admiring his pink plush carpeted toilet seat, a rarity in the late seventies, we played on his front lawn.

He pulled down his pants and showed me his penis and then asked me to show him my most private of spots. I pulled down my pants and showed him it. I really did not think much of the whole experience that is until I revealed to my parents at the dinner table what had happened. My father was so enraged that he marched directly over to the Burger house to confront Jason's mother. I had thought nothing of it until I blurted out to my parents what we had done. Uneasiness and panic washed over me as I stared down at my fuzzy blue house slippers. We were two small children innocently exploring each others bodies. We hadn't even touched each other inappropriately, but I was made to feel shame for what I had done. We were basically treated as if we were adults, held accountable for engaging in such irresponsible behavior, but I was four years old. I did not know that penises and vaginas were forbidden parts of the body, filthy rotten blemishes hidden from the world. I was not aware of the stigma that accompanied these most private of parts, but from that day on I did. I was taught to believe that this most forbidden spot of mine should fill me with shame and embarrassment.

I was a disgrace for bearing this vile emblem of femininity. This fleshy flap of skin sliced in half disgusted me from that day on. My breasts, my vagina, my behind, almost my entire body repulsed me, especially when unclothed. Therefore I always made sure to cover up as much as I could, to disguise my flesh, and therefore conceal my sexuality. I did not want to be a sexual being. I only wanted to be an innocent child, but I could never be one. I was dirty, and I did not know why.

I only had a baby sitter one time as a child when I was four years old. She was an older woman, perhaps sixty-five or so. I can remember pulling my pants and underwear down and spreading my lips open. I desperately tried to get her attention and show her my private spot, but she remained indifferent. Even at the age of four I had felt so foolish, trying to flaunt my privy parts and being completely disregarded at that. At a very young age I was discovering that people either tried to shun sexuality or developed a great deal of hostility towards it. There was no middle ground, no level of comfort to express one's carnal appetite. Therefore I suppressed that side of me, a natural and normal part no one was supposed to know about. My babysitter must not have been too incensed at my display, because in the morning I found a couple of Tootsie Rolls and packages of Laffy Taffy that she had left me the night before.

By the age of five I was growing more and more ashamed of those parts of me which celebrated my individuality. I was developing an odd phobia concerning my freckles. In the summer months I'd wear long sleeve turtlenecks to school or a sweater to conceal the freckles covering my arms. I cannot remember anyone pointing out these amusing sun specks, but for some absurd reason, they disturbed me. My freckles made me feel vulnerable, like less of a person. Therefore I shrouded them in secrecy, proudly wore long sleeves in the sweltering heat. I noticed that no one elses freckles annoyed them, but this did not matter. I thought that they were the strange ones for embracing their speckled surface. I would tell people that I was afraid of my freckles, and they thought I was an absolute lunatic, but I did not care. As long as my brown splotches were hidden and forgotten from the rest of the world I was happy.

I try to delve into my subconscious, scoop out some significant memory to provide me with peace. I begin to remember a janitor in our building, an older man, probably about sixty-five. He was lanky, his hair sparse, with wire rimmed glasses. He would wear a navy blue mechanics uniform, the sleeves rolled up to his bony elbows. He lived in the building with his wife, a pleasantly plump woman with a thick set of rose colored glasses and thinning hair teased out in several places to give a fuller look. Her graying hair was dyed red, but had a pinkish hue, especially when reflected off the light.

Every day I would bring the janitor a present. Some days I would take a plain white piece of construction paper and create a colorful masterpiece with my box of crayons. Other days I would find a small trinket in my room and deliver it to their apartment. One morning, out of the goodness of my heart, I decided that I was going to give the janitor and his wife my life size plastic vacuum cleaner. I loved my vacuum cleaner, especially the realistic cranking noise it made when I glided it along the carpet. I marched over to the janitor's apartment, excitedly tapped at the door and proudly lifted up the vacuum cleaner when the janitor's wife opened the door telling me she couldn't accept it. I thought she would be flattered, honored to receive my beloved blue plastic vacuum. Dejected and blue, my head down, I pushed the vacuum back to my apartment, into my room, and far back into the closet. I did not want to be reminded that my generous offer was cast aside. I felt so foolish. How could I have gotten so carried away, bringing almost complete strangers a different present every morning? Why was I bringing this old couple who I have no memory of a present every morning? I have no memories of this janitor. I do not even know why I knew where they lived. I do remember playing outside in the courtyard unsupervised every day, pretending that I was being abducted by aliens and dismembering my shiny blue bicycle piece by piece, untwisting every last bolt and screw until a pile of rusty pipes, fasteners, my bluish leather banana seat, white ribbons, and rubbery handlebars laid in the center of the sidewalk. I hunger so badly for some sort of memory, a traumatic tale of abuse to account for my dirty attitude towards sex. Could. I have been exposed to some sort of pornographic material, smutty pictures of abducted Mexican teenagers doped up on narcotics with their legs spread wide open. Could there have been Polaroid pictures taken of me in suggestive poses? Was I forced to behave like a full grown developed adult and engage in sexual acts? Was I violated, touched inappropriately, or forced to fondle a grown man's penis? I needed my past brought to light, to rationalize my present.

OVER ON THE EAST SIDE

At age seven I can remember rummaging thorough my parent's dresser, looking for a small treasure to entertain me for the afternoon. My mother's dresser drawer held dozens of wadded up bundles of flesh colored nylons and fuzzy bootie slippers, a small golden square jewelry pill box decorated with colored rhinestones in a heart shape filled with antique bronze earrings, and a pile of her cotton grandma bleached white underwear. My father, on the other hand, always had a drawer full of the same old boring contents; his brown and black woolen socks, a half dozen torn and stained underwear, and a couple of undershirts.

On one particular afternoon though snooping through his drawer I found something completely different; something which I had never seen. Buried underneath the balled up socks and underwear was a magazine. When I lifted the magazine from out of the drawer, the glossy cover startled me. Emblazoned in blazing yellow bubble lettering was the word, PLAYBOY and situated underneath the word was a topless bleach blonde women with feathered hair saturated with hair spray. Her mouth was slightly open, and her rosy cheeks conveyed a look of sexual gratification. I assumed that the woman was a former Dallas Cowboys cheerleader as she was proudly waving her pom poms and wearing a beige suede cowboy hat and the Dallas Cowboy insignia imprinted on her white thong with turquoise fringes. She looked to be in her late twenties, almost thirty, her tan giving her skin a leathery texture. I first dropped the magazine in disgust. This gallery of nudity belonged to my father, the same man who made me laugh, comforted me, walked me to the candy store. He was supposed to be a virtuous man, incapable of sin, a man not easily influenced by trashy money hungry women spreading their legs open or flashing their breasts. This was my dad. My father was now a stranger, an intruder in our house, a sexual being, not a caretaker. I felt like he was abandoning my mother, giving up on their marriage to ogle these naked women.

I didn't even want to imagine where this magazine had been. Could he have brought it into the bathroom, flirtatiously stared at their oiled buns, their plump breasts as smooth as butter, and their intimate golden thatches. Could he have gratified himself, used the magazine and these unrealistic symbols of perfection to fulfill a missing element in his life? I did not want to think about it anymore. How I wished to lay these troublesome images of my father gaping at these strange women to rest, but I couldn't. My wicked side opened the magazine and began thumbing through the pages. As far as I could remember, I had never been a witness to such vulgarity. The innocence of the world was slowly beginning to fizzle away, my sickly sweet outlook on life dissolving as I turned each page. PLAYBOY was supposed to be one of the more tasteful periodicals, but to my seven year old mind, these pages might of well been emblazoned with images of the devil himself. I flipped to the middle of the magazine and pulled out the centerfold spread. The same platinum blonde as on the cover was sprawled on a tan bearskin rug, her legs stretched out, revealing her shaven mound. Her round breasts balanced perfectly on her chest, her pinkish nipples as flushed as her cheekbones. I neatly folded the centerfold back into the magazine and placed it back underneath his socks, trying to position it perfectly so as not to arouse suspicion from my father. It sickened me that my father was getting aroused by women young enough to be his daughter. Eighteen year olds posed, girls who were still teenagers. These girls had fathers who still thought of them as their little girl, and my father and men older than my father were getting aroused by them. How long would it be before men my father's age found me sexually appealing? How long would it be before my father's little girl induced tingling and erections from men three times her age?

I tried to forget about the PLAYBOY, tried to pretend that my father was untainted, that he and my mother had a romantic relationship void of porn. I pitied my mother, regretful of the fact that my father needed a glossy pictorial to produce pleasure, that he needed to bury his desires among his underwear and socks. I couldn't forget though. Every time I looked at my dad's drawer I was reminded of the nudity concealed within, the stark naked women provocatively posing for the men of America. I could hear the moans from the women inviting me to explore their secretive places. I could hear the pages crinkling up, the enthusiasm in their voices. I could stand it no longer. Softly, I tiptoed to my father's drawer, cautiously opened it, and pulled out the PLAYBOY. I studied each page again, the curiosity within me practically bursting as I once more pulled out the centerfold of the brazen blonde bombshell, but my excitement was short lived. I could hear my mother's footsteps scuttling outside the bedroom door, her house slippers sliding along the slippery floor as she twisted the doorknob to their bedroom. As swiftly as I could I tried to stuff that centerfold back into the magazine and toss it into his drawer, but it was too late. My mother had already caught me. Again, I was filled with shame. I couldn't understand why I was drawn to something which repulsed me, why I was filled with the compulsion to stare at these naked women. I cannot remember my mother's reaction, but I believe she only scolded me a bit. I do not know if it was more upsetting to her to find her daughter reading a PLAYBOY, or that it was hidden in her husband's underwear drawer. I felt like a dirty lesbian, a little girl guilty of exploring grown women's bodies. No, I was not a grown adult, but I felt as if I was, an evil sexually confused seven year old not able to exercise the right amount of self control to shun a PLAYBOY. I did not comprehend that this magazine objectified women, that these women were portrayed to be icons of perfection, airbrushed to appear flawless. All I understood is that it felt dirty to look at these unclad women, that nudity was shameful and should be hidden.

At seven years old I felt I was too knowledgeable about sex, but my angle on the subject was distorted. To be sexual with someone you love is beautiful. To be intimate and share a side of you that is forbidden from others, but I did not see it that way, and to this day I cannot see it that way. To me, sex is only about penetration, about two naked, sweaty, and horny animals humping.

One afternoon, at the age of seven, my four year old sister and I simulated the act of sexual relations. We were both unclothed, one of us pretending that they were the women, the other pretending that they were the man. My mother and father opened the door to the bedroom and discovered what we were doing. They hustled into the room like they were officers of the law, shouting at me to stop. They screamed: "*What are you doing?*" They were mortified, humiliated that their seven year old daughter was experimenting with sexuality. I felt dirty, ashamed, like a child molester. I felt like I needed to atone for my sinful afternoon of indiscretion.

After that dreadful day, my parents never mentioned the incident again. After they scrambled into their bedroom like soldiers on a mission, I slipped my Wonder Women underoos on, my violet knickers, and Looney Toons T-shirt. I began to put together a puzzle. The amount of guilt I felt was stifling. I put together my puzzle, agonizing about how evil I was. I thought I was pregnant, that my stomach would begin to swell in only a matter of months, that I was going to give birth to my sister's baby. I also thought that I was infected with the *A.I.D.S* virus. The previous night I had watched a news story about Rock Hudson, an out of the closet homosexual and movie star of the fifties who got the virus in an age when people were not aware of A.I.D.S and shunned the people who got it like the plague. Imagine a seven year old girl assembling her Bugs Bunny puzzle, searching for the right piece and worrying if she was pregnant or dying of a sexually transmitted disease. My parents instilled the fear of God in me.

They neglected to inform me that I was not a rotten sinner or a perverted child molester. They forgot to let me know that I was not a horrible monster preying on my little sister. No, this was a dirty little family secret. I thought that if only people knew what I had done, they'd abandon me. My friends would cut off contact, my grandparents would think that there was something horribly wrong with me, my teachers would believe that I had some sort of malfunction. If only they knew, I thought. If they only knew what I had done, they'd hate me. If only my parents would have approached it differently, then eleven years of my life could have been redeemed. From the age of seven to eighteen I walked around with this burdensome weight on my shoulders. I did not confess to one human soul about what I had done. I was only seven years old at the time, but in my twisted mind I felt like I should be punished as an adult. By suffering from extreme guilt I was disciplining myself, sentencing myself to eleven years of self inflicted punishment.

The guilt trailed me like a shadow or a mysterious smoky cloud drizzling raindrops of shame and scandal wherever I went. My parents could have told me that I wasn't a bad person, that many sisters and brothers or just children in general engage in sexual experimentation. In fourth grade, while playing on the playground, I had overheard that a girl in our class had done the same thing with her sister. I stayed silent while the girls gossiped about how disgusting the girl was for experimenting with her little sister. This had confirmed my feelings of disgust within. I hid behind a veil of deception, persuasively nodding my head in agreement with the girls, but they did not know that they had just condemned me, sentenced me to an eleven year guilty sentence. I was so impressionable, molding myself to be what others would like or found acceptable. I was just thankful that I did not expose the truth which would have left me leave susceptible to attack.

Plain and simple, I was the product of a dysfunctional family. We were perhaps not any more dysfunctional than any other family, but to say the least we were not as mentally healthy as we should have been. To obtain some normality in my life I would spend the majority of my time at my best friend, Theresa's house. Her family was absolutely perfect. Her father, Larry, a lawyer, was the subdued one of the bunch, always walking their beloved pet bulldog, Brandy. He was the introvert of the family, generally keeping to himself. Carol, her mother, was the most pleasant woman I had ever met. It was just comforting to be in her presence. She was strikingly attractive, lean and tall with dark brown hair. She had a special way of making me feel like I was part of the family.

One afternoon Theresa and I were playing a game of tag on her front driveway. I tumbled to the ground, skinning my knee. Hot tears began to well up in the comer of my left eye as I looked down at my bloody knee, gravel and dirt embedded in the gash. Carol stopped those tears fight away. Unlike my mother she didn't panic. With her soothing voice she reassured me that I would be just fine. She walked me into the house and handed me one of my favorite chocolate bars filled with nuts and caramel that they kept in the freezer. She patted me on the head, indulging my sweet tooth and need for comfort. Carol was the mother I always wanted, and this was the closest I would get. Natasha, Theresa's older sister, was the stereotypical perfect blonde and popular homecoming queen. She never had to try to be popular, because people always flocked to her. Theresa and I loved when she would let us pester her by hanging out with her friends and listening to Duran Duran records in her room. Theresa was my best friend from age seven to age thirteen. Besides her mother and sister she was one of the most composed and well adjusted people I knew. She was one grade higher than me with brownish-red hair and delightful freckles which dotted the bridge of her nose and cheeks. Ironically, I met her on one of the most terrible days of my grammar school career.

Lately, I had gotten in the habit of wetting my bed. I can remember waking up in the morning, sunlight streaming in through the sheer gray curtains. I knew that I had to go to the bathroom, but I was too lazy. I'd lay in my bed, the mildly heated urine dribbling down my legs and soaking the sheets beneath me. I could have laid in the smelly puddle of urine all day if my mom didn't force me to get up for school. After wetting my bed she wouldn't make me take a shower. In fact, I'd go an entire week without taking a shower. Every single morning I'd wet my bed, so this was five to seven days of peeing on myself and not cleaning afterwards. I cannot even imagine the odor emitted from my oily urine clogged pores. The foul smelling excrement clung to my legs creating an uncomfortably sticky surface for my red polyester pants to adhere to. It was not long before the children at school began ridiculing me, squeezing the tip of their noses as I walked by. Their laughter penetrated deep within me as they pointed their fingers and told me that I smelled like piss. My class mates began to keep their distance. I would sit alone at the long orange lunch table, munching on my bland peanut butter sandwich and butter cookies, each wrapped tightly in cellophane, and study my Mork and Mindy lunch box. The cafeteria was swarming with obnoxious children, giggling and pointing, shaping paper airplanes out of their lunch bags and propelling them in my direction. I just continued to nibble on my lunch though washing down the dried peanut butter sandwich and butter cookies with the fruit punch from my thermos.

Theresa had recognized me from a kindergarten tea party a year before. Theresa was not like the other children. She inquired if anyone was sitting at my table and then politely asked if she could sit down. She unwrapped her lunch, offering me one of her milk chocolate Easter eggs wrapped in gold foil. Unlike the other children, she seemed to be immune to the putrid odor of urine radiating from my filthy flesh. That afternoon after school, Theresa invited me to her house. I fell in love with her house and her family immediately. They lived on an affluent block, one of their neighbors the Byer family who owned a museum which had mysteriously burned down years later. Theresa's house was by far the most modest house on the street, but by no means was it shabby. In their backyard was Lake Michigan, tranquil blue waters and sand which they could swim in whenever they wished. The interior of their house was like nothing I had ever seen, enormous picture windows, long corridors, an Oriental carpet splashed with rich colors of Turquoise and Magenta. Their pet bulldog, Brandy, so homely, yet so adorable, with her crinkled neck and freckled fur was the friendly family mascot. Playing with Theresa, meeting her family, and seeing her beautiful house and lakefront made me forget how cruel the kids had been at school earlier that day.

Every day at school I'd excitedly count down the hours until I could play at Theresa's house. She had an impressive collection of Ken and Barbie dolls, a hot pink three story Barbie townhouse complete with elevator and a camper. I grew very envious of her collection, resentful that she owned at least three Ken dolls while I had none. I possessed plenty of Barbie dolls, Barbies with twinkling pink dresses, gaudy diamond earrings, Mexican Barbie, Hawaiian Barbie with a hot pink neon bikini, but no Ken dolls. I became so consumed with my Ken obsession that I sheared off one of my Barbie's platinum locks leaving her with a short spiked do. I tried to overlook the fact that my newly created Barbie had breasts or was not anatomically correct. Each time that Theresa and I played Barbie, I felt a nagging compulsion to engage Barbie and Ken in sexual play, but Theresa had no interest in changing the tone of our innocent childhood game. I would find myself experiencing a strange state of arousal when I peeled off Ken's black leather pants and exposed his tanned rubbery legs and spot where his penis should have been. I would then strip off all of Barbie's clothes and mount Ken on top of her, smacking their atomically incorrect genitalia against each other. Emulating sexual activity through my dolls was a way of relieving myself, an indirect expression of my pent up sexual energy.

As I became a little older though I wanted to explore my sexuality even further. Theresa and I were trying on my mother's clothes, playing dress up as all little girls do. Theresa slipped on a gaudy fur coat and a Russian mink hat. I did not want to play dress up though. I tore off my clothing and tossed it to the floor and began to strut around on the bed.

I flipped the knob of my radio to Madonna, and suggestively pranced from one side of the bed to the other. Theresa basically ignored my dance, not wanting to partake in my game of striptease. I am mystified as to why at the age of nine I'd want to imitate a stripper. I pivoted my hips, my underdeveloped naked frame swirling to Madonna's spicy new single, Like a Virgin. Amazingly, at the age of nine I could visualize my audience, older men with salt-and-pepper hair nursing their bottle of beer. I could feel the men staring at my breasts, my buttocks, my most private of spots. The men, their hardened faces due to exposure to the toxic chemicals at the factory across the street, sat hypnotized by my raw nakedness, the subliminal vulnerability I conveyed by my nude forbidden dance. I imagined that my flattened chest, looking like two bee stings, were round ripened breasts drawing the men into a hypnotic state of arousal. As the song faded, I was transported back into my unripe frame and youthful mind. I felt so ashamed as I hopped off of the bed and slipped my clothes back on. Like all children I remained curious about sex, but my unhealthy attitude was beginning to eat away at my conscience. I felt like I was not developing quickly enough for my thoughts. On one hand, I was impatiently awaiting my development, the moment when I would enter adolescence and begin to blossom. On the other hand, I tried to ignore my evolving body, the slightly swollen protuberances jutting out of my chest, the pubic hair sprouting up, my newly curvaceous thighs. To me, developing into a woman was to be equated to something dirty.

The first time I got my period instead of rejoicing I mourned. I pulled down my underwear to go to the bathroom, and screamed in shock as a nauseating squeamishness overcame me. The center panel of my panties were spotted with blood. I felt so disgusting. I hysterically wept as my eyes remained fixated on my blood soiled underwear. I was now a woman, an unsanitary sexual being ready to give birth at any moment. My mother ran to the bathroom to witness what all of the commotion was about, and surprisingly at this life altering moment, she was supportive. She kissed me on the forehead, wished me congratulations, and informed me that I was now a woman. She then reached into the bathroom closet for a ridiculously large sanitary napkin and handed it to me. I slipped it into the center panel and walked bow legged to my room, where I laid comatose, reflecting on my induction into womanhood.

Theresa and I never discussed that afternoon again. Again, silence seemed to be the response to my naughty behavior. I was filled with shame once again as we waited in line at recess. Theresa was one of the most innocent wholesome girls I knew, and I had. tainted her perception. Even though she never expressed how she felt about that afternoon, how did she really feel? Did she replay the image of me dancing on the bed, stark naked, as she stood there uncomfortable, or did she repress what I had done in order to instill the sweetness and normality back into her fife?

My best friend, in the fourth grade, Jessica, was very different from Theresa. Jessica was very unique looking. With her pale skin and full head of sandy blonde curls, she looked like one of those children displayed on an eighteenth century painting. She appeared almost cherubic with her cloudy blue eyes and ruddy pink cheeks. Jessica and her mother became my second surrogate family. Jessica's mom, Nancy, was one of the most charismatic people I knew. She had such individuality and style infecting those around her with the same enthusiasm she shared in life. Nancy was much younger than my parents, around thirty three, and gorgeous. It was from Nancy, her mom, that Jessica inherited her thick mop of curls. Nancy made clothes and owned a clothing store, naming the store after her daughter, JESSICA.

It was the year 1985, so naturally the clothes she created were quite flamboyant, ranging from sweatshirts with faces sporting painted neon spiked hair and shirts with different pastel colored bandana pieces sewn on. Jessica was always the most stylish dressed girl at school. I loved going to her apartment which was so tastefully decorated. Her mother instilled the same showy theme that she used in designing her clothing line. The walls in the den were covered with life size professional black and white portraits of Jessica sporting her mother's designs. These pictures were used for advertising purposes. The bathroom was colored in only black and white giving it a cold sterile feeling. The tile on the floor was a shiny white color, absolutely spotless. A scale sat in the corner, dark ebony. The shower curtain had black and white stripes, and black and white pictures of women, their faces angular, their hair funky and spiked hung over and across from the toilet. My favorite part of the house though was Jessica's room. Upon walking into the room, you almost felt like you were walking into a game of Candyland with her red and white bold striped bedspread, shiny satin red pillow in the shape of a pair of lips, and gigantic oriental fan hanging on the wall directly above her bed. A breezy lace curtain separated her room from a sunroom which was neatly stacked with dolls, a dollhouse, and various stuffed animals. The entire house was always kept immaculate, cleaned by their Mexican housekeeper, Dora. Dora would always become irritated with Jessica and I, secretly following her around the house, and peeking at her. She'd annoyingly flail her arms, mumbling to herself in Mexican about how terrible of kids we were.

Jessica's parents had recently separated, perhaps to the fact that Jessica's father was much more subdued than her mother. He was a simple and quiet man, thirtysomething, pale with a receding hairline of black hair. He lived in the heart of Chicago, near Wrigley Field, his neighborhood obsessed with baseball. He may have been modest and a conservative, his friends, typical Chicago yuppies driving their shiny black Saabs, but he was not unconnected to his succeeding generations. One evening he took Jessica and I to see Friday the Thirteenth, a horror movie definitely not recommended for two impressionable ten year old girls. Jessica and I excitedly sat, munching on our hot buttered popcorn as the movie began, but ten minutes into the movie, Jessica's father realized that the mature content of the movie outweighed our appetite for fear. After we witnessed a teen couple stripping off their clothes on a picnic blanket in the woods, engaging in sexual relations, and then lynched on a tree by Jason where he tightened a belt around their eyes and popped their eyeballs out, it was time to go. At least he did not try to blame his poor judgment on us, unlike my mother who entirely blamed me, at the age of eight, for taking her and my sister to the movie, Gremlins, tame in comparison to Friday the Thirteenth.

Jessica and I had a very different relationship from Theresa and I. First of all, Jessica might of have had an angelic look about her, dripping an aura of innocence wherever she went, but by no means was she innocent. Theresa brought out my wholesome side, the same sugar sweetened qualities that I displayed in the classroom or with people I didn't know well. Jessica, though, brought out the evil side of my ten year old self.

One early evening, after school, we were playing in the park. We slid down the spiral aluminum slide a couple of times, our hot sticky legs making squeaking noises as they glided down the scorching metal. We watched from a distance, on the bench behind the recreation center, as an older group of boys and girls from our school were talking and skateboarding. For some strange reason, one of the boys, Daniel, a chunky skater, dressed in an alternative punk black T-shirt had left his skateboard unattended and behind the recreation house. I took one look at Jessica, into her devious baby blues and knew right then and there that we were going to hide that skateboard. While the group was preoccupied, skateboarding down ramps in the park, Jessica and I grabbed hold of that skateboard and hid between a wall of the recreation house. We casually strolled over to a mound made out of dirt by a construction crew, and sat on the top of it. Watching Daniel and the others anxiously scramble and look for the skateboard provided great comical relief. We must of sat upon that hill watching them until the sun went down. Daniel never did find his skateboard, and sadly neither Jessica nor I confessed. To be slightly wicked felt sort of nice, to be rebellious and inflict misery upon others felt even nicer, and to be the sole cause of someone's loss of material possessions felt the nicest. So long as my sinning wasn't sexually oriented, then I did not worry, but I would not remain lucky for much longer.

To escape from my dysfunctional household I'd spend at least two to three nights per week at Jessica's house. We would sleep in the same queen size bed, side by side, pretending that we were sisters. On one particular night Jessica decided that she wanted to pretend to have sex, to emulate two grown adults engaging in intimate relations. I was very hesitant to join her in her little game of sexually impersonating a pair of adults. I protested, making it quite clear that I did not want to partake in this fantasy of hers. She was very adamant though, and despite my protestations we began. The guilt I carried on from a few years before began to trickle back into my memory as I stripped off my shirt and pajama bottoms. Jessica did the same and then asked me to climb on top of her. I obediently complied, knowing that if I didn't my commanding friend would make me suffer the consequences the next day. She ordered me to lay on top of her and begin moving back and fourth in a way that we assumed was sexual. I was not very enthusiastic as I rocked my pelvis back and fourth.

Our cold bony chests smacked against each other as I tiresomely moved. Jessica was not pleased with my performance, flaunting the fact that her other best friend, Amy, excitedly humped her and even convincingly moaned. Amy would even talk dirty to Jessica, uttering phrases such as "fuck me" every so often, and she even removed her underwear. I quietly grunted to appease her but kept my underwear on, and that was the extent of it. As I rolled off of Jessica, she belittled me by telling me how boring and monotonous our friendship was, but I did not care. All I could think about was how disgusting I was, a sick twisted pervert somehow finding herself in these sexual circumstances, predominantly lesbian. As I stared into my bowl of colorful fruit loops the next morning, the loops floating to the side of the bowl, I harshly gazed at my reflection in the puddle of milk. If Jessica's mom only knew what we had done the night before, that we had simulated a grown man and woman having sexual relations, that we had imagined that Jessica was a curvaceous big busted woman and I was a hairy muscular man, she would have disowned me as her surrogate daughter. Jessica and I never told another living soul, but when the boys at school cruelly called us lesbians, I was devastated. I must have projected a homosexual vibe which others could detect. I began to imagine that I would transform into a hardened stocky muscular female who preyed on lovely and delicate ladies. Clumps of my rich brown hair would fall to the ground, and platinum spikes would sprout up. From now on I would only wear button up Polo shirts, Khaki pants, and brown boots. In all reality I was still the cute little girl with all effeminate qualities, a girl who loved to dress up, play with dolls, and had crushes on plenty of school boys. If I only realized that I was not a psychopathic sex offender, but a child.

To add to my list of worries, it certainly did not help that none of the boys at school thought I was attractive. I delve into my childhood repeatedly, struggling to pick up the shattered bits and pieces from my past. Many of the pieces have disintegrated by now, but a few have remained intact. It was not until I was eighteen years old that I realized that a seven year old child should not have to carry the weight of the world upon her shoulders. It breaks my heart when I stare into Ivy's face, this small creature, her delicate face splashed with sun specks. She babbles incessantly about Barbie dolls, macaroni and cheese, and Hilary Duff. She is so innocent, her high pitched voice so childish sounding. Was this what I was like at the age of seven? Was I this petite infantile sounding child, not the wicked dirty monster that should be held culpable for all of her wrongs?

Age seven definitely had to be the turning point, the period of my life when the world and the people in it changed. I remember sitting in class celebrating one of my classmates, Sarah Marthaler's, birthday. I could not stop fixating on the glazed lilac butter cookies piled high onto a crystal serving plate and carved into the number seven. Sarah seemed so carefree, no burdensome secrets buried deep within her soul that would alter everyone's opinion of her. She held no uncertainties about who she was, whether she was a sinful lesbian, pregnant, dying of A.I.D.S. Sarah, like most of her classmates, radiated a worriless existence. Like most children her age, she was only preoccupied with the trivialities that a seven year old should. She loved Dr. Seuss books, especially Cat in the Hat and was obsessed with the color purple. She was not contemplating whether she should go back to her father's dresser drawer and dig around for his Playboy.

Not only internally was I straggling with the differences I felt compared to the other children, but externally as well. I was not given the gift of common sense by my parents. This is why I urinated in my bed regularly and failed to bathe every day. This was why I floundered in a self made puddle of guilt for eleven years concerning choices I had made as a child.

From birth until about age eighteen we are supposed to be given the tools to survive by our parents, but to me the world was a frightening place. I'd stay up for hours at night sitting in bed and shivering, envisaging life after a nuclear attack. Visions of babies swaddled in bloody rags, toothless women in doorways muttering nonsense, and dead bodies piled in puddles of vomit occupied my thoughts. Tiptoeing to the bathroom in the dark, I feared squishing cockroaches with the bare soles of my feet or feeling them scuttle in between my toes. I worried about rats living in our toilet bowl and sharks swimming in our bathtub. Footsteps heard on the stairwell prompted me to press my face against the kitchen window and search for burglars.

Ridgeview Mental Home was located only two blocks from our apartment building. The mentally ill roamed Main Street at all times of the day. I'd curiously watch these interesting but frightening persons wander the streets. They were like storybook characters with their peculiar mannerisms and non traditional appearance. There was the man with one eye, a quiet elderly man whose only companions were the books which lined the library's shelves. I'd casually lift my head up while reading at a table and study him, speculating what unimaginable tragedy could have touched this poor man. Was he born with a disfiguring disease? Had he been in a horrible fire? Would God really be that cruel to disfigure a man for life instead of introducing him to the pearly gates of heaven? A sunken cavity was placed where one of his eyes should have been, a smooth gorge blinding this man to half of this world. One of his ears were also missing, a hole the only part remaining in this area. Part of his nose was smashed flat, only one nostril left to smell life's sweetness. He'd wear the same attire every day, a long tan trench coat, white blouse, black pants, and a top hat. I'd feel so sorry for him as he breathed heavily, his face remained buried in the book. His mind had probably been the only place where his adventures lived, and for him reading had been the entryway into a life of adventure. In this library he could slay dragons, romance beautiful women, cradle fearless children in his arms. His literary companions did not judge him or ostracize him for being different. He was not suppressed in any way, free to explore the mysteries which life contained. The fire had not only scarred his outsides but confined him to a prison. The smoldering flames would always hold him back from exploring life, but through reading he could taste the delicacies that life had to offer.

It was not only the people who roamed the streets that we were frightened of, but people who broke into our house. Every Sunday afternoon my parents went grocery shopping, and they gave me the choice to either stay home or accompany them. On one particular Sunday afternoon they gave me a choice, but for some reason I felt like I needed to go. When we got home the front door was bashed in, wooden splinters dotted the floor, and upon entering the house was a mess. Our clothes were strewn everywhere, dresser drawers were left opened, papers were littered everywhere, and most importantly a key to the house was missing. Nothing of real value was stolen, but worse our safety and security was compromised. My father every night slept with a steel pipe under his pillow in case the burglars decided to come back. I thanked the lord that I decided not to stay home that Sunday afternoon. What would have happened if the burglars would have found me in the house. Would I have been raped or even worse killed? I could have been a twelve year old girl who'd have her first taste of sex through force, an innocent little girl bent over and raped from behind forced to bear the truth of the world upon her tiny shoulders. How tragic that would have been!

After the burglary I was consumed with thoughts and fears of the burglars coming back and killing us all. A sixth grader shouldn't have had to worry about intruders coming into her home, shouldn't have had to fret about roaches crawling into her shoes, climbing the stairs of her dollhouse, killing her goldfish, but I did. There was never a time in my childhood when I can remember being totally safe. It is sad, but it's the truth.

CHAPTER 3

I developed an interest in boys long before they noticed me. Let's just say I had not yet blossomed. I was infected with what they call the "ugly duckling syndrome", a condition in which an extremely attractive woman spent her childhood and high school years being unattractive. Therefore, she develops a good personality and warm heart, because that is all she has. She carries this sentiment with her into adulthood, even though she has thrived and flourished into a beautiful woman. This was me even though I still cringe when describing myself as beautiful. As a young girl I was unaware as to how homely I really was, but when I look at pictures of myself as a child and throughout adolescence I am stunned. Who was this girl with the beady brown eyes and the pasty blemished skin, the girl with the kinky permed hair and crooked teeth? I study my class pictures and that naïve look in my eyes. I can remember posing for my class pictures, flashing my crooked teeth to the camera, trying to smile like a Hollywood movie star. I was oblivious to my state of homeliness. When I looked in the mirror I saw nothing wrong, that is until people thoughtlessly made it known to me.

I can not recall the initial incident that sparked my interest in the opposite sex, but scattered bits and pieces occasionally do come to mind. It began in the fourth grade, my hormones bubbling, butterflies aggressively fluttering throughout my belly. As soon as my pencil tapped my notepad I scribbled my passion for the opposite sex, how I loved boys, wanted to kiss them, hold them close, touch them, do every dirty deed imaginable to man. My gawky unripe loins screamed for attention form man, shouted to be stroked and fondled and kissed, but I was not yet a woman, a delicate being with soft skin and supple breasts. My mind developed long before my body and was brimming with all sorts of grown up desires, I'd lie in my bed, staring at the ceiling in the darkness of the night and envision myself as a woman all grown up, seducing hordes of men with my short skirt and bounteous curves. I couldn't wait until any body caught up with my mind.

To the boys at school I was invisible, an indiscernible fleck scattered among the other insignificant crumbs and scraps. Boys had crushes on girls like Lizzie Butterfield, the popular angelic faced heartbreaker with radiant skin, high cheekbones, and transparent golden yellow eyes identical to an imperial topaz stone. I did not contain that magical radiance to lure boys in. They did not care to become acquainted with a pale skinned foul smelling girl with greasy hair who had her nose in books all the time and loved to write essays. The few boys I had crushes on, namely Neil Snow, the borderline albino, or Steven Schecter, the diminutive boy who resembled a crinkled up raisin, rejected me. Therefore, I concluded I was not appealing to the opposite sex. Instead I was an androgynous being floundering in a sea of good-looking starfish.

By junior high I was at my most awkward stage ever. Being tongue-tied and homely was not a recipe for popularity. Acne was sprouting up all over my face, especially my reddened cheeks. My teeth contained gaps wide enough to stick a finger into, and my once slender frame was beginning to chunk up in places. Of course it did not help matters that I bathed only once a week and sprayed my crispy do' so high that I'm sure radio stations could get signals from any hair. I was a prime target for ridicule, especially from the boys at school who stopped at nothing to make me feel like I was the most disgusting creature on this earth.

Continuing to take showers once a week enabled me to be a breeding ground for bacteria, causing my acne to flair up and my black stringy hair to lie limply. It was not until Becky Chapman, the popular other half of the powerful twin twosome, Becky and Vanessa Chapman, inconsiderately hollered at her friends how disgusting my hair looked, and how I needed to take a shower. It was remarkable; how all those years I carried on bathing only once a week when all I needed was to be teased by my peers to shock me into a routine of cleanliness. At the time I was broken hearted, filled with an undesirable amount of hate, ready to ground popular little Becky's face into the cold tile floor, but I was too cowardly. Instead I made sure to shampoo my hair every night, condition those ebony tresses, scrub every section of my body until my skin squeaked and my hair shined. Never again was I told that I smell or look dirty, except for Carl, my boyfriend. Carl reaffirmed my feelings of dirtiness, how I needed to douche my stinky pussy and scrub my hairy armpits.

Unfortunately, my new and improved hygiene habits didn't coax the popular kids to accept me or the boys to trip over their shoelaces as I passed by. Instead, I remained a favorite object of ridicule for the most popular boys. My band partner, Greg Myers, was the most obnoxious of them all, not to mention Matthew Swanson, Aaron Marnstein, and Jeff Pogany. Every day after school, as I attempted to peacefully walk home, they'd relentlessly hound me, sarcastically screaming "I love you", "You're so beautiful!" Finally, I just became so fed up with the teasing that I screamed "bitch" at them, which of course brought about more childish mockery from the boys. Mortified, I ran into my lobby only to be backed into a corner by Matthew Swanson, the cute sandy haired Swedish boy I had a crush on for a year. I should've kicked him in the nuts, struggled to be let free, something, but I did nothing. I meekly cowered, begging to be let free while he coldly laughed and spit in my face. I couldn't take it anymore! Why couldn't I be like the popular girls, the girls that boys like Matthew Swanson and Greg Myers swooned over, a girl they'd excitedly pull into the closet during one of their weekly spin the bottle games. No, I was a joke; a self-conscious, spineless, four eyed, pizza faced drip.

Band was the fourth and most dreaded period of the day. Each and every fourth period Greg Myers basically tortured me. He'd vary his torture session every day to make it less monotonous, one day stating at me like I was the most nauseating creature on earth, the next day telling me how gross the volcanic whitehead sandwiched between the crease of my nose was . Instead of pummeling his puny little face like I should have I put up with it. I tried to ignore his teasing by playing my clarinet or staring at the wall, but inside I was dying. My sense of self worth was slowly being chipped away by this obnoxious brat who I am sure was suffering from the Napoleon Complex. He was an inch shorter than me, and bear in mind that I was only five feet tall. Some days he didn't even need new material to come up with, such as days that I collapsed in my folding chair, falling back and provoking laughter and drum rolls from the band. The most peculiar factor of this story though is that I secretly held a crush on this dweeb, a secret which was a little more noticeable than I thought.

You see, Greg could be the nastiest little twerp, but other days he could be the most polite and sweetest boy imaginable. It was on those days that I felt like the most special girl, pretty, thin, popular, the complete magical package all rolled into one. I am not sure what clued Greg or his friends into believing that I liked him. Perhaps it was the lingering stares or the glazed over look in my eyes, or possibly it could have been the high pitched giggle when he joked around or the never ending grin plastered on my face. Whatever it could have been didn't matter. What did matter was that his friends teased me about it on the walk home from school. They yelled "YOU LIKE GREG!" like it was the most hysterical joke ever. Why was it so amusing that I liked Greg? Why couldn't I invoke tingles of pleasure in these boys, hold the same amount of magnitude as the popular girls. Instead I was the laughing stock, an insignificant paltry gremlin with a big pointy nose, bad skin, and beady eyes. I was livid, upset with how transparent my feelings were to other people. If Suzanne Bouvair or Vanessa Chapman would have liked Greg, he and his friends would be thrilled, slapping each other on the back, giving high fives. All I could do was lie in my bed and cry, feel the hot tears gush down my cheeks. I wanted revenge so badly, but a girl with no sense of worth could not defend herself.

Discouraged and mortified I set my sights on older men, men in the eighth grade. Seventh grade was a year of new beginnings for me, a year of self discovery. It was the late eighties, a period of rebellion for not only me but for many other kids around America. It was the beginning of heavy metal, a new culture phenomenon that introduced bands such as Poison, Twisted Sister and Gun N' Roses. Rotem and I became obsessed with heavy metal quickly. We loved the long haired babes, the glamorous outfits, the heavy eyeliner, but most of all we just loved the music. We could relate to these pop idols that screamed their angry lyrics into the microphone. Through their songs they protested parents, school, and laws. Rotem and I soaked up every aspect of pop metal culture. We ripped our jeans and scribbled Poison all over them, wore band t-shirts and bandanas, read heavy metal magazines, watched Headbangers Ball every Saturday night, covered our bedroom walls with pictures of our favorite hard rock idols. My parents went crazy when they discovered my latest hobby. They became fanatical extremists on a mission to save my satanic soul. They tore down every poster that covered my wall hoping that would cool my fascination with the devil's music, but it didn't. It only prompted me to rebel as all teenagers do.

There was a group of boys at school, Lee Wasserman, Leo

Levkovski, Mike Polocki, and Jeff Sneidelman who exemplified heavy metal perfectly. They were the bad boys at school, the rotten seeds with bad attitude and long hair that you'd never want to bring home to your parents. Rotem and I became infatuated with them, especially Lee and Leo. With his golden tanned skin, long auburn locks, and chestnut colored eyes, Lee Wasserman was the most gorgeous one out of the group. Leo, with his shaggy hair, big nose, and pale skin was more of the less attractive sidekick, but he was mysterious, and I loved mystery. I believe Leo began a new chapter in my life, the bad boy phase. After Leo there would not be one boy that would turn my head who didn't smoke, drink, or break the law. Rotem and I never technically spoke to Lee or Leo, but our green imaginations would create fairy-tale fantasies which satisfied our overactive hormones for the time being. So much as a teeny look from them would provoke riotous laughter or excited jumping and encourage us to either follow them or harass them with prank calls. They were the victims of our unwelcome advances one afternoon when we spotted them at Old Orchard Shopping Center and stalked them for hours hollering obnoxious compliments like "Nice Ass!"

At the time we had concocted this idealistic fantasy, a sweetened delusion of ours which was not based on reality. We really believed that Lee and Leo liked us, but when I look back on it now I realize that they were the victims of two delusional teenage girls. We were so desperate for attention from the opposite sex, once even painting our phone numbers on our t-shirts and calling a radio station and begging them to put our phone number on the air. How desperate! My friend told me that some day boys would be lined up at my door wailing to see me, but I just didn't believe it.

It wasn't only the boys that validated my feelings of worthlessness, but my own friends also. Rotem had been my best friend since the sixth grade. Upon first impression, Rotem seemed like a sweet quiet foreign girl, but upon closer examination Rotem was a sinister conniving bitch. With her warm brown skin tone, coal colored hair, strong accent, and thick bushy eyebrows Rotem could have passed for Arab, but she was Israeli. Rotem and I were inseparable. We walked everywhere together, wore the same outfits many days, babysat, stayed up all hours of the night talking on the phone about boys. I would have never guessed that my best friend would have become my worst enemy.

OVER ON THE EAST SIDE

I am uncertain as to what initiated Rotem's hatred for me, which brain cells shifted in order for her to treat me like I was some sort of diseased animal. I really do not understand how a human being could be quite so cruel to another. The most ironic part of the story though is that she couldn't accomplish her nasty deeds by her lonesome. No, she had to have an accomplice to help her achieve her dastardly exploits. Michelle Oertel was Rotem's co-conspirator in this heartless ordeal. Michelle Oertel shouldn't have been so willing to gang up against me, but like a hound dog she could sniff weakness a mile away. She had no logical reason to pick on me, only the possibility of making herself feel better by attacking someone weaker than she.

Both Rotem and Michelle decided to make my life a living hell, at least a living hell to a teenager. It might not have been as devastating to a girl more sure of herself, but to me it was a nightmare. They completely ignored me and whispered amongst each other how I had thunder thighs. I admit I did look slightly plump in my tight polyester gym shorts digging into any pudgy flesh, but I was at an awkward stage in my life.

I felt so lost without Michelle or Rotem. At one point I got down on my hands and knees, folded my hands, and begged Michelle to take me back as my friend. All she could say though was *nope*, but I didn't want to take no as an answer. I skinned my knees as they quickly traveled across the cold tile of the gym locker room, as I pleaded for her to be my friend again. How pathetic! They had such control, and I didn't think enough of myself to preserve my self worth, but it was their actions at a sleepover party that I really took to heart even to this day.

A friend of mine, Hillary Weiss, had invited me to a sleepover party, an event I had been excited about for weeks. The awful part though was that Rotem and Michelle were going to be there. Emotionally, I was a very frail girl, but I decided to gather up what little strength I had and decided to attend the sleepover. It was difficult to ignore the continuous whispering of Michelle and Rotem while I sat on the other side of the room, but I tried. Their whispering was only a small taste of what I would receive later that night.

Both Rotem and Michelle asked me to follow them up to the bedroom where they would be waiting to talk to me. Foolishly, I thought they desired to make up, apologize for all their wrongs, but they didn't. Instead they maliciously insulted me: **"You're ugly, No boys will ever like you, All the boys talk about how ugly you are and how you wear your make-up funny!"** To this day I take those words with me wherever I may be. Unlike a stronger person, I took every filthy word they spit out of their mouth to heart. The voices began to swirl around me reaffirming what I had always thought. **"You're ugly! You're fat! No boys will like you!"** Their insults whirled through my eardrums, traveled down my throat finally entering my heart. They began to nibble away at my center until I could no longer stand it. I got up from off the end and ran down the stairs, wailing like a baby. I took to heart everything they said about me, how I was fat, ugly, how no boys would like me. The rest of the girls at the party stuck up for me, but that didn't help. I didn't stand up for myself, and this is what I should've done.

For the longest time I believed Rotem and Michelle. I'd stare for hours in the mirror criticizing my every flaw, picking at every pimple, cursing myself. Rotem and Michelle have a lot to do with how I feel about myself to this day. I don't care how many men are knocking at my door. I'll always feel like that insecure teenager at the slumber party, running down the stairs, arms flailing, tears streaming down my cheeks, taking every word they said to heart. Those words ate at my heart, nibbled every artery until it was a veinless lump of nothing. Thank you Rotem and Michelle.

OVER ON THE EAST SIDE

Who are my enemies? Who should I hold responsible for my diminishing sense of self-worth? Should I point the finger at society for brainwashing us, by subliminally convincing us that we should succumb to their ideas of beauty? They feed our hungry minds with stereotypical standards of what is considered beautiful. Young is beautiful! Thin is beautiful! Big breasts are beautiful! Blonde is beautiful! Tall is beautiful! We surrender to these notions, fill them with life, give them meaning. We cannot turn the pages of a magazine or watch television without being bombarded with this idealistic imagery. Billboards, posters, movies, music videos: All of these methods of marketing broadcast unattainable standards of beauty. Men assume that women are supposed to be perfect and are expected to resemble our rivals, the airbrushed embodiments of perfection splashed on glossy magazine pictorials. Therefore to appease them we dash to the nearest drug store to find that miraculous shade of lipstick or sprint to the mall to search for that amazing outfit that will make us look like a supermodel.

I am most passionate about this issue, but I too, like so many others are a product of this dysfunctional culture. Though my words convey strength and preach individuality, my actions reveal different. I am a fraud. I am society's next victim. I strive for perfection each and every day. While I preach to others that they are beautiful and perfect just the way they are, I squirm with revulsion as I glance upon my naked breasts in the mirror. I eagerly pour through beauty magazines searching for a life changing miracle and secretly hating the models that promote them. I scour the malls wasting my money on fads that will go out of style by next season. I compromise my sense of uniqueness by desperately trying to look like everyone else. I hide behind my boring brown eyes with sea blue contacts. I give in to the belief that blondes have more fun by coloring my chocolate brown mane a lemony yellow. I wear a water bra to enhance my less than ample bosom. I exercise like a maniac for fear of becoming obese. I am also a slave to society's way of thinking, grappling with issues such as plastic surgery to make others notice me.

Fads materialize out of nowhere and then vanish just as quickly. Each era introduces a new obsession impossible to attain without some sort of sacrifice. In the eighteen hundreds the rounded shape was celebrated. Plump women were the subjects of colorful masterpieces, their curves beautifully translated into works of art. In the Victorian age it was no longer in style to look healthy. Therefore women restrained themselves from the joys in life by strapping themselves into corsets to cinch their waists until they had that sought after hourglass shape. In the nineteen twenties women bandaged their breasts and cut their hair trying to pull off the boyish silhouette that was so in style. In the sixties Twiggy hit the runways making the undernourished look so sought after. The seventies though; this was the decade that changed everything. From this moment women would strive to be perfect and do anything to achieve this goal. The supermodels were anything but boyish. Women and men alike were obsessed with Farrah Faucet, Christie Brinkley, Cheryl Tiegs, and therefore the California blonde was born.

To have that bottled blonde, golden tanned, long legged look was in, and culture's acceptance of these qualities unfortunately excluded women who were different. For example, look at the popular seventies show Three's Company. Chrissie, the dense bubbly blonde, was adored by America while Janet, the intelligent serious brunette was ignored. It was not trendy to be intellectual, brunette or flat. The cosmetic surgery craze began. It was no longer acceptable to age gracefully. Breast size increased every year presenting the message once again that what we are given by God is not beautiful. I face this dilemma every morning as I slip my shirt off and look into the mirror. My shapeless breasts sadden me, how the elasticity of the skin has loosened, how my areolas hide underneath each breast instead of perkily pointing upwards. My breasts are not necessarily tiny, but they droop, and that is not good enough for me. My natural mammories are looked down upon, unlike the artificial helium inflated goodies swollen with silicone. If only those simple people from the eighteen hundreds could witness this craze, how saline bags are implanted into breasts, how time can be reversed with facelifts, how people can lose fat with liposuction. They would think, "What a crazy warped society, how these people are so obsessed with appearance!"

I'll never be that California girl, the Pamela Anderson bombshell women aspire to be and men dream about. I could tan until my skin is toasted brown and can be peeled off like the skin of a chicken, exercise until I collapse, bleach my hair until clumps fall out, inject my boobs with helium until they explode. I will never be Pamela Anderson or any blonde bimbo for that matter. I mourn for my failure as a woman to project sexiness, to entice men with my breasts, my baby blues, my rounded ass. I mourn for my daughters, for their uncertainties about who they are, about their lack of self-confidence. I wish they could see themselves as I do, how special they are, how beautiful, how precious. I only wish I could perceive myself in this way, through a mother's eyes, cradle my inner child. I wish I could travel back in time and sit down at that lunch table with that lonely little girl, the girl who knew that she smelled like pee but did not know why, the girl who watched all of the other children eat together while she sat alone. I'd ask that little girl her name, why she looked so sad, why no other children sat by her. I'd tell her that she is beautiful and that it is not her fault that she smelled like pee. I'd tell her that I love her and that I will always be there for her, that she can always rely on me. Then I'd hug her. I'd wrap my arms around her and squeeze her like her own mother never did, and she'd finally feel what it was like to be loved and nurtured. As I write this I realize that this is exactly what I do to my kids. I will look over at my kids and for some reason feel terribly sorry for them, perhaps they conveyed a sorrowful expression. I cannot bear to see them hurt. Therefore, I'll make an effort to hug them or say I love you. This enables both my children and I to free ourselves of this pain.

I've never comforted my inner child. In fact I've neglected her terribly. I have cursed her, degraded her, constantly reiterated the message that she is not good enough. I have never protected her from the abuse, emotionally and physically. She must be frightened to death, cowering in the corner afraid of life. Until I enable my inner child to heal, she will never grow. I will take her to my death, to my grave, and into the heavens for all eternity.

Lately, I've framed a picture of me as a beaming toddler and set it beside my bed. This way I never forget that I was once my daughters, as small and innocent and precious as they are. I was once that chubby faced adorable toddler with dimples widely grinning for the camera. I once placed my faith in two people, my mother and father, and had no comprehension that some day I would be an orphan, not literally, but emotionally.

I can remember when I was in the advanced stages of Rosacea. Acne and red patches covered my entire face. I'd stare into the mirror for hours examining each bump and how inflamed my skin looked. My forehead, nose, cheeks and chin would remain flushed for hours. Sections of my skin would swell causing lumps to form. I'd pray for hours, damning my luck. I was lost as to why this happened to me. Every day I'd scour through beauty magazines snipping pictures of girls with clear perfect skin. I creatively arranged them into a photo album creating a sort of collage I could refer to when my skin condition intensified. I'd gaze at the pictures and daydream, fantasize about how one day I'd have clear creamy skin.

From the moment of conception until the day that we say goodbye to our parents we are damned. They create this recipe, a formula for who we are going to be, and for the remainder of our lives we are to fix those mistakes. My father added the sugar and flour to the mixture. My mother poured in the chocolate chips, the vanilla, the egg, the baking soda, but it was as if they both forgot to mix the batter. I contained all of the primary ingredients, but I was not well blended enough to create a batch. Without surgery we are not able to alter our physical traits, but we can change our physical ones. I had to reinvent myself, nurture and care for my soul as others never had.

I despised myself, hated both my character and my appearance. I detested my black hair, beady brown eyes, hook nose, acne, and thunder thighs. I loathed almost every feature that God gave me. I had to change in order to live with myself. Otherwise I'd try to take my own life, destroy myself for all eternity. I was tired of looking out at the world through my boring brown eyes. I wanted vivid blue ones; eyes as translucent as the skies above, and my dull brown hair; I needed shiny golden tresses, hair as yellow as yolk that I could teasingly toss and wrap around my finger. My skin exhausted me; my large pores, the red spots. Milky clear skin is what I wished for, and how I hated my body; how short and chubby I was. I was the antithesis of the American sex symbol. I needed men to walk into walls when they saw me, be so transfixed by my beauty that they remain speechless. Why couldn't I be that sort of girl?

At the age of sixteen I was friends with a girl named Patty. I loved

OVER ON THE EAST SIDE

Patty! She was quirky and caring and easy to talk to; at times flaky, but other times serious. Patty was sort of the Goldie Hawn type, blonde, beautiful, flaky, but intelligent. The horrible troth though was that I hated being her friend. It seemed that men were hypnotized by her, spellbound by her bubbly character and bleached hair. She'd dress in white leather mini skirts, cropped fringe jackets and high heels. To this day I cringe when I think about how we'd all be standing in a group and I'd hear guys talk about how "hot" the one in white was. Comments such as that was enough to make me shrivel up and die. I thought that somewhere there would be a man who would love me for me and not be as shallow as all of these other men out there. Did all men only want breasts and a body and blonde hair? Did guys even care about the face? There were many flaws about Patty that I could pick out if I wanted to be catty. She had horse teeth, her chin was much smaller than it should have been, she was too thin, but the more I put down Patty in my mind, the more guys she got. The sailors would always ask,"who's your friend? That is a good looking woman!" In in the meantime I was standing there, so taken aback that I was nearly speechless. If she was a good looking woman, what was I? Why was I constantly supplied with the message that I was not good enough? I tried not to compare myself to her, but it was extremely difficult, considering every man that passed us stared or tried to talk to her. The flattery was never-ending, so horrible that it caused Katt to run into the bathroom, bawling and muttering nonsense that she was ugly. Katt was a very pretty girl, blue eyes, blonde hair, an attractive figure. She had absolutely nothing to cry about, but this superficiality was killing her. There was nothing that made us feel uglier than a friend who won all of the men's attention.

Patty hid a dark side though, a part she let only her closest friends see. Patty was an obese child that miraculously shed her baby fat. Her father and mother had been divorced for years. Patty's little brother had once chased her around the house with a knife, finally stabbing her in the back. He spent a year of his life in the county mental hospital, something Patty felt terrible about for years. She lost her virginity to her longtime boyfriend, Todd. They didn't have a condom. Therefore they used a plastic baggie. Todd's father tried to make the moves on her while Todd had been sleeping, and Patty wound up having to push him off of her. Patty didn't think of herself as beautiful. Instead she cursed herself for being so irresistible to men, and secretly I cursed her also.

As cliche as it may sound, we were to put it, plain and simple, sailor groupies. To a doe eyed fifteen year old girl this new world was glamorous; older men, limousine rides, hotels, on a better night the penthouse suite. We received the royal treatment, were treated like a queen in this world limited of any sign feminine. We knew everybody. For once in my life I was popular. Those simpletons in my school had no conception of reality. I was part of the real world; dating real men, drinking, partying.

While most fifteen year olds could be found scouring the malls, going to the movies, attending homecoming dances I was encountering a whole new world. The problem was that I was unprepared. I bore no shield. My insides were visible and vulnerable and accessible to anyone who could manipulate them. When a tree is chopped into half one can discover the age of the tree by inspecting the tree trunk. This process is called dendrocinonology. The number of growth rings present on the surface determines the age. I had very few rings inside me. I was one of the ripe trees, undeveloped, new to the world. I was surrounded by massive weeping willows, giant oaks, sturdy elms, their trunks broad and expansive. Then there was I, a tiny insignificant tree, its leaves still blooming, growing alongside the others. Physically I was developing. My breasts were blossoming, my hips were curvier, pubic hair had sprouted, but inside I was still a child. When confronted regarding my youthfulness I became angry and resentful, insisting that I was an adult, fully developed in every essential area. I had no conception of what it truly meant to be an adult, but I would learn soon.

To think that McDonalds could be the centerpiece of one's existence sounds absurd, but it was. Every Friday and Saturday night Rock 'N Roll McDonalds was the gathering spot for teens and young adults alike. Crowds of young people entertained themselves in the parking lot, and others circled their cars around the building showing them off and performing all sorts of car acrobatics. Inside was even more spectacular. Miniature jukeboxes sat at every table, fifties memorabilia lined the wails and dangled from the ceilings. Florescent neon lights framed the Elvis and Marilyn photographs. Fifties and sixties music blared from the loudspeakers placed in the corner of each room.

The place was always packed. Kids stood anywhere they could, outside the building at the round tables, in the parking lot, at the booths and tables inside. The only drawback was the ridiculously overpriced food, but that didn't matter because most people didn't go to Rock 'N Roll McDonalds to eat. They went there to have fun. It wasn't actually McDonalds that excited me though. It was what passed through and around it every Friday and Saturday evening. The first moment I laid my eyes on these identically dressed service men marching towards us I thought I was dreaming. This massive cluster in their dress whites and black ties, sailor hats propped among each of their heads was surreal. I had never seen sailors in person before, only in the movies, and usually only the classics.

We had our own little soap opera with its own revolving cast of characters, Katt, Big Rachel, Stephanie, Becky, Patty, Liz, Melynne, Cathy, Jennifer, Gloria, Amanda, Janet, and the U.S. Navy. I had found a family, a group of girls who didn't judge me, call me uncivilized or a slut.

What I didn't realize was that I was still a little girl tossed into a heartless world of adults. While most fifteen year old girls discovered excitement in dances and high school boys, I stumbled upon mine in hotel parties, limousines, and sailors. The first time I set my eyes upon those seamen fully clad in their dress whites, I knew in my heart that this was where I wanted to be. There must have been a hundred of them banded together, not walking further than an inch apart. High school boys had never expressed an interest in me, but older men in the military fighting for their country. This was an adventure. The world was mine for the taking, and I was going to grab it by its coat tails. Through my doe eyes the world was sugar coated. I perceived only the sweetness in people and was blind to the bitterness which inhabited their souls.

Most of the uniformed sailors that walked the streets of Chicago were fresh out of boot camp, Ricky Recruits they were nicknamed by the civilian dressed sailors. I loved the booters. They were always in good spirits, grateful to have graduated from the hellish confines of boot camp. They were always ready to party and drink, and I loved to soak in their enthusiasm and genuine appreciation for the things we take for granted. I almost felt that through the sailors I was going back in time. While most men dressed in the latest hip hop fads, blasted their rap music, shouted obscenities to scantily clad women, sailors remained a world apart. Their timeless uniforms exuded an elegance lost on our generation. They most always held the door open for us and called us maam instead of baby. Through sailors I felt like I had traveled the country. I could be talking to a sailor from New York and then instantly be transported to the south when his buddy from Louisiana stepped into the conversation.

My parents were not at all thrilled with my new hobby. They held a much more cynical perspective of sailors, the sex, the drinking, the girls waiting at every port. Understandably, they did not want me to just be one of those girls pining away in the background while her love sailed the high seas. They wanted more for me, and I was too immature to realize this. I had no aspirations, no plans for the future. I thought that I could mature through the eyes of another, be coddled by a protector, but I was so naive, blinded by my youth and fearless of the dangers which lurked in the near distance. I thought I was invincible. I hopped into cars with total strangers, spent nights with groups of sailors in hotel rooms, rode around in limousines with sometimes almost twenty sailors. I was shielded by my naivety. I could have easily been raped or killed, but someone was protecting me. I don't know why or how, but there must have been a guardian angel traveling by my side throughout my journey. I needed my life to be anything but ordinary. I dreaded the monotony of a normal day, had to spice up my life with drama and romance. I even discovered that tragedy was pleasurable compared to the tediousness of everyday life.

It was difficult to keep my new thrilling life a secret from my parents, especially at the beginning when they were my only mode of transportation for traveling to downtown Chicago. On one occasion they witnessed me squeezing out of a limo crammed with sailors, and that was just about enough. Because of that incident and my parents toughening up, I devised various plans on sneaking out of the house and to hang out with the sailors. Sometimes I'd lie and say I was babysitting, then ride the train and bus to Chicago. On one particular occasion my friend and I even rented a limousine and had him drop us off at Rock 'N Roll McDonalds. It started out as Rotem, my best friend, and I. Rotem, a native of Israel, loved the attention from the sailors almost as much as I did. On our second trip we met a sailor, Jason, newly graduated from boot camp. With a crew cut, the blonde stubble beginning to show, mad his lanky build, he was moderately cute, but that uniform made all the difference. Like so many of the sailors he expressed his nostalgia for home, reflecting on family and the good old times and drowning himself in alcohol. He passed us two bottles of lemon chilled wine coolers, our first introduction to alcohol and how adult we felt as we sipped the intoxicating blend. Grown men, fancy hotel rooms, alcohol; it is all we could have hoped for and more. That is, until he threw up, spewing out a thick chunky stream of projectile vomit. Drinking was just never the same after that.

I didn't bare the hardened view I presently have regarding men. Sailors were like children to me, caring and impressionable beings far away from home, just searching for something familiar. They were lost little boys, and I was there to take care of them. What I neglected to do though in the meantime was take care of myself.

Every day I was drifting further and further away from my family. The sailors and a new group of girls had become my new family unit. Rotem had disappeared, not literally, but from my life. She had thought I was uncivilized. Actually, her choice of words was a slut. I prefer to believe that she was just jealous, because I received more attention. Girls are so catty. My new family was composed of Big Rachel, Katt, Stephanie, and Becky, a group of girls who lacked family structure and loved the sailor scene as much as I did.

I had met all of these girls at Rock 'N Roll McDonalds. Big Rachel, sixteen, was the ringleader, but extremely venomous. Her innocent looks and sweet as a peach Georgia accent deceived all who crossed her path. She possessed this heart shaped face, pale ivory skin, big brown eyes, and she had this sweet southern drawl that melted the sailors' hearts. At age fifteen I was a weakling. I had not developed a real sense of self worth. I had absolutely no confidence in myself, and I let others order me around. Big Rachel took great pleasure in dragging me around by the arm, grabbing me by my shirt collar, throwing solid objects at me such as the telephone. Basically she dragged me around like a rag doll scolding me like a child when I didn't behave to her satisfaction.

Katt, fifteen, a petite pretty blonde, emanated innocence and intelligence. Katt was an honor student and took great pride in the fact that she never placed her lips upon another. From the start Katt and I shared a deep connection. We certainly shared the same sense of humor and dislike of Big Rachel which bonded us even further. Katt possessed delicate features with her sea blue eyes, small straight nose, and slim pink lips.

Stephanie, eighteen, was the mother of our new surrogate family. She nurtured us, protected us, gave us advice when we were in need. She was like the big sister we never had. Unfortunately though, Stephanie was often put down for her weight. I was aware of the whispers and stares as she'd walk by dressed in her leopard mini skirt, but like her, I tried to ignore it. She didn't care what others thought, and that was what was so beautiful about her. Stephanie, by no means, was a homely girl. In fact she was striking with her bright aqua eyes which changed with her moods and milky flawless complexion. She could have been compared to one of the great beauties of our time, Elizabeth Taylor. Stephanie's chestnut brown hair framed her movie star good looks perfectly. She was absolute perfection. It was just a shame that people could not overlook the weight issue. Stephanie was definitely the wisest of the group. She taught us about things we had never even heard of. As a matter of fact she boasted about her lovers and built up this mysterious facade of how experienced she was. She taught us about how she did flying Hawaiian (sticking his penis between her breasts to emulate sex) with her sailor boyfriend Matt.

Becky Passman, sixteen, could have easily passed for a twelve year old. She had the mind of an adolescent but her body and face lacked the maturity of a fully grown adult. She was about 4' 11" tall with sandy blonde hair and thick rimmed glasses. Her complexion was baby smooth. I don't think she ever had even one pimple, and she didn't grow body hair. She never had to shave her legs. In fact she was on special medicine to get her period. I loved Becky, the comedian of the group. She was always cheerful infecting us with her optimism. She never fooled around with a lot of the sailors but instead chose a select few. Sad to say the sailors made her look comical when they were with her, very mismatched, as if they were dating a child. One episode extremely disturbed me regarding her and a sailor named Chad.

Chad and Becky had been fooling around earlier in the evening. Becky had to leave for curfew at twelve o' clock, and we were all smashed into my friend, Melynne's car. What disgusted me greatly was that Chad asked his friend if his fingers smelled. I was so disgusted!

I was only fifteen years old, but practically everyone I associated with was older than I. Therefore, I became accustomed to a more grown-up way of life. Stephanie was a student at Columbia College, a local art school in Chicago. She lived in the dorms located on the corner of Clark Street. These dorms were filled with artsy college students struggling to be recognized and establish themselves as artists, whether that be painter, actor, photographer, dancer. These young people craved to be noticed, and it was obvious by their choice of makeup and dress. Stephanie's closest friend at Columbia, Julie, was a four hundred pound lesbian who only dressed in black, powdered her face white, and painted her lips black. Her hair was black as ebony and shaved on one side. Her other friends consisted of Kate, a pretty twenty year old with long blonde tresses and delicate pale skin who always talked in a breathy voice and had a boyfriend with one testicle and Mary, her roommate, a snobbish dance major who detested all of Stephanie's friends, including me. She basically assumed we were bimbos only interested in screwing sailors. We found ourselves continually defending our reputation. Hanging out with sailors every weekend was staining our sugary sweet image. We were not whores as everyone insisted though. We were only looking for love in that one perfect guy. We just didn't realize the incredible heartache we would suffer as a result. Sailors did not want to commit. They were only looking for a short fling until they left and traveled to their next port.

Stephanie, being the only legal adult of the group, was overwhelmed with responsibility. She became our surrogate mother providing us with a second home, wiping away our tears when we were dumped, spending money on us and providing us with meals. She had been the daughter of an air force officer that died in a plane crash, and therefore she received money every month as a dependent. She was the only role model we had at that time seeing that we rejected our parents. Stephanie influenced us to believe that it was acceptable to sleep around with different sailors. She loved to have fun, and this left little time for school and other activities, hence I dropped out of school shortly thereafter.

Men were plentiful, and I had my choice of many. New Years Eve was the night I had my first kiss, a quick peck on the cheek by Jimmy from Kentucky. Jimmy was shy and quiet, fresh out of boot camp. He was not traditionally handsome with his bushy eyebrows and reddish brown hair but was considerably sweet, a real gentleman from the south. He had ridden into the city from Great Lakes Naval Base on the party bus, a luxury coach that transported the sailors from the base to Downtown Chicago. It always stood on the same corner, Clark and Wabash, and usually left to go back to base at 1:00 a.m. There were many nights spent on the party bus by the girls and me.

Jamie, a dark haired sailor from Boston, was the second sailor I had met. By this time I was dressing more provocatively, black thigh high stockings with a short skirt outfit. I could have passed for a prostitute, but I didn't care. I lavished the attention I got from dressing slutty, even if it attracted the wrong men. That night the girls told me that they overheard Jamie saying he was going to get a piece of ass. I had no idea what they meant. My unseasoned mind assumed he was talking about wanting a piece of pie. I mistook his sexual cravings as flattery and rewarded him with only a kiss on the lips but then became heartbroken when I never heard from him again. I could not understand why these men made no effort to keep in touch. Didn't they miss me as much as I missed them? I was becoming quite used to seeing their face one last time as they waved from the party bus.

Saying goodbye to these first few men in my life hurt, but I had never really felt genuine heartache until James Ludwig. With James I could taste the misery. He was not an ordinary man to me but an icon. He symbolized all I wanted in a man. Of course I overlooked how he let Big Rachel sit on his lap and how their tongues tangled as they joined together in a kiss in the back seat. These were minor setbacks in my infantile mind. His hormones may have been stimulated by Big Rachel's overt actions, but our minds were connected. We were soul mates. We walked by the Chicago River holding hands, me slightly shivering as he wrapped his strong arms around my small body infusing me with a sense of warmth I never felt before. His exquisite features were arranged perfectly, almost magical. My stomach fluttered each time we touched. Only one day together, and I was in love. Saying goodbye we engaged in one enchanted kiss, not obnoxiously trashy like his and Big Rachels, but innocent, like a mother that spoils her baby with tender smooches. He obviously felt the same way, considering he wrote me a note the following night and had his friend deliver it. As I unwrapped the folded up note scribbled on notebook paper, I became overwhelmed with both joy and grief. It stated how special our evening together was, and it urged me to keep in touch, listing his address in Florida. *"This is for James!"* I screamed at a group of sailors, slamming my head onto the table and weeping for the one I loved. I was excessively dramatic, pronouncing my love for another in front of the entire Rock 'N Roll McDonalds, but I wasn't concerned about making a scene. My intentions were to spread my sorrow around the room, infect others with my despair. I held no concept of how foolish I appeared so I just let it out, let my tears wash away my garish makeup. I sent James a letter, scribbling all my fears, declaring my love for him, threatening suicide if I never saw him again. Adolescent angst over a boy; it was insane, but I bathed myself in the misery of it all, scrubbed the aches away until I was numb and ready to move on to another man.

Wayne Moler; this was the next man I wasted my energies on. Wayne was also exceptionally handsome; tall, tan, rich brown eyes which complimented his chocolate brown hair perfectly. For some odd reason he singled me out, romanced me with his penetrating stare, spoiled me with the attention I craved so badly. We went to the movies, shared a buttered tub of popcorn, and for the first time I felt my heart jump as his greasy hands fondled my perky breast. We rode in a limo all the way back to base where he got a hotel. This was the last and only time we had sex, a bland experience I might add. He crawled on top of me, doing missionary position, humping me like a sick dog until he satisfied himself. We ate breakfast with his best friend and his girlfriend. I finally felt like a normal couple, but I was unaware that this was the last time I would see him. Two weeks later I ran into Wayne's friend who notified me that Wayne had been cavorting with another girl, Monique. He had brought her onto base, let her into his cozy confines of the gunners mate building where she played pool with the sailors. I hated this new temptress, this seductress tempting Wayne with her beauty and brilliance. Who did she think she was? Wayne was mine! Did the special night we spent together mean anything to him? I waited for a phone call, a letter, a visit, anything to let me know that I was not forgotten. I sipped on Jewish cooking wine in my room, wallowing in my grief, listening to *Total Eclipse of the Heart* over and over until the tape wore out and the words ran together making Bonnie Tyler sound like she was slurring.

My father knocked and knocked on the door. He could not imagine what could be wrong with a sixteen year old girl. What could possibly be so tragic in a teenager's world? I got drunk on Jewish cooking wine, sitting in the dark singing sad songs. Wayne was my savior, the cutest man alive, my soul mate. How could he do this to me, toss me to the side like rubbish. I was more than that to him, so I thought, but I wasn't shit.

For three years I continued the cycle. I fooled around with at least fifty sailors, some I got to know well, some I didn't. I was used bad, but I grew strong from all of these experiences. I bore a pathway of heartache which each sailor happily stomped on. Every time my heart broke a piece crumbled, but each piece grew back. Like a starfish it regenerated. Like a starfish that didn't use their muscles, I didn't use my heart. A starfish clings to a rock using an intake valve while I clung to each sailor with hopes and dreams that were never fulfilled and eventually like a starfish I was washed away by the tide wandering the salty seas in search of my rock.

OVER ON THE EAST SIDE

CHAPTER 5

If anyone expects me to embrace man they are truly mistaken for I will never accept one of these hairy insensitive creatures as my own. Man has disappointed me time and time again. In times of need man has deserted me. At times in my life when I have desperately clung to life, man has dismissed me. When I have doubted intentions, man has attacked me. No individual man will revolutionize the entire race, for man is unconquerable. Man will triumph over woman for all eternity.

I have been exploited by man, chewed like a wad of bubble gum and spit out shortly thereafter. Yes, traveling from one sailor to another was titillating, but the anticipation was far more stimulating than the outcome. Should I be held responsible for how man manipulated me and then tossed me to the side like moldy leftovers. Because of man I have no identity. Because of man I have no heart. Should I be held accountable for the fact that I had fooled around with more than fifty men by my eighteenth birthday, or did an impressionable young girl such as I not know any better. Could it have been construed as more than coincidental that four of my first sexual encounters occurred in the short span of two weekends, and that two of these men were best friends? I was bubbling with naivete, exuding this raw aroma, my insides rare and pinkish in color, and man sniffed my juicy red meat from miles away. Can I justify why man nibbled and bit at my skin until bloody juices rose to the surface. Do I have a good explanation as for why I boasted about the fact that I had eleven hickeys spread all over my body from four different men, why wine colored bruises decorated my chest and neck. Can I defend my actions as to when I describe the circumstances that surrounded these affairs? Does it sound almost as naughty when written on paper as when it is running through my mind?

I squirm in revulsion when I remember it all, how I abandoned my beliefs, sin-rendering them to fit in and feel accepted. I can remember how my first kiss took place in a cheap hotel room on a snowy night packed with seven people, how I was drunk on orange juice and vodka dry humping a sailor topless, how he sucked and twisted my nipples when all I wanted was to be with was his best friend.

I can dredge up unwelcome memories of the first time a man went down my pants, how dirty I felt as he roughly fingered me, jabbing at my insides until they ached. I wanted to scream STOP, but my lips froze, and I surrendered. I parted with my body as his head moved under the covers and in between my thighs, as he began to greedily lap at my vagina. Tightly shutting my eyes did not remove my feelings of uncertainty, how I doubted if I even liked this individual, how his huge head oddly resembled a giant pumpkin, how an orgasmic wave washed over my body as he continued to lick. How disgusting I felt, how I could engage in intimate acts and remain emotionally uninvolved with the person. I didn't even know what had happened, why pleasurable sensations swirled through my intimate spot, why it still throbbed, the drumming pulse still evident. I had had my first orgasm, but instead of cherishing the moment I fled, hopped out of that bed and speedily put on my pants, scurried out of the darkness into the familiar hallway, and I cried. I rolled into a tight little ball and wept, mourning such loss of innocence. I did not even know this man that ate me out let alone like him. I only let him do these things to me because he wanted to, and I thought it was cool to act like a slut. I didn't respect my body enough to guard it, shield it from the famished wolves that lurked.

Feelings of shame wash over me as I think of Lee Yarber, that charming sailor with the thick southern accent. I was supposed to be on a double date with his friend, Mike, while my friend, Big Rachel, was with Anthony. Mike was useless to me though. He failed to stir passionate sensations within me. The first time I laid eyes on Lee I knew I had to have him. What my inexperienced mind did not think about though was how I'd only have these men for one night. I planted myself on Lee's lap while Mike reluctantly chauffeured us around. Lee's hands wandered, groping my breasts and eventually ending up in my pants. Mike parked and pretended to fall asleep as Lee and I crassly kissed and fondled each other, and then the night was over. While I romanticized about Lee, imagining how grand life would be with him, he had already forgotten about me. Like so many others I had just become attached too quickly.

Jeff, the final fling, was the original boy who had peaked my interest only a few weeks earlier, but little was I aware that he was bitter about my night with Dave. Dave and Jeff had plotted a revenge plan behind my back. Jeff was going to use me, play with my body and then abandon me so I'd feel as shitty as he did. We kissed and he fingered me in Big Rachel's dark bedroom and of course he added a hickey or two to my collection, and as soon as he felt that he had used me enough he strangely became distant and hailed a ride back to the base. I did not grasp the reality of it all, how men were using me for their own selfish purposes and then disposing of me like a piece of trash. To them I was human waste, a pile of feces they'd stomp on. I was the girl they'd fool around with and then brag to their friends about. I was not the type of girl they'd marry or keep around. I was an anonymous face and body, my heart and soul irrelevant in their adolescent diversion. Luckily, at that stage of my life I was not scarred yet. I was too lighthearted to understand the implication of it all. I look back at that same girl with pity, but she did not feel sonic for herself. To her it was amusing, a game of how many hickeys she could get and by how many different guys. Those eleven purple bruises scattered over her breasts, her neck, her shoulders were her badges, emblems she could proudly show off to anyone that would listen. She finally felt like a woman.

I was not taught to deal with heartbreak as most teenage girls were, to slowly pick up the shattered pieces of my fractured heart and hurl myself into sports or painting or schoolwork. Instead my girlfriends taught me to get over a guy by getting another one, and this is exactly what I did. No one man could break my heart for long. I was not about to grant them the satisfaction. Each sailor was another notch in the bedpost. I actually carved their names in the back of my closet door, excitedly adding to the list almost every weekend.

Two weeks after Jim Mauritzen, the catastrophic world changing event of my life, I fooled around with a sailor named Dave. We walked to the river, arm in arm, and I sat on his lap as he fondled my breasts and fingered me. As a souvenir for the evening I compensated him with my brazier, which he discreetly tucked into his rain coat pocket. I felt so much better having sacrificed my body to yet another sailor. In my twisted little mind Jim Mauritzen had no longer won. I had literally given a piece of myself to someone else. "How special could Jim have really been?" I thought.

You see, to sailors we represented the unattainable. In their predominantly masculine culture civilian girls were a rarity, a gourmet delicacy with our long flowing tresses, soft young bodies, and fragile features. The sailors that had just gotten out of boot camp were the worst. These "Ricky Recruits" as they called them were only in boot camp for eight weeks, but it was as if they had been locked up in a prison for a decade. Eight weeks had completely transformed these men, trained them to be identical by shaving their heads and having them wear uniforms. They were brainwashed to be part of a cult and abandon individuality. Generally what the NAVY had done was they broke each sailor down and then built them up to be just like each other. The booters hungered desperately for a woman, to smell and taste their sweet skin. They'd catcall at practically anything that walked by, cleverly yelling metaphoric phrases such as *"Make a hole"* when a woman had to walk through a crowd of them. Certain sailors respected women, calling us maam and apologizing for their rowdy shipmates, but others were sexually starved bundles of hormones. On one particular occasion whispers circulated the McDonalds as a sailor was witnessed entering a back alley with a well known black prostitute that loitered Clark Street every weekend, and sure enough twenty minutes later the same sailor ran back to his friends and boasted about how the hooker gave him a blow job for $20.00. On other occasions a small group of sailors would be seen leaving Puss 'N Boots, a local strip club on Clark Street. I was a sixteen year old girl who did not understand the impact that strip clubs would have on me later in life, but my friends and I still had a shallow understanding of these places as we'd quietly utter *"pervert"* as the sailors exiting Puss 'N Boots strolled by.

Carl had told me that sailors were responsible for starting the strip club craze, but I did not want to believe it. How could these men who had brought me such laughter, joy, and memories be the object of my hatred, the culprit of such exploitation? Naval life was so exciting and glamorous, tempting to a group of teenage girls bored with high school life.

Two weeks later Melynne, Katt, and I had been hanging out at Sing Has, a Thai restaurant/bar that specialized in serving minors. There were three places we'd drive by and check out before going inside, Sing Ha's, Tommy's, another local bar, and Rock N' Roll McDonalds. Most likely on a Friday or Saturday night a group of sailors could be seen gathering in front of the picture window and merrily celebrating their graduation from boot camp. I loved walking into Sing Ha's, past the string of sailors sitting on their barstools, each slowly turning their heads as I walked by.

On one particular Sunday afternoon Melynne, Cathy, Katt, and I decided to try our luck and drive past Sing Ha's. Surely enough a group of sailors could be seen jovially drinking and toasting each other. It was the end of the summer, a bitter chill in the air, unusual for this time of the year, but they still wore their dress whites. The girls and I casually strolled into the bar, taking a seat at a table against the wall. Despite our efforts not to appear obvious, it was not long before we had the entire bar full of sailors kissing our feet. One sailor, in particular, intrigued me. His name was Jimmy Kimball, and he was from Flint, Michigan. I would not say that he was traditionally handsome, but he possessed this indescribable sex appeal. He reminded me of that actor, Sean Penn, only with darker hair, less pronounced features, and an amazingly droll sense of humor. The one quality that attracted him to me most though was his ego. This is what set him apart from that room full of sailors, that he presented a challenge. On that eventful Sunday afternoon I had made it a point in my mind that I was going to get that man, and what I wanted I always got. We teased him, calling him the "Hunk", flattering attention which he gobbled up.

The sailors in Sing Ha's were becoming quite rowdy, severely annoying the Thai wait staff, who told them to quiet down. The sailors failed to obey, taking no notice of a gentleman complaining who sat nearby. Instead they chanted what sounded like a name of one of their shipmates; *Fritz, Fritz, Fritz* while they banged their fists on the table and bar in unison while the bartender poured 1 ½ ounces of 151 proof rum and 8 ounces lager into a shot glass. He than poured a beer into a mug about two thirds full. "Hunk" leaned ever and whispered in my ear that the drink was a flaming orgasm which was a drink wherein one lights the shot, drops the shot glass into the mug and then drinks. They say the flame is supposed to improve the taste if it is done properly, meaning one is supposed to heat the liquor in the spoon first and steadily hold the spoon while the vaporized alcohol collects above the spoon allowing the alcohol fumes to be lit. The flaming alcohol is then to be poured. They say not to hold your head close to the spoon which might have been what Fritz did, because as soon as he lit the drink, the entire front of this body and the table burst into flames, brilliant hues of blue and orange blazing. The entire restaurant went into panic mode as the fire continued to spread. Customers rose from their seats to inspect the commotion. The staff panicked, running around in circles and squawking like a chicken with its head cut off. Some of the more inebriated sailors inappropriately cheered while his closer friends stomped the fire out with the surrounding napkins until the last flame disappeared.

The sailors were scolded by the wait staff, and the manager finally asked them to leave, unfortunately causing us to say our goodbyes for the evening. I hated goodbyes. I do not think that anyone had to say more goodbyes than I. The "Hunk" tipped his hat and gently grabbed my hand to kiss it, saying 'maaaybe I'll see you around." My heart sank. *"Maybe I'll see you around."* What was that all about? We had shared a moment. We had chemistry, and all he could say to express the moment was *"maybe I'll see you around."* I watched the sailors fade away into the distance, looking like little action toy figurines small boys played war with. All I could do was daydream and hope that I'd run into him the following weekend. The boys were only in town so long before they were shipped to their home base. That night I squirmed in my bed silently screaming out for *"Hunk"*. My adolescent hormones were energetically dancing desperate to find an outlet for their frustration. I wanted the *"hunk"* bad!

Sure enough, like in my dreams, the following weekend I ran into the *"Hunk."* I acted casual, remaining aloof as not to arouse suspicion that I was secretly in love with him already. Hunk and his friend were in need of a ride back to the base, and who was more willing to give them a ride but my friend, Cathy, a cute bubbly Chinese girl who I had grown close to. Cathy, a pretty oriental girl with a heart shaped face, creamy skin, and reddish-brown hair, the color of fall leaves, spoke with a gentleness and babyish tone of a child. Hunk's friend, Tim, was interested in Cathy, so it had worked out perfectly. On the ride back to the base, Tim sat in the front seat with Cathy while I sat in the back seat with *"hunk"*. After all those nights of dreaming about this man, he was sitting right next to me! I wanted the car ride to last forever, me and "hunk" in the back seat of a Chevrolet. His intentions were not as innocent though. Jimmy was not daydreaming about our future, the 2.2 children, the white picket fence. No, Jimmy was only thinking about one thing, and that was sex.

"Hunk" placed his hand under my blazer and began to squeeze my velvety breasts. He aggressively tweaked nay nipples while I looked out the window at the scenery passing by. At times he pinched my nipples so hard that they stung, but I ignored their throbbing as I shut my eyes. I finally turned my head whereupon he planted a kiss on my lips. Our tongues joined together as one and began to salsa, our electricity fogging up the windows. We were oblivious to the passengers in the front seat as he pawed my breasts and slipped his hand underneath my skirt.

His fingers slowly crept up my leg like a spider inching it's way up a web. Like every other inconsiderate sailor he thrust his finger into my vagina. His boldness surprised me, but I didn't protest. I never took pleasure in these sessions of groping, fondling, mauling. In my dreams I never imagined that I'd be his sexual toy, an object of his sexual frustration. No one ever had the courtesy to ask if they could put their hand down my pants or play with my breasts, but I guess that is not something you ask for, huh? I was too weak to say no, to express how sickened I was by their selfishness, how they only pleased themselves for their own damn gratification. I worshipped the "Hunk. I had built him up to be this glorified individual. I had characterized him to be the perfect man, my knight in shining armor, but he was nothing as I had thought. I was in love with his outside, that superficial shell used to deceive young naive gifts such as myself. I was a hundred steps ahead of where he was.

We finally arrived at the Great Lakes Train Station parking lot. Cathy and Tim got out of the car and walked over the railroad tracks towards a row of bushes. I assumed they were going to have sex. Apparently that was why we were all there. Jimmy and I remained in the back seat. Being a chilly night Cathy had left the car running and the radio playing, the only noise to break the uncomfortable silence between us. We were two strangers that knew practically nothing about each other about to engage in a deeply personal act with one another. The hunk cleared his throat of phlegm and began to kiss me again, gently pushing me down so I laid my back flat on the seat. I stared at the ceiling, focusing on the car light in the center of the roof of the car, while he unbuckled his belt, unbuttoned his pants and pulled a condom out of his pocket. He tore the silver wrapper with his teeth and slipped the condom on his penis, climbed on top of me and guided his penis into my vagina with his hand. I squirmed in pain as he coldheartedly thrust his penis into me. Silently, I prayed that Cathy and Tim would not come back to the car and see Jimmy's rear end rhythmically bouncing off of me. The only sound I heard was the wind whishing outside the window. I searched "Hunk's" face for some sort of expression, hopefully one of warmth, but there was nothing, only a frosty look in his eye. I had had sex with him in hopes of getting closet, but I had never felt so distant from anyone.

For two more minutes, in evenly spaced intervals, he continued to pump into me until he climaxed, where upon he suddenly pounded more rapidly until he exploded, his semen gushing forth like a waterfall into the protective rubber. Jimmy, the only one breathless, laid silently upon me as he recovered, pulled off his condom, and than buttoned up his pants and buckled his belt. Awkwardly, we sat, speechless, unable to vocally respond to what we had just done. He picked up the slick rubbery sheath he had laid on the seat and reached for the rearview mirror tying the condom to it. It limply dangled from the mirror, swinging from side to side, the semen swishing.

"You know, you could have moved a little during sex, gotten more into it." He said.

I was humiliated! How experienced did this man think that a sixteen year old girl was. He had came. He got what he wanted. Now he had to critique my performance and display his cum for the world to see. I was beginning to come to the realization that hunk and I were not going to end up happily ever after.

Cathy and Tim ran back to the car and quickly pecked each other on the lips signaling that the night was about to come to a close. "Hunk" placed his lips on me one more time and then shook my hand.

"I suppose I'll see you around sometime" was all he said. How fulfilling, fucking a sailor that just got out of boot camp so that he could brag to all his friends. When Cathy and I made it back to McDonalds we headed to the brass coin machine where I typed in the inscription: *"I fucked hunk and I loved it."* What a joke! I should have put that on the coin.

OVER ON THE EAST SIDE

I ached for weeks afterward. Through my daydreams I had developed a fictitious love affair. As I sat in my room I'd listen to a song by Nightranger which eerily described our night together perfectly and still brings a tear to my eye.

What do you do when it's falling apart
And you knew it was gone from the very start Do you close your eyes and dream about me A girl in love with a gleam in her eyeI was a younger boy all dressed in white
We're older now, do you still think about me
I remember we learned about love in the back of a Chevrolet Well, it felt so good to be young, feels like yesterday Or (No good for an old memory to mean so much today) When you close your eyes do you dream about me When you close your eyes do you dream about me Do you still dream about me

My guess is no.

CHAPTER 6

We knew everyone, the limo drivers, the McDonald employees, all the kids who hung out there, all of the sailors. The limo drivers would actually use us to lure sailors into their limousines. This strategy boosted their profits, not to mention the handful of pretty girls was an additional benefit of offering a limo ride. We never thought of ourselves as prostitutes, per se, but that is exactly what we were; objects being sold for a cost. These girls became my family. We banded together, a group of rebellious teenagers with one thing in common: We all came from dysfunctional households.

Big Rachel had been my first friend that in my new surrogate family. We called her Big Rachel, because she towered over me by about seven inches. She was 5'9". I was 5'2". I met her the week before New Years Eve in the bathroom at Rock 'N Roll McDonalds. From my first impression of her I did not think of her as overly pretty girl. Yes, she was tall, a trait admired by society and the fashion industry, but her face struck me as average. She had a lovely heart shaped face, but her skin was heavily oiled. She had translucent brown eyes, as brown and clear as a glass of tea. I could tell she was glowing from excitement, her cheeks pinkish. She radiated innocence, but in all reality was manipulative, scheming, and wicked.

Big Rachel originated from Georgia, obvious from the southern twang she tried to emulate whenever she met anyone from Georgia. She wasn't like Chicagoans or any Midwesterner for that matter. Instead she deceived others into thinking she was a down home southern girl. Big Rachel was the first girl who persuaded me to act like a slut, but a minute later she'd turn around and tell me that I was acting like a whore and embarrassing her. Only minutes before fooling around with Dave Herman, the amateur boxer, I was shocked to see Big Rachel pop out from under the covers, topless, her less than voluminous breasts flapping against her chest. I was disgusted, but at the same time was pressured to imitate her. She was a role model to me. Sadly, I looked up to Big Rachel, so much that I'd lose myself in the process. Big Rachel had found just what she wanted in me, a feeble puppy dog she could mold and train to be her mirror image. When she had found me I was a damp chunk of clay, someone she could mold and sculpt, creating a twisted self made prodigy only she could have power over. I idolized Rachel and soon became her best friend, a title which Rachel eagerly appointed me as the second that we were together. I obediently followed Rachel as she'd literally drag me or lift me by my shirt collar if I didn't obey her wishes. Now when I think back on it I cringe in shame; how I allowed another human being to demean me, to physically assault me like I was a nobody. I was not handed the tools that were necessary to survive in this corrupt world. My parents never taught me how to stand up to people, to be my own person. All I considered was that I had finally been accepted by a clique. I finally felt popular.

Big Rachel might have acted like an angel to her school mates, embodying that she was a straight A student. Amazingly, she was the valedictorian of her Senior class. Big Rachel harbored secrets though, skeletons in her closet that would alter everyone's perception of her. In confidence she told Katt and I that her stepfather, Jay, allegedly was a homosexual, that five years ago he had had a sex change and that his mother loved him regardless of sexual orientation. This family secret had devastated Big Rachel, a deeply disturbed girl trying to masquerade as an all American sweetheart. What would her boyfriends think of her if they knew that Rachel's "daddy" was really a woman? Big Rachel had also neglected to inform us of her violent past, an episode of insanity that her mother openly discussed with Katt's mother. The family secret of Rachel's step dad being a post operative transsexual disturbed her so deeply that in a moment of madness Rachel had chased her stepdad around the kitchen table with a butcher knife. Big Rachel was not only a calculating control freak but a homicidal maniac unable to differentiate right from wrong.

Our moods all revolved around Big Rachel, one moment all of us laughing, the next moment all of us crying from the insensitive remarks she made. I can remember one particular afternoon in which Katt, Stephanie, and I were all laughing about our sailor friends until Big Rachel called and began to tell us these horrible rumors tactlessly informing Stephanie that one of her boyfriends was using her. In the matter of less than a minute the mood in the room transformed, all of us uncomfortably silent and at a loss for words. Stephanie flung herself on the couch, buried her face into a pillow and sobbed. Big Rachel's evil wrath had touched us, and she was not even present. Of course no sailors ever used Big Rachel. She had several long term boyfriends, the first Chris Nye, the second Kenny, but she was never faithful. Men to her were more like toys, playthings she could manipulate into getting exactly what she wanted. It was not uncommon that Big Rachel forced me to date a sailor just because he was friends with the guy she wanted to go out with. There was no end to Big Rachel's evil wrath.

One sailor she had been dating, Scott Shope, a friendly blonde from Georgia, had a friend named Chris Trevino. Except for the obvious fact of being Italian, Chris was not my type. Chris had red hair and freckles, an unusually dopey face, and was quite chubby. I would have never considered dating a man like this, but Big Rachel had persuaded me, told me how much he liked me and how rich he was. I knew in my heart that I could never fall in love with this man, but I was trying to please Big Rachel, sacrificing ray happiness for the selfishness of another. Chris bought me dinners, gave me money, gold jewelry, Girbaeu shirts and belts, but my heart just wasn't in it. Eventually Chris demanded that I give him back his clothes, on the sidewalk in front of his Gunners Mate building of all places. Big Rachel's plan might have backfired, but the fact that she had already moved on to another victim spared my punishment in that incident.

Big Rachel had been convinced that she was more beautiful than any of us. When Katt and Rachel would talk on the phone to sailors, they'd ask for them to describe themselves. Big Rachel would talk for both of them, explaining that she was gorgeous, but Katt was just ok. She basically brainwashed everyone into thinking she was stunning. She even brainwashed me. I felt inferior compared to the tall striking goddess that stood before me.

Eventually Katt wound up telling Big Rachel off, and we never saw her again. I was relieved, and to this day I'll always hate Big Rachel.

OVER ON THE EAST SIDE

CHAPTER 7

I was young when I lost my virginity unripe and poorly seasoned when faced with life's challenges. Losing one's virginity was a contest between my friends and I, eagerly racing to see who could lose their treasured cherry first. As excited as we were at the thought of shedding our unripened fruits, we still wanted to lose it to the right person, and not just anyone. For me that special person was Jim Mauritzen. In all actuality Jim was not exceptionally unique, but a horny twenty-two year old sailor, but in my youthful eyes he radiated sex appeal, mystery, and individuality.

We had met at Rock N' Roll McDonalds. The very first time I laid my eyes on him I thought I had traveled back to the nineteen fifties. He looked like a poor imitation of Fonzie with his black leather jacket; outdated black acid washed tight jeans and plain white t-shirt. His hair was greased up into some sort of chocolate chip shape making him look as if he jumped off of the GREASE set. I was not much better though. The first time I had met him I was dressed like a Navy freak. I wore a NAVY sweatshirt, patriotic jean shorts with the flag enblazoned on the front two legs, and my dog tag collection around my neck. In fact the first words he had said to me were: *"Are you in the Navy?."*

I lost my virginity with Jim at the Hotel Tokyo, a historic hotel which should have been abandoned years ago. When we got to our room I decided to go downstairs I decided to go downstairs and explore. After all, I loved historic buildings. Deciding to be brave, I turned into a long Corridor and pushed open a wooden door, the paint terribly crackled. An enormous nineteen twenties ballroom stood before me. I closed my eyes and imagined that I was back in that ballroom in the roaring twenties. The floor before me was immaculately polished, glossy maple wood set in a parquet flooring pattern. The buttercup yellow wallpaper, thick and heavy, was splashed with delicate floral garlands. The ballroom with its fourteen foot tin roofed ceilings gave me the clue that the hotel had been built in the late eighteenth, perhaps early nineteenth century. A giant chandelier was suspended by an iron link chain from the center of the ceiling, thousands of radiant ovular glass crystals dangling. Mahogany armchairs, the top rail carved with dragons and vases of fruit sat in each corner of the room.

I walked into the room, a small orchestra arranged on a slightly raised platform.

A trumpet lazily wailed while a base cello was heartily plucked. A spicy oriental scent floated throughout the air as the men and women exchanged in polite conversation with one another. The men were impeccably dressed in their black tailcoats and top hats. Some of the men donned crisp white shirts with pleated yokes while others wore bow ties and shirts with white wing collars. Their black patent leather shoes glistened while they glided along the dance floor. The women wore cotton and wool flapper style dresses, the wealthier women dressed in beautifully embellished silk. The dresses were mostly close fitting, hemlines directly below the knee. All bore stockings in colors such as honey beige and teatime. The women were not rounded but had masculine silhouettes, their chests bandaged flat. Their hair was sleek and short, first bobbed then shingled, and then Eton cropped. I envisioned their faces, neatly powdered in shades of peaches and cream, deep rose and berry shades of rouge smeared but not blended on the fullest part of their cheeks. Their thin brows were darkened and elongated, and every inch of their eyes were lined thickly and then smudged. Their lashes were curled and ox blood lipstick was affixed onto their cupid shaped lips. How badly I yearned to be back in that time!

The elevator, situated in the front of the lobby was one of the only old fashioned elevators left in the city complete with an attendant. The attendant looked about as old as the hotel, with his pale skin deeply weathered and sparse gray hair. As we rode up in the elevator he recounted an old ghost tale which originated from Hotel Tokyo.

Corrine had been a guest at Hotel Tokyo and decided to attend the grand ball on a rainy night in 1925. Unable to find her beau on the ballroom floor, she went up to her room and found him fucking an unknown prostitute in their bed. Walling, her cries audible to all the inhabitants still in their rooms, she ran down the hallway into the back stairwell. Corrine hysterically ripped off her dress, constructing a homemade noose which she tied to a pipe line in the ceiling. She was found two hours later by a maid dangling from the pipe line in the ceiling and wearing only her latex girdle and suspenders attached to her stockings.

OVER ON THE EAST SIDE

The attendant claimed that he had been in Hotel Tokyo as a child, actually the grandchild of the maid who had found Corrine in the hallway that rainy night in 1925. On a rainy night he said that one could still hear the haunting wails of Corrine and her feet scuffling down the hallway. Even more terrifying was the rumor among the staff that if brave enough one could look into the bathroom mirror in the dark, only a candle lit, and catch a reflection of Corrine staring into the mirror back at you, her neck and face bloodied and red.

Looking back on the attendant's story, I wondered if Corinne was having a post traumatic stress syndrome disorder attack like I had in Roxy's. One could draw many of the same parallels in both of our stories. Like I, Corrine had a most violent reaction, running down the hallway screaming and crying. Also, Corrine had suicidal urges which she hastily decided to act upon. Had the sight of her beau and a prostitute been that traumatic to trigger suicide? Were the brothels of the 1920's the equivalent to strip clubs today? The sight of naked flesh must have shocked her in a time when values were more traditional and females sporting the masculine silhouette were all the rage. At a time when women bandaged their breasts flat or wore tight fitting bras to conceal their womanly attributes it must have been a shock to see this woman's creamy full breasts and long flowing hair cascading past her buttocks.

As the tale has been spread over the decades there is one element of the story that never changes, and that was Corrine's beauty. She was said to have resembled the great late movie goddess of the twenties, Jean Harlow. Corrine had platinum blonde hair, smoldering corn blue eyes, and perfect little cupid bow lips. She was envied by many women, but her fiance had been known to circulate the city brothels. Corrine despised prostitutes and everything they stood for. It was no consolation to Corrine that prostitutes abused alcohol and drugs and were infected with a multitude of diseases. They were known to live short tragic lives. Therefore no matter how many gentlemen pursued her, she would always feel less than complete. The night of her death Corrine was said to have worn the most exquisite dress to the ball. She was said to have looked like a sweet angel in her long flowing white dress, the same dress that would be used to kill her later that evening.

How I wished I could travel back in time to save her, but it was too late. The best I could do was comfort her spirit and hopefully bring peace to her wounded soul.

Hotel Tokyo, to bluntly put it, was a run down roach infested dump. In fact, as the elevator attendant conveyed his tale to us an enormous juicy cockroach crawled above his head, the type one might find in the humid jungles of Africa. The building had such charm and potential with its old-fashioned architectural structure, but it might as well have been abandoned. It was surprising that they charged $20.00 a room for one night. Shabby red carpeting lined the hallways, the only vivid color to light up the morbidly dull corridor. The corridor itself was extremely narrow with a long rectangular window placed at the end of the hallway. The room itself was even spookier. Bare mattresses laid upon the bed frame, no silk sheets or fluffy comforters to wrap oneself in. No curtains hung from the window. There was a small round wooden table placed in the comer of the room and two metal folding chairs were stacked against the wall. The only bright part of the room were the brilliant lines reflected from the vertical Hotel Tokyo sign hung from the side of the building. Certain areas had been shattered, but red, orange, and yellow bulbs still lit up the night sky.

I never questioned Jim as to why he was taking me to a $20.00 roach dump to lose my virginity. I did not believe I deserved better. I was only grateful to be graced with his presence. He had probably never spent more than $25.00 on me, but at least he was actually taking me to a hotel. The previous time we had went out we had roamed the streets of Chicago until dawn and then ended up at the beach. He had tried to have sex with me, but I refused so he had left me alone in the middle of the night left to find my way home all by my lonesome. Real nice guy, huh? Sure, there were things about Jim that bothered me such as his clothing and hygiene, but I chose to overlook these small shortcomings. I had never had the opportunity of seeing him in his dress whites. He was allowed to wear civilian clothes since he had went through boot camp and resided on main side.

He'd wear tight black acid washed jeans, a black t-shirt, black leather jacket, and grease his hair back with globs of hair gel. The gel solidified his hair so badly that little white flakes would eventually form giving him that salt and pepper look. He looked like a nineteen fifties greaser, but he didn't seem to notice that he was lost in his parent's generation. Jim took showers but once a week. His bunk mates always told him to take a shower, calling him by his nickname, *stinky*, but he shrugged it off. Again, I overlooked this minute flaw. To me, Jim was the Elvis look alike I always dreamed of. His hair was luxuriously thick, the color of creamed coffee and his puppy dog eyes, the color of caramel, made my heart melt. His lips were full like Elvis, especially when he puckered them.

It was not only his looks I was infatuated with but his background. Jim Mauritzen originated from Brooklyn, New York. He was a mix of several different nationalities, Greek and Puerto Rican, but to me he looked one hundred percent Italian. He could have been perfectly cast in any mafia movie alongside Robert Dinero and Joe Pesci. He just had that look about him. Jim had a mother and a father, and a younger sister who he said was a dwarf. His father was a detective with the NYPD, and just like his father he aspired to be a detective as soon as he got out of the NAVY. James was a dreamer, a lost sailor with a pipe dream of becoming New York's most celebrated detective. I let him carry on his absurd fantasies, how he would detonate booths, catch spies, perform daring car chases. At the age of sixteen his delusions of grandeur fascinated me. I was going to marry a New York detective. How exciting! A nai've sixteen year old girl was probably the only human being who would actually listen to his improbable flights of the imagination. He barely had any friends in the NAVY, but instead associated with a group of black men that sold newspapers in a newspaper stand at the corner directly across the street Rock N' Roll McDonalds. The white square shack painted with black highrise buildings, (the skyline of Chicago) was not only a newspaper stand but a meeting place. In fact the night I had lost my virginity I spotted James in the newspaper shack sipping on a bottle of whisky wrapped up in a brown paper bag. The other men nicknamed him *Brooklyn*, a name which I loved. To me, James was dangerous, an exciting action hero from the tough streets of Brooklyn. It seemed that choosing men with nicknames had become a leading theme in my life. Brooklyn was the first, then Hot Rod, and finally Biggie. Like movie stars with one name, Madonna and Cher, it made me feel important to be with such "famous men" important enough to be nicknamed by their friends.

Losing my virginity was such a momentous event in my life. For months I had searched the faces of my fellow service men, pondering who would be the one to pluck my cherry. My infantile imagination expected to be with him for all eternity, not for him to discard me like any common tramp. I thought I was special, that my first would magically be in awe of me, love me so intensely that he could never leave. I was not thinking about the pain that would accompany my loss of virginity. To have my vagina ripped apart by an erect love muscle did not perturb me in the least bit. I was willing to sacrifice blood loss, stitches, skin tom to shreds for the love of my life. To have this toxic snake stab me, wiggle around in my most intimate of spaces intrigued me. I had no idea where Jim's penis had been or in whom, but those were frivolous fears I did not want to contemplate at the moment. *Brooklyn* could have fucked hundreds of women for all I knew. His penis could have been swarming with small parasites, infested with crab eggs, or splattered with Herpes sores, but I didn't care.

We had sex in the dark that night on the bare damp mattresses. It was the middle of August and humid, and of course Hotel Tokyo had no air conditioning. Our sweaty bodies stuck together as he savagely humped me. I cried out in pain, but he did not care. I squinted and whimpered as his erect muscle poked at my insides. It felt like he was parting the great sea. The room was dark, but I knew that he could hear me sniveling and taste my salty tears as he kissed my cheeks. He was not as tender and gentle as I would have liked. I was a virgin, an impressionable delicate blossom, but he could have cared less. With his palms he put pressure on my forehead, pushing my hair back as he faintly murmured *I love you! I love you!* I was too stunned to question his intentions. Was this something that all men said when they had sex with a woman? Did all men proclaim their love for another while their penis explored our insides? I could not believe that he had felt the same way as I did! I tried to focus on his words, on the car horns blaring on the busy street below, anything to alleviate the stinging I felt, and then it was over. Before I knew it he rolled off of me and lit a cigarette while I turned over staring at a cockroach scurrying across the wall. I did not know if I should feel different. I was no longer a virgin. Someone had finally deflowered me. I had completed my passage to womanhood. I was a woman now. I felt unbelievably sticky as I got dressed and went to sit by the window, the cool breeze feeling heavenly on my sweaty skin. Jim did not bother to get dressed. He reminded me of an ape in the monkey house at the zoo, so uninhabited and primitive, wobbling around the monkey house, oblivious to the onlookers pressing their face against the window, picking at chunks of banana embedded in his fur.

I enjoyed bonding as he related his hopes and and fears to me, his adventures when aiding his detective father, the good old days when he sang in a cover band playing Journey songs, and his enthusiasm and love for New York. I felt like I was visiting an unknown mysterious place, allowed into his adult sophisticated world. I never wanted the night to end.

As the time passed I began to feel more comfortable around Jim, less inhibited, and finally able to enjoy sex. Our last time together we humped like two wild animals, completely naked, both of us moaning. It felt so dirty, our sweaty bodies squirming on the soaked mattress beneath us and groaning in ecstasy, but it felt nice to be with someone I loved. I finally felt special.

Later that evening we had to part. We sat at the bench in front of Rock N' Roll McDonalds talking and watching the people roam by. A little boy with his father walked by holding his toy truck and accidentally dropping it by Brooklyn's feet. Brooklyn picked up the truck goodheartedly handing it to the little boy, calling him buddy and chuckling as the boy stood still studying him. I could see his fatherly instincts shining through, how he was tough but gentle with children. At this point I did not only see him as a lover but a fatherly figure, a man perfect to start a family with.

As I saw the bus roll to a stop I knew it was time to leave. Jim kissed me one last time and made arrangements to meet the following Friday at 9:00 in front of Rock N' Roll McDonalds. I did not give him my phone number nor did he give me mine. I assumed he'd be there like he said. Why wouldn't he? He said he loved me.

As the following Friday rolled around I excitedly got dressed and rushed over to McDonalds to meet Jim, but I might as well have waited forever, because he never showed up. I searched different faces for a glimpse of Jim, perhaps those chocolate colored puppy dog eyes or caramel colored hair or puffy Elvis lips, but Jim was nowhere to be found. I sat in my pathetic low cut shirt, jean shorts and black flats sulking. Jim not showing up was not good for my perfect fantasy world of marriage, 2.2 kids, and a white picket fence.

Every weekend night I went back to McDonalds hoping to see Jim, but every night I went home even more dejected when I realized that he was never going to show up. My parents had known that something was not right, especially when my nosy father discovered an unopened condom package stuffed into my jeans pocket. I did not know how to explain myself so instead I spilled my secret; how I had sex with James without a condom, how I would never see him again, my fear of pregnancy. My parents were stunned. Their nightmares were turning into a reality. My father threatened to call the police and have twenty-two year old Jim arrested for statutory rape, but I desperately pleaded with him not to. It was just as much my fault as his, I told him. I knew what I was doing.

Almost instantly my mother called Planned Parenthood and arranged to have me come in the following week for a pregnancy test. Secretly though I hoped that I was pregnant. It would be the one way to hang onto James. I yearned so badly to carry Jim's baby, to carry a part of him in my womb, to nurture his seeds, an unborn miracle. How badly I wanted to see a combination of James and I be born. James would never be able to leave me. He'd be forced to know me for the rest of my life.

The following weekend Katt and I went to the base to visit some of our gunners mate friends. We ran into one gunners mate who had been friends with Jim. He told us that Jim had been in the brig for the past three weeks, and they just shipped him off to New York. I was speechless. Katt looked at my pale blank face and knew not to say anything. I wanted to cry, but I couldn't. For the past three weeks I had basically mourned a death. Finally, I could have closure.

That evening at home I let it out, crying harder then I ever had in my sixteen years. My parents had no idea how to comfort me. My eyes were so sunken in, my puffy cheeks reddened, my lips swollen. All I could think about was my plan, how I desperately wanted to travel to Brooklyn and knock on every door until I found him. The world was black and white. The sky, as blue as the ocean, was full of fluffy cotton tails, but I was color blind. The cars whizzed by, their stereos blaring. Kids were screaming, but I could not hear them. The only sound I could hear were my footsteps.

I laid in bed, playing Open Arms by Journey over and over, wallowing in my self made puddle of pity until I choked on my own tears. No one could reach me, not my mother, not my father, not my sister, none of my friends. In my adolescent mind I had met the love of my life, and tragically he had been snatched from me. I'll always hold Jim close to my heart. He didn't fulfill my hopes dreams and wishes, but he added a spark of magic to my life. That sixteen year old girl still lives within me and she'll always think of Jim fondly.

CHAPTER 8

There was always this undercurrent of sexuality within my father, a suspicion I never explored until now. I am not confessing that my dad sexually abused me, because I have no recollection of this. What I am saying is that I believed my father acted out in an inappropriate way toward his daughters. In fact both of my parents did. For some unexplainable reason my father had chosen to call me a whore, not on one particular instance, but several. In fact the night I lost my virginity I was a whore. Two years later I was still a whore. At twenty-eight years of age I was a bitch. To this day I am a bitch and a whore, a no good selfish bitch.

The night I lost my virginity I was on cloud nine, fantasizing about my first lover, how we were going to get married, have children, live happily ever after. At sixteen years of age I was planning my wedding, how I was going to be a Navy wife and move to Brooklyn, New York the remainder of my days. I sat at a bench at Howard Station, my head in the clouds, oblivious to the fact that the last bus had already came and left an hour ago. The creepy little Mexicans slithered by me, blathering in Spanish, winking and whistling as they walked by. I was hesitant to call my father for a ride home, but it was 2:00 a.m. in the morning, and I refused to wait for four hours until the early bird bus rode by. My father at the time was working as a limousine driver, one of the perks of the job being that he was able to take the luxury cars home. When I stepped into the pearl white Lincoln Town Car with the burgundy plush interior there was nothing that could rouse me out of my fantasy, I had thought. My father was infuriated, understandingly so considering his naive sixteen year old daughter was stranded at a bus station at two in the morning. He was foaming at the mouth, bubbles of saliva fizzing at the corner of his lips. I had not confessed to what I had been doing all evening, having sex with a sailor six years my elder in a roach infested run down hotel, but somehow he knew. He might not have been able to recount all of the sordid details, but father's intuition gave him a clue.

The entire car ride home, all thirty minutes of it, he hollered that I was a whore. His first born was a whore, the same little girl he bought the blue tricycle for, the same little girl he played Snow White with, the same little girl he walked to the park. I was no longer that cute innocent youngster, but now a fully developed woman. My swollen breasts, blackened hair sprouting forth from my legs, underarms, vagina, my menstrual periods; all of these things made me a whore. He could not see me as to what I really was; a lost naive girl with a broken heart; a teenager too blind to see that she was just taken advantage of by some horny sailor. No. I was a slut traipsing the streets, standing at corners soliciting whoever would have me. Despite my protestations that I was not a whore, he would not have any of it. How could he think that his own daughter was a whore, a being he created that should have remained innocent in his eyes, in a father's eyes.

Two years later I was still a whore. What had made my father believe that I was a whore at the age of eighteen? It was my lipstick, a harmless ninety-nine cent tube of cherry red lipstick. I had romanticized this tube of lipstick, how upon application it would transform me into a timeless glamour queen. Women were daringly wearing the color, and I did not see the harm in it. The creamy textured makeup instantly brightened my other features, brought out my dark eyes, my olive skin, my dimples. It was the accessory I had been searching for. It was late at night, but I ate my sugar sweetened cornflakes at the kitchen table, trying not to disturb my father sleeping in his room. He ran out of his room, enraged that I was eating at this time of night. He marched over to the table, and swung his fist at my face, punching me in the nose. The impact of the punch was so great that I fell off of my chair. *"Look at you. You look like a whore with your red lipstick on!"* He scowled at me. I did not understand why he was calling me a whore again. Did red lipstick automatically make me into a whore? Should I have slipped on sequined pasties, a g-string, sparkly heels and spun around a pole? Was red lipstick the beginning, the first sign that a woman is developing into a whore? Daddy's little girl had again disappointed him. I was only eating cornflakes, but the red lipstick; that had been the trigger. Something about that red lipstick spread unto the lips of his daughter induced such fury and hatred of women. I was like every other woman to him; my mother who cheated on him, his ex-girlfriends who perhaps hurt him, the women in the Playboy I had found in his drawer her legs spread wide open teasing and taunting him. Women were no good, all of them whores, even his own daughter.

The blow to my nose had startled me, the impact of the punch hurling me to the floor. What had gotten into my father? It was as if he was possessed by the devil, dominated by a higher being who knocked women off of their pedestal and sent them screaming into the fiery depths of misery. At this time of my life I was very lonely, the cold winter insulating me in my father's trailer. I had no friends there, not much family. I was tricked by my mother to stay in Indianapolis. I would think that my dad would have been concerned about me, feel pity for his eighteen year old daughter munching on cornflakes at the kitchen table alone on a Friday night. No, these loving feelings did not enter his mind.

Perhaps I reminded him of my mother, Margie, that same woman who carelessly informed him of her engagement to another man while she was still married to him. Was I Margie? I was her offspring. For nine months I had been completely dependent on this woman, relied on her for food, slept in her, kicked in her. I did not choose to be her spawn, the seed planted in her uterus by my father, but it did not matter. Did my mother wear red lipstick on her first date with my dad? Did those girls in Playboy wear red lipstick? Did his past girlfriends wear red lipstick? Could there have been a porno he watched, red lipstick smeared on the women's lips? What was the correlation between red lipstick and whores, and why was I a whore? Maybe it was my past, the amount of men I had been with, the clothes I wore.

I am not going to say that as a child I was a victim of abuse, physical, emotional, or even sexual, but I will go so far as to say that I was a product of a dysfunctional family. I suppose some of what I am going to relate could be interpreted by some as physical or emotional abuse, but this type of behavior was typical in our household. I do believe that at certain stages of my childhood that I was neglected, a consequence of having a mentally ill mother. In certain respects she was a model mother. Every morning she had my lunch made, a paper sack, *TUESDAY JONES*, scrawled in capital letters. It was never filled with goodies like the other kids had; miniature Snickers, Milkyways, or Three Musketeers, but at least silently it showed me that she cared. My mom usually prepared the same sandwich, peanut butter and jelly spread between two slices of white bread, the peanut butter and jelly warm and smashed, but the bread always cut into four evenly squared pieces. She'd wrap the sandwich tightly in clear saran wrap, along with an apple or orange, and complete the menu by adding a juice box. The only day that I'd buy a lunch was on Tuesday, pizza day. I looked forward to the rectangular baked pizzas garnished with sausage seeds and spices. On one particular Tuesday though my pizza was not baked quite to my satisfaction. Instead of the usual golden brown, my pizza was a drab gray. There was no way that I was going to be stuck eating a gray pizza, so I marched to the front of the lunch line, a disgruntled frown spread across my lips and complained to the lunch lady, She was not going to put up with any whiny snot nosed kid insulting her cooking. Therefore, she marched me right back to my seat and stood over me shouting until I finished the entire slice. Needless to say, that was the last time I bought a lunch at school.

My mother was consistent when it came to helping me with my school work, teaching me Hebrew, or preparing me meals, but for some strange reason hygiene was not practiced or taught regularly. I do not know what prompted me to urinate in my bed every morning before school, perhaps laziness, but the fact that I did not bathe after wetting myself was something which puzzles me to this day. My mother had to know that I wet my bed. The sheets would be sopping wet, but I suppose she did not feel it necessary to bathe oneself after peeing in the bed. Every single morning this happened, me peeing in the bed and getting dressed directly afterward. I cannot even begin to imagine the rotten odor emitted from my skin. After five days of urine soaking into my skin, marinating my exterior, I am sure I smelled horrible. I was not taught to bathe regularly as most children were or the consequences if1 didn't, but the children pointing and avoiding me gave me an indication. I feel such pity for that little girl sitting at the lunch table by herself. She knew that she smelled bad. She accepted it, but she did not know that her mother could have helped her avoid this. She did not have to smell like urine, be teased by her peers, or forced to sit at the lunch table by herself. Wetting the bed could have been her little secret, not a rumor spread by the first grade class that she smelled like piss.

My mother frightened me. She would erupt into these rages that none of us could control. I mourn for the loss of a mother figure. I might have a mother and father, but I'll always feel like an orphan on the inside. Sad, huh?

CHAPTER 9

Scattered amongst the occasional grocery store and trailer park were strip clubs and not just one, but six nestled on a strip of land behind a corn field

Having these clubs located so close to their homes influenced Sarah and her friends, manipulated their gullible fresh minds by false promises of money, glamour, excitement. Every girl that Sarah knew, including herself, aspired to be a stripper. It was sad that these fourteen year old girls had such low ambitions, that they'd be willing to degrade themselves for money. Sarah's was set on becoming a stripper as soon as she turned eighteen. Her friend, Misty, was a stripper, and Sarah loved to hang out at her trailer and listen to tales of Misty's new glitzy world. Sarah would sit in a chair, spellbound, her hands folded under her chin, and concentrate on every word that trickled out of Misty's mouth. She loved hearing about the parade of endless men, some businessmen, others factory workers, some older retired rich men looking for girls to spoil. She loved to hold and smell the bundles of money Misty laid on the table after a hard night's work, but most of all she liked to slip into Misty's glittery heels, close her eyes, and dance. She'd imagine she was a stripper, spinning in her sparkly sequined g-string, the crowd of men mesmerized and waving fresh green dollars. She could hardly wait - only four more years and she would be living the life of luxury.

Sarah again looked at the worn faces encircling her, the bored gifts dancing on stage, absorbed the stench of pungent whisky, vodka, tequila. She watched the girls gulp down shots of cheap liquor, the devil's brew which gave them their courage. She observed their faces, their sallow skin, their vacant eyes, the creases in their skin which contained stories of betrayal, heartache, woe. Where was the glamour, the riches, the sparkling costumes? Most of the men in this place couldn't scrape together two pennies, let alone a bundle of cash. Sarah had only made eighteen dollar thus far. What had Misty been talking about?

Sarah felt like she was selling her soul to the devil, letting the evil spirits below nibble at her heart until only crumbs were left. She had never been taught to respect herself, let alone let others give her the respect she deserved. Her mother had practically abandoned her at the age twelve, left her alone to fend for herself in this crazy mixed up world. She didn't have a mother figure to guide her. Therefore, it was no wonder she was drawn into an environment so incredibly degrading to women.

At the tender age of fourteen Sarah had been giving blow jobs to the local boys in the trailer park. She had actually been forced by one boy four years her elder, threatened that if she didn't give him a blow job that he'd smash her head in with a baseball bat. She was essentially treated like a whore by the neighborhood boys, even succumbing to her second cousin, Lee, for sexual favors. Lee was the neighborhood "stud". Girls swooned to him like bees on honey. Not one girl could hide her feelings about Lee, except Sarah who burrowed her secret deep in her heart. She not only liked fooling around with her second cousin, but she had fallen in love with him, and no one in the neighborhood could find out. While Aunt Goldie was working nights at Wonder Bread Factory and Uncle Bill was watching t.v., Sarah and Lee would do every thing that two people can conceivably do, except for intercourse. Sarah and Lee were not prepared to care for a baby at fourteen years of age, especially one sprouting horns and a tail. Lee's own mother; Cindy, had given birth to him at age twelve, and Aunt Goldie had practically raised him.

Sarah's mother was barely a part of her life anymore. Only one year earlier Sarah had visited her, and her new husband, Oscar, in Chicago, and now they were barely speaking. Marge's new husband, Oscar, had propositioned Sarah for sex, stating that she should let him place his penis by her hole so they could test out sizes. This way when she was ready to have sex, she'd know what size penis to shoot for. Sarah, of course objected to his suggestion but was dismissed as a liar when confronting Margie. Margie did not want to believe that her husband would do such a horrible thing, therefore she pretended they were all lies. Sarah was shattered by her mother's rejection. At a time in a young girl's life when a mother's support was essential, Sarah had none. At one time Sarah had been a part of Marge, absorbing Marge's nutrients, dependent on Marge for food and warmth. How could her own mother choose a man over her, this woman who was supposed to nurture and protect.

Having a mother is so important, especially to a girl. I love my mother. How can I not love the woman that gave me life, but to say I like her; that would be an overstatement! It's sad when a daughter has to learn about the basics of life from others, when she could have avoided heartache, depression, abuse, exploitation. I use to be a lot like Sarah regarding men. I would let man after man use my body like a toy, and when they were done they'd throw me away, toss me into their pile of worn and unwanted playthings. Sarah and I were not equipped with the tools we needed to survive; the most essential tool common sense. After dating over sixty men I have finally learned that it is not alright for men to use my body, to treat me as if I am nothing, but I do not know if my sister has learned this lesson. Instead of experiencing life she disappears, goes into hiding so she will not sleep around with different men. When she is thrown into a bar environment she cannot control herself. She has let strange men finger her on the dance floor, fuck her behind a bar at a club, fucked men in cars outside the club in an East St. Louis parking lot. She has let strange men fuck her up the ass after meeting them in a bar.

Sarah was obsessed with one loser, Bob, for years. She imagined that she was Vivian Leigh and he was Clark Gable and that they were having a passionate silver screen romance, but there were a few differences that set these two couples apart. First of all, Bob looked nothing like Clark Gable. Bob was not tall, dark, and handsome. Bob was short, fat, and unattractive. Second of all, Bob did not court Sarah. Bob's idea of a date was to take her into the back alley of the bowling lanes and force her to give him a blow job. He never once took her out to dinner, and even bragged that he used to waste all his money at strip clubs. If our mother had been there for us we might not have gotten mixed up with these worthless men. If she had spent less lime stressing how important algebra and Hebrew were and more time educating us about men, we might have avoided years of heartache.

I am uncertain as to what happened to my mother, as to why she stopped caring about her appearance and developed into such an angry woman. It frightens me; the heated look in her eyes when she gets mad. It saddens me; why a pretty woman such as herself would gradually let herself go. When I was a little girl, about three years old, I would perch myself upon a stool and eagerly watch my mom apply her makeup. I loved smelling the beige tube of pastel pink lipstick, and smearing the sapphire blue eye shadow onto my tiny almond shaped eyes. My mom would pin her raven black hair up into a neat little bun, and then she'd curl my deep warm chocolate tresses into adorable Shirley Temple ringlets.

She had a collection of stylish dresses, some feminine florals, others bright paisley patterns. There were gingham checkered blouses with pointy collars, polyester fabric suits, wrap around jean skirts, bell bottom jeans, ballet shoes. She was very fashionable, but as the years passed by and decades changed her closet stayed the same. Her soft ebony black hair turned gray and now had a wiry texture, and she wore no makeup. Her once warm gray eyes had now cooled and would swiftly dart from side to side when angry or excited. Her patience and temper had deteriorated over the years. It was as if everyone was out to get her. Both my father and my mother had that mentality. She wore gray thick framed glasses which hid her cloudy eyes, and her hair remained disheveled.

I believe at some point in her life my mother lost hope. Her life did not turn out as she expected. She did not marry a rich Jewish lawyer, her children were not perfect; she was not wealthy. She hoped to recapture some of her past dreams when she married Oscar, but again her choices failed her. She became a very angry, judgmental, and miserable woman, such as I had become.

Both my mother and father contained optimism when it came to their future. I believe they were so disappointed later in life because of their idealistic expectations. They both had talent. My mother was a singer and a dancer, her voice so fluid and harmonious that she won a singing contest. She was also an artist who loved to splatter canvasses with vivid oil paints and do charcoal black and white drawings of the female form. She held such artistic promise, this woman who stuttered when she spoke, but fluidly sang. She had even shattered a light bulb with her high pitched operatic arias. Her creative inclinations attracted her to other creative individuals, one namely, Tony Sprino, her boyfriend of four years. Tony was an Italian artist that became obsessed with my mother, so passionate that he stalked her, resulting in my mother getting a restraining order against him.

My father was in the air force for four years. No, he did not guide significant aircraft to top secret destinations. He was a typist in the air force who spent a majority of his duration in Okinawa, Japan. Despite the lengthy period he spent in Japan he only learned one sentence, moko ha killie ha nashke kudasy which meant speak more clearly please.

My mother and father met in a Jews for Jesus meeting which is very ironic. Considering how she drilled in our heads how important it was to be Jewish. Yes, my mother held high hopes for the future, clung onto my father's false promises that they would attain financial prosperity, flourish from the riches they would accumulate. This never happened though. Every year my mother would languish further and further, a piece of her would disappear, descend into the fiery depths of misery until she was a weathered up elderly rendition of what she used to be. It is sad when I think of how my mother's dreams crashed, how life didn't turn out how she expected, and how she let life's inconsistencies and small problems gobble her whole. I'll always love my mother, appreciate the fact that she gave me life, but to like her. My mother is not my friend. I do not call my mother when I am strewn out on the couch wailing like a baby. My mother would not understand. She shows no compassion, but that is who she is, and that is how I'd have to be.

OVER ON THE EAST SIDE

CHAPTER 10

Please God, please stop me from having one of my crying attacks. Please quell the lump in my throat, that same lump that begins to form whenever I have the overwhelming need to cry, when my remaining self confidence leaks through every pore, when my spirit fizzles away and is replaced by a faithless bantering phantom. Nobody knows. Not a soul can discern my waning heart or my somber eyes, how the sapphire specks once dancing gaily are now at a standstill. No one would guess that this girl behind the wide bright smile was disheartened at that very moment, craving so badly to hurl herself onto a bed and wildly flail her arms and legs, pummel the headboard until her knuckles and palms bled, like on that life altering night outside of Roxy's. I talked, I walked, I laughed, but I was only going through the motions. I was not my natural self but a synthetic reproduction. I would probably not be myself for weeks. Why was I so different from everyone else? While other women remain fascinated with stripping, I am devastated. They embrace stripping like other deep-rooted traditions, rattle off their experiences in the clubs as if they were reciting folklore. They talk of women teasing the audience as they tug at their panties, pulling them up and down over their thighs. They talk of women baring their naked breast to the room as if it was merely an arm or a leg. They say these are beautiful women, exquisite feminine beings swollen with pride, but all I can see before me is ugliness. An enormous blanket of darkness swaddles me, blinds me to the good in the world, that sweetened land awash with peppermint sticks, chocolate, laughter and silliness. Gone is that place.

Am I any better though? Do I in all reality set a better example for all of womanhood to aspire to? Wasn't I repeatedly smiling through the heartache, allowing man to abuse me, belittle me as if I was a common street whore. Wring my throat like it is a sopping wet wash rag, slap my cheek so powerfully that it is the shade of raw bloody meat, squeeze my breast and call me a dirty bitch. Call your friends and tell them how my pussy stinks, how I need to douche, how I don't shave my armpits. Reduce me to a blubbering puddle of flesh, a shadow of that formerly strong woman, the same woman that said she'd never let a man hit and demean her. Am I the same woman who wipes away her tears after having her legs spread open and snapped like a wishbone, acts like everything is perfectly normal after her underwear is wedged up her ass so hard that it begins to bleed. Yes, I am that woman. Was Carl right? Am I no better than a stripper, a street walker, a crack whore?

I don't understand God. I don't understand how women can be treated as if they were dogs. "Roll over and I'll give you a bone." "Spread your legs and I'll give you a dollar." What is the difference? A trick for a treat. When will mankind see stripping as a masochistic form of servitude? Tell me how a man is supposed to make a distinction between a stripper and me. Tell me that a man who enters a strip club is not staring at the outline of my breasts in a snug fitting sweater as I walk by or fixated with my crotch or ass in a tight pair of jeans. Reassure me that the same man who is ogling these strippers will not try to rape me as I walk to my car, because he has lost all respect for women and thinks of them only as pieces of meat.

God, I am beside myself, baffled as to how a stripper can come home after a long nights work of riding customers as if they were ponies at the zoo, tuck her children in after she flashed her crotch while men casually swig their beer, lay her head down on the pillow and see the faces flash before her as she closes her eyes, the wrinkled dirty old men, the cocky businessmen, the college boys wet behind their ears. Why am I the one who cannot fall asleep? Why am I the one who cannot get the images out of her head?

OVER ON THE EAST SIDE

CHAPTER 11

My heart drifts from one man to another never settling in one place. My heart has no home, no warm cuddly pillow to lay its warm head upon. I long to kiss him, to stroke his face, to squeeze him tightly and never let go. I know it's evil of me. I know it's wrong, but my heart is so cold that I don't care. I never intended for a simple crush like this to get so twisted. How did a thought residing in my head become so distorted? How did it get so gnarled by people's words and cruel rumors? Perhaps I shouldn't blame others though. Maybe it is I, myself, who thrives on the drama, who desires to dabble in the world of the forbidden, to taste the fruits those impish sprites dangle past my lips.

The scene opens in any bedroom on a peaceful Sunday evening while enjoying a tranquil slumber. Suddenly, I am rudely awoken by the piercing hollers of a furious man, too inconsolable to calm down. He is foaming at the mouth, the spit flying everywhere, sprinkling me in the face as I rub my tired eyes. He sends the children to their room and brutally grabs any wrist, squeezing it until it mutates into a deep shade of plum, and I plead with him to let go.

"Alright, you have thirty seconds to come clean or I'm ripping your arm off. What the fuck were you doing with Donny all night?"

"What are you talking about? I wasn't doing anything, I swear." I desperately insisted.

"Bullshit Tuesday! Donny told Chris! All Donny's friends said you did it! What kind of sick mind games do you think you are playing with guys minds? Chris said Donny wouldn't even go for your nasty ass anyways."

I could feel my tear ducts begin to prepare for another endless trail that would soon drain from the corner of each eye. Sadly, I was not crying because Carl was accusing me of a most wicked lie, but instead I was weeping because Donny didn't want me. This just confirmed my belief that I was a piece of shit, too ugly to seduce the biggest whore of them all, Donny Ortmann.

"What the fuck did I do? I told you, all that happened was Donny asked me where you were and then walked away."

"Then how come Donny told everyone that you were all

over him, and he turned you down. He said you followed him all night. Even Larry Parmley said it!"

"Carl! They're all on crack! There is no way I'd follow some guy around all night. I didn't even go up to him. He went up to me. Come on, Carl. You know me! I wouldn't do that. I swear on my children's lives, and you know how much I love my kids."

"Everyone's pissed at you, Call, Chris. They can't believe you'd do something like that to me."

"Carl, first of all. You are not my boyfriend anymore. You have no right to barge into my house and accuse me of Something I didn't even do."

"Tuesday! You liked my buddy. Then he says that you guys did something. I'm sorry. That is just a little too weird."

"Yey, I know it sounds weird, but I didn't do it. I told you, I swear on my life and my kids. 1 told you I liked him. I was honest enough to tell you that. Don't you think I would have told you if I did something like that?"

"No, Tuesday. I don't. You're a whore just like all girls are. You spread yore legs for anyone that will have you, and you just had to do it to my friend, huh?"

"You need to talk to your supposed "friend"! I wouldn't follow some guy around all night like a puppy dog. Don't you think I would have been a little more upset than that if I did that? I do have some pride, you know."

Maybe it was my persuasive story or perhaps my perseverance that calmed Carl down and caused him to release hold of my now throbbing wrist. My heart was broken yet again. I could feel it burning to a crisp as Carl's words continued to echo in my mind: *"Chris said Donny wouldn't even go for your nasty ass anyways!"* How humiliating! My crush on Donny had been a secret, my own little flight of the imagination I could visit when my heart wept for some sort of stimulant so it wouldn't simply perish. I was keeping my heart alive. Was there any crime in that? The Donny in my daydreams was not the real Donny. This Donny wasn't a drug addict, didn't shoot up heroin and meth, didn't share needles with his loser friends, didn't take girls to the dumpster behind Woodrows and fuck girls he had just met, wasn't a woman beater and a womanizer. No, my Donny was completely different. My Donny was perfect, fell in love with me and completely changed, and I was different than any girl Donny had been with, because I had forgiven him for all his sins. I had never done that before. Carl had turned me into such an angry women, a bitter merciless woman unable to forgive anyone, especially a man, but Donny was going to change all that. Through Donny at last my heart would soften, its frosty coating would thaw allowing true love to again penetrate its once icy exterior. Why couldn't I ever get anything I wanted? Why couldn't I for once in my life be happy?

No one would understand how I felt, how I could feel for this man I barely knew. To someone that didn't know me it sounded like an unhealthy obsession or an adolescent crush gone wild, but it wasn't. It was simply my little secret, an idealistic modest romance I had created and locked away deep in my mind, but now everyone had the key, and I was made to look like the fool. I can't explain why I'd pick out the biggest loser to like. I have no excuse for singling out one of Carl's friends. I can only justify my choice by explaining how I'd feel with him. Fantasizing about Donny keeps my spirit alive, basks my heart in sunshine when it ordinarily would be brooding in the shadows of solitude. In my mind I can create a storybook romance where no one gets hurt, where I can taste his sweet tongue and kiss his soft lips as many times as I please. I am so lonely, but these fantasies of mine; they aid me when the loneliness becomes unbearable. If I can't find the perfect man out there in the real world then why can't I invent my own? Why can't my fantasy man inhabit the body of Donny Ortmann since he embodies what I am physically searching for in a man?

There had to be something there. Didn't there? When we looked into each others eyes was there nothing there? I had never gazed into such empty eyes, incredibly bleak eyes but so absorbing. I yearned to place a kiss upon his lips and replace all that he had lost; love, trust, goodness. I wanted so badly to fill his barren eyes with what had vanished, to make his pupils dance with such feverishness. I know he felt something when he looked at me. He had to! I am not dim-witted or inexperienced in the matters of love and attraction. Somewhere deep inside of him I know that our "look" transcended beyond the ordinary and stirred feelings he thought he never had.

For once G-D, allow me to experience the sort of pleasure that happily married couples do. Try to tolerate the simple fact that Carl and Donny are friends, and realize that two embittered souls need each other.

Chris and Cali do not realize how lucky they are. Yes, Cali always emphasizes how their marriage is hard work, but I would love to have to work at something as sacred as the union of marriage. To be married to the person you love, to have children with that person, to witness the miracle of birth before each others eyes, to grow old with that person and commit until death do you part, How beautiful and how sad that I most likely will never feel such joy! At one time I did. Through the grief and the fog Carl and I used to be that happy. I spent many a time daydreaming about Carl and I exchanging vows at the alter, sprawled out on our bed in the honeymoon suite after a meaningful session of lovemaking and telling each other how deeply we love one another, but along with my heart those dreams are dead. I have new dreams with a new lover cast, but this vision only exists in my head. I feel foolish, entertaining this delusion over and over again until my soul yearns so badly to just touch him, to stroke his forearm, the same forearm patterned with a trail of track marks. I long to hold his hand, the same hand he used to pound his wife in the face. I hunger to passionately brush my lips lightly against his, the same lips used to kiss Shannon, that stripper at PT's. I crave to rub our bare bodies together, the same body he used to bend Kitty over the dumpster behind Woodrow's and fuck her.

Why God? Why do I wish such unhappiness upon myself? He will treat me no different than any of these girls. To him I will also be his drug, his beaten wife, his stripper, his whore. I will be all of these things even though I am none of them. Please quell my addiction, my hunger for these wrong kinds of men. Allow someone good to enter my life, a man to really love me, protect me, to respect me like never before.

I hate Carl! I hate Donny! I hate Chris! I hate them all for tinkering with my fantasy, for meddling with the gears in my head, those same gears I used to chum out incredible whimsies of the imagination that filled me with a split second of content, at least for the time being. I would have never acted out on it, but now they are tampered with, and I will never know again how it feels to be happy, even though it was only a dream. Carl stared at me hunched over the bed, bawling like an infant. He saw the anger in my reddened fists clenched so tightly that the ligaments ached. Perhaps a moment of truth bit him in the face, and he realized that his friend had created the entire story.

OVER ON THE EAST SIDE

"Tuesday, look at me." He gently whispered, placing his index finger under my chin and raising my face to look upon his. I looked into his eyes misted with tears which only made my cry harder.

"Tuesday, I don't know babe. I just love you so much, and the thought of you with Dooon." he started to say. "The thought of you and Donny. I don't care who else you'd be with, but not Donny. I don't trust him, and I don't trust yon. My worst nightmare has always been you and Donny ending up together for some strange reason, and now my nightmare is turning into reality."

"You don't have to worry. I would never do that to you." And with those final words Carl leans by my side at the foot of the bed and embraces me, squeezing me so tightly that for a moment I have trouble breathing.

The curtains are drawn and the scene closes with me internally exploring what I had just told Carl. I always had to reassure Carl in every way that I had honorable intentions, but in my heart the most of intimate of secrets was kept hidden. I did have a crush on Donny, and despite the objections of Carl, Chris, Cali, practically everyone; my feelings were not going to fade. I was told to mourn the fact that Donny and I would never end up together, to bury my feelings deeply where neither sunshine nor air could touch them, but I can't do that. Yes, Donny is a drug addict, a womanizer, a woman beater, basically a man that I would most likely find repulsive, but I cannot deny the direction in which my heart guides me. My heart is my compass, and it navigates me to destinations most foreign and exotic. Yes, Donny and Carl are friends, but to be honest; I don't care! Carl has hurt me enough, and now it was time to hurt him.

Two weeks later as I had hoped I saw Donny at Woody's. As soon as I saw him my heart plunged to the bottom of my stomach. I couldn't hear that geek Justin anymore. All I could see was Donny. Justin kept talking and talking, and I wished so badly that he would just for one moment shut up so I could soak in the excitement of the moment. Was it finally going to happen? Was for one time in my life something going to turn out how I had hoped? I excused myself from Justin for a moment and casually walked to the back of the bar where Donny was talking to a friend of his. I walked right past him, the same way I had walked by him in my dreams, but he didn't notice, or at least he pretended not to notice.

"Dammit!" I thought to myself as I walked to the back bar to get a refill of my drink.

I walked back to the front bar to talk to Justin again, but every other minute I'd glance in Donny's direction hoping he'd walk by me again, but instead he walked downstairs. Justin kept blabbing, excitedly saying how no hot girls ever talk to him, but I didn't care. I pretended to care, falsely professed how cute he was and how those girls would be idiots not to talk to him, but I could only pretend for so long. I had to talk to Donny! I just had to, so I apologized again for excusing myself and descended downstairs where I casually walked right past Donny to the bathroom, but just as I had hoped I felt a strong hand pull me in its direction. Donny stood before me, and just as in my dreams he glanced upon my heaving bosom, my shimmering golden lips, my sun kissed cheeks, but he was nothing like in my dreams. He looked tired is the simplest way I could put it. The shadows under his eyes said it all, explained the inner turmoil; how his wife had cheated, the guilt he felt from abusing his son and wife, the high he yearned for so badly as he'd jab needle after needle into his forearm poisoning his veins with that elixir he was addicted to. I felt badly for him, felt pity for this once so handsome man that was deteriorating before my very eyes, but it didn't change my feelings for him in the least bit. I wanted him more than ever, ached so desperately just to place a kiss upon his lips, a kiss so long and deep, a kiss so intense that we'd both never want to stop.

"So, why'd you break up with Carl?" he asked.

I had to think of a good reason, something which didn't incriminate me.

"Cause I didn't love him, and he was abusive."

"Yey, that's what I'm trying to take care of right now. I use to do that to my wife, but I'm trying to control that now. We're back together." He bragged, lifting up his left ring finger to show me the gold band squeezed onto it.

My heart plummeted. I tried not to look upset, struggled to somehow congratulate him for taking back that ugly hoosier bitch, but my best wishes were anything less than sincere.

"That's great." I quietly uttered as all my dreams crashed down before me.

"Wait, that's not great." I bravely retorted. "I'm mad at you for getting back with her. I had a big crush on you." I spit out, my arms to my side, and not thinking of the repercussions I'd have to reap later.

"But I didn't know that, and you were fucking Carl anyways."

"Yey, so?"

"You were fucking Carl!"

"Yey, what's your point?" I asked. Could he have been jealous? God, I hoped so. I needed him to care. He looked confused at that moment.

"Here, let me get your phone number." He asked.

"But you're married."

"I know, just to be friends."

"Uhhhh."

"Alright, then don't worry about it."

I wish I could've been valiant, turned around and walked away, but of course I dug around in my purse for a pen as he grabbed a napkin off of the bar, and I scribbled my number on it.

"Here, not like you'll call it or anything."

"I'll call you, I promise." and just like that he was done, moved on to one of his buddies who hadn't seen him in awhile.

I walked upstairs over to the bar where I saw Rob, a friend of mine. We talked for awhile, and then there he was again, Donny, a man who had more power over me than any man in my life ever. Rob walked away and Donny sat on a stool casually turning his head in my direction. Our eyes met. Plain and simple we were having eye sex. If his eyes were a pool I could've drowned in them, sunk to the bottom never to come up for air. I was submerged, put under a spell. The music was drowned out by his stare, the people around us vanished. All was peaceful and still in our own little world until he looked away, and I looked down at the floor, my cheeks hot and flushed with excitement. Justin walked over to me again along with Rob.

"Great!" I thought to myself. The only person I wanted to talk to was Donny, and instead the two shortest guys in this place wouldn't leave me alone. I wasn't in the mood to talk to some midget who cooked bratwurst outside of Woody's with his father. My feet scooted in Donny's direction even though my brain told me not to.

"I don't mean to cock block you." He shouted trying to be heard over the music.

"You're not cock blocking me. Don't worry." I casually replied.

I really wanted to tell him how it would be almost impossible for him to cock block me considering that I wanted him more than any man ever before.

"I still have to pick up the kids". He said almost falling off of his stool.

"You're picking them up?" I questioned surprisingly.

"Well no. They're at my mom's house. My wife is there."

"Oh."

"Yey, I wouldn't drive them drunk. I just don't get it though."

"Get what?" I asked.

"I just get so jealous. She can't go anywhere without asking where she's going. She wouldn't even fuck me for two months."

"That's because she cheated on you. Why are you back with her when you can't trust her? When I was with Carl...."

"I know." He interrupted me. "You fucked him every night."

"No, that's not what I was trying to say."

"I know, when you are with that person you are really with that person."

"You know, your wife is really lucky?"

"Why?" he asked stumbling again.

"Because.....She has you."

That had caught him off guard. I don't think any girl had every said anything so sickingly sweet to him before.

"Why are you with her when you can't trust her?"

"Cause I'm trying to practice forgiveness."

My heart sank. Did Donny's wife know how lucky she was? To come home every night to Donny Ortmann. This was what I wanted. I could've grabbed him and whisked him away to Las Vegas and married him that very moment. I had no doubt in my mind. He stood up and walked over to the trash can hurling his beer bottle into it and staggered back in my direction. He stood over me, his 6'2'' frame towering over my tiny 5'2" one.

"So, you want to be friends, huh?" I flirtingly asked.

"Yey."

"What kind of friends do you want to be."

"Any kind of friend you want me to be." He teasingly answered.

"So, what size are those anyways?" Donny asked.

"They're D, but when I got measured at Fredericks they said I am a 32F.

He looked quite pleased.

"Let me see them."

"Noooo, not here."

"Come on, just a peek."

"I can't."

He lifted the fabric of my top and peeked down at my nipple.

"Come here." I said motioning him to listen closely to a secret I was about to tell him.

"If you ever leave your wife I'll fuck you good." I whispered.

His jaw dropped open and he stepped back which I knew was not a good sign.

"I'm sorry. I shouldn't have said that. I'm so sorry." I said ashamedly shaking my head.

He placed his index finger under my chin and I raised my face softly placing a kiss upon his lips, but he pulled away.

"That's ok, don't worry about it." He said walking over to the bar to get another beer.

I could've punched myself in the head. How could have I of said something so blatantly slutty to him. *"When you break up with your wife I'll fuck you good!"* God, how stupid I was. He talked to some other girls and we just stared at each other. The smoky air didn't lessen the intensity of the gaze. I sweetly smiled at him hoping to reel him in once again. An invisible rope was strung between us as I desperately tried to pull him in my direction, but he didn't walk over as I had hoped. I could tell he was struggling with this. I knew in my heart he wanted me, but he couldn't. He was trying to work out things with his wife, and as badly as I wanted him I couldn't have him either I would always love Donny Ortmann even if nothing would ever happen between us. I'd love him forever I knew what I felt in my heart, and my heart was never wrong.

CHAPTER 12

Apollonia, a name bestowed upon only the most powerful. In fact, the literal meaning of Apollonia derives from a Greek myth in which a martyr had her teeth knocked out and suffered from a toothache her entire life. The name also signifies strength and power; Apollonia is the feminine form of Apollo. The real Apollonia who I am going to describe was not a Greek Goddess, but instead a mother of a little girl who suffered from her own kind of aches her entire life, and these pains were inflicted by men. Apollonia Thomas was a stripper. She had worked at Ms. Kitty's for over four years, but was fired after getting in a fight with Hank's wife, a regular patron of the establishment. It started out as basically every lap dance she gave in which she wildly grinded for a mere twenty dollars, but when she felt a soft hand grab her shoulder she knew there was going to be trouble. This angry woman, Estelle, grabbing her shoulder had been wondering where Hank had been going every Friday and Saturday night, staggering in the door smelling like cheap sweet perfume. She thought he was doing either of two things, having an affair or going to those damn strip clubs she detested. After hearing from her friend that she had seen Hank's pick up truck parked in the parking lot of Ms. Kitty's, she had to see for herself what her husband had been doing.

When she saw this strange woman completely naked, writhing on her husband like a jungle snake she simply lost it. How could Hank have done this to her? They were high school sweethearts, had five children, went to church every Sunday. She couldn't stand it. She walked over to her husband and Apollonia engaging in this sordid lap dance, placed her chubby freckled hand on Apollonia's chocolate colored shoulder and pulled her off with such force that Apollonia landed on the linoleum floor beneath her, her bare behind landing with a thud and briefly knocking the wind out of her.

It was against club policy to attack a customer or anyone for that matter who walked through Ms. Kitty's doors, but Apollonia couldn't restrain herself. She clutched a thick strand of Estelle's hair and yanked it so hard that Estelle's head flipped back, and she also landed on the floor. This gave Apollonia the perfect opportunity to pounce Estelle like a famished tiger fighting for its prey. They rolled on the floor knocking over flimsy tables, folding chairs. Drinks fell to the floor making the linoleum so slippery that Estelle and Apollonia almost glided along it like two overwrought seals. A crowd of men cheered and clapped egging them on, but the manager did not share the same opinion as the crowd. He fired Apollonia on the spot even though Estelle had started the fight. Apollonia didn't possess many skills. She thought she had no other way to earn money and had to take care of her five year old daughter, Victoria. She had always been a stripper and she would always be a stripper until she was too old.

Through a friend she got a job at a massage parlor in Brooklyn. These massage parlors were cleverly disguised as an alternative to the regular strip clubs, but in all reality the women inside did not just strip and massage. They actually performed acts of prostitution regularly, and Apollonia serviced customers just to survive. She dreaded going to work every day. Her jaws, her arms, her calves, her entire body was worn out, exhausted from blow jobs, hand jobs, intercourse. Her calves were severely bruised due to the impractical high heels she danced in every day. As soon as she left work she'd tuck away her experiences, bury them deep in her mind where even she couldn't unearth them, but sometimes she simply could not forget. Wherever she went, people constantly reminded her of her sins. She had been deeply involved in a religious group, and they relentlessly pestered her regarding her profession, plaguing her with their warnings that if she did not stop what she was doing both Victoria and her would take their last breath in hell.

At first the devil painted a pretty picture for Apollonia. He dipped his brash in a palette of vibrant colors creating a rich masterpiece to lure tbe vulnerable woman into his work of art. Satan promised Apollonia glamour, riches, gold, diamonds, furs, a new and prosperous life, but he didn't specify the price she'd have to pay to acquire such worldly possessions.

By no means was Apollonia an introverted woman, but she would not have labeled herself an exhibitionist either. However, stripping appeared a more attractive alternative to her and Victoria starving on the streets. She'd just close her eyes and imagine that she was in another place, a peaceful garden with Victoria where no one could touch either of them. Victoria was oblivious to what her morn did. Apollonia stressed that she never wanted Victoria to find out.

Victoria actually had a chance at a future, a good future, therefore she surrounded Victoria with people who she thought would have a positive influence on her daughter, namely Larry, a flea market vendor who formed a close bond with Victoria over the five years he rook care of her. Larry had spent countless nights listening to Apollonia's tales of woe, comforted her when the flood of tears would not end. He pitied this poor woman who had been beaten, raped, had such repulsive acts of violence committed onto her that it was a miracle she was not dead. It was his duty to make sure that Victoria would not end up like her mother, would not be abused by men, would be self sufficient and strong. He treated this sweet little girl like his own, taking her to the park every day, to the flea market. He even typed up words on the typewriter and taught Victoria how to read. He emphasized to Victoria that she was to be treated with respect, to follow his fundamental rule in life: ***Treat every woman like your daughter, mother or sister!***

Larry did not know that the last time he was asked by Apollonia to watch her daughter that it would literally be the final time he ever saw Victoria again. He knew that Apollonia was troubled, but he never foresaw the impending misfortune stealthily tiptoeing in his direction. Apollonia had been extremely uneasy the past few months leading up to her breakdown. She felt like she was living two lives, one of a stripper/prostitute, the other of a devout fanatical church woman. Every Sunday they preached about the evils in the world, sex, drugs, pornography. They looked down on Apollonia, reminding her that once her daughter and her entered the gates of heaven, they would be forgiven for all of their sins. She devoted herself to these people and to the bible faithfully reading every day, but when she entered work every night the rules of the bible were laid to rest. It seemed to her that since she joined this religious group that her profession haunted her; even when she wasn't working. She began to see this outline, a slimy ghoulish figure swiveling round and round a pole, slapping its skeletal ass, spreading its emaciated legs for anyone who gave a damn. Gradually this ghoul began to follow her, materializing in any reflective material in which she passed, mirrors, hubcaps, windows. Eventually, she could not break away from this phantom.

It became a part of her, and all she could think of was what the people told her at her church: "*When you and Victoria die, you will go to heaven."* She was convinced that she was caught in the devil's firestorm, that satan himself stood outside her door with a pitch fork ready to burn her and Victoria to a crisp. The guilt was beginning to nibble at her soul, gobble up her heart, eat into her flesh. She was beginning to see the devil in the faces of her customers as she straddled them and feel their flesh disintegrate as she rubbed them down. She couldn't break away from the evil spirits which lingered by her side. She thought the only thing which would set her and Victoria free would be death. She wanted to go to heaven with her daughter, spring from cotton candy clouds into the forgiving arms of angels, strum golden harps. She was hearing voices, a haunting devilish song telling her to kill her daughter to send her into the gates of heaven. She thought she had to do it, especially when the devil bounced back at her from her reflection in the mirror chanting DO IT! DO IT! Apollonia knew she must dull her toothache, numb her and Victoria of the pain they felt on this earth.

As she got Victoria ready for a shower, she grabbed her .357-caliber Magnum revolver and pressed the cold pistol against Victoria's right temple. She pulled the trigger, but as Victoria tumbled to the floor, and her eyes rolled back in her head, a moment of reality hit her. She thought Victoria might still be alive. She thought she could still save her so she picked up her warm bundle of joy from the floor, held her close, squeezed her so tightly causing Victoria to release those last few gulps of air. She had given this little girl life, and now she had taken it away. It was five years ago, but it seemed like only yesterday that after ten hours of hard labor Apollonia held her new baby swaddled in silky pink blankets. She was at a loss for names, but finally decided on Victoria, a latin name meaning "Victory". She wanted her daughter to have a chance at a good life, be victorious, a winner, and for those short five years she was. Regrettably, her mother's world mixed with hers, and she was forced to pay for her mother's sins.

To this day Larry cannot say Victoria's name without shedding a tear. Every December 5th Larry visits Victoria's grave and puts balloons, a bouquet of roses, and Victoria's kindergarten picture, the one where she is grinning widely. He'll always love her like a daughter and bear the emptiness a parent feels when their child dies. He will never recover, all because a stripper's soul was tortured.

CHAPTER 13

Each and every day I find a nagging compulsion to maintain the thinness which I have attained. My obsession with perfection began at the age of fifteen. As a child I never was a rail, but I wasn't obese either. I generally consumed what I desired substituting chocolate cream filled pies and entire bags of cheese puffs for dinner. As I entered my teen years though eating unhealthy caught up with me, and by the age of fifteen I was pleasantly plump.

My parents had sent me away for three weeks to visit my Aunt Goldie in Indianapolis, Indiana. My Aunt Goldie was by no means a petite woman. She could have easily weighed three hundred pounds, but her height compensated for her massive weight. Aunt Goldie towered over many men, her stature reaching six feet. Every morning I would rise to the heavenly aroma of zesty sausage, syrupy pancakes covered with butter, crunchy slices of bacon coated in grease, sugary sweetened french toast, flaky biscuits bathed in an ample amount of gravy, and hash browns so delicate that they dissolved in your mouth.

Lunchtime would arrive a short time later consisting of honeyed ham, velvety mashed potatoes doused with butter, green beans and corn sprinkled with tiny bacon scraps, and luscious breads slathered with sweet honey butter. Shortly thereafter dinner was served. I devoured such delicacies as salmon sweetened in a tart lemon sauce, new potatoes adorned with garnishes, massive stalks of broccoli sprinkled with parmesan cheese, and salads crammed with shredded cheeses, scraps of chewy bacon, crunchy croutons, and drowned by creamy dressings.

Over the three week period I had become accustomed to scarfing down these slovenly portions of edibles, and had become blind to my swelling physique. Staring at my figure in the reflective looking glass which covered one wall of my room did in no way jolt me to recognize that I had become an inflated simulation of myself. It was not until I traveled home and reunited with my mother that the entire concept of what I really looked like was altered forever. My mother in such a brash mariner informed me that I had become quite "stocky" in the past few weeks. How considerate of my mother to use the word stocky instead of fat. At the moment that I was notified of my weight gain, there was no other concern that could have been of greater importance. I envisioned myself as a blubbery mass of lard dripping of fleshy plump fat deposits, wobbling as I waddled to and fro. How could my plentiful frame fit through doorways? I saw how others would retch as I teetered by. In my mind, there was no one as overblown and bloated as I. I was befuddled as to how I did not recognize what I had developed into, and so in response to this fresh perception of myself, I became obsessed. Food was no longer a source of delight, but instead an adversary which taunted and teased me mercilessly.

Each night as I lay in bed, my stomach rumbling, I would be bombarded with visions of how remarkable my life would be with a new slender shape. The maximum amount of calories I would consume in a day never exceeded seven hundred. On holidays such as Thanksgiving, when almost every American feasted, I could not. My mother fixed me a turkey sandwich marinated in a delicious dressing which I gobbled down, and as I took my last bite the gratification which accompanied the sensation of such a tasty sandwich dissipated. I contemplated exercising the entire night to redeem myself for whatever foolish misdeeds I had perpetrated, but instead I lay under my covers sobbing, regretting that I could have ever let myself relinquish the discipline which I had instilled in myself.

My best friend expressed concern in my state of emaciation, stating that my head was not proportionate to my body. Sadly, I interpreted her concern as a compliment, indulging the fact that I resembled a human lollipop. Many of my friends would commend me on my weight loss which would only reinforce the idea that maintaining thinness is applauded, while plumpness is shunned.

Finally, I could shop for the clothes I at one time only fantasized of wearing, but cute clothes and compliments did not compensate for the incessant hunger pangs which crept in every other minute. Being so consumed with my body image was becoming quite monotonous, and eventually the importance of not starving superceded my devotion to remain flawless. Therefore my starvation routine gradually diminished to where I was basically consuming an adequate amount of food each day, but again, I am paranoid about gaining weight. As I write this I can feel my stomach swell, the bulge making my jeans tight. I'll never be happy with my body, because man has been engineered to be attracted to thin big busted women. It's sick how men expect us to be perfect.

OVER ON THE EAST SIDE

He took to heart the suffering I had inflicted onto him. He felt there was a point that to be established and injuring himself was the only way he could express the grief which congested his heart. The previous evening I remained detached, cold and aloof, yearning a bit of solitude. Unfortunately, Carl interpreted my distance as a personal attack reminding me of how his first girlfriend craved seclusion. Equating me to an individual whom obviously did not respect others as well as herself filled me with such loathing. How could he compare me to a girl who administered such a sinister punishment upon him.

Her name was Brandy, and Carl usually refers to her as his first piece of ass. I will classify this relationship in a more humane and tactful manner and refer to her as his first girlfriend. Carl was eighteen years old, and Brandy was fifteen, but Carl was not as experienced as most eighteen year old boys. He lacked self esteem, and the fact that someone showed interest in him was mystifying. Over the past decade Carl's body had transformed. Only a year before he was an exaggerated caricature of himself, fleshy and overblown, almost 300 pounds. He had been rejected by almost every girl at school which made him doubt any wonderful qualities he was even close to thinking he had.

Therefore, when Brandy entered his life, he felt so fortunate to be graced with her affections. Carl spoiled Brandy, tending to her every whim. He purchased lavish quantities of jewelry to pacify his qualms that the relationship wasn't working out as he had planned. Brandy, at the age of fifteen, was almost childlike, too immature to appreciate the quality of man that Carl represented, thus she dumped him on prom night. It was not only the act of rejection which clouded his perception on women. Carl was haunted by the lies, an unsettling truth that his son was not his. For six years Carl took care of Shannon and his son, Daniel. Even though Daniel was half black Carl was oblivious to the fact that his son wasn't his. Daniel had been what had gotten Carl out of his drug habit. He had overdosed twice on cocaine, but knowing that he had to straighten out to be Daniel's father saved him. When he stared at the DNA results he was dumbfounded, but I always knew. I knew the first moment that I laid my eyes on Daniel that that boy wasn't his.

Now I was paying for Shannon's mistake. I was to bear the lies, the hurt, the deception. Because of Shannon, Carl would never trust a woman again, and every time he hit me, choked me, kicked me, smothered me, or threatened to kill me he reiterated this message loud and clear. **ALL WOMEN ARE WHORES!**

OVER ON THE EAST SIDE

CHAPTER 15

Dear Carl,

It is so difficult to go on each day when my mind is cluttered with such distressing thoughts of you and your past. It is as if the past exists as the present. To this day I am still trapped in the past. I cannot distinguish between the past and the present. Time exists as a circular continuum, and I cannot escape. The love we partake of continues to ripen each and every day. This is why I cannot understand the disintegration of our affair. In all reality I recognize that you are a wonderful man with morals and values, but some bothersome notion continues to corrode away at my heart and soul to where I am left with a small morsel of what I entered into this relationship with. You revealed to me each and every detail of your past with noble intentions, but to this day I am plagued with disturbing visual images which permeate each and every crevice of my mind. I am a disturbed individual bothered by events which would net affect someone a bit more sane.

The first time I met you, I could sense an aura of goodness around you. Never before in my life have I become enamored with someone who possesses such a humane demeanor. My entire life I have encompassed myself with the sinister portion of society. I have always surrounded myself with vile men, but then I met you. Just as I felt the goodness in you, you sensed the goodness in me. Deep in my soul I recognized that you were my soul mate. When I gaze into your eyes I am calm. This is why I cannot comprehend the distance I impose upon us. It is as if I am jeopardizing the very entity which fills my existence with such perfection. In all actuality do I wish to be miserable and desolate, a shadow of my former self going through the motions of life, but not really experiencing or relishing them?

At times I will imagine our parting, and all I can envision is me perched upon my bed weeping until the last liquidy teardrop drizzles down my tear stained cheek. It is as if I need to expunge the dreadful grief which buries itself deep within me before I can experience the blissfulness I yearn for. I welcome misery to pervade my life. I have determined a self inflicted punishment for myself. I have surrendered any likelihood for normalcy in our relationship. This union is not only amid you and I, but between you, I, and all womankind. Could there be a justification for my insecurities, or in all rationality am I being preposterous? Is it probable that I can rekindle the faith I once placed in you? I crave the intoxicating giddiness which encompassed my heart at one time, but instead the exhilaration and animated chatter of our partnership has been supplanted with uneasiness and apprehension. The justifications which dribble fourth from your infected lips does not satisfy my uncertainty, for you have tainted the perception I once kept of your sweet soiled soul.

I wish that you never divulged every mystery that you endured. Every night I pray that I can absolve you of all of your sins, but my heart is not filled with such humanity. There is only aversion to what you have witnessed. Were you an innocent bystander or a perverse fiend satisfying a wicked hunger? For you cannot only commit sins through physical acts, but through sight, contemplation, and longing.

OVER ON THE EAST SIDE

CHAPTER 16

It was six years ago that I initially made an entry into the realm of transgression. My friend Katt and I were entertaining the possibility of becoming cocktail waitresses. Money was scarce and in ample demand, therefore exploring strip clubs for the cocktail position seemed to be a clever resolution to our dilemma. I had not yet grasped in sll actuality that contributing to these portals of wrongdoing in any fashion was immoral. As I stepped into the entrance the thrill of a familiar blaring melody dubbed *"Missing You"* by *Everything But the Girl* filled my eardrums. As I proceeded further into the facility, the initial tingling subsided, only to be replaced by a severe realization. It was at this exact moment that my entire conception of mankind altered. No longer could I hold onto fanciful sentiments and sugar coated reveries of how man regards women.

To me my body has forever remained shrouded in secrecy, These unclad women exposing their most sacred regions was incomprehensible. These women were making it so effortless for men to glimpse these performances of vulgarity. It was as if not one being in this chamber of immorality had a conscience. There was no heart flowing through the soiled atmosphere which beset me, only frigid replications of what an individual should subsist as.

Stark naked women were gyrating provocatively to the pulsating rhythmic symphony. The lights glimmered intermittently to the tempo of the melody reflecting off of their bosom, genitals, and rear. One particular woman spread her legs wide open while one gentleman glared defiantly at what lay betwixt her extremities. Another woman performing a lap dance whirled her hips in a circular gesture simulating the act of intercourse, while the man she was roosted upon sat in a trancelike state.

The point which I am attempting to attain by illustrating this is as follows: By being an eyewitness to his spectacle, my perspective of Carl is ravaged. Why did he have to indulge in such a depraved sport? To frolic in strip clubs Carl exploited women. He thinks I am cold towards him, but I don't mean to be. It is just that I have encountered a predicament and do not know how to confront it. I wish my suffering could magically dissolve, but it won't. When I glare into his eyes I only wish to identify with what he underwent, but how? The only sentiment I can conjure up is fury. My conscience is occupied by the sort of fervor which terrifies me, because if I cannot suppress animosity towards Carl, how can we endure? Realizing these truths, my heart forever is blemished. The gnarled damp mixture used to reflect warmth and optimism, but I have relinquished any possibility of recovering my confidence in humanity. Throughout eternity I will prevail as a bitter soul mortified of what this planet has evolved into. This realm is supposed to be a cradle of humanity displaying compassion and appropriate ethics. It should not be a playground for the deterioration of the nurturers of civilization.

Carl professes his disapproval in women stripping. He says there is no portion of his being which roused feelings of arousal, but how can I presume that his confessions are genuine? Each and every day I struggle with the reality that he has been an observer of such foul nauseating behavior. The dilemma which mystifies me most though is the reality that I am completely envious of these strippers. These women lured him into their atmosphere. Carl claims he despises these shameless women, but I remain bewildered as to his recurrent visits there. Men have no conception to the grief they impose upon women.

OVER ON THE EAST SIDE

CHAPTER 17

Whenever my mind deceives me and regresses back to the dismal abyss, I will revert to that one special night, the night which I will treasure forever. That was the night that the movement amongst us came to a standstill, the voices hushed, the lights dimmed, and the symphony amidst us ignited the passion which had concealed itself among the shadows. For one night my senses were awakened, the disgust was lifted, and everyone around us vanished. Many who had tried to sabotage our relationship surrounded us, especially one wicked symbol, but we conquered all. Your tender chocolate colored eyes dissolved my bitterness, healed my sorrow, drained the teardrops swimming in my liquid pools of remorse. We swirled along the dance floor, spellbound by our love, entangling our tongues, and intimately embracing. I prayed that this one night would blot out the painful visions, bury the nude girls slithering down their poles, destroy the image of you spreading Shannon's fleshy legs open while you fucked her. At that very moment all that mattered was our love for each other, our genuine meaningful expression which we so strongly displayed to each other that evening. Could that dance salvage our relationship, absolve you of your sins, mend my broken heart? I hadn't danced in years, but my feet glided along the floor, my fear melted away, as time stopped. Never before had I felt this way. Never before had my love for another man been reciprocated.

My mind drifted to a conversation that my sister, Garrett, and I were engaged in a year ago. I became aware of some knowledge that should have been put to rest years ago. This passage of enlightenment I was about to follow would haunt me, force me to delve inside Carl's conscious and relive the events of his journey with Shannon in that sordid motel room. Sadly, it comforted me to accentuate her flaws, stress her shortcomings in order to alleviate my insecurities, subdue the neurotic pangs that ceaselessly pestered me. Shannon had become an inflated character, an overblown caricature who I despised more than anyone. She never won Carl's heart, but I was still envious, resentful of the time she had spent with Carl before me. Despite Carl's protestations that their relationship was not emotionally or sexually satisfying, I still was resentful. To me, Shannon had snatched an essential part of Carl, no matter how frequently I struggled to deny this. She had captured

117

Carl in all his youth, a naive, polite, and overly nice boy who at this stage in his life was not mistreated by destructive girls who did not share the same intentions as him. Carl had never been a player, always boasting about how selective he was when it came to the women he chose. I, for one, did not understand how Carl could describe himself as picky though, considering that each girl he was with had something wrong with them.

Brandy, his first, and the only girl he claimed to be his girlfriend besides me, was dwarfish in size, barely five feet tall, almost small enough to fit into his pocket. Her scrunched up rat face was blemished by acne, as so was her back. She was only fifteen years old, and nasty as they come, once wiping her bloody vagina with a rag in front of Carl, then casually tossing the rag to the side of the bed while crudely laughing. Julie, a hefty Puerto Rican, with Herpes, had fucked half of Carl's friends and unknowingly to Carl, had a boyfriend. Her own mother warned him to stay away from her, told him that he was too good for her, and after that day he ran and never turned back. Laura, a skeletal twenty eight year old crack addict, had it bad for Carl, but he could not get past her emaciated frame. He was only eighteen years old when he had sex with her, one drunken clumsy experience he wished he would forget. And then there was Shannon. Shannon was not only fat, but grossly obese, weighing in at close to 320 pounds. Many girls that size would have been tormented by their peers, brutally chastised for their plentiful figure, but not Shannon. Shannon had grown up tough, taught to instill fear in others before they had a chance to instill fear in her.

Her own father, the few times be watched her, taught her to fight, forcing her to throw punches at him. Shannon's mother, not prepared to accept the duties of motherhood, would basically drop Shannon off at her grandmother's house, leaving Shannon to practically fend for herself. Despite her excessive weight, Shannon practiced ballet, the only feminine hobby she could ever claim, but as she became older, life's evil temptations derailed her original plans. To survive, she had to be thuggish, take on black mannerisms, join a gang. As part of the initiation she had to fight a group of five seventeen year old boys. She was only fourteen at the time. She made it look effortless, flinging those boys to the side like a cook flings a burger with their spatula. No one intimidated her.

OVER ON THE EAST SIDE

Carl's dad and Shannon's father had been in the same jail years ago. Now, years later when they ran into each other in the trailer park, no one could be more surprised. This was how Shannon and Carl became acquainted with each other, not to mention Joe, Carl's best friend. The three of them began to walk to the bus stop every morning. They became a tight knit threesome, Carl thinking of Shannon as one of the guys.

Shannon had loved Carl since the beginning though. She cleverly disguised her adoration for him by teasing, calling him crocodile teeth or fat ass. Carl had no suspicions at all that Shannon was in love with him. She was clever not to expose her true feelings, how strongly she idolized him, how badly she wanted to make mad passionate animal love to him. In her heart she knew that Carl did not reciprocate those feelings, but after quieting the struggle within herself to ignore her gut, she desperately tried everything she could to win his heart. At the time Carl was also over three hundred pounds, but it did not matter. Unlike the other superficial girls at school who never would consider Carl, Shannon celebrated his weight, indulging in the fact that just like her, he was big also. Carl believed that big belonged with big. To Carl, Shannon was masculine. Perhaps due to the absence of a mother figure, she lacked all feminine attributes which would make her attractive to the opposite sex. Carl has no rational explanation as to how he and Shannon began to fool around, except that heavy drug use, drinking, and desperation were involved. They only kissed once, Carl describing this first and only kiss as disgusting. To Carl, he could be sexually intimate with Shannon, but kissing was an expression of much more.

It bothered me, but I could accept that Shannon and Carl had a sexual relationship. To provide me with some consolation though, I was always told that their sex life was terrible, Carl only caring to satisfy himself, so drugged out on meth that he barely knew who or what he was doing. I would have preferred to been spared the intricate details, to be able to rationalize their intimacy as an accident, but I could no longer do that. Garrett had exposed to something which I would have preferred not to have knowledge of. His intentions were not malicious, but as sensitive as I was, my heart plummeted. My mind retreated back to the conversation Garrett, Sarah, and I had had a year ago.

119

"I just don't understand how he could be with her. She is huge." Sarah said.

"I know. Don't ask me. I saw it firsthand." Garrett chuckled

"You saw what firsthand?" I blindly asked, not expecting to hear what I was about to hear.

"That one night that Melissa, me, Shannon, and Carl went to Tunica. We stayed in this motel room, and it was hard to miss Carl's big ass spreading Shannon's legs open. She was naked as a jay bird and believe me, it was not a pretty sight."

At that moment my heart plunged, descended into a molten puddle of lava, left to dissolve in the boiling pool of volcanic heat. My face numbed and turned ghostly white, my manner becoming lethargic as Sarah and Garrett continued to talk. There was only one thing I could think of asking.

"Garrett, did he ever love her?"

"No. He never loved her. I can promise you that. He did what he did for Daniel. That was it."

I did not understand how spreading Shannon's monstrous legs and humping her like an animal was helping Daniel. Garrett could sense that I was lost in thought.

"Tuesday, you know that Carl was fucked up on meth that night, don't you? He was never in his right mind to fuck her."

"I guess. You have just described their sex life differently than what Carl tells me, that's all. What you described sounds pretty steamy, like hot steamy sex, not that boring shit that Carl told me about."

Flustered, Garrett half chuckled. "It wasn't, believe me. It wasn't."

Garrett's attempts to pacify me were not alleviating the visions, an image of the motel room on that sleazy fun filled night. Slowly, I walked into that motel room, a modest setup with two queen size beds, a floral print in a light pink frame hanging above each bed. The room was dark, except for the light from the street lamp outside which shone through the open crack between the blinds. Garrett and Melissa were sitting up in their bed, Melissa giggling and guzzling on a bottle of rum. Garrett took a drag from his blue plastic bong, the bubbles simmering, a venomous cloud drifting over to Carl and Shannon's bed. Garrett, dressed only in his boxer shorts, walked over to the bathroom, but stopped and squinted his eyes in order to see what Shannon and Carl were doing. The only sound at that

OVER ON THE EAST SIDE

moment was the heavy inhaling and exhaling of Shannon and Carl, Carl thrusting his manhood into Shannon's never-ending ravine. Carl's palms lay flat aghast the inside of Shannon's pale doughy knees as he stretched out her legs as wide as he could. Shannon laid motionless, her shallow breathing and grunts of gratification quickening Carl's rhythm as he callously thrust himself into her. Chunks of her blubbery flesh jiggled as Carl penetrated her. Her thighs looked like the thighs of a prize winning pig, fatty and pink. Carl suckled on her overblown breasts, lacking form, and dangling to her side. He looked like a calf pumping milk out of it's mother. Garrett scrambled to the bathroom, chuckling, as Carl climaxed. Carl lay on top of Shannon for a moment, their damp skin clinging to each other. As he rolled off of her their sticky skin adhered to each other, making moist squishing noises. Envision a wad of bubble gum clinging to the sole of a shoe, the gluey gum extending as it is pulled off of the shoe. Carl, disoriented, fumbled for his pack of cigarettes and lighter on the nightstand, accidentally knocking a black leather bound bible situated at the left hand corner of the table to the floor. Shannon's bulbous figure wobbled to the side of the bed, where she grabbed her pack of cigarettes, her obnoxious booming voice and laughter echoing as Garrett ran out of the bathroom.

The intimacy between them was so impersonal, so very different from Carl and I after we had sex. Carl remained indifferent, detached from this woman and what they had just done. So badly I wanted to snatch him away from her domineering grasp, entice Carl with my feminine curves and soft skin. I never wanted Carl to belong to Shannon, not now, not in the future, and not in the past, but it was too late. Shannon would always possess a part of Carl's life that I never could, his past.

In my mind's eye I dashed out of that room as fast as I could, running until my legs violently trembled and my breathing ceased. I squatted down, placing my head between my legs and quietly sobbing, mourning a lost piece of my heart that I would never recapture. Carl might not have loved Shannon, showered Shannon with sprinkles of tenderness, or even respected her, but she had some sort of unnatural hold over him. Shannon was such an eccentric personality that people would always talk about her. Therefore her monstrous shadow would constantly pursue me, eclipse the rays of blissfulness attempting to fill me with peace. That night I had felt like I lost Carl, lost him to Shannon and their past. His account of their relationship was appearing quite different, especially that devilish night of events which Garrett so generously informed me of. That night I wrote a letter to Carl.

Dear Carl,

I just am writing this letter to tell you how much I love you. Tonight your brother told me about you and Shannon in the motel room. It hurt me a lot to find out that you shared such a personal moment with her in such a vulgar way. I am selfish, because I only want to think that you were with me in that way. Rationally, I know that it is not going to be that way. We are both not virgins, but I just want you to promise me that you never loved her, not the same way that you love me. Please, promise me that. I just love you so much. I have never loved a man like the way I love you. I have never experienced love like this. I just do not want to think that Shannon had the same thing that we have now. My heart feels like it is breaking at this very moment. I want to see you so badly, to touch you, to feel you. Please let me know that you want the same. I love you.
Love,
* Tuesday.*

I folded up the note and placed it under my pillow, tightly hugging the pillow, pretending that it was Carl. The next day I wanted to confront Carl and probe into his past. I wanted to find out what his intentions were with Shannon. As soon as he saw my ashen face, he could sense that I was troubled. We sat outside on a bench in front of the park while my sister and Garrett talked in the house.

"Carl. I need to talk to you about something."

"Uh, oh. What did I do now?" He cautiously asked.

"Nothing." I quickly reassured him. It has nothing to do with you now. It has something to do with what happened in the past, but I don't want you to get mad, alright?"

"I mean, I can't promise that I am not going to get mad. What is it? You are starting to scare me." He defensively retorted.

"It's nothing bad. It has something to do with what your brother told me last night, but please. You have to promise not to say anything to him. I don't think he meant to hurt me. It just came out."

"What is it already?"

"Well, do you remember a trip you took with Shannon to a motel room a couple of years back?"

"Yey. Uh, oh. Where are you going with this?"

"Well, Garrett told me that he saw you and Shannon having sex, that you were spreading her legs wide open, and he saw everything."

"What are you talking about? I was on meth, drugged out of my mind. That is the only way I'd fuck that bitch. If you think that the sex was good, then you are out of your mind."

"I didn't say the sex was good. It's just different from how you described it."

"You know what. I don't have to take this shit. I'm outta here. I'll give you a call tomorrow, alright."

"Alright." I quietly said, my head down, praying this wasn't the last time I'd ever see him.

CHAPTER 18

You supposedly fell in love with me, because you said that I was different from all of the other girls. You thought I was classy. You placed me upon a pedestal. You called me an angel. If respecting myself was such a turn on to you, then I can't even begin to understand why you visited strip clubs, especially when you so adamantly denied any association with those places.

"Sure I was with dog ugly girls. Sandy, she looked like a rat, and God did she break out. She had really bad pimples all over her face and her back. It practically covered her entire body, but strangely I was whipped. Maria, the Puerto Rican girl. Sure, she was a bit on the heavy side, not as big as Shannon, maybe about half her size, and she had a boyfriend. She was just fucking me on the side, but boy she put a spell on me too. Barbara Jean, she was just ugly, and she also had a boyfriend, but oddly I was whipped by her too, and then there was Shannon. I don't know what in god's name made me end up with her, but a guy like me thought he couldn't get anybody, until you came along. I thought you were so hot. My friends actually thought you were hot. I never ever have had my friends compliment me on my girlfriends, but with you they did. You were the innocent looking girl that everyone wants. That's why I thought that it was strange that I was not whipped by you. When I walked into that strip club, I realized that what I had at home was so lame. I thought I'd think different. I thought I wouldn't even be tempted. I thought that you were so beautiful that when I laid my eyes upon other naked flesh, that they'd be pale in comparison, but I surprised myself."

He angrily split my shirt open revealing my naked breasts in the mirror.

"These, you see unfortunately are way too saggy." he sneered, abrasively squeezing at my right breast and then releasing his firm clasp causing it to ricochet back like a boomerang against my chest. My elongated droopy breasts hung lifelessly resembling two summer sausages unwrapped from their casing, raw and exposed.

"They should be much higher. You are twenty-eight years old, and you look like an old lady. Not the girls over there, oh no. Their breasts are firm and round and high. They don't hang down to their bellies like yours, and speaking of bellies..." he brusquely brushed his fingertips over my plump round belly adorned with crinkled white stretch marks. "This is not what a stomach should look like you fuckin old ugly bitch. The girls over there. Their stomachs are completely flat. God they are sexy with their tan flat stomachs and adorable belly buttons. Your ass," he proceeded to criticize next. Now that's a shame." He ripped off my pants humiliating me even further. Not one dimple those girls have, not one.. You could fling a quarter off of one of their cheeks and it would bounce right off." He disgustingly chuckled making my insides curdle and feel like they were going to decompose right then and there. "Look at your white flabby ass. Girl you need a tan or something." He said fiercely smacking the left cheek and leaving a bright red imprint. "Maybe it's a Jewish thing or something. Maybe you Jewish chicks just sag earlier in all the wrong places. I think that's why I was never whipped by you. How could I possibly get whipped by a girl who has the body of a seventy year old woman?" he evilly cackled. "After I get done with you no one will ever want your ass. I'll make sure of it."

"Stop, stop please. I don't want to hear this. I don't know why you are doing this to me. You have already hurt me enough. Please, Carl tell me that you are lying. You won your game, alright. You can stop. Tell me that those girls weren't hot like you told me before. At least give me that."

"I don't have to give you shit. God, you are a pathetic excuse for a female. All you care about is if you look better than everyone else. You constantly compare yourself. Give it a rest already. You women are so god damn competitive. It's ridiculous."

"How can I not compare myself to other girls when you throw it in my face. You are the one downing me. You are the one telling me that I am not good enough. I might not have big boobs or a tan, but I have substance. I actually have a brain. I'm sorry that you can't appreciate that."

"Why should I appreciate a brain? Brains are boring. You know, I would love to tell you different. I wish I could tell you that you are the hottest chick out there, but I can't do that. That is one thing I do not do. I never lie. There is always going to be someone prettier and hotter than you. That is something that you are going to have to get used to."

"I don't need a lesson in self esteem Carl."

"Shut up. I'm talking dumbass, Unfortunately all of those girls in those places are hotter than you. You might be able to measure up to them if you maybe got a boob job or worked on that stomach of yours. Other than that sweetheart. You are a lost cause. I'll see you later." He walked out of the apartment slamming the door behind him.

OVER ON THE EAST SIDE

CHAPTER 19

I shut my eyes and began to drift off. I was walking down a city street with a teenage boy. He struck a match and lit the tip of a cigarette. We both sat in front of a store on a bench, smoking and observing the vast assortment of people who walked by. Suddenly, a female officer approached the boy, inquiring him about his age. She placed a breathalyzer into his mouth and took a reading. Amazingly, despite the fact that he was inebriated his reading was below the legal limit showing that he was not legally drunk. I sighed in relief, because I knew that I would have been held accountable for contributing to this boys delinquency. The people continued to walk by, the street becoming livelier as the night progressed. Suddenly, I could hear booming shouts echo from across the street. It was Carl. He was bundled in a camouflage army jacket and wore a navy blue baseball cap. He dashed up to me, his arms frantically flapping at his sides, but instead of attacking me, he maintained about a foot of distance between him and myself. He stood there, blaring obscenities and accusing me of infidelity. His scolding became more severe, his deafening screams causing a crowd to gather. He began to scamper back and forth, shoving people to the ground as he dashed past them. They crashed to the ground, and cracked in half as their bodies hit the pavement. They looked like eggshells, their brittle casings shattering, their yolks splattering as soon as they hit the concrete. I tiptoed through the chaos, the soles of my shoes sticking to the gooey yolk. I bellowed for help as loudly as I could.

"Help me. Please. Help me. He is crazy!" I pleaded to the female officer.

I looked around and Carl had vanished. He was nowhere to be found. My heart sunk, and my terror changed to concern. I had this nagging fear that Carl was dead. I hysterically ran through the city streets, stepping over the body bags lined up on the sidewalk. I cried out for Carl, praying that he had not departed from the living, but my hope was fleeting for as I treaded over one body bag in particular, an eerie sensation washed over me. I slowly unzipped the body bag and was confronted with what I had been dreading. Carl's beautifully sculpted face was barely discernable. His eyeballs had been gouged out, leaving his emptied sockets to decay. His bronzed skin was splattered with blood and clumps of his abundantly thick hair had been pulled out, leaving several bald patches. I caressed his few remaining ebony strands and placed his battered head into my lap. I cradled him back and forth, my teardrops trickling into his vacuous sockets. The same man that I had feared only a short while ago was the same exact man that I was weeping over at this very moment.

My dream paralleled my life with Carl. In one respect I feared Carl, but in another regard I pitied him. At one moment I would try to liberate myself from his domineering grasp, but during an ensuing moment I would treat him like a child, comforting him and gently patting his head in an attempt to smother his insecurities. Our relationship was never normal. Instantaneously, I would assume an authoritative role only minutes after being coddled like a child. There was never a middle ground, and that is all I wished for. I only craved the stability that all other fortunate couples took for granted. I yearned for friendship, for mutual respect, for a degree of intimacy which was not only sexual, but this did not seem likely. Instead of nurturing each other we pounded each other down. We were not friends nor were we enemies. Instead we continued to engage in an unhealthy co-dependency, neither of us courageous enough to sacrifice our union for a more healthy life of lone*liness.*

The following night I dreamed that Carl was having sex with three beautiful women. One of them was Puerto Rican, the other was Asian, and the third girl was blonde. I patiently waited outside the room while Carl fucked all three of them. At first it did not bother me that he was making love to three women simultaneously, but as the dream progressed I became quite envious. I questioned Carl about the encounter, gently prodding him as to if I made love better than those girls, but he was quite hesitant to tell me the truth. I could not rationally justify my reason for interrogating him, but as usual my competitive nature clouded my logic.

I do not know why I always have to compare myself to other women. Logically, I realize how superficial I am being, but it does not stop me from continuing to probe. No matter how much I inquire about Carl's past, hoping to uncover an answer which will completely pacify my insecurities, I realize that this will never happen. He constantly stresses this to me, but I refuse to listen for I need to know that I am the best he was ever with or the best he has seen. I need to feel that I am the best. I need physical proof laid before me to alleviate my lack of confidence, because until that moment there will be no hope. My unquenchable thirst to attain superiority in his life is absolutely sickening, and my dreams only reinforce my obsession to be perfect.

We never had a chance. From the beginning we were doomed, chained to our pasts, predestined to a life of heartache. The tragic reality of it all is that we controlled our own fate. If I really wanted to I could have steered our relationship in an entirely different direction, but I sabotaged any chance for happiness. I honestly think I would rather be miserable than happy. If something isn't tragically wrong in my life, I am lost. Therefore I created a problem to regain some sort of control. I chastise every component of Carl's life, his past ways, his present ways, his future. I nit-pick until we are both physically and mentally drained. This is who I am. This is who I have become, and I hate it. It would be so much easier not to care, to be one of those airy headed girls comfortable enough with themselves and their sexuality. I would love to be free, not to have such a strong sense of morality ingrained into my conscience. How I wish I could peel off the restrictive layers which confine me to a world of innocence and dance upon a table controlling the room as I gyrate stark naked. Then I wouldn't care. I would remain oblivious to the wickedness that brews in this world, because I would be a part of it. My sensitivity would not destroy me and neither would my conscience, since I would not have one. I would be consumed with only immoral thoughts. Acts of sin would manipulate my every move and every action until I was a dim-witted, synthetic reproduction of what I used to exist as. Never again would I have to be envious of these artificial women, because I would be one of them. I would never have to compare myself or think I was not good enough, because men would be paying their hard earned money to see me. Instead of being the girlfriend at home curled up into a ball and mourning the innocence that is lost in the world, I could be one of the instigators. I could stop hating, stop bearing the weight of the world upon my tiny shoulders and get lost shedding my inhibitions. Morally sound girls would weep over me, would despise me but secretly wish that they were me.

In reality I did not wish for this, but it seemed easier. To detach my mind from my body seemed like a tempting option, to have my spirit mingle with the devil's children, to burn to a crisp in the underworld. This is what I secretly wished for. No matter how pure and righteous I was, there would always be a portion of me that secretly craved to be identical to what I despised. Until I dabbled in a world which repulsed me, I would remain fearful, frightened that sin would snatch my Carl away from me. How could I hold the same appeal as such blatantly slutty women? I couldn't, therefore I would just wait for Carl to toss my lackluster self to the side and dive into a world of stimulating spicy women. Never mind if they were dreadful conversationalists, or contained absolutely nothing in their hollow heads. Men did not care about that. As long as they could strut their pretty little bodies along a stage, protrude their swollen breasts, and spread their legs wide open, men would be drooling. I was not comfortable enough with myself to expose my vulnerabilities, because maybe if was, I could regain the control that I had been searching for.

CHAPTER 20

"You know I used to be such a loving little boy. I had about twenty different girlfriends. I was so well mannered, always said please and thank you. I had the prettiest head of hair, thick dark curls that the girls would love to mess up. I loved my life until I met that fat bitch! To this day I blame my dad for introducing me to Shannon. If my father and her dad wouldn't have been in jail together I would have never even met her!"

"Your fathers were in jail together?" I asked.

"Yey, for two years. Yep, they were buddies, the kings of that prison boy. Nobody crossed their path."

"It has to be more than coincidence that they ended up at the same trailer park."

"I guess. A small fucking world. At age eighteen I was still in church. I would preach to people who did wrong. *I* lived my life strictly by the bible. I was going to save myself for my wife. I did not believe in sex before marriage. To me that was the ultimate sin, but I guess I was tired of being alone so when the first girl showed me attention I was ready to jump."

"Let me guess. You are talking about Brandy."

"Yep. I could not believe that a girl showed interest in me. I had never even kissed a girl. I was the fat kid that no one wanted, and she was my first piece of ass. It did not matter to me that she looked like a little rat or was a fuckin midget. She was so small you could practically fit her into your pocket, and that girl was fucked up."

"How?" I curiously asked.

"She was only fifteen, lost her virginity at thirteen. We were driving through a field one night, and she made me stop the car, started becoming real hysterical, screaming and shaking. She said that she had just seen her dead aunt and that she was coming for her to take her to hell."

"Didn't that make you think that this girl might have been crazy?"

"Yey, but I didn't care. I couldn't afford to be picky. After having sex I pretty much ruined what God had planned out for me, so I started smoking pot. One afternoon Joe handed me a joint, and I took a puff and I liked it. I liked it so much that I kept puffing on it. Nothing had ever made me feel so good, and from then on I couldn't stop. When I smoked weed, my problems with Brandy were forgotten."

"So why did you guys split up?"

"You would never guess, for the most stupid reason. We broke up on the night of prom. I wanted to go to prom, but she had to go to Motorcross, and she broke up with me over that! I cried for maybe a day until I realized that she wasn't worth it. That girl was not right in the head. Do you know what else she did?"

"What?" I asked in a monotone voice, rolling my eyes.

"I found out that she had called me on the phone while we were going out while she was fucking some guy. Can you believe that? What kind of girl would fuck someone else and call their boyfriend up?"

"She sounds like trash to me. You should be glad that she dumped you. It was a blessing in disguise."

"Yep. I would have never found a hottie like you otherwise."

"Well, what happened after she dumped you then?"

"That was when I got with Shannon. Well, I never actually got with her, but that was when we started fooling around. Actually, I think I started fooling around with her when I was still going out with Brandy."

"If you were so in love with Brandy then why would you cheat on her with someone that you didn't really like?"

"I don't know what was going through my head. I liked pot, and Shannon was the biggest pot head in the trailer park. She was like a dude. She was cool to hang out with like one of the guys. That is why I can't understand how I could even stick my dick into her."

"You must have liked it somewhat." I snottily retorted.

"No, Tuesday. It wasn't like that. You could get anyone you wanted. I couldn't. Girls were not lined up at my door to go out with me so I had to take what I could get. That bitch wouldn't leave me alone. She was always calling me, dropping over at my house with weed. She knew how to trap me. We would walk to the bus stop together before and after school. She was cool to hang out with until we started fucking. I had stopped talking to her for a couple of months and then one day I got a call from her. She told me that she was pregnant and that it was between me and another guy. My jaw dropped open. I hated myself. I did not want to face the truth that I had gotten that fat bitch pregnant. For that entire year I partied so hard. I snorted Coke every moment of the day to forget. For one year straight I was high on Coke. I almost died twice. If it wasn't for

Joe I would have died, but I did not care. He had to carry me out into the snow when I was so drugged up or I would have died. You don't understand. You think that me and Shannon had this wonderful thing going, but we didn't. I couldn't stand that bitch, and I couldn't face that I was with her. It was easier to be all coked up than to face the truth. I missed the ultrasound. I missed the birth. I was never there for her. When I got a call from Shannon that she was at the hospital with Daniel, I saw her. My mom and I went and when my mom held Daniel, the first thing she said was that that baby wasn't mine, but I didn't listen. I should have had the paternity test right there, but I couldn't leave that little boy's side."

"I don't understand why you wouldn't have the test if you hated her so much. I mean if you don't want to be with somebody, I would think that you would try to go to extreme lengths to find out that that baby wasn't yours."

"You would think, but you have to keep in mind how lonely I was. When I got to that hospital, the first thing I asked was, where's the other guy, but she couldn't even tell me."

"Do you even think she told the other guy about the baby?"

"Honestly, I don't. I think she knew that she had a sucker. She knew how sensitive I was. She was like one of those preying mantis bugs. She knew what my weaknesses were. When Daniel was born he didn't look black. He looked just like me. He had my pug nose, brown eyes, and bent ear. He was light. You couldn't tell that he was black at all. I thought he was mine, and Shannon never tried to tell me different. For another year I stayed coked up. I wasn't in that boy's life for the first year. I partied and partied and partied, snorted thousands of dollars of coke up my nose, until one day I realized what I was doing. I realized that I had a kid out there, and I could not believe what I was doing. That boy saved my life. If it was not for him I would have died."

"So how did it get from you starting to see Daniel to you moving in with him and Shannon?" I asked.

"I was stupid. My dad wasn't there for me, and I didn't want to be like that. I thought that you had to live with your child to provide for them in every way. Everyone told me that I didn't have to live with her, that I was making a big mistake, but I didn't listen. My mom begged me not to move in with her. My friends begged me not to move in with her, but again I didn't listen. We were cool at first. I mean I didn't like her like that, but we got along. From the beginning I told her that we were not together, and she seemed cool with that."

"Carl, how can you tell a girl that you are not with her if you are moving in with her, helping to take care of her child, and fucking her?"

"I know, it sounds bad, but if you were there, you would have seen how clear I made it to her. I bought a trailer, and she tried so hard. Even when we fought she would wait on me hand and foot. Every night she had these huge dinners on the table. The laundry would be done, but I didn't care. I couldn't stand that bitch. I would get home from work, make her cry, she would go to her room for hours, I would leave to go out and then when I got home she would be sleeping. You think that we fight bad. That is nothing. At least I love you. When I fought with her I hated her. You should have seen how many holes I punched in that wall. So many times I wanted to hit her, but I thought that was my kid's mom, so I didn't. I was scared to meet anyone else. I thought that if I met someone that I really liked that she would ruin it. Yey, I fucked other girls, but those girls meant nothing to me, until I met you. With you I didn't care. I knew that I could live with you and I wanted to spend the rest of my life with you. You were the prettiest thing I had ever laid my eyes on. I mean there are ugly girls out there and pretty girls, but you beat them all. I could tell that you were special. You were not like these other Missouri girls. You do not understand how hot you were to me. I had never had a hot girl. That night when I left Woody's you should have heard me. I could not stop looking at that little slip of paper you wrote your phone number on. I thought it was the wrong one. I was like, *Joe, can you believe that I got a hot girl's number?* You were the classy girl that I always dreamed of. You were my fantasy girl. You were the most ordinary, I mean extraordinary, is that the word?"

Yey." I replied glowing and giggling simultaneously

"Anyways, you were the most special angel I had ever laid my eyes on. I knew that we would be together forever. It was love at first sight. I was still scared that Shannon would fuck it up, but I had to try this time. It was different."

"She almost did fuck it up."

"Yey, she did, but not in the long run. You have to understand. I love you so much. When you constantly don't think that you are good enough it hurts me. To think that those cheap whores are better than you is unbelievable. If you could only see those girls."

"I know, Carl, but don't you see? You are supposed to be my good guy. You are not like that, and that is why I don't understand how you could go into those places."

"I don't either, but I never went there alone. It was not like I thought, *hey I want to go to a strip club today.* It was something to do with my friends."

"Couldn't you have found something else to do?" I snottily asked.

"It was always late at night when everything else was closed."

"Couldn't you have gone to the Oz or Pops?"

"Yey, we would go to the Oz and Pops, but like I said it was just something to do."

"I don't see how looking at naked women is just something to do."

"1 don't either babe, but it just happened. You cannot hold it against me. You have done some stupid things in your past, and I have done some stupid things in my past. You can't hold that against me for the rest of my life."

"Yes, I can." I ignorantly answered.
"I don't even see how you can judge me. You have been with how many guys?"

"That is normal though, Carl. I looked at each guy as an individual. I didn't clump them together in one big lump. I don't even understand how you can like one girl when you were so use to looking at them as one, just a crowd of naked women without feelings or personalities, just bodies. Don't you see something wrong with that?"

"Of course I see something wrong with it. That is why I don't go to those places. They did nothing for me. I am sorry, but it takes a little more that a pair of tits and pussy to turn me on."

"I'm sorry, Carl, but I just can't believe you. If it didn't turn you on, you wouldn't have gone there every day!"

"Who said I went there every day?"

"You did, genius."

"No. I would have to meet the boss after work to get my check, but I would usually meet him outside in the parking lot."

"If you met him outside, then how did that black girl try to give you a hand job?"

"That was the last time I went in there. After that I met him in the parking lot."

"Carl, your story is just not adding up. One minute you tell me that you went in there every day, then you went in there every Friday. Now you never went in there, just in the parking lot. Give me a break. How many times are you going to change your story?"

"I'm telling you the truth Tuesday. Why are you trying to pick a fight?"

"Because, I hate you for what you have done. I hate those girls and I want to punish you for looking at them. I try to be so good, such a nice classy girl, but it doesn't matter. Why should I try to be good? Yey, you like me, but you also liked them. If you didn't you wouldn't have kept going back."

"Tuesday, don't start this again."

"Why? It bothers me bad. It will always bother me. I want a nice guy, and a nice guy doesn't go to strip clubs every day. A nice guy doesn't tell me that he likes those places just because he is a man. A nice guy doesn't tell me that he almost got a hand job by a stripper at a bar. A nice guy doesn't tell me that he used to like looking at the pussy, but he got burnt out on it. A nice guy doesn't tell me that he enjoyed a few of the strippers, especially the ones that looked like school girls, whatever that means. You can pretend that you are a nice guy, but I will never believe it!"

OVER ON THE EAST SIDE

CHAPTER 21

It was New Years Eve, a time of festivity and jubilation, but in my abode a conflict of immense proportions was about to commence. Once again I became cool and reserved, my former spirited self dwindling away until I completely diminished. Reality was soon to be replaced by a demented rendition of what I presumed the truth to be. I disregarded that he displayed distinct qualities which no other male that I met had. This was the one man that never abandoned me. It seemed that not one man in my life ever found me fascinating enough to keep around. I was not the class of woman to convert a man into commitment. There was not one individual who ever yearned to see my grinning face when I felt content, or wipe away my tears of sorrow when I was dispirited and dejected, but the man beside me did. This man cherished me more than all the worthless males put together that I dated, yet I continued to be blind. For the only thing I could see in front of me was a twisted and corrupt pervert instead of the misguided, upstanding man that he actually existed to be.

I could sense his fidgety matter and how apprehensive he was to show any tenderness towards me for the fact that it might not be returned, but I was deadened. Anyone in a paralyzed state such as I was experiencing was indifferent to the torture I administered onto him. Instead of attempting to conceive the agony I endured, he became defensive and hostile.

> "You better start shaping up, or I'll leave you, just like I left Shannon."

Hearing this made me question the validity of our relationship. To equate his and Shannon's partnership with ours made me feel as if our entire union was a deception. My mind repeatedly would falsify the accuracy of the circumstances, leaving me with a demented interpretation of what in all actuality transpired. Hearing what he had just said, I dived towards him pulling at his shirt, shreds of the flannel pattern descending to the ground. Slapping him relentlessly, my hands bloody, chapped and raw, until he could no longer tolerate the misfortune bestowed upon him. With a most destructive glare, he hoisted me up against the wall deliriously cupping his fingers around my neck, squeezing out any last breath which engulfed my insides. My eyeballs spurted forth suspended like two springs in midair, and never in my existence did I feel so defenseless. At that moment I likened myself to a scrawny, soiled puppy dog, its fur matted down, dampened and dingy, mistreated by its owner, being berated unceasingly for any minute infraction it perpetrated. It was as if all of the vital juices which coated my insides squirted forth as teardrops, and as soon as his fingers unclenched my throat, I descended to the floor cowering in a fetal position, weeping like a newborn.

OVER ON THE EAST SIDE

CHAPTER 22

It was time for a change. The flaxen mane which I had enjoyed for years had been looking dull lately. I wanted to liven things up a bit, spice up the color with ginger undertones and buttery highlights. I wanted to brighten up my features which had been looking so dull lately. I decided on getting my hair colored at P.C. Nickels hair salon, a beauty shop planted on the first floor of a department store. Carl had been ill all day. His throat was terribly congested and his forehead was feeling hot and clammy. All day he had confined himself to our bedroom, tossing and turning every two minutes. His haunting moans echoed throughout the apartment. Upon entering the bedroom, the stench of sickness drifted throughout the air. The stale air floated into my nostrils and down my throat, filling my airway with a sour taste. I lovingly stared down at Carl, admiring his handsome features. Even when he was ill his splendor shined right through. His cheekbones were deeply flushed, and he was heavily perspiring. I gently stroked his forehead, the sticky sweat covering my fingertips with a moist layer. He looked like a peaceful little boy not capable of instilling fear in another. He fluttered his eyelids finally looking up at me, his gentle brown eyes emitting such warmth that I practically melted.

"Hi mama." Carl softly uttered.

"Hey. How are you feeling?" I compassionately inquired.

"I feel like shit." He replied coughing.

"I know you do," I said stroking his forehead. "You feel like you have a fever. Just keep sleeping and you'll feel so much better."

"I can't. I have to pick up Daniel."

"You need to rest. That is why you always get sick."

"I know, but I have too much to do to just think about lying here."

"All right. Well, I have to get my hair done. It's probably going to take a while. They have to do quite a bit to it."

"I don't want my mama to leave. I will miss you. Who is going to take care of me?"

"I'll be back soon. Don't worry."

Carl was quite good at giving me guilt trips. He had always been searching for a motherly figure to take the place of his own. In one respect he needed to assume an ultimate position of authority, controlling me to the point where I could barely breathe. In an entirely different regard, he wished to be taken care of by another, just as his mother had babied him. At certain times he craved to be reprimanded and treated as if he were a child, but at other times I was the child being scolded and overpowered. I never knew which role I was going to play. Was I going to be the vulnerable child, immersed in her own web of fragility, too timid to find her way out? Was I going to be the maternal figure, her motherly warmth radiating, having Carl suckle at my breast to obtain the nutrients from the sweet milky fluid which he so desperately needed. Both of the roles depleted my energy and lessened me as a woman. I was neither Carl's mother nor daughter, but I continued the charade, for fear of the consequences if I did not.

"Well, give me a kiss. I'll be back when you get here." He said.

Carl puckered his lips, and I reached down to plant a warm kiss upon them. The warmth emitted from the kiss instantly surged through my veins filling me with a brief moment of contentedness. The syrupy flavor from the cough medicine lingered on his tongue. His sweet chocolate kiss sugared my lips. I licked his tongue, his gums, his teeth. Our sticky lips were held together by the syrupy concoction, and I couldn't have felt more at peace than at that moment. I treasured these brief moments of tenderness from Carl for I knew that his compassion was bound to vanish sometime. The horrible moments were terrifying, but the good moments were absolutely wonderful, and I always forgot how terrible things had really become. I lived in the moment, never looking beyond to the future. I could not confront the truth that my relationship was slowly unraveling and destined to end in heartbreak.

I felt like I could have floated out of the bedroom that afternoon. How could such a sweet innocent man instill such an intense degree of panic in me at times? Today was going to be the day of total transformation. My drab lifeless hair was going to be painted in vibrant golden and reddish hues, and my relationship was going to become one of perfection. We were going to be a couple that others envied. There would be no more violence, no more jealousy, no emotional abuse. Never again would I be the battered woman that others pitied. There would be no more bruises, no more burns, not one wound to arouse suspicion in others. I would never shed an ounce of blood again to symbolize that love damaged the ones it touched. From this day on our love would be untainted. Dirty sex would be reserved for dirty people, not a pure perfect couple such as us. From now on making love would be an expression of our devotion to each other, not just an indulgence to titillate our senses.

I walked into P.C. Nickels in good spirits that afternoon. The receptionist at the desk had the most striking shade of red I had ever feasted my eyes on. Her red hair was the color of the juicy pulp from within the core of a pumpkin. That was the shade I wanted, the shade that would rejuvenate my senses, add life to my tired skin, subtract years from my aging face. Red hair brought back memories of my youth, transported me to a simpler place and time void of the complications that maturity had brought on. My eyes scoured the salon for the fortunate soul that would be responsible for changing my life. I was hoping not to suffer at the hands of someone too intimidating. I wanted an artist, someone to sculpt these lifeless strands into a masterpiece. There were certain stylists that I would have preferred. Some appeared kinder, gentler.

"Tuesday." A kind looking blonde with a soothing voice called.

I rapidly stood up and followed the woman to a chair.

"Hi. My name is Pam. So, what do you have in mind today?"

Already, I felt a strong connection with this woman. I estimated that she was probably in her middle forties, but she was absolutely striking. Her shoulder length blonde hair was highlighted with bright lemony highlights that accented her twinkling blue eyes perfectly. She had the most gentle smile, a beam which conveyed not only delight, but wisdom well beyond her years.

"Well, I was wanting a change. I have had blonde hair for a while, and I used to have red hair. I was wondering if I could possibly go back to red hair, not something really dark, something light to where if it washed out, it would be more on the blonde side than brown. I just don't know if it will work on my hair though. I don't want it to streak."

"Wow! It sounds like you know quite a bit about hair."

I eagerly shook my head in agreement, thankful for the recognition of my knowledge in that area. "Why don't you take down your hair so we can have a look at what we are dealing with."

I unfastened the ponytail holder, and the ashy mess tumbled onto my shoulders. She gently picked at the top layer inspecting it.

"Well, your hair shaft is relatively strong considering that you have bleached your hair so many times, but I am not sure if red would work. I have to warn you that changing your hair to red would be very expensive and timely. I have the time, but I am not going to guarantee that the color will blend evenly." I appreciated her honesty, but the lack of optimism proved disheartening.

"You know what. I think I'll just stick to blonde then." I replied realizing that my dream to go back to red had died.

"Alright. I just try to be honest with my clients. So, you just sit here and I will be right back. I'm going to mix the bleach."

As promised, a couple of minutes later she returned with a plastic bowl full of a baby blue liquid mixture. She stirred the concoction with her plastic spoon and began to section my hair, beginning with the back.

"Yey, I try to educate my clients about hair. Instead of promising them something that they can't have I try to teach them to be realists. Like I told one client today who worked in a club, you have to take care of your hair, use the right products, or it won't respond. She was a stripper and hair is very important to them. A lot of the girls are able to afford hair extensions, but she could not. She said one of the girls wear very long blond hair extensions, because the men like the long blonde hair."

I was feeling so wonderful just a few minutes ago until I had to hear about strippers. What Pam had been telling me confirmed my insecurities. Visions of lean tan bodies with their long flaxen manes bouncing off of their buttocks consumed me. I could see or hear nothing else. These women sounded as if they were high maintenance, not the crack whores that Carl had recounted in his tasteless tales. If they were conscious enough to have hair extensions put in and get breast implants, they could not have been that sore on the eyes. I stared in the mirror as Pam tugged on my hair. How could Carl have settled for someone as lackluster as I when he had been witness to all of these sensational looking women out there?

A flamboyant hairdresser walked up to Pam at that second inquiring about the previous client she had that afternoon.

"So, that girl looked pretty young today." He said.

"Yey. She had her kid and her boyfriend with her. I just associate that lifestyle with drugs. You know, having to stay up all night and sleep all day."

"Yey. Do you think she was trying to just make a quick buck?"

"I'm not sure. I think she has just gotten use to that lifestyle and knows of no other. She seemed like a nice girl."

"I guess to each his own, huh?"

"Yep."

"Well, I'll see you later. I have to go to my sisters tonight. She's having some sort of dinner party." "Have fun."

He made his way over to his cubicle and began sweeping the hair into a dustpan. From that moment on I was miserable. I never wanted to hear about strippers again, but that did not seem likely. No matter how hard I tried to bury Carl's past, it always resurfaced, only to slap me in the face harder each time. There seemed to be an unnatural notoriety and thirst about strippers and their lifestyle. The glamour as well as the danger captivated people's interest like no other profession. No one felt the same way as I did. No one saw stripping off your clothes for a living as immoral. No one exhibited the anger that I did. Pam dipped her brush into the gooey mixture and began to paint individual strands of my hair until my entire head was saturated with dye.

"Alright, I am going to turn on the timer for about twenty minutes. You can just sit and relax. Would you like a Coke or something?"

"No, thank you." I politely replied trying to conceal how insufficient I was feeling inside.

Pam placed a crisp dollar bill into the soda machine and planted herself in the chair directly across from me.

"Gosh, I am just so tired these days. It has not been a good year. My husband died just a few short months ago, and I just haven't been the same. He was the most wonderful kind man and he died of a heart attack."

"I am so sorry." I meaningfully replied, feeling selfish for a moment that I was worrying about strippers while this woman had experienced so much worse.

"Thank you. I just have trouble getting up in the morning these days, and now my finger is infected." Pam said showing me her finger which was wrapped in a plastic glove.

"I have to wear this glove at all times so it doesn't get infected,"

"Yey, things are tough. I know, believe me. I've been on anti-depressants for the past few months."

"Oh, are you depressed?" Pam asked.

"Yey. I have been for years, but lately I have been using them to deal with my boyfriend."

"Is he abusive?"

"Yeeeey," I reluctantly answered. "Emotionally and physically."

"That sounds like my first husband. We had three children, two boys and a little girl. For thirteen years I stayed until it just proved to be too much."

"How did you finally decide to leave?"

"I Just had had enough. He would threaten me all of the time, tell me that if I left he'd kill the kids and me. That was basically why I stayed, but when the kids got older, I finally had the courage to leave. I was like, if he wants to kill me, let him kill me. I was not going to live in fear anymore. I moved out into my own apartment, and sure at night I was scared, but gradually day after day it got better."

"Did he ever put you in the hospital?"

"No, but I blacked out a couple of times. He would choke me, sit on me, use the back of his hand to slap me when I was pregnant. For some reason they know what to do, so they won't get in trouble. He was an alcoholic, and that was when he got the meanest. Finally, when I found out that he had two girls in two different towns on the side I decided that enough was enough."

"Oh, my God, he had two girls on the side?"

"Yey, it's ironic isn't it? I couldn't go barely anywhere without him asking me where I was going or accusing me of cheating on him, but he was the one who was cheating on me. He begged me not to go at the end, but at that point I was numb. I hated him so much that I did not care. If you are going through something like that I strongly recommend that you see a violence counselor. You don't have to tell your boyfriend. You just need to get some sort of help before he kills you!"

OVER ON THE EAST SIDE

CHAPTER 23

I despise myself for the suffering brought onto you because of my selfishness. To behold the sight of you crouched against the wall expressing the state of your heartbreak gnaws away at my conscience. I never wanted you to have a nervous breakdown. The state you were in reminded me of my father ten years before.

It was a chilly evening. The sort of night where all you desire is to remain snug and sheltered, shielded from the wintry elements which linger outside. I had been residing at my father's house for several months, prevailing as a pariah concealed away from the bustling surroundings which laid outside my doorway. Remaining so detached from civilization had transformed me into an elderly, ill-tempered, irritable woman, and not the type of mature woman who evolves into a seasoned blossom. Continuing to be so confined only contributed to my transformation into a moronic unsociable oddball.

Not possessing an animated life full of vitality caused me to criticize and condemn my father with no reprieve. He craved to be alleviated of the anxiety I imposed upon him, but I could not recognize the anguish which brewed beneath the surface. I poked and prodded at him incessantly until he finally ruptured. My father sat in his recliner remaining oblivious to any presence which attempted to revive him. No one could rouse him from this state of unconsciousness he had descended into. He resembled an inanimate object, stationary and silent, his mouth gaping, and eyes open but expressionless. His vegetable like trance filled me at once with complete dismay. I felt so defenseless. Would I trek out into the fluffy, frosted snowfall which scattered the earth, or did I maintain the competence to awaken him from his peaceful slumber. For what seemed like an endless eternity, I wailed and pleaded desperately, hugging him, trying to resuscitate his former self.

At last my father regained awareness, but only to be transposed into a whimpering mass of misery. The teardrops declined to cease, and for this I was remorseful, but gradually, after each sip of coffee, my father regained the strength he formerly retained. It dismayed me that any presence could bring on such ill effects. Could my critical demeanor be severe enough to send an individual into the depths of insanity, losing any connection to mental normalcy they once maintained?

My father was the first casualty, and now Carl was duplicating this disturbing calamity. There existed to be a vital discrepancy in Carl's affliction though. While I could rouse my father out of the ailment I induced upon him, the prospect of alleviating Carl's breakdown was scant. Sadly, I could not muster up even a kernel of compassion for I still harbored such hostility towards him. Any semblance of decency he possessed was obstructed by a perverse compulsion to condemn his as an immoral individual. I misconstrued the image I once held of his sweetened spirit, relinquishing any possibility of perceiving him in a sensible mode.

I yearn to restrain myself and exercise self composure, but I can't. The confession that his insides were deadened shattered any perceptions I conceptualized as the truth. I aspired to harm him as intensely as he did to me, and I would.

OVER ON THE EAST SIDE

CHAPTER 24

I removed my shirt and twisted the shower nozzle until the sprinkle from the showerhead was hot enough to produce a cloud of steam. My head was throbbing with a burdensome headache which I had become quite accustomed to lately, and the only remedy to alleviate my discomfort was this manufactured thundershower before me. Unfortunately though Carl contained the same vision as I. He casually opened the door, clad in only a pair of creamy white boxer shorts and a tangerine colored towel he had draped around his shoulders ready to invade my paradise.

"Carl!" I screamed as he opened the shower curtain. "Why are you in here? You knew I wanted to take a shower. You've been home for how long, and you are waiting to take a shower until now?"

"It'll just take a minute. I just got home from work anyway. Look at my leg, Tuesday." he said showing me his hairy calf encrusted with a thick coating of mud. "See, I think I need a shower a little more than you. I've have been working hard all day, twelve hours."

"I've working hard too. You're not the only one who works here, Carl. It's not my fault that you worked twelve hours."

"Tuesday, can you stop your bitching for one minute? I told you. I'll be done in just a minute." He casually retorted climbing behind the floral shower curtain and into the bathtub.

"Still, why do you always have to invade my space? I was just about to hop in the shower, and of course you have to want to take a shower at the same time as me!" I annoyingly groaned concealing my two fleshy mounds by squeezing them with the palms of my hands and my fingertips. The remainder of my breasts bulged fourth from between my fingers, the excess flesh, resembling two light fluffy muffins spilling over the edges of a muffin tin.

"You know Tuesday, I already had a bad day. I've been fighting with ignorant jerks at work all day and now I have to come home to you and fight. I was in an alright mood until you started your shit!" he irritably hollered, his voice dramatically echoing.

Carl twisted the nozzle into the off position forcefully tugging at the shower curtain and grabbed the towel off of the toilet. He fiercely rubbed himself down with the towel, blotting every last drop of water glued to his skin.

"Why don't you leave Carl? I am so sick of you."
Infuriated by my insensitivity, he thrusted the door against my arm, the unexpected whack spawning a wine tinted stain.

"I hate you! Get the fuck out of my house. I hate you." I hysterically shrieked enraged by the continuous physical abuse inflicted upon me. I think you are disgusting! You are a pig! You are not different from anybody else out there. You repulse me! Why am I even with you? I don't understand it! How could I be with a guy that has done the things that you have done? Why did you have to go out with me?"

"That's alright, Tuesday. I'll be out of your life tomorrow morning. I promise this time."

"Sure, you will. You always say that."

"No, this time I mean it Tuesday. I don't care if I have to sleep in my car. Who wants to put up with a nagging bitch when they come home from a hard days work. I don't deserve that kind of treatment, Tuesday. If you want to be a bitch, then you need to find one of your faggot boyfriends or something, because I'm not one of those nerds. I won't put up with it."

Slowly, I slithered my body into the shower winding the knob until a scorching hot downpour scalded my skin and misted the mirrors. I began to cry, my curdling wails reverberating off of the ceramic tile.

"You are such a baby." Carl taunted. "When you are ready to become a grown woman
let me know. In the meantime, I'll see you later."

"Where are you going?"

"What concern is it to you? I disgust you, remember. You hate me, remember."

He turned off the light switch leaving me to fend for myself in a shadowy abyss surrounding me in gloominess.

"Please God, let me die." I repeated, as the black hole enveloped me. I pressed my back against the chilled tile and slinked to the floor like a slippery snake. My backside cooled instantly as it pressed against the frosty porcelain tub. The door creaked open and I heard miniature baby steps scuttle to the edge of the tub and then turn on the light switch.

"Mom, are you alright?" Madeline asked.

"Yey, honey. I'm fine." I snivel. "I'll be out in a minute. Alright."

OVER ON THE EAST SIDE

I spread my damp naked body across the floor of the tub, watching the downpour splatter off of my slick flesh. A shallow puddle began to develop in my belly button, and for a brief moment my tribulations were erased as I amusingly splashed at the pool of rain water swimming in my navel. The pads of my fingertips begin to crinkle up prompting me to finish my shower. I looked like I had ten golden raisins affixed to the ends of my fingertips. I lazily draped a towel around myself and retreated to the kitchen where I surprisingly found Carl cooking toasted ravioli for supper.

"I thought you were going somewhere." I annoyingly asked.

"No, I'm hungry. Is that alright with you?"

"Yey. I suppose. I just don't know why you are cooking dinner when you said

you were going to leave tomorrow."

"I have to eat."

"Yey, Carl, but I don't want you here tonight if you are going to leave me tomorrow. That's just too painful. You know what I mean?"

"Well. I guess you'll have to call the cops to get me out tonight then."

"Carl, I just don't want you here tonight. It is going to be too painful."

"Why, you are the one that said you wanted me out of here."

"No, Carl. You are the one that decided to leave."

"I like how you turned this around. Do you remember screaming that you thought I was a pig and disgusting and to get the fuck out of your house? I like how you conveniently push it off on me as my decision when you are the one that started this whole thing. I was in a good mood until you started your shit, remember."

"I'm sorry. I just think that this relationship is beyond repair. Too much has been said. There is no mystery. I'm sick of hating you."

"You know what. I just don't care anymore.   He indifferently replies tossing the crispy golden brown pouches of ravioli onto a porcelain saucer with a side of meat sauce.

"If you don't care anymore than why are you here? I will always think that you are a pig. I will always be a bitch to you. You will always be an asshole. It will go on and on."

"I'm not a pig, Tuesday!"

"You did it to yourself, Carl. You made yourself look bad. Don't you remember what you told me? *I'm a man, of course I liked it. I liked the pussy at first, but then I got burnt out on it. Show me your tittles!"*

"Tuesday, shhh. Don't say that stuff in front of your daughters!"

"Why? You weren't careful about what you said in front of me."

"You're not a child, Tuesday."

"No, I'm not, and you're not either. That's why you should've known not to say that stuff to me. It's all about common sense Carl! You should have been smart enough to know not to say that shit in front of me. I need to go out with someone more intelligent than that, someone who is not stupid enough to say those things."

Upon hearing my declaration to stray, Carl quickly rose from his chair and chased me into the kitchen, squashing my body against the wall until my insides felt like a lumpy heap of buttered mashed potatoes drowned in gravy. I could remember how my father used to chase me throughout the house when I did something bad. I'd sprint through the hallway trying so badly to run away from him and lock the door behind me, because if I didn't he'd punch me in the nose, pull my shirt, whatever he deemed necessary to scold me for a punishment.

"Someone less stupid? I don't ever want to hear something like that come out of yore mouth again. Do you understand me?"

"You know I didn't mean it that way. I'd never think about seeing other people." I meekly responded, shriveling against the wall like a snail.

"The next time I hear you even mention the possibility of seeing someone else, I will kill you and your new faggot boyfriend, understand?"

By this point his forehead, bulging of veins, was smashed against mine. His peppery scented breath was so hot that it practically broiled my chin and neck. His intimidation terrified me, causing me to cringe and crumple up into a ball.

"Please, don't hurt me Carl!" I miserably pleaded.

"Do you understand?" he reiterated gruffly unexpectedly

jolting his foot into my thigh, a mist of slobber spewing out of the comer of his mouth and drenching my face with salivation.

The potent blow to my thigh propelled me against the silver-plated wash basin, the solid metal surface instantly bruising the bony segment of my loin. I gasped for air. The wind had been knocked out of me. The fresh air which formerly circled through my veins and purified my blood could be felt fizzing out through every orifice of my body. The indignity inflicted upon me began to stimulate a warm trickle to spill down my cheeks, incensing him to even greater depths and inducing spasmodic convulsions. At that moment his practically epileptic fit and trademark eye twitch could have easily branded him as a psychopath.

"Carl, Carl, don't hurt me. Please. Please." I implored searching his eyes for a glimmer of recognition that he once did love me and attempting to revive him out of his psychotic spell and transport him to an ethereal fairyland of absolution.

I could hear my children scurry into the other room for refuge, their sanctuary providing them with an aura of serenity. They looked like two terrified cockroaches, their crunchy shells about to be crashed by the sole of a shoe. For a brief moment an expression conveying rationality emerged as he backed away from my limp body. My crying for the time being took a brief interlude so as to muffle the intensity of the situation and not to inflame Carl's temper any more than needed.

"Why do you hate me, Tuesday?" I'm the one guy who didn't fuck you over, and I am the one who gets treated like shit."

"Carl, I don't hate you. You know that my head is just fucked up..." I chimed in, in an effort to calm him down.

"Shut up! I don't ever want to hear another word from you. You are not going to make it seem like everything is cool when it is not. Yon started this, and I will finish it." he threatened, lifting the fragile china plate topped with about a dozen crumbly pouches of toasted ravioli and a modest plastic container holding the red sauce filled with meat an seasonings.

I flinched and dipped down to the floor as he hurled the plate in the air, aiming it directly for my head. In slow motion, the plate shattered as it collided against the wall, ceramic scraps and slivers crashing to the floor. A watery stream of sauce dribbled down the wall, followed by hearty chunks of meat. A blood red stain situated itself in precisely the identical spot where my head had formerly rested just a minute ago, and I thanked God that the saucy mess above my head was the meat sauce and not my blood.

"God, Carl, why are you so destructive? You are going to wind up destroying this entire house!" I screamed, my feistiness returning.

"If you weren't such a psycho bitch, it wouldn't come down to this. I have to go. I don't like what this is doing to me at all. I'll see you later." He said removing the blue crystal bottle of cologne off of the kitchen counter and spraying a fine mist of the ocean shore scent onto his collarbone.

"Where are you going?"

"Again, it is none of your concern."

"Carl, if you walk out that door, you are not coming back. You cannot just leave and go out doing God knows what and expect to come back like everything is normal."

"Alright, if you are going to play like that, then give me my ring back."

"I'll give you your ring back when you get all your shit out of here and really leave."

"I can't get all of my stuff out now. I'll get it out when I feel like it. Now, give me the ring back, or I'll cut your damn finger off." He callously threatened.

Carl reached into his pants pocket and pulled out his polished black pocket knife painted with the likeness of George Washington, Thomas Jefferson, Abraham Lincoln, prestigious patriotic landmarks such as Mount Rushmore and the Grand Canyon, and the American flag.

"Don't hurt me Carl."

"Then I recommend that you do what I say bitch!" he harshly spoke, flicking the shiny silver switchblade. Without hesitation I quickly twisted the ring off of my finger, tossing my future to him and dashed into the bedroom, mournful that I most likely would never take delight in the three twinkling crystals embedded in the golden white exterior again.

I climbed into my bed and under the comforter, any passionate feeling within me chilled. At this point I was detached from the world among me, left to wilt away in a realm of solitude, but I could not place the blame upon another. I had constructed my own kingdom of isolation, a dispirited princess left to wander in the garden among the hushed immobile greenery. The front door closed and the heavy clomp of his work boots could be heard treading up the steps. I breathed in a sigh of relief. I could sense that my children, presumably burrowed deep beneath their covers craved to be comforted by their mother, but I could not conjure up the strength to do so. I remained indifferent, too engrossed in my own problems to aid my children. Therefore, I pined away in my bed wrapping my arms tightly around my chest in an effort to console myself and thwart off the devilry that brewed within these closed confines.

I could feel myself begin to drift off into a dreamlike state. *I was on a tropical island, cracking coconuts against the bark of a palm tree. I held the severed coconut above my mouth, holding out my parched tongue while sweet droplets of milk saturated it.*

"Tuesday!" Carl screamed dangling his water bottle above my head and squirting out a stream of water from the spout so it splashed off of my face. Startled by Carl's stinging voice and jangling of his car keys, I awakened from my blessed fantasy and explored my lips and skin with my tongue and fingertips for remnants of moisture from the sweet coconut milk, but realized that the dampness was none other than water.

"God, you are such an asshole. Why do you have to do that shit to me?" I growled.

"Because, you are not going to sleep. If you think that you are then you are more stupid than I thought." He amusingly chuckled.

Like a small child I rubbed my eyes and sluggishly arose from underneath the covers, my ruddy cheeks stained a pale shade of pink.

"You are not going back to sleep, at least not until 7:00 tomorrow morning if you are lucky. Tonight I am going to torture you. You know like they do in the movies, well they have nothing on what I am going to do. You are fucking with the wrong guy. If you even try to go to sleep, that's where this hammer comes in handy." He warned, scooping the canary yellow rubber handed tool out of the plastic bucket at the side of the bed.

"Your face might not look as pretty all bashed in, but at

least it will shut you up."

I nervously giggled as I always did when Carl and I brawled.

"Do you think this is funny? That's the problem with people. They underestimate me. They don't think that I will go crazy on them, but they'll think different when their head is sliced open by this hammer, won't they?"

I cautiously scooted towards the rear of the bed away from Carl in an attempt to create an obstacle if he so chose to use the hammer on me and turn my face into a rare ground beef patty.

"What do you think you are doing?"

"Nothing." I meekly replied slouching my shoulders to convey an air of vulnerability.

"Are you scared?" he mockingly questioned, his tender voice conveying concern, but not genuine in the least bit.

"I rapidly nodded my head." Scooting back even further until the skin on my back rubbed against the cold metal rail of the bed.

"Good, but this is nothing baby girl. The fun has just started. Yep, by the time this is done you will have never felt like such a piece of shit."

He perched himself on the edge of the bed, and pulled out his box of cigarettes from his pants pocket.

"You know, you are one nasty bitch."

"Whatever," I defiantly rolled my eyes, exhausted from his belittling remarks. "Shut up! Did I say you could talk?"

Carl pulled a thick joint tightly wrapped out of his cigarette box and moistened the tip of the joint with his lips.

"I could tell you were a whore from the very beginning."

"I'm not a whore, Carl!"

"I warned you to shut up. This is my time. Anyone that gets into sex the way you do. I'm sorry. You are not a good girl. A good girl wouldn't have a stinky pussy like yours. What you need to do is douche and wipe your ass. That's for sure. I don't know. Maybe Jewish chicks stink down there or something."

At that moment I could sense that Carl was radiating with glee as he ridiculed me. He delighted in my vulnerability. With Carl I was susceptible to whatever afflictions he passed my way. I felt a fatty tumor swelling in the center of my stomach. This growth was a glutton, gobbling away at the ambrosial pleasures in life, such as laughter, calm, and cheer. Carl instilled such fear in me that the familiar sensations remained as I feared for my life.

"You know, sooner or later you will cheat on me. You already hate me, but you will wind up hating me so much that it will drive you to be with someone else."

He fired up the tip of his joint, the end of the paper flaming, ashes descending to the floor as he deeply inhaled and breathed out a hearty puff.

"The last four nights I have had dreams that you cheated on me. You were doing everyone, and I was powerless to stop it. Do you think my dreams are trying to tell me something?"

"Carl, it was just a dream. You know I wouldn't do that to you." I reassuringly offered.

"It was a rhetorical question dumb ass. You still are not allowed to talk. You know I should rape you. You are the kind of girl that deserves to be brutally raped."

He disgustingly chuckled, clearing his throat of phlegm and spitting out a congealed ball of slobber onto my face. Ashamedly, I put my face down, and shut my eyes hoping to be transported to another time or place.

"You didn't like that, did you? It's payback baby.
What comes around goes around. You treat me like shit, I treat you like ever bigger shit. You think I'm such a bad guy, such a pervert after all of those guys fucked you over. If I wasn't so sensitive I would've cheated on you by now. In fact I should go to strip clubs. I might as well, since that's what kind of guy you think I am. I have had a million chances to cheat. Yey, when I was fat no girls looked at me, but now I am noticing that girls look at me differently. A girl walked straight up to me at a bar and asked me to dance, but I didn't. I was so proud of my girlfriend! All I talk about is you. All I think about is you, but in your fucked up world, that is just not good enough."

I sat there dumbfounded by what he had just said.

"You should have danced with that girl Carl."

"See, there you go again, assuming that everyone is out to get you, that everyone wants to hurt you. I didn't want to dance with that fat chick. That was not the point I was trying to make. I am just trying to say that if I wanted to cheat I could. Anyone could go into a bar and pick up a fat chick, but why do that when I have something good at home."

"You know, it doesn't matter what you tell me. To me you will always be a pig."

"But why, Tuesday? What I did before you is none of your concern! It shouldn't matter."

"Of course it matters. If you were a serial killer before you met me, then that would be alright? The things you do before me just like the things I have done in the past make us who we are today. In my eyes, the past is a strong judgment of character."

"Tuesday. You are not my judge. You are not my mother. You are not God. This is a free country. If I want to drink a beer in a bar then I can, and you aren't going to tell me that I did something wrong."

"No, if you just went into a regular bar, but you didn't. Why did you have to go into a naked bar?"

"Look at what you did, fucking all of those guys, the threesome. You fucked guys you didn't like. I don't judge you."

"I had the threesome one time, Carl. I didn't like it, so I didn't do it again, unlike you who went there every day. I dated guys, looked at them as if they were people, not pieces of meat."

Carl began to giggle hysterically. "Date guys. What a joke. More like fuck them. That's all you did, Tuesday. You are a bigger whore than those strippers. All you are is a fucking hypocrite. And not to mention your threesome. Now that's a whore. Ask my friends. That's worse than anything, and my friends said that you had to have liked it."

"I didn't. I swear."

"Shut up. Did I say you could talk? If you wanted to fuck one guy you would've. You obviously had it set in your mind to fuck two."

"I only did it once. Look how many times you went to strip clubs. I didn't like it. So I never did it again. I didn't even get any pleasure out of it. If I would have liked it, I would have done it again."

"What am I going to have to do to get you to shut up? You know, those straps would look good with you tied to the bed. You'd really be scared then, wouldn't you? I just want to tell you now, that if we break up you will lose your apartment and your job. Your entire life will never return back to normal. It will be destroyed. You will never have a boyfriend again. I'll make sure of it. I have enough friends in this town to tell me if you are seeing someone else, and don't even think about going back to Woody's because everyone there will know to stay away from you."

"Carl, stop!" I pleaded. "You know I don't want to be with anyone else anyway."

"No. I guarantee that you will have a dick stuck in you in a week. You are a dirty whore. That's alright though. I'm tired of one pussy anyway. It's all stretched out. You had your threesome. Why can't I have mine? Let me have my chance. I want two pussies."

"If you want a threesome, go find some other girls."

"No, only if you are there."

"I can't believe you are such a pig. You know me. I wouldn't do that. That is the one good thing we still have, our loyalty."

"Come on. Don't pretend to be Ms. Innocent. We know you are far from that. Why wouldn't you do it?"

"Shut up. For once can you try to be different from every other pig out there? I'm not like you think

"And not all men are the same". He quickly retorted back.

"Well, you could have fooled me. Sorry, Carl. You are such a great guy, wanting to have sex with two girls, just like every other man on this earth. Is that a fantasy programmed into every guy's head or what?"

"You know, I should have listened to everyone about you."

"Who?"

"Mike and your sister. They said you were a bitch. I didn't know what I was getting myself into."

"What about what I was getting myself into? I didn't know that I was with a disgusting pervert."

"You shouldn't have gone out with me then. You know what. You're not my mom. You are not God. You cannot judge me. There are forty million girls out there. I don't know why I'm wasting my time on you. All you females are alike. You are just like Shannon, Brandy, all of the other girls. I just would love to be free, to leave this state and never return. I would leave my son. I don't give a fuck. I have nothing keeping me here. I want to have my own house, my own car and have all the girls cry over me."

"Nice fantasy, Carl."

"Well, I've never gotten to experience that because I went from one bitch to another. I was a sucker, the good guy, and look where it got me. I am one unstable motherfucker." He growled, clutching a tuft of my hair. "I will wind up really hurting you if I don't leave and not just physically either." He threatened spewing a wad of phlegm into his coffee cup. "That would've been a good one, don't you think? By the time that this night is over, you are going to wish that you were dead."

At that moment I wished I was dead. To be buried alive beneath layers of mud, devoured by filthy parasites, the dirt particles obstructing my airway, stifling me, until I am numb. My body is only a wrapping for my spirit, a receptacle to sustain the tribulations and inconsistencies that life tosses my way. At this moment I would greet death with a broad smile, flirt with the prospect of complete nothingness to console me. I would dance with the shadow of darkness himself, tantalize him with irresistible proposals in order to secure a position in the underworld. I am not concerned with how mundane the frivolities will be which will take place in this burning inferno. My skin will be burnt to a baked crisp, my bodily fluids boiled, my hair fried, until I am a baked carcass. These are only physical forms of torture that will vanish as soon as I am departed, but the emotional anguish will not. Each and every day when I awaken I will have to relive the abuse I suffered as a result of being weak, leaving my morale to be spoiled.

For what seemed like an eternity Carl held me captive in our bedroom. His soulless eyes, devoid of all compassion patrolled me, entrapping me in a fictitious dungeon. I laid in my bed immovable, any heart mutilated, anticipating the moment when Carl's eyelids would flutter, finally closing for the night, and just as I hoped, they did.

"Nice torturer." I sarcastically uttered under my breath, not expecting Carl to hear me.

".Shut up." He groggily mumbled, pulling the comforter over his head.

OVER ON THE EAST SIDE

CHAPTER 25

Our house had been shrouded in blackness for two days due to the power outage. The flame from the candle flickered merrily, its jovial dance casting shadows on the ceiling. Carl and I lounged on our bed, sprawling on the soft comforter, my arms draped around his chest. We were trying to enjoy the evening despite the gravity of the situation, but without a doubt, those incessant images began to slink into my head.

"I can't believe you went to Roxy's. That is like the pervert strip bar of all strip bars. We used to make fun of a waiter, Paul Potter, at my old work who went there all of the time." "What do you care? You didn't know me then."

"Who cares if I didn't know you. Can't it still bother me?"

"Yey, I guess. Just don't take it out on me."

"How can I not? It was you who did it. I can't get it out of my mind. I see you going into those places, showing them your ID, drinking your beer, looking at the women. I play it over and over in my head. I'll never be able to get close to you, because I'll never trust you. I don't know what kind of guy you are."

"You know I'm a nice guy, Tuesday. Get over it."

"You are not a nice guy, and I can't just get over it. Don't you see? I will never be able to stop thinking about it, because I am obsessive. I have a disorder. I can't just snap my fingers and be rid of it. You know what, this won't work. You need to get out. I hate you."

"Tuesday, don't tell me that we are going to go through this again?"

"Yey, you know what we will always go through this, because I hate you. You are a pig." I hollered running into the living room.

"You know, you are nothing but a big nosed, no tittied, big stomach Jew. You look like a Jewish tellytubby." He screamed.

I hurled myself onto the couch and began to weep hysterically, burying my face into my hands, but summoning up enough strength to yell back.

"Come on Tuesday. You know I don't like those girls."

"Oh, they are so gross." I sardonically whined." They have big tits and flat stomachs. That is repulsive."

"Tuesday. You know I don't like that."

"So, what are you saying? Look what you told me. I have a big nose, no tits, and a big stomach, but those gifts have big perky tits and a perfectly flat stomach. Yey, Carl I can understand why those gifts are so gross and I am a beauty queen." I sarcastically retorted.

"You need to get some confidence, for real." He said walking into the living room.

"Maybe it's hard for me to feel good about myself when my boyfriend keeps telling me that I am basically disgusting. You know, either those girls were nasty or they weren't. When you describe nasty girls I think of something else altogether, not skinny little bimbos with boob jobs and flat stomachs!"

"Why does it matter so much what they looked like, Tuesday?."

"Because, I will never think that I am good enough. You have already seen young hot bodies dancing seductively, spreading their legs. How can I beat that?"

"I'm sorry Tuesday, but it takes a little more than tits and pussy to turn me on. You don't think normal. You can't compare yourself to every other girl out there. They are just bodies. Everyone has them."

"If they are just bodies, then why do you pay to go to those places? Why do those girls make so much money? Why does everyone make such a big deal out of them?"

"Fuck, I don't know Tuesday. This has been going on since the beginning of time. There will always be sin in this world. You can't blame me for everything that goes on out there."

"How can I not when you are so clearly a part of it. I should have never gone out with you. Why can't you just get out of my life? Please, just get out. Leave already. I don't want you here."

Carl, afflicted with severe abandonment issues, sprang on top of my body like an Olympic vaulter, smashing my brittle bones as he applied pressure with all of his body weight.

"I'm sick of you trying to get rid of me. You are not going to get rid of me!" He screamed biting my arm. I wiggled, like a worm, helplessly beneath him wincing in discomfort as his teeth sunk into the fleshy part of my arm.

"You are a worthless bitch! I don't even know why I care." He nonchalantly said, flinging himself off of me and sitting his breathless body onto the edge of the couch.

"You are such an asshole. Does it make you feel like a big man to beat up on a woman. Now I know why Shannon couldn't put up with you."

"That bitch would take me back in a second. She did everything for me."

"Well, if she did everything for you, then get the fuck out of my house and move into hers. I'm sure she'd be thrilled to have yon back."

"Get the fuck out of my house and move into hers." He insensitively mimicked me.

"What? You say I'm so terrible, that she did everything for you. Why should I want you here? I do a lot for you. What did she even do for you?"

"She had dinner on the table every night when I came home. She did the laundry. That bitch did everything."

"Well, yey. I could do that too if I didn't work full time. She didn't have to do anything except take care of Daniel. If I sat on my lazy ass all day like her I could do everything for you too. I still clean all of the time and do laundry, take care of my kids, and I work. What did she pay for? I had to pay all of the rent last week. How many times did she pay rent or anything else? How many times did she give you money? She lied, remember? She hurt you more than she helped and you are acting like I am the bad one."

"I know she lied. She tried really hard though. It was pathetic, but that is what you do for someone you love."

"She only did that to try to trap you. I am not going to go to ridiculous extremes to try to trap a man. If you like me you do. If you don't like me you don't. I have never tried to trap anyone. If you are so happy with her fat ass you need to go back, because, obviously, to you I am just the most terrible girlfriend."

"Well, you don't act like you like me. You hate me."

"Yey, of course I hate you. You are a scum bag."

"I'm going to tell my morn that she raised a scum bag. We'll see how much she likes you then. In fact she'll come over and beat your ass for calling her son a scum bag."

"You are such a little baby. *I'll call my mom and she'll beat your ass.* How old are you, five? The only way that I can stand you is when I am on my medicine."

"I'm sorry, but if you go back on your medicine, I will find someone else."

"That is so sensitive of you, Carl. You don't even care If I feel better. All you care about is the sex. Yey, you are not a pig." I cynically uttered rolling my eyes.

"Damn right, I'm a pig. In fact I will take the bitch into your bed, fuck her, and then make you suck my dick, spunk on you, and then you'll taste her pussy."

"God, Carl. How could you say such a thing? You are disgusting. If I take my medicine we will get along better. I won't hate you. I'll still have sex with you."

"I don't want to have sex with you while you are on your medicine. You lie there like a fuckin zombie. You don't get into it at all."

"Oh, well. There you go being selfish again. Isn't it better that we not fight? You know all of the side effects go away after awhile."

"It doesn't matter. I didn't get a girlfriend so I could jack off every night. Maybe you are just too old for me."

"I am only two and a half years older than you, Carl."

"So. Two and a half years might not seem like a lot, but it is. You are supposed to be in your sexual prime and look at you. I need sex every day."

"You are ridiculous. You demand way too much. I am not your sexual slave."

"No, you are not, but you are my girlfriend, and you need to start acting like it."

"How do I not act like it?"

"Well, for one thing Tuesday. You are a cold bitch. You never want to go anywhere with me. You never kiss me when you get home from work or put your arms around me. I need to know that I am loved."

"You are like a little child. I can't pay attention to you twenty-four hours a day. I'm not that cold. I'm sure that your girlfriends weren't very affectionate.

"They were more affectionate than you until you dumped me. Just don't be surprised if I need a little action on the side to show me some lovin."

"God, Carl. Why are you such a pig? We're completely incompatible. Can't you see that?"

"Yey, of course I can see it. The only thing that we are good at is fucking. We should just get together to fuck and that's it."

"Another wonderful comment made by my boyfriend. I don't know why you insist on saying those horrible t/tings to me."

"I rather say horrible things to you than beat you. A lot of the guys I know beat their old ladies until they are black and blue. You think I beat you? Oh, no. Believe me, you have not seen beaten."

"I don't know which I rather have. It might be less painful to beat me."

"I know it is. This is why I say those mean things. I know how to hurt you, and I use that to my advantage."

"I just get so scared that there is going to be something out there that you will notice."

"Like what do you mean?"

"I don't know, like what your cousin said at the family reunion, about how he had his old lady, but all of these hot women were walking around in their bikinis, and he couldn't help but look."

"You know I wouldn't do that."

"Yey, but what if you see a hot girl at the beach in a bikini with a great body. You're not going to look?"

"What do you mean by look? Of course I look, I have two eyes, I'm not blind."

"That's not what I mean, Carl. I mean are you going to turn your head and notice her tan body slicked down with baby oil and her boobs bursting out of her bikini top?"

"Tuesday, you are absolutely crazy. You put way too much thought into this."

"You know I can't stop thinking."

"It doesn't matter. Who do you think I am? I'm sorry, but I have never lusted over a girl like that. I have never looked at a girl like a piece of meat. It takes a little more than that to turn me on."

"So you wouldn't?"

"No, of course not. What about when I go camping or rafting? Those girls are going to do things that might bother you. What am I supposed to do?"

"What are they going to do Carl, show their boobs, lie naked and pour beer all over each other?"

"No, I am not saying that."

"You are acting weird. Did something happen in Lesterville that you are not telling me about?"

"No, nothing horrible. Two of these fat girls, I mean fat as Shannon, were sitting in tlae back of a pickup truck topless, and Mike and me almost puked. I screamed, put your shirts back on, and Mike told me to shut up."

"What? You saw two half naked girls and you neglected to mention this to me until today. How could you not tell me?" My voice began to quiver as I envisioned Carl ogling two pairs of breasts.

"Tuesday, are you insane? They looked like two baboons sitting in the back of a truck."

"I don't care how fat they were. You fucked a fat chick, remember? A fat chick got you off. How do I know that you don't like that kind of stuff?"

"Tuesday, how sick are you? Listen to yourself. You are pathetic, getting jealous over two fat chicks."

"What kind of people are these anyway? Who sits in the back of a pick up truck topless just waiting for people to pass by? If I knew that Lesterville would have been like *Girls Gone Wild*, I would have never let you go."

"You see, this is why I never take you anywhere, my point proven exactly. What about when we go to Bass River or the Party Cove? There is a lot worse stuff that happens there. Old women and country girls flash you their tits all of the time. You can't think anything of it. Are you going to restrict me from going there too?"

Suddenly, a bubble full of envy and rage began to swell in my stomach, finally erupting. I could no longer restrain myself. Images of breasts danced through my mind, milky white breasts, chocolate brown breasts, golden bronzed breasts, perky breasts, saggy breasts, petite breasts, colossal breasts, breasts with pink nipples, breasts with toasted brown nipples. By that point I was delirious, my mind overflowing with these indecent visualizations which I could not control. I was blinded by jealousy, forced to succumb to my weaknesses and insecurities.

I began to punch and stomp Carl, wildly flailing my arms and legs, not knowing or caring where I would strike him next.

"Why didn't you tell me? Why didn't you tell me?" I repeatedly screamed. "I hate you, you sick pervert!"

Carl's entire body flinched as I jolted my foot into his ball sac. Trying to ward off my oncoming blows he finally grasped my wrists with one hand and my ankles with the other and wrung them like a wet mop.

"You are going to quit your bullshit, do you understand me? This jealousy thing has got to stop!"

Carl flung me off of the bed, my back slamming against the

wooden sock drawer. I could feel a throbbing tender bruise begin to develop in the center of my back as I tried to raise myself up onto my reddened scraped elbows.

"Why do you have to start your shit today Tuesday, why? We were having a perfectly normal conversation until you had to start again!"

"Perfectly normal? Girls flashing their breasts is a perfectly normal conversation. I guess it would be for you since this always happens in your world."

"My world? This is the 2000's baby. This is what happens in the real world. It is a free fucking country. I do not know what kind of fantasy world you are living in, but it's just not real. Not everyone hides behind big baggy clothes like you."

"So what if I hide behind big baggy clothes? At least I have some class, way too much class fur a hoosier like you!"

"A hoosier like me? *A HOOSIER LIKE ME*?" he screamed, clutching my waists tightly and flinging my arms back as he hopped on top of me, smothering my frail body.

"Ahhhh...." I bawled, the hot tears instantly welling up in any eyes in response to the excessive pressure placed upon any wrists.

"Ahhhhh..." He nastily mimicked, his tan face reddening as he continued to squeeze my wrists. "I'm a nasty hoosier? I must not be that nasty, since I make you feel real good huh?"

"Carl, please let go. Please don't hurt me!" I desperately pleaded, my pride slowly withering away as I continued to beg.

A brief wave of compassion slowly washed over Carl's face, and he released hold of my wrists. I weakly rolled over, burying my face into the sheets. I could not stop sobbing. I soaked the sheets with my tears, the endless stream creating a damp spot underneath in which I rested my head. Carl turned me over, my limp lifeless body resembling a rag doll.

"Tuesday, come on. Stop your crying. It's not that bad."

"Not that bad. That's easy for you to say." I sniveled, a yellowish trail of mucous dripping out of each nostril.

"Come on. You need to stop your crying. You are going to wind up having the cops called."

"I can't just stop crying. I don't have a faucet that I can just turn on and off. What do you expect? You hurt me. I'm going to cry!" I wailed, my crying becoming louder as I struggled to emphasize my point.

"Stop it Tuesday! If there is one thing I cannot stand, it is crying. I can't stand when the kids do it, so why should you be any different?"

I could not stop crying though. A sea of tears gushed through my tear ducts, enough tears to fill up every body of fresh sea water, every ocean, every lake, every river. I did not know if the tears would ever cease for my faith in man was shattered. Each and every being who represented a member of the opposite sex disgusted me and every member of the same sex I remained envious of. I was transforming into a bitter old woman, an elderly rendition of my former frisky self. Nothing or no one could pacify my misgivings, tranquilize the throbbing which would not cease. I would never feel at peace again until death. Therefore, for the remainder of my life I would be waiting to breathe my last breath, to float through the big pearly gates at the portals of heaven. There would only be heavenly thoughts from then on, not the repetitive nagging compulsions which disturbed me in this lifetime.

"Tuesday! I told you to stop crying["

Carl brutally roiled me over, placing his hands around my neck and wringing it like a wet sponge. My moistened eyes began to roll into the back of my head. I couldn't vocalize a plea for help, but I imagined that the slight gurgling noises conveyed a message of helplessness. I closed my eyes and was instantly greeted by cottony clouds and blue skies. The clouds swiftly swirled by me as I floated through the heavens. Not since I had been a little girl had I felt so free. At last I was liberated, free to frolic among the cotton candy bundles and savor each sweet cottony morsel which the angels hurled at me. The gleaning pearly gates of heaven loomed in the distance. The angels plucked at the strings of their sparkling golden harps serenading me with a hospitable melody to welcome me. I soared towards the gates, the tranquil harmony warming my soul and melting every speck of chilliness that resided deep in my spirit.

Suddenly, the angel's chores faded, and a haunting melody replaced their sugary childlike voices. My body began to feel heavy, so weighty that I began to plummet back to earth. The brilliance of the beautiful blue skies were replaced by a shadowy evening void of the moon, stars, or any trace of light. My eyes snapped open just as

OVER ON THE EAST SIDE

Carl's hands released their overwhelming clutch. I gasped for air as I tried to raise my wilted body from off of the bed.

"Don't get up Tuesday. You are not going anywhere."

I disregarded his order, stumbling off of the bed and massaging my sore throat as he leaped off the bed. Quickly, I hobbled over to the closet in an attempt to get dressed and salvage what little dignity remained.

"You think I am going to let you get dressed. Nope. You are going to stay naked the entire day."

I stood there, naked and vulnerable, shivering and clutching my raw throbbing throat. I tried to reach into the closet for a pair of my pajama bottoms, but he slapped my hand away from the closet.

"You never listen to me you worthless little hoar. You think you are somebody. You are a nobody. You think you are better then everyone else out there. What makes you better than a stripper or a prostitute. Nothing. Today you are going to be naked, as naked as any stripper. You are going to feel what they feel. You are going to do what they do. Today is the day that you will learn the lesson that you are not better. You are just like every other worthless whore out there."

How could he have not known that he hurt me, that his words ate away at my heart like maggots, those filthy slimy larva gobbling away at my self confidence, love, and trust. Would he have realized the damage be had done if he found me dead, strewn across the bathroom floor peacefully sleeping forever? If I had sacrificed my own life, succumbed to my inner demons, gulped down countess pills? Would hc then finally take responsibility for what he had done? Would he have wished he could reach inside of me and grasp my heart, plucking away word by word until all former harmony was restored? I am impressionable as a small child. Would seeing my lids eternally shut, my lips slightly parted, my skin ashen reawaken him, force him to realize that time does not erase the bitterness. I will forever carry his words within me. Long after I am departed his words will continue to linger causing pain to generations hereafter.

Again, I am descending into the depths of despair, my very own personal hell. There is no one or nothing to rescue me as I sink deeper and deeper. I envision a portrait of vengeance, how by taking away my own life could inflict pain in others.

Submerged in a sea of sorrow; a sadness that won't go away
Dark clouds mist my happiness; a cheerfulness which never stays
Envious thoughts creep in every hour; make me cringe and shut my eyes
Denial of one's past existence shut down any nearing cries
Visions swirling round my head; visions now forever dead
But visions that will stick with me; forever, always, constantly
No release will be near in time
Living life as in a wholesome nursery rhyme
Gingerbread houses, cookies, and tea replace drugs and drinking that used to fill me
No way to escape my gray skies; sunny skies prevail outside
Here I live inside my box; this is where I always hide
I represent weakness; weakness is me
When my lips attempt to speak they express stupidity
Therefore I live in silence; hide my expressions, thoughts, and fears
I drown my face in pillows to muffle endless tears
Before I can feel happy this blackness must leak out; from every tear, from every scream, from every solemn pout
Then I will be so happy, all sweet and tingly too; feel toasty warm from sunshine rays
Never again will I feel blue

OVER ON THE EAST SIDE

It was a little over a year ago that I again set foot in the domain of wrongdoing. My sister, Sarah had recently relocated to St. Louis to reside at my house. I was in dire need of money, and by Sarah utilizing my dwelling it was only expected that she alleviate the seriousness of my financial state. Sarah did not give credence in maintaining a practical vocation which utilizes her skills. She insisted on searching for an effortless alternative, even if the consequences were less than honorable. My sister did not regard stripping to be an impure profession as I do.

Yes, Sarah was pondering the unthinkable, but unbeknownst to us she had us believe that she was interested in becoming a cocktail waitress. Katt, Sarah, and I piled into my gray '88 Chevrolet Celebrity oblivious to the dangerous territory we were about to embark on. It was a perfect spring day, the air a tad humid for the time of year, but in St. Louis this was to be expected. I was dressed in my floral red capri outfit, my golden hair beautifully contrasted against the blood red stain applied upon my lips. I continually snuck a glance in the side mirror and rearview mirror admiring my pretty face and silently wondering if I was better looking than the East Side Girls. It took about twenty minutes for us to get over the river into East St. Louis. The past fifteen minutes had been filled with spontaneous laughter, but the giggling faded as we saw cross after cross planted into the side of the highway. A different person must have been killed at every block we passed. How had they died? Were they innocent bystanders hit by drunk motorists, were they prostitutes diced into pieces and stuffed into a garbage bag? From that moment on the mood was somber. There was complete silence amongst the three of us, but I could still hear the cries, the pleas of help from the prostitutes being beaten by their tricks, blackened tears streaming down their roughened cheeks, their short jean skirts riding into their panties. I heard the howling toddlers, their eyes bulging, blood trickling down their forehead as they stared at their mother's tom limb from limb after being hit by a careless drunk driver.

We drove down Mississippi Avenue through Sauget, and turned left on Washington. The neighborhoods got worse and worse as we traveled westward. The houses lined up reminded me of the house my grandfather was murdered at, the shack like structures and peeling white siding similar. There must have been a liquor store at every corner. There had to be. How else could the citizens of these communities cope with the poverty? Katt became edgy as we slowly cruised the neighborhood streets. A group of black men rocking themselves on a porch swing yelled as we drove by causing me to put my foot on the accelerator and press on the gas. Sarah and I giggled, but Katt just mumbled how we were going to die. We pulled up to the comer on Kingshighway past Forest Avenue on the left and we pulled into the parking lot of C-Mowe's. I cleverly pulled in between a van and a beat up Cadillac as to not arouse suspicion. A lime green beat up station wagon with the wooden siding pulled into the front entaance. The driver kissed the short haired blonde and watched her enter.

"How dysfunctional!" I uttered to Katt.

I wondered how boyfriends could drop their girlfriends off at work knowing that countless men were going to see her naked every night, possibly have her ride them in a sinful lap dance.

Sarah confidently walked into a club. Her favorite movie idol, Sam Elliot in biker gear from the movie Mask was sloppily pasted to the wall. His bushy eyebrows were cocked upwards and his mustasche was cuffed at both ends. He was sitting on a silver and black Harley Davidson, his arms confidently folded upon his stomach. Sam Elliot was such a compass of moral stature, Sarah thought to herself as she stared at Sam. In Mask he had befriended a deformed young boy, took care of the family, romanced Cher. How in the hell could they put his poster in the hallway of a strip club?

The first sight Sarah saw upon walking into C-Mowes was only one girl dancing on stage topless. She might have looked normal from a distance, but upon closer examination Sarah noticed her coarse looking skin and heavily sprayed hairdo molded into some sort of helmet shape, a hair style solely meant for Farrah Faucet. Sarah expected glamour. Her upper lip was covered in a thick layer of fuzz, the blonde almost looking like she had a milk mustasche. Sarah held onto some idealistic belief that all strippers were beautiful, long blond hair, big boobs, long thick lashes.

There were about seven other dancers in the bar. The bar was right in front of her, and to the left were tables. On one side of the room was a long stage. She looked away from the stage and at the few men scattered throughout the bar. Most of the men were overweight wearing trucker hats and wrinkled flannel shirts. They all looked like rough Harley guys. About six of them sat up at the bar, and the rest sat at the tables with the dancers. It looked to Sarah as if some of the dancers went up to the customers at the bar while others went directly to the customers sitting at the tables.

The girls wandered from man to man asking if they wanted some company. One of the girls, a short brunette, her squinty gray eyes crying for love, crinkles at the corners of her lips and outer edge of her eye walked around the joint holding a paper cup in her left hand collecting money for the juke box. Her frail bony hands made the cup shake, the few coins clinking against each other. The dancers appeared as friendly as could be to the customers, looking like pathetic pets vying for attention from their owners. As a dancer walked by Sarah though she cast her an icy stare silently letting Sarah know that she was not welcome in her territory.

The club had an upstairs, a mezzanine section, but it was not open. Strangely the stage was covered with a thin layer of lime green carpeting. *If anything this place needed some updating*, Sarah thought to herself. The center table caught Sarah's attention. Sitting upon a skinny biker with a shaggy red hair and beard, a layer of freckles spread over his forearms was a topless redhead doing a lap dance. Her moves reeked of sexuality, similar to the grinding done onstage by the Farah Fancett hairdo girl. Her moves were so blatantly crude, and overly suggestive in their manner. Her long sandy blonde hair swayed from side to side exciting the man and causing him to lean his head back in ecstasy.

Sarah drank in the excitement. Finally, it was her chance to shine. With her chocolate brown mane and porcelain skin she was much prettier than any of these girls. She could not wait to show off. Approaching her was a short obese woman, kinky black curls falling out of her scarf. Draped around her chunky frame was a floral mumu. Oddly, she greatly resembled Sarah's late aunt Goldie, except for the fact that Goldie was taller. The skin on her forehead was wrinkled as an acorn, and pock marks dotted her flabby jowls.

"Is there something I can help you with hon?" the woman suspiciously asked in a country twang.

"Yes, I wanted to know if you were hiring?" Sarah assertively replied, trying to act more grown up than she really was.

"Hiring?" the woman laughed. "We are always hiring."

"Here. Sit at the bar and I'll have you fill out an application." The woman offered, wobbling over to the bar and reaching under the counter for a thick pad of generic applications and brusquely tore off the top piece of paper.

Sarah sat at the bat secretly wondering if she could work here. She didn't see any cocktail waitresses or female bartenders. She assumed all there was to apply for was a dancer. Hmmah scribbled in her name and address, but the woman aggressively snatched the application before she could finish.

"Don't worry about that hon. So, do you think you could start today?" "Uh...t..today?" Sarah stammered.

"Yey. One of the girls called in sick, and we need a replacement. You can dance till closing."

"Uh...My sister and friend are waiting for me. I can come back tomorrow"

"Alght. I'll see you tomorrow at 2:00, 2:00 in the afternoon."

Sarah quickly walked out of C-Mowe's and ran to the car.

"So, what did they say?" I curiously asked.

"They said I can start tomorrow, but I said I'd have to think about it."

"For a waitress?"

Sarah paused, the anxious look on her face enough to convey to Tuesday that she was digging herself a hole she might not be able to get out of.

"Sarah, please don't tell me that you are going to be a stripper."

"Sarah!" Katt chimed in sounding more than shocked.

Katt and I both shook our heads in disbelief as Sarah sat quietly in the back seat. We were about to enter onto the highway when Sarah pointed to a club, Ms. Kitty's, a western looking tavern. I sighed and reluctantly pulled into the parking lot.

Sarah jumped out of the back seat and almost skipped to the front door. There was a sign on the door that said there was a two dollar cover charge and a two drink minimum. Sarah opened the door and was immediately approached by a man behind the bar asking to see her I.D. Oddly, he resembled an old western cowboy, his thick furry mustache curled up at the edges. Sarah reached into her pocketbook for her i.d. and pulled out her Ohio drivers license.

"Ohio, huh?" the man asked looking from the license to Sarah and back to the license again, finally looking content and handing it back to Sarah.

They both uncomfortably stood for a minute or so until Sarah got up the courage to ask if they were hiring

"Yey, we are hiring for dancers."

"How about cocktail waitress?"

"Nope." He said looking away and drying a beer glass with a clean white rag. "That spots been taken. We have a spot open for one more dancer, but you'd have to start right now. How about it?"

Sarah paused and looked around the bar and up at the stage at an older looking woman, her coarse looking skin making her look at least ten years older. Her emaciated frame did not move much until a customer sat down at the stage. She then eagerly hopped into his lap (Sarah assumed a regular customer) and began to wildly gyrate to the country song blaring through a cut-rate sound system. They provocatively rubbed against each other as she fondled her nipples and vagina. The country song ended, and the couple left for a private dance in the back room.

"Alright. Let me just tell my sister and her friend. They are waiting for me outside."

"O.K., but a few rules first. You mainly earn your money from private dances. You are to charge about $25.00 for each dance, but since it's your first night you can give a couple free ones. You can choose to either wear your underwear or not. If you choose not to wear it your tips of course will be bigger. The men are not to touch you. You are to tell them to place their hands behind them and sit on them. If you let them touch you that is your choice, but you are not to let anyone see. This can only be done in the back room. You will work until 2:00. You are not allowed to leave until then. If you take a break you take it inside. You are not to go outside while you are working. I cannot stress how important it is for you to follow these rules. You are not to have any girlfriends visit you during your work. Women are not allowed as customers. They take away the attention from the dancers. When you are ready you can go into the back room and Misty will show you what to change into. Are we clear?"

"Yes." Sarah gulped, rapidly shaking her head up and down. "I'll be right back."

"Then tell your sister and get back in here. If you have any more questions my name is Mick by the way."

Sarah walked outside to Tuesday and Katt impatiently sitting in the car and broke the news.

"Guys. They want me to start right now."

"Start what right now, dancing?" Tuesday disgustingly asked.

"Fuck Yey." Sarah snapped. "It's my damn life. Let me do what I want."

"Daddy won't like it." Tuesday condescendingly replied. "How can you do that? Waitressing is one thing. Stripping is another thing Sarah. This place looks dangerous. I don't like the looks of it. That big fat dyke keeps giving us dirty looks. I think she wants us to leave."

"Just pick me up at two." Sarah brusquely said running back into the club.

Sarah confidently strode into the back room and approached a slightly overweight brunette with kinky hair.

"Excuse me. Are you Misty?"

"Yey." The girl snottily replied, looking Sarah up and down as if she were studying her.

"Hi. I'm Sarah" she eagerly introduced herself, her friendly tone not moving Misty in the least bit. "I start today. Mick told me that you'd tell me what to do."

"Well, first you have to change. What are you wearing underneath your dress?" "Uh...This two piece lingere set." Sarah shyly replied lifting up her floral dress. "That'll be fine. Just wear that and take off your top. You can keep on the bottoms if you want. You can borrow a pair of my heels. You have to give them back by the end of the night though."

Sarah walked back into the club to a few cat call whistles and evil stares from the girls. By now the bar was more crowded, and several of the girls were doing lap dances on the men. Sarah immediately walked onto the stage, her heels clicking as she walked up the linoleum covered stairs, but two of the dancers taking a smoke break at the bar began to scream at her to get off of the stage. Sarah was speechless. These girls were acting as if they hated Sarah, but she tried not to take it personally. The world of the dancer was all about money, extremely competitive. The girls were hustlers. A thin cracked out blonde, her hair pirmed up into a bun lazily danced on stage and then proceeded over to the corner to give an older man motioning his hand a lap dance. Sarah again walked onto the stage. She basically danced as if she was at the clubs. The only basic difference was that her breasts were displayed for all of the world to see. She moved her feet from side to side and swayed her hair from shoulder to shoulder.

Two men sloppily guzzling on their beer in the corner screamed that she had some big nipples. An Indian gentleman, bordering on middle age in a button down paisley shirt reached into his acid washed jeans for a crumpled one dollar bill. He tossed the dollar, reeking of body odor, onto the stage. Sarah casually looked over at the other dancer spreading her legs open wide, her nakedness displayed for the world to see in all its grandeur. The chubby factory worker wolfed down his bottle of beer as he explored the inner workings of the female genatalia, the clitoris, the labia, the pinkish tinge, the dirty blonde stubble. He pulled a twenty dollar bill out of his flannel coat pocket and placed it on the stage directly in front of her vagina. The customers at the bar scurried towards tbe stage. Apparently, they knew what was about to transpire.

The stripper moved her ass to the side and scooted forwards making sure the balls of her feet made contact with the floor of the stage. She almost looked like she was in a position to do the splits. She then placed her vagina directly over the twenty dollar bill contracting her vaginal muscles until it picked it up. She had such muscular control of her vaginal muscles, so much that it appeared as if as a magnetic pull was drawing the bill into her slit.

The small crowd assembled around her cheered and tossed more bills onto the stage. Sarah was beside herself. How could she beat that performance? Sarah sat down on her behind and spread her legs causing a few of the men from the other crowd to walk over. An older man, his scruffy gray beard hanging past his collar, motioned for Sarah to leave the stage and crawl upon his lap. He held a twenty dollar bill between his index and middle finger as Sarah walked down the steps and into his arms. Sarah lifted her long legs and sat upon his lap. She moved his dirtied wrinkled hands, his fingernails embedded with dirt and placed them behind his back. She began to rock back and forth, pretending that this disgusting scum bag was bringing her extreme gratification. She continued with the sordid dance as the man leaned his head back. From a distance they looked like two lovers tangled in an exotic web. She could feel his stiff manhood but tried to ignore it.

When the dance was over Sarah excused herself and walked into the bathroom hoping to spend some time alone, but it was hopeless. Misty had followed her into the bathroom with a slinky red velvet dress.

"Here, put this on." ordered Misty

"All the way?" Sarah asked.

"No. Let your tits hang out of it." Misty ordered.

Sarah climbed into the dress, letting the top half of her show and walked over to the bar. A reserved black man hidden by a baseball cap sat in the comer.

"How long you been working here?" asked the man in a friendly tone.

"I just started today."

"You need to be careful. My friend was a stripper here two years back and she was shot in the head out in the parking lot.

"Oh my God!" Sarah gasped

"I just want to make sure yon are careful."

Sarah was puzzled as to why a customer at Ms. Kitty's was concerned about her safety. Could her guardian angel be disguised as a pervert?

"Hey Beautiful" yelled a man in a New York accent.

Sarah turned her head only to be surprised by this good looking guy showing her interest. He smoothly rose from his seat and walked over to Sarah, his steps so smooth it looked like he was gliding across the floor.

"My name is Chad and you are beautiful."

Sarah blushed, her cheeks turning pink as a bunny's nose. Chad was not like the other creeps at Ms. Kitty's. He was actually movie star handsome with his gelled black hair and clear blue eyes with small violet specks. He was taller than the other men in the bar, about 6'3" and muscular in stature. The only flaw which could be picked out was his slightly crooked nose which he claimed had been broken in a boxing match.

"Would you like to go back to my hotel with me?" Chad

bluntly asked.

Sarah could barely contain herself; images of Sarah and Chad getting engaged, dancing at the wedding, standing in front of their perfect house with their 2.2 kids and puppies danced in her mind. Or maybe he was in the mafia, Sarah thought to herself. How dangerous and exciting! He was Italian and from New York. He fit the general stereotype of a mafia guy with his slicked back hair, gold chain, and hairy chest.

"I can't. I have to work. It's my first night."

"Ohhhh...." Chad sighed understandingly. "How do you like it?"

Sarah was speechless as she looked around at the impish spirits around her. "Here." He gently grabbed her hand, pressed a ten dollar bill into it, and closed her palm shut. "At least get on stage and do a dance for me. Since it's your first night I'll even show you some moves."

Sarah shyly backed away, held her breath and then turned around, her cheap shiny heels clicking as she walked to the stage. Chad grabbed his beer and followed Sarah to the stage, eyeing her buttocks as they swayed from side to side. Sarah began to move her feet from side to side, wildly swinging her hair and bending to the ground. "Do that again!" Chad ordered. "And this time, move your hips more."

Sarah again bent down to the ground, sticking her butt out as she stood up.

"Yey. That's it." Chad yelled as he tossed five dollars onto the stage.

Sarah continued to dance controlling the crowd with her moves. Out of the corner of her eye she could spot Mick motioning her to come over to the bar.

"How much have you been charging a dance?" Mick asked.

"About twenty dollars."

"You can give away a couple of free ones tonight."

Sarah obediently shook her head softly mumbling yes and proceeded back to the stage. As she danced a thin man in wire rimmed glasses, his greasy black hair parted to the side motioned her to follow him to the back room. She had never been to the back room. Together her and the man walked to the back room. The room was shadowed in a cloak of darkness, objects and people barely visible. The only light left to stream on the naked bodies was a bright red heat lamp affixed to the center of the ceiling. Sarah could hear the whispers, the groans, the thumping from the *Prince* song, *Cream* in the background. At one point she claimed she could even hear the devil mischievously snickering. Sarah placed the man's hands behind his back and climbed onto his lap and began to ride him. Every half minute he moved his hands and tried to grope her, but she'd move them back into place. He persisted countless more times once sticking his finger into her vagina. Sarah jumped back.

"You better get your damn finger out of there!"

"Oh, sorry." The man softly said in an embarrassed tone.

Her vagina stung, but she continued to ride the man. Little did she know that this quiet mannered man she had been riding was a convicted sex offender about to go to prison for a six year sentence in two weeks.

"How much for the lap dance?" The man asked after she was finished.

"It's on the house." She said.

Mick had told her to give a couple of free lap dances, so that's what she had to do. Nipples, another stripper, gave her a dirty look, but Sarah could not see through the smoky air and darkness. Sarah walked back into the dressing room while Nipples followed her, grabbing her shoulder and forcefully turning her around.

"Why the fuck are you giving out lap dances for free?"

"Hell no!" the other girls chimed in.

"B...Becau....Because Mick told me I could." Sarah meekly answered in a soft tone.

The other girls changing looked over at Sarah while Nipples started to complain.

"I'll be damned if you are going to be giving out free lap dances. That could be money going into my pocket bitch!"

"I....I...I'm so sorry,." Sarah began to apologize, tears welling up in her eyes.

"Why the think you are in here anyway, a goodie two shoes like you?" Nipples asked, shards of spit flying out of her mouth and wetting Sarah's face.

"I swear. I didn't know. I was only doing what Mick said." Sarah pleaded, her eyes searching the girls for a kind face, but all that stood before her were angry hard faces.

"Listen. Mick is an ass, He'll tell you anything just to fuck with ya. Just don't do it again." Nipples ordered, backing away.

"Mick tries to be our dad since most of us don't have one." Misty said.

"Yey. Me and my dad get along pretty well." Sarah said.

"You're lucky. I don't have one."

"Neither do I" the girls chimed in.

Sarah was saddened by these girls lack of parental figures in their lives. It was no wonder they had been led to this path. They had no one to look out for them. How would these parents have felt if they knew their daughters were displaying their crotch to dirty old men, getting fingered and fucked for a measly twenty dollars. These girls were no longer looked at or treated as people. They were pieces of meat, juicy pieces of flesh to ogle, grope, molest. These were no longer individuals to these men. Instead of they were thought of and treated collectively as whores, strippers to fondle and point at, live breathing blow up dolls to manipulate. The room was quiet for a moment, the girls silently mourning their lack of family, that missing ingredient in their lives which could have salvaged them from these places.

"Here." Misty said tossing a short black dress at Sarah. "Put this one on next." Sarah slipped into the black dress and walked back out into the main room. Chad, the New Yorker, pulled her hand and signaled for her to go into the back room. Chad sat down at one of the booths and grabbed Sarah's hand plopping her on top of his lap. She hopped upon him like a frisky puppy and began to gyrate back and fourth. Sarah felt sickened, disgusted that she bought into the whole concept that strip clubs were glamorous.

Chad was the last lap dance of the night, and when Sarah counted her earnings she was disappointed.

"$35.00." She thought to herself. *"All those free lap dances."*

Sarah was supposed to give the manager a cut of her money, but to give him a portion of her measly thirty five dollars. What a joke. Sarah got dressed, pocketed her money, and when no one was looking she sprinted to the car where Katt and I sat.

"Quick. Start driving!" she yelled as I opened the passenger door and she hopped in. We drove off into the darkness of the night grateful that one of us was not shot.

CHAPTER 27

When darkness falls among the land.
I shed my clothes and wave a hand.
My beau, he starts to follow me.
To a magical land of fantasy.
I swivel my hips and thrust out my chest.
He licks his lips as he stares at my breasts.
I sit on his lap and straddle him.
And cross the threshold to a land of sin.

Only at certain times did I shed my shield of purity. Only when darkness fell among the land and a full moon glowed in the night sky did my wild playful spirit escape. Like Dracula, werewolves, and witches I flourished among the shadowy skies and as always to aid me in my wicked diversion my two best friends were present, cocaine and marijuana. Tingles of excitement would swim through my stomach as Carl poured the magical powdery substance onto the table. He would always take out his credit card and divide the pile of snow white dust into four even lines. He'd then take out a dollar bill and roll it into a skinny cylindrical shape. We'd take turns placing the cylinder into each nostril and snorting the sandy granules. The free particles burned my nasal passages, the stinging sensations feeling like a cool menthol rush. It was slightly painful but also strangely enjoyable, in fact pleasant enough to repeat again and again. Cocaine was the one drug which made me feel glamorous perhaps because it had been glorified in the movies and society as the *"rich man's drug"*. It also made me feel powerful and confident, two traits of which I lacked. I craved the numbing sensation under my nose so badly, wishing that my entire face would deaden.

He'd then pour the miraculous plastic bag of grass onto the table and break it up with his fingers twisting the smelly weed between his fingers until it was fine enough to roll into a joint. He'd place the crumbled mixture into the thin paper wrap and roll it into a thin cigarette, licking the ends to make it stick. Carl would light a flame to the end of the joint and inhale, the strong taste so pungent he'd spastically cough as he exhaled. As I would exhale puff after puff eventually I'd feel as if I was about to float, so peaceful and content. In slow motion I'd breathe out the cloud of smoke, the swirl of fog filling the air with a sweet-scented aroma. My sexual appetite would blossom, causing the blood to rush to my most intimate of places. I could feel my breasts swell and become tender, my nipples thickening and hardening more every minute. I craved for my nipples to be fondled, behind to be stroked, vagina to be petted. I needed my body to be explored in detail by his tongue and fingertips, but first I'd have to tease him.

It was at this time that I'd wave my magical wand causing supernatural sparkles to drift throughout the air. I'd enter my room, strip off my shirt, pants, and shoes only to be left in my thong panties and push up bra. I'd slip my black fishnet stockings over my legs, pulling them just slightly under my thighs, and glide on a pair of black patent leather heels. The light would be flicked off, the strobe light turned on, and a dance CD placed into the CD player, and then the show would begin.

Carl knocked at the door and proceeded over to the bed, obediently sitting at the edge while I took my place on the floor. For a moment there was sheer silence, the only sound to be heard the flickering of the strobe light. Finally, the music began. I fluidly swayed my hips from side to side holding my hands high above my head. My body flowed gracefully as I sexily danced. I removed my bra rubbing the black lacy fabric over my milky breasts and erect nipples and then tossing it to the floor below me. I'd squeeze a glob of the coconut massage oil and smear the tropical scented lubrication on my breasts and stomach. The oil glistened as the flickering light reflected off of my shimmering skin. I'd then pull down my panties ever so slightly, but then immediately pull them up again mercilessly teasing him.

Carl pulled a twenty dollar bill out of his pocket and folded it in half, smoothing out any crinkles. I walked up to him seductively sticking out my thigh. He pulled on the side of my g-string, slowly placing the twenty into the strap and ever so smoothly grazing my thigh with his rough calloused hands. He then snapped the g-string back into place. I grabbed both sides of my panties, pulling the side strings upward allowing the fabric covering my vagina to gather itself into the slit. I could sense Carl salivating, but I continued to torment him relishing in the fact that I was punishing him. Gradually, I slipped my panties off, sliding them past my buttocks, thighs, knees, and finally calves where they ended up bundled into a neat little wad on the carpet floor. I turned my backside to him, knowing that my rear end was his favorite trait of mine. I wiggled my plump ass from side to side, bending over so he could have a good look. I then grabbed the coconut oil and smeared a dab on both cheeks generously buttering my fleshy buns. I sat my behind on the floor and spread open my legs practically torturing him and then finished the dance by roiling onto my stomach and stepping back up.

It was time to give him a lap dance. I climbed onto his lap forcefully putting his hands behind his back reminding him not to touch, and then I began to rock back and forth. I could feel his manhood stiffen as I rubbed against it. He excitedly wagged his tongue as a drop of his saliva fell on my thigh. I placed my index finger into his mouth so he could slurp on it, and he did the same to me. I arched my back sticking out my breasts as far as I could finally pushing him backwards on the bed. I naughtily slapped him on his right cheek a couple of times causing him to mischievously laugh. With the greasy coconut oil now on both of us, we resembled two slippery playful seals flipping on a sea deck. I grabbed his penis and placed it into me as we both moaned in satisfaction. I gyrated my hips to the music almost forcefully moving them back and forth. He pinched both of my nipples with his thumb and forefinger squeezing them until they were red causing me to rock back and forth harder and harder. His tongue hungrily lapped at my nipples and between both breasts as he rubbed his thick head of hair between them. I kissed his chest repeatedly, brushing my fingers over his chest hair. Our tongues entangled into one as the tingles became stronger and stronger finally inducing an incredible rush of ecstasy. I looked into Carl's eyes as waves of elation flowed through my insides making me groan, and when it was complete I giggled and collapsed on his chest.

"Oooh, you cane hard. Did you like that baby?." he asked flipping me over onto my stomach as I submissively got onto my knees and he shoved his penis into me again.

He aggressively slammed his penis into me his thighs slapping my behind. I loved how he could make me feel like a slut. I loved pretending that I was something that I wasn't, and then he let it out. He howled like a dog, letting out every last ounce of stress that had accumulated over the week as he gently pulled out his penis and squirted it all over my behind. We both breathed heavily as we got off the bed and he wiped off my behind with a damp rag, and he quickly placed a kiss upon my lips.

There was nothing I liked more than to be exploited by Carl. He made me want to try to be something that I despised, demoralize myself in order to make him feel manlier. I could only play make believe when I was intoxicated or high. I loved being his sex slave, how he could cause stirrings of arousal by calling me a slut or whore or tramp. Why did I like pretending that I was something I was not, a symbol I despise? Carl was convinced I was a whore because of it. I just tried to detach myself from these nights. That girl that danced for Carl was not me. She was a girl I hated.

CHAPTER 28

My beliefs about stripping extend far beyond jealously. Some might view me as a small-minded prude resentful of those who use their bodies to acquire wealth. Others might perceive of me as a green-eyed beast prepared to obliterate the sex industry, but only I know the truth. It is only I who can admit why I am obsessed with women's bodies. Only I hold the key to the mysteries hidden deep within my soul. I cannot divulge my secret to anyone, including myself, for if I do my sexuality is questioned. If I admit to myself that I am attracted to women, then my entire life is a lie. From the age of nine, that defining moment when I realized that I loved boys, that crucial turning point when I recklessly scribbled in my Hello Kitty notepad my attraction for the opposite sex. Could that have been a lie? Was my childhood crush on Nicholas Jukubco, Coby Turner, or Eric Bloom a hoax, how I fantasized about kissing them and laying my head on their bare underdeveloped chests. Could all of those lonely sixth grade nights when I'd lay in the darkness visualizing those spin in the bottle parties I was never invited to be a fraud, how I'd imagine Larry Fugate, the popular redhead getting a blow job in the closet. I had wished I was that girl succumbing to his desires, rubbing my cheek against his cinnamon tinged pubic hair.

Overhearing the spin the bottle stories from my oversexed friend, Michelle Oertel, my mother decided to keep a tight rein on me. Sex was only received in the spicy narrative my friends would relate to me. The slanderous gossip spread like wildfire and transformed my fellow schoolmates into whores. Sex was unattainable, reserved only for the most popular. I can remember that fresh-faced honors student, Katt McCoy, the gifted freckle faced girl all too high and mighty to socialize with the likes of me. I might have detested her, but was more so disgusted when I learned of how she had been the girl servicing Larry Fugate in the closet. How my opinion of her had changed. To me Katt was no better than a prostitute, sucking dicks behind closed doors.

I'd hear the rumors wishing that I was one of those girls. It made no sense to me, how in one regard I resented them, but in another how I wanted to be them. I was that shy quiet girl no one wondered about, the girl that slumped her shoulders in the locker room while the other girls hollered loudly, obnoxiously chasing each other in circles while their towels dropped to the ground. I dared not look at what lay beneath those towels, probably for fear that I'd like it. I'd always drape the towel tightly around my plump waist, gripping onto the flimsy thin fabric for dear life. During showers I'd cleverly maneuver the soap suds onto my intimate spots to prevent having to remove the entire bathing suit. I was not comfortable in what my body had developed into. I'd hold a washcloth over each breast as I slipped mybra on, squat down to the floor as I struggled to place each foot into the holes of my panties, hide behind the locker door as I put on my shirt and jeans. I must have appeared odd to the other girls going to such great lengths to cover up, but I was different fiom the others. I was a man in a locker room full of girls. I'd bury my head in my locker to avoid the forbidden, those ripened bouncing breasts and bushy triangular patches. If my eyes grazed these parts only once they'd burn to a crisp, be reduced to ashes, burn until they were two blistering hollowed eye sockets. Through the corner of my eye I caught a glimpse of Katt McCoy, completely naked, standing proudly, feeling no shame for who she was. The tingling in any intimate spots told me that I enjoyed seeing her in a state of undress, but my mind quickly dismissed these feelings. I liked boys, believe me I did, but I always hid my face behind the locker, my head down, grunting if asked a question. I concealed my desires and my sexuality to appear normal.

To this day I am in denial as to my sexuality. My heart is firmly implanted in masculine soil, but a few of those seeds have strayed into feminine terrain. I could not have a deep emotional connection with a woman, but the female figure ignites passion in my core which I cannot explain. I will never explore that side of me though. It would change who I am and everything I stand for.

In times of desperation, when I partake in pleasuring myself, I'll close my eyes and make believe. I massage my vagina with a wet washcloth imagining the dampened rag is a tongue. I visualize a gorgeous tan stripper, her buttery golden mane sweeps across her buttocks. Her swollen breasts barely bounce as she sways her hips from side to side. Her stiff perky nipples are as pink as pencil tips. She turns her back to the crowd and slowly bends over, sticking out her plump ass as she crawls down to her knees. Her translucent aqua eyes, the lids heavily painted with glossy blue shadow gradually close as she spreads her legs open. In her mind she travels to another place, a fairy tale land with rainbows and leprechauns and pots of glittering gold. No one can read her mind though. They believe she is there only for them, especially Carl. Carl sits at a table, mesmerized by the stripper's beauty. His eyes, reddish brown, the color of fire wood, remain fixated on her pussy, the flaxen hair neatly trimmed into a narrow strip. He guzzles on his beer, ravenously wiping a drop of ale from his lips.

Another stripper struts onto the stage as the crowd crudely hollers. This girl, her hair the color of caramel, wildly gyrates her hips as the blonde rises to her feet. They begin to dance together, teasing the audience as their breasts briefly touch. Their gleaming lips, generously polished with chocolate pink gloss, converge as one. Their tongues dance in each other's mouths and hungrily lick the watermelon flavored gloss off of their lips. Hoots and hollers emanate from the corner of the room encouraging the girls to go further. They rub against each other creating such friction that sparks begin to fly. Their hips grind one another to the echoing base of the dirty melody, and then they begin to emulate sexual acts that transcend even the nastiest imagination. The blonde lays flat on the stage, her tanned skin twinkling, as the brunette places her head between her legs. The men chant crude phrases, their foul language and smelly crinkled dollars thrown onto the stage egg on the exotic auburn haired dancer to wildly flick her tongue along the clitoris. Cocaine induced moans of ecstasy echoed from out of the blondes lips as she wildly grinds her hips and her breasts engorge.

Carl hungrily wags his tongue, his curiosity heightened by the yelling from behind a curtain separating the rooms. He slowly rises to his feet, walking into the back room and discovering a shower stall complete with two naked women massaging and scrubbing each other. The soapy suds look like whip cream gliding down their silky smooth skin. The raven haired dancer squeezed the redhead's breasts freckled ever so lightly and licked her nipples. The girls cheeks are flushed, the hot steam also reddening their nipples. Their nipples resemble juicy strawberries doused in whipped cream.

I wring the washcloth, droplets of water dribbling onto my chest, my belly, my clitoris. I imagine the water is my body's juices, the boiling liquid swimming in my belly button. My fingertips speedily diddle traveling to my breasts, pinching my nipples, rubbing my thighs, my waist, my neck, and then a wave of self induced elation washes throughout my insides. I moan as I scream Fuck me Donny! Oh fuck me Donny!

CHAPTER 29

I thought that by being exposed to this phobia embedded so deep within my soul that I would be healed. I thought that the naked bodies encircling me would provide me with peace and comfort, that I could confront the secrets buried in my subconscious. I thought that uplifting melodies would swirl through my eardrums finally allowing relief, that the heaviness in my heart causing it to sink to the base of my stomach would be replaced by the weightlessness of a light fluffy feather. I thought my heart would float through my inner recesses, a wild current of ecstasy gushing throughout every orifice. I thought I could at last be free, free of this self inflicted agony This is what I hoped for. How childish of me. How foolish to believe that I'd be comfortable in such a seedy environment, prepared to submerge myself in these devilish waters, to be drenched by these nude sinners which inhabited Roxy's. How I yearned to stare into their soulless eyes and feel compassion for them, to glance upon their bare flesh and unearth some hideous flaw to console me. I craved to empathize with these women, to be able to understand why they have to resort to being demeaned and exploited by men.

This morbid obsession was destroying me, this destructive compulsion to find the truth. I wanted to look into these women's faces and be startled, stunned by their rough skin sprinkled with craters, their disproportionate features, their youthfulness drained. I needed to see lopsided saggy breasts, plump stomachs, stretch marks, bodies devoid of any sign of perfection. Why can I never get what I want? Why do I sit here, my eyes welling up with tears yet again, the swollen bags beneath my eyes darkening until every speck of sunshine contained within my eyes sets beyond the horizon.

I thought I could suppress my disgust, be a neutral spectator critiquing these women as if they were nothing to me. He begged me not to go, not to take him back to a place he tried hard to forget, but I could not let the issue rest. I was tired of comparing myself to these women, questioning their beauty. I needed a boost of self esteem, and I thought this would do it. I thought that if I dolled myself up, slipped on my pink and black floral dress which hugged my every curve, wore my water bra so that my swollen breasts gushed fourth from out of my revealing neck line, dabbed on the perfect amount of plum wine lip gloss, golden glimmer eye shadows, and donned sunlight kissed cheeks that I could lift myself above this place.

Carl was nervous, frightened to expose me to Roxy's, but I insisted. I needed to be a part of him, and I thought this would complete us, rid me of the jealousy that was budding like an umruly field of wild flowers and pemit my entrance into his world. His nervousness only agitated me. Why did he not think that I could cope with a place he described as disgusting, swarming with undesirable and unattractive women? Could he have been lying to me, falsely reassuring me and filling me with hope only to have my entire world crash down before me? I did not want them to be attractive, or thin, or completely nude. Carl always emphasized that they wore panties, that big screen televisions were built into every comer, broadcasting the sports game of that day. He told me that it was not just a strip bar, but a recreational venue not only for perverts, but for the hard working man desiring a refreshing bottle of brew, to sit back and recline and watch a game of football. These women were disgusting he said, the rough looking Harley type of woman covered in tattoos. They had no figures, emaciated bodies, haggard skeletal redneck faces oozing of pimples. This was not a place to get aroused. If he wanted to go see hot women, he'd go to a regular bar, not into this nauseating dump his friends and boss dragged him into. *A man could look at naked flesh and not lust*, he said. Why couldn't I believe him? Why couldn't I have enough faith in my man? Just because he is being swarmed by nameless faces displaying bare breasts, buttocks, and vaginas, this should not faze him, right? Could I be desensitized like Carl claimed he was?

Carl sat on our beige couch, his eyes tearing up. He knew that he should not take me there, but there was no convincing me. I was stubborn. My head was aching, my eyes were puffy, my skin was sallow. This obsession had transformed into a sickness with the symptoms beginning to reflect in my appearance. We sat in the car, silent, our fate solely based on my opinion towards the place and how I would react. The blackness enveloping us sucked us into a vacuum. We were exploring unfamiliar territory, entering a devil's paradise that would either spit me out or suck me in, a Bermuda

Rachel Gunn

Triangle of dirty indulgences.

I could remember entering Brooklyn once before, by accident of course, but I remembered every road, every turn, every torn down building we passed on the way as if it was yesterday. A gigantic billboard displaying the Hustler club overwhelmed me with fear. An exotic Asian woman laid flat on a grassy pasture, her dark black hair drenched, water droplets clinging to her tan oiled flesh. She was doused by a rain shower, an odor of dew almost permeating onto the highway from the billboard. I prayed that this woman was just a ploy, a trick to draw gullible lonely men into these places. If these girls were attractive, I would simply die, my self worth to have vanished forever.

We made our way onto a dim deserted road, under a bridge, and past a small rectangular white shack that had a sign reading *"Girls, Girls, Girls"* on the top of the triangular ramshackle roof. I commented on the sign, how these places boast about their females inside as if they were beauty queens. It nauseated me, how society was geared towards the fantasies of men without any regard for women. Carl said the place was a whore house. I could not argue. I had never been inside. An old man in a flimsy plaid hat and long white beard rocked himself in a rickety rocking chair while a pudgy middle aged woman rotated smoked sausages with her metal tongs. A thin stream of smoke wafted from over the barbecue, leaving a gray cloud of smoke to linger in the air, the zesty smell seeping through the crack in my window and entering our nasal passages. It was comical how every strip club always had a team of people barbecuing outside. Was barbecue and nudity a mandatory combination? Did the taste of juicy smoked sausage somehow provide some magical aphrodisiac to lure these men into their strip club?

I could hear my heart thumping in my chest. Carl and I held hands, his calloused fingers stroking my sweaty palm. By holding hands we were clinging to each other, so absorbed in comforting one another, and hoping that this night would end pleasantly. He was trying to make me feel secure, shield me from what I was about to see.

Finally, I recognized the lights in the distance, and as we drove upon the dilapidated wooden shacks adorned with neon signs, my heart plummeted. In the far left hand corner of the parking lot, was the smallest building, a poorly constructed house, covered in gray shingles. A fluorescent yellow sign, reading massage parlor, was affixed in the center of the front of the house. There were no windows in any of the buildings, and if there were, they were tinted. What transpired inside these buildings was only to be witnessed by the men who entered. I was facing my fear, and for better or for worse, I promised Carl that I would not break up with him. Carl circled the parking lot, searching for that perfect parking space until I hollered for him to just park. I was becoming quite agitated and impatient, my fear simmering in the pit of my stomach, the bubbles violently fizzing, giving me heartburn. He parked in front of a wooden fence and turned the car off. Usually, Carl would sit in the car for a minute, dipping his one hitter into his dugout and puffing on it one last time until he was ready, but he knew better. He realized that I had been building this up for years, and I was finally going to do it.

I opened the car door, my heart thumping louder and louder. I looked directly ahead of me and saw the Platinum Club, another strip bar directly to the right of Roxy's. A yellow school bus was parked in the parking lot, probably a bus used for a bachelor party. A severely obese black woman walked off of the bus with a plastic name tag hanging off a string around her neck. She placed her hand around her greased black hair tightly wound in a bun, and tightened it as she carried on a casual conversation with one of the men in line. He looked exactly as I expected these men to look. He wore square rimmed glasses with a clear frame and had strawberry blonde curls, several unruly ringlets moist with sweat and sticking to his forehead. The man was creepy just like every other man who stood in line. The man talked to the black woman about work just like it was a normal night and a normal place. Did not anyone here realize where they were, aware that they were about to enter satan's shack of delight? Roxy's looked like a shack, a poorly constructed shed intended for sin. I walked up to the end of the line, my legs jiggling like jello as I tried my best to stand there still and sneak a peak inside. As the line moved up, the bar became visible as did the sounds of the music and the smells. The intoxicating scent of hard liquor and cigarette smoke gave me a head rush. A fragrance of pure wickedness swirled throughout the air, making me want to turn around and never come back, but as the line moved up further it was too late. I caught a glance of one of the strippers, her bare ass bent over.

"I don't think they are wearing underwear." I said to Carl coldly as he stood behind me. Carl looked as shocked as I was, his face also searching for a dumbfounded expression to express his confusion. A younger nerdy looking man wearing a cheap tuxedo, his thin spiked dirty blonde hair spiked with globs of hair gel stood behind a glass counter.

"Eight dollars." he said to Carl and then his beady eyes looked over to me.

"Sign here sweetheart and you get in here for free." He lifted an official looking log book, the page displaying several signatures.

My unsteady hand trembled as I reached for his pen and shakily signed my name. I could feel him stare at me, and I could sense a snide smirk on his face, but I ignored looking at him. I came here for one thing, and that was relief. I was not going to let anyone or anything deter my mission. A fairly attractive woman, wearing a black mini skirt and sequined tube top had me raise my arms as she patted me down and gave me the ok to make my entrance. *This was it*, I thought to myself. My footsteps gradually slowed as I walked ahead. I was not even concerned with where Carl was, because I knew that as soon as I stepped into this place that I had made a mistake. It was not at all as Carl described. I looked ahead at the buffet of naked women. There were at least five or six of them entertaining the crowd. None of the girls had underwear on. I looked up at the front stage. A thin girl stood, her vagina shaved, the slit completely visible, only a thin path of brown hair accenting the area. Her small firm breasts did not budge as she turned around and smacked her ass. She did not dance. None of the girls actually danced. I expected seductive gyrations, hips twirling, buns and breasts jiggling, not this pathetic display of trashiness used to entertain these easily amused perverts.

I could not hear the noisy chatter at the bar nor the steamy *Prince* song blaring from the speaker system. All I could see were the women, these anonymous nude women, their bodies displayed for the world to see. They were filled with mystery, each story, each struggle, each heartache tucked away deep inside as they provocatively moved, putting on a front to tantalize these men. These men did not think of these women as individuals. They could have cared less if these women had a mind. They were just bodies, anonymous bodies satisfying these men's twisted need for sexual fulfillment. Each women dancing had a story, a tale woven throughout her soul, buried deep within her heart. How many tears had these women cried, how much abuse had been inflicted upon them, what drove these women to get to the point where they would be objectified by men in such a manner? These women were once little girls, modest little girls twirling around in front of the mirror, their bright pink lipstick sloppily applied, a floral plastic handbag hanging off one shoulder, glittery pink heels placed on each tiny foot. They had such high hopes for the future as they looked into that mirror. They were going to be movie stars, singers, ballet dancers. They were oblivious to the perversion they would encounter as adults; how they would contort their bodies into all sorts of sexual positions to earn a dollar here and there. They would not even be able to imagine how they would have to gulp down countless glasses of alcohol to numb them, snort lines of coke to make them lose their inhibitions, smoke crack to feed their addiction. If only they could look into that mirror and see what would become of them, maybe they could've stopped it.

If only men wouldn't have developed this perverted belief about women that they are just bodies. Do these men comprehend that these women are real, that some of them are mothers who tuck their kids in every night before stripping off their clothes. All of them are daughters who belong to somebody. Daughters whose parents worry about them every moment. Some of them are sisters, sisters of big brothers who tried to protect them from men. Many of them are girlfriends or wives who crawl into bed with the same man every night, a man who has to straggle with the fact that the girl that they love shows all every night.

It was hard to be so compassionate at this moment though. It was hard for me not to despise these women. Such hatred I held in my heart. I was guilty of the same wrongdoing as the men in the club. I also only looked upon these girls as pieces of meat, soulless women, the bleak look in their eyes not touching me in the least bit.

I critiqued these women, looking them up and down, any eyes

gazing every inch of their bodies. They were not as flawed as I hoped for, not tattooed from head to toe. They were perfectly thin, not plump in the stomach as I was, their behinds not puffed out as mine, their breasts small but firm, their nipples pointed, not finding below the breast like mine. It was an optical illusion of sorts, these so called *"nasty girls"*, a handful of naked women surrendering their values and prepared to do whatever it takes to con these men into giving them money. My heart began to descend as my eyes quickly darted from one woman to the other. It was dark among us, the light perhaps distorted to conceal many of their flaws. They all had long hair, which I had feared, lengthy luxurious locks, golden as honey wheat. Their hair swayed from sided to side, brushing each cheek of their behind as they moved. My eyes quickly dashed to the front stage again, upon the nude girl, her shaved vagina facing the room. In horror I stared at this woman, so enraged, so blind to acknowledging her as an actual woman. I squinted my eyes, searching her face for something to console me, a hideous wart, terrible ache, unattractive features. A moment of relief hit me for she was not attractive as I had feared.

Her skin was rough and weathered, prematurely aged. I looked into her crinkled eyes, but she did not acknowledge me, each eye a dismal abyss. She was a soulless puppet, her actions controlled by the men in the audience, her masters manipulating her every move to trigger tingles in their intimate places. The woman mechanically rotated her body, her behind now facing the audience as she lifted her man to the side and slapped her left cheek, leaving a pinkish imprint as her hand fell to her side. She was trying whatever she could, teasing and taunting the audience with her body. It was no consolation that her face frightened me, that she resembled a rotted corpse, her soul slowly decomposing before my very eyes. She grinned wide, her eye sockets empty, a decaying pumpkin head, no candle within to light her eyes. I found no solace in her hideousness, as she used her sexuality to pacify these men's insecurities. She made each man feel special, as if she were here only for them. In their lonely little minds, she was theirs.

"You lied to me." I continuously cried to Carl. "They're not wearing underwear. You lied to me!"

He kept insisting that he didn't lie, that they used to get in trouble for removing their panties, that they removed the big screen televisions. It was nothing like it was now, but I didn't believe him. How could I believe anything he told me? Right in front of my face, not less than five feet away was a shaved vagina, completely bare for everyone to see. At that point I could not distinguish him from the others. He was like all the other guys in here, lonely disgusting men that didn't give a shit about women, only their bodies.

I needed to see the others. I had to see their faces, be comforted by their ugliness, but all I could see were breasts, behinds, and long hair. I was invisible in my pretty pink dress, my face rich with color, my hair perfectly pinned up. I was clothed and therefore useless to these men. I was boiling inside with anger, usually able to draw attention towards me, but not in Roxy's. I marched up to the far left stage where the blonde was dancing, her back facing the crowd. At least two of the other strippers, topless, walked by the stage and I walked fight in front of them, trying desperately to sneak a peak at their face in the darkness, but it was so hard. The illusion was overwhelming me, the misconception that these were female goddesses of perfection with perfect faces and perfect bodies. No matter what I saw, my body was beginning to go into shock, my disgust overpowering me. I prayed that the blonde would turn around and surprise me, shock me with warts, a pointy nose, a witch's face, but she never turned my way.

The rage could no longer stay inside of me. Panic set in. I had to leave this place. A spirit overtook me, shoved me towards the door, made my footsteps quicken as the magnetic pull overtook me. Carl tried to stop me, tried to force me to be rational, to actually stay and take a look at these women's faces, to not make rash judgments, but I couldn't. I hated him by this point. He was a liar. He liked the places, he didn't. He went there every day, he didn't. He liked the girls, he didn't. They wore panties, they didn't. What else did he want to lie about? How could I even sleep with this man, this stranger, this chameleon of many colors who changed his story only to appease me.

I shoved Carl in the shoulder, pushing him away as I searched for the door. Laughter and applause circled us, intoxicated men misinterpreting my hitting him as if he was in trouble. They had no conception of what I had been through for the last two years, how I was not hitting him at that moment for taking me there in the present, but for the past, for all of the lies, for fooling me. The hot tingling he felt in his shoulder from my slap was no consolation for the emotional torture he had put me through. How could I be with someone who would sit in a place like this? Was he oblivious to the wickedness, the foul stench of liquor floating through the atmosphere, the poor worn-out women too drained to even dance that they only stood there pacifying these pervert's desires.

I desperately searched the room for an exit, my teary eyes scanning the cheap wooden paneling for a door. *I found it!* I forcefully thrustt that door open, the warm night air wafting through my nostrils, providing me with a brief moment of relief. My heart ached, tbe sore muscle painfully contracting, squeezing my entire chest. I had never been so heartbroken, never! All the men that had stomped on my heart, not cared about me, abandoned me. They no longer mattered. Only Carl mattered, only Carl and his lies, lies he told to save me. I ran towards my car the distance eternal as my pretty pink heels clicked against the pavement. Winded and hysterical, I ran towards a wooden fence. My clenched fists pounding at the splintered wood, I began to scream, my cries echoing throughout the parking lot.

"LIES, ALL LIES, YOU LIED TO ME! YOU LIED TO ME!" I screamed.

I did not care who heard me, because at that moment I was insane, unaware of the people who curiously watched me, oblivious to the stares, the whispering, the snickers of the creepy little men sitting inside of their cars. He had betrayed me, the one person whom I had come to trust. Those lies had continuously poured forth from that filthy orifice of his, and I had believed them! What an idiot I had been! How could I have believed that these girls wore underwear or had layers of fat hanging off of their stomach and thighs? Where were the big screen televisions broadcasting the major sport plays of the day? Where were the fifty year old crack addicts with their saggy skin and wrinkles, the emaciated meth heads so stoned out of their minds, the rugged motorcycle women with the Farah Fawcett hairdos and covered in tattoos from head to toe. I suppose I expected to encounter a traveling circus, a freak show, hideous ogres. Wishful thinking, because all I saw were naked women. It did not matter how unattractive they might have been in reality, because they were only pieces of meat. How could I see them as anything else?

OVER ON THE EAST SIDE

I punched that fence until my palms bled. At that moment the fence was not a fence. It was Carl, it was the perverts in the bar, it was the naked strippers slithering down their cold aluminum poles. I beat that fence until I felt Carl's muscular forearms wrap around my waist. I was sobbing, my tears blackened by my smudged eyeliner, goblets of mascara streaming down my soaking face.

"Get her out of here man! Why the hell would you take your girlfriend to a strip club?" "Get her out of my lot!" a hefty black man standing on the opposite side of the lot hollered.

"Get in the car, or you're going to get the fucking cops called." Carl reprimanded, forcefully squeezing my waist and dragged me into the car.

I crumbled into the seat like a wounded puppy dog, burying my head between my knees. There had never been a moment in any life that I had felt more pain. Not one event in my life could compare; not labor, not my first love, not my broken pinkie finger dangling off of my hand. No physical form of torture, no heartbreak, not even death could I imagine had ever equaled to the grief I was experiencing. Squeezing my own children from out of my loins had not caused that sort of pain. I was grieving the death of my idealized outlook, a romanticized view of relationships and what mine would be like. I wanted Prince Charming, not some pervert that hung out in strip bars ogling at pussy all day.

My boyfriend had vanished from this planet, my adorable pure beloved. His childlike charm, his boyish good looks, his sugar coated compliments. None of this mattered to me anymore. In my heart Carl was now dead. No amount of buttering me up, crying spells, or begging would bring him back from the departed. He was dead to me, and I wished that I was too.

I lifted my head up for a brief moment. Carl was slowly transforming into a gigantic penis, a diseased, infectious penis dripping of a creamy foul smelling pus. He was not of the clean circumcised breed, but instead the dirty uncircumcised kind, his filthy flap's discharge spilling over the tip. Bleeding sores were now sprouting up like wildflowers, the bubbling blisters of bacteria attempting to leap onto any skin. I did not want him to taint my sparkling clean soul, this spirit which I had struggled so hard to protect. He needed to go back to Roxy's, return to his sinful beginnings, infect his dear stripper friends instead of me. At this point I did not care if he wiped his poisoned tip all over their shaved vaginas, their smiling entryways into hell, their deceivingly clever cavities of temptation. For all I cared he could ram himself into each and every one of their rotten anuses, stroke their marshmallow soft ass cheeks, tease them, taunt them, ensnare them into his web as he did to me.

I buried my head back between my knees. Oddly even during this heartbreaking moment of my life, I was still self-conscious. I did not want to see the man who screamed at Carl to get me out of here, the disgusting perverts peeking from within their cars to witness the commotion, the illuminated shacks of immortality, the yellow school bus crammed with hollering drunk idiots. I wanted to forget I ever came here, retreat back to a time when strip clubs were prohibited, go back to an era when that yellow school bus was packed with innocent screaming children excited about a field trip or their first day of school, not dirty drunk idiots jacking off.

My shouts were muffled, stifled by the flesh of my inner thighs as both sides of my face remained pressed against them. I was shrieking as if I was being murdered, my violent screams echoing far beyond the scrunched confines of my car. I slowly raised my head when I felt it safe, and slammed it back onto the headrest. I yelled to God for help, prayed with a vengeance so fierce I was sure that he heard me. I rocked back and fourth, mumbling gibberish I am sure not even the lord could understand. I believed that the end was near. There was nothing left to live for in this sick world, this place that I had once loved, but now loathed. I placed my hand on the cold plastic handle of my door and began to pull it towards me, aware that I was about to inflict such horrible pain onto myself. I was going to commit suicide, roll out of my car onto the highway and make my demise from the terrible world. I would never feel anything again. I am sure that at first my soft skin scraping against the pavement at sixty miles per hour would sting, but how could that compare to my inner suffering? How could the crumbled asphalt and jagged pebbles embedding themselves into my newly formed cuts throb as badly as my broken heart? I had never before attempted to jump out of a fast moving car, never held such little hope in my heart. I began to open the door and shift my body weight towards it, leaning into a miserable destiny which I was forcing onto myself. The wind outside fiercely whistled, violently pushing itself through the opening, welcoming me into the afterworld, but it was not my time. Carl's bellowing screams and forceful grip of the meaty section of my upper arm awakened me out of my daze. I reluctantly slammed my door shut, infuriated that the same man who had induced my suicide attack was the same man who was rescuing me from it. The sound of the wind lulling me into a world of my own had disappeared only to be replaced by my crying.

Carl was shrilly hollering at me, attempting in the only way he knew how to revive me out of this smoggy haze I had plunged into. He thought I had lost my mind, that I had permanently excreted every brain cell I carried. I was no longer a rational woman, but a powerless paraplegic, my facial expressions paralyzed for the time being. Only a thin stream of drool trickled down my chin as I painfully groaned and babbled nonsense.

I resembled my dearly departed Great Aunt Katie who my mother had treasured as a child. We only visited her in the nursing home on one occasion, when I was a small girl, but the powerful scent of disinfectant lingering still stirred in my nostrils. Even as a little girl I realized how precious life is, how it can be snatched away from us at any time. These once fascinating persons loitering the hallways were at one time animated, but now were only shadows of their former selves, ghosts before they lay dead and buried. I pitied these poor souls, how their families probably forgot about them, because they could no longer make an impact on this world. I felt so badly that the highlight of their day was needlepoint or creating mundane crafts for family members who rarely visited, or being spoon fed the gooey multicolored marshmallow mixture in pastel hues. It hurt my mom so to see this once strong beautiful woman dwindle away to this skeleton, this ancient wrinkled frame. Katie had nurtured my mother as no other family member had, and now as my mother tried to connect, Katie could not reciprocate.

I felt as Aunt Katie had, dead to this world, numb to the persons whom inhabited it. I held no regard for life, dismissed its joys and wallowed in its heartache. No one could stir me out of this self inflicted coma. My mouth was viciously chattering, my teeth clacking away as if it was twenty degrees below zero. Carl could not comprehend what I was going through, how a strip bar of all places could cause me such grief. He thought I had gone insane. I was not insane, just overwhelmed with disgust and jealousy. My spirit had been severely dampened at first by Carl's tales, and now as they were brought to life in vivid color, my body went into shock. I was suffering from a sort of post traumatic shock syndrome similar to what Vietnam War veterans had experienced, but instead of being besieged by explosions and enemy snipers I was bombarded with a barrage of nakedness. I no longer wanted to be a part of this world, this nauseating garbage dump crawling with trashy inhabitants. Those people I saw tonight were like cockroaches, greasy creepy-crawlies infected with all sorts of disease.

At this moment Carl was also one of the undesirable vermin. I violently swatted him away as he tried to control my outburst, but I didn't want him to touch me. I wanted so badly to get out of the car, run away from Carl, from this town, from this state, but I couldn't. Images of blowing my head off seemed so appealing, but without a gun hardly practical. Pills would have to suffice. I'd swallow pill after pill, drown down the bite size colorful tablets with mouthfuls of water until I had finished the very last one. I'd take them all, the yellow capsule antidepressants, the round white Lexapro tablets, the diuretics, both bottles of antibiotics, and if that did not world I'd gulp down a bottle of household ammonia until my insides were washed away, destroyed. I could forever sleep and not have to preoccupy myself by these tortuous thoughts and images. No strippers, no tittie bars, no disgusting perverts, no lying boyfriends, only sweet clouds and angels to whisk me off to a higher plain and rescue me from this hell.

I held such high hopes for this evening. I foolishly thought that I'd magically be healed, cured of bad self esteem, self hatred, intrusive images of naked women dancing in my head. This was the end. I used to be loving, generous, non judgmental, accepting towards all people regardless of race, religion, or occupation. No more. The car ride felt like it would never end, the endless motion lulling me into a deep trance. I felt claustrophobic, stifled by the tainted air which Carl and me shared. As I took in each breath I felt as if I was going to choke on the toxic fumes I shared with this stranger beside me. Despite the promise I had made earlier in the evening, I screamed *"It's over!"* until my hoarse voice could no longer endure the strain, and I had gagged on all my tears. Carl played like he didn't care, buried his humiliation and heartbreak, damaging me even more.

As soon as the car screeched to a halt, I leaped out of my passenger side and sprinted towards the door, shooting up the stairs as quickly as I could. All I could think about were the pills I was going to take, how pleasant an afterlife would be, no bodies, no temptation, only souls and the warm soothing light which bathed all of God's children.

As my jittery fingers tried to fit my jingling key in the keyhole, I could hear Carl stomping up the stairs. I knew that ending my life was going to be a challenge with Carl's overbearing shadow hovering over me. I ran to the bathroom, making sure to lock the door behind me, and unfortunately catching a glimpse of my reflection in the mirror. How pretty I had looked just a couple of hours ago. My lipstick was smeared all over my lips, the plum wine color staining my teeth. My cheeks were no longer sun kissed but flushed a hot pink shade. My eyes with gobs of mascara and eyeliner smeared round the edges made me look like a raccoon. I resembled a demented Raggedy Ann doll. My entire face was slick with tears, my forehead soaked in perspiration from all of the kicking and screaming in the car.

He had won. They had won! All of them! The strippers, the dirty old men, the starving sex crazed hormonal idiots barely out of their adolescence, the promoters of these places, the owners, the world! They were all winners, and I was the big fat loser. I was the one who way laying in a rolled up heap on the chilly bathroom floor shedding tear after tear after tear. Not the strippers! They were the ones who had to live with the decision they had made, not me. Then why did I hurt so bad? I was not the girl wildly gyrating on strange men's laps, wiggling my naked ass for a stinking dollar. I was not the girl bending over on stage, displaying my genitalia in front of a multitude of nameless faces. I was not the girl jiggling my breasts, inducing erections in almost every creep who entered the place. If I was not one of the girls who did this, then why was I bringing the shame they felt home with me, or did they feel no shame? Did these women objectified and exploited by these men enjoy what they did? Were they in all reality exhibitionists that enjoyed electrifying their audience? Did everyone condone this sort of behavior? Were there no morals left in this world? Why were strip clubs legal? It was barbaric, animal like, sexuality stretched to ridiculous extremes. Why was the legal age for drinking twenty-one, but eighteen to strip off your clothes.

Eighteen year old girls were practically still children, confused adolescents endangering their lives for a cheap thrill. Men, old enough to be their fathers gawking at their little girls. Daddy's little girls. These men could have chosen an honorable path, but instead of being a father figure, they carried out these perverse fantasies of fucking their daughters. Society was sick, twisted, and I wanted no part of it. I was bewildered as to why I carried the burden of the world upon my shoulders. Tale after tale circled through my mind making me dizzy. Such dirty gossip traveled in my time. I thought back to a story I had heard from a Navy wife, also a friend of mine, her husband traveling through Europe and Asia. Her husband had gone into a strip club with his Navy buddies and actually witnessed firsthand his friend finger fuck one of the Taiwanese strippers in front of everyone. How fucked up did a woman have to be to let a stranger or anyone in that matter stick his finger in her vagina, especially in front of a cheering crowd? Was any amount of money worth losing one's self-respect? How many viruses were crawling in these women's genitals? Did these men even care? Was this the example our service men were setting overseas?

I removed my dress and sweater, carelessly tossing them onto the fluffy purple mat. I wanted to shred my pathetic pink dress into a million pieces, shove it in the garbage and forget it ever existed, this bitter reminder of my devastating night. I slinked down to the floor, my damp crimson cheek pressed against the unpleasantly cold tile floor, and I continued to cry. The crying would not stop, and I did not care. It almost felt good to cry, letting go of all the pent up anger I carried.

Carl thumped at the door loudly, his knuckles I imagine raw from his persistent pounding. How could I open the door and look him in the eye? I was fearful of what I'd see. I would look into the windows of his soul and see one of two things, the latter my worst fear. If he was honorable I'd look into his chocolate brown eyes and only see the innocence of the world reflected back, children giggling, puppies scuttling, first loves pecking. If he was shady though I'd look into his muddy brown eyes and only see the wickedness of the world echoed back, the naked strippers twirling round their poles, their admirers cheering them on. I mustered up what strength I could to twist the handle only to be faced with what I had feared most. When I opened up that door and gazed into his eyes, there was only darkness. There was no purity from within to light up those murky brown eyes of his. Every naked girl, every vagina, every breast leapt forth from those vile eyes of his, brutally gouging me in the face. His tears failed to drown the images but only magnified them. He was uncontrollably sobbing, begging me for another chance, but I was numb. His grief did not move me for all I could see in him was evil. His eyes expressed sorrow, but I was deadened to what he felt. All I could think about were his damn eyes, how those same eyes that cried tears for me now had at one time stared at the naked strippers, followed them from one stage to another as they performed all sorts of tricks for their masters. As they spread their legs open Carl fixated on their vaginas, as they spun, he stared at their breasts, as they bent over, he mentally devoured their ass. How could he even cry for me now? How could he cry for one girl when he was using to seeing them collectively? The signs outside of Roxy's read *Girls, Gifts, Girls*, not girl. I was only one girl, and what good was one girl when there were so many naked ones under one roof? I was the one that hurt, my shattered ego spread out for him to reduce to rubble. He had no right to cry, no right to hurt. He did not feel as deeply as I. No one ached as I did.

I callously pushed him out of the way as if he was nothing to me, but he could not let me go. Carl clutched my forearm, foolishly thinking that his touch would melt my frosty heart. Didn't he know? Did he not realize that I had no heart left? Words can kill, and his words slaughtered me. Physically I was still here, but mentally and spiritually I was dead. It was enough that my imagination could mold his words into artwork, create a canvas, each word a different oil shade spread on. His words were now put to life, the reality far more graphic then I'd ever realize. Each time he opened his mouth, the brush was dipped deeper, adding yet another vibrant color to his masterpiece, and now that the painting was finished I could not bear to look.

He bawled like an infant, pleading with me to give him another chance. How many times was he going to tell me that he wasn't like those men in there? How foolish did he think I could be? It was enough that he took me into Roxy's. What did he think would really happen when he brought me in there? Perhaps the strippers would slip on their panties and bras, sit still, and humor Carl and me, shield me from their usual duties.

I struggled to be free of him, but he had trapped me underneath him. His head was buried onto my shoulder, the tears dampening my neck and chest. I wriggled from underneath his powerful embrace, but every time I had slid away, he dragged me back towards him, the friction of the carpet rubbing against my elbows burning. Normally his crying would have touched me, but I was deeply wounded. I did not believe that Carl genuinely wept for me. He had been caught. His lies had finally caught up with him, and he was embarrassed. All I wanted was to leave and drive away and never look back, search for comfort from anyone other than Carl. I needed to be hugged by a friend, not an enemy such as he. We both lay on the floor weeping, me wiggling to be free of him, him crushing me beneath him so he could never let me go. There would be nothing to save us though, except perhaps death, and not even that could truly keep our spirits together, only our vacuous wintry cold bodies. I hoped that his frequent excursions to the strip clubs were worth losing me. I hoped that him and his friends had fun living it up at the expense of women. What a selfish race man is!

I forcefully squirmed, my face reddening due to the pressure from his body weight. My arms and legs flailed about like the tentacles of an octopus, desperately trying to free itself. He was not going to let me go though. I was not a person to him but a prized possession he had acquired. In the past he knew that he had treated me badly by calling me names and hurting me, but deep down he knew that he was lucky to have me. I can remember on our first date how I sort of leaned against him and placed my head against his chest. The way he looked down at me was so sweet, like he had never been loved before. A girl was actually opening herself up to him without demanding the material possessions in life as other girls had. Other girls only wanted money, jewelry, cocaine, but I didn't care about that. I got a certain sort of energy from him, a liveliness I had not felt in years, and security. I flourished from his love. We were the nourishment each other needed.

OVER ON THE EAST SIDE

I think that as I squirmed underneath him he realized that he could not keep me where I did not want to be kept. He'd have to let me go, and he did. I grabbed my keys off of the coffee table and sprinted out the door and down the stairs. I felt like a frightened child running away from an imaginary monster, but in my mind the tyrant was Carl. It would have truly taken a miracle for him not to run out that door. He wanted one last opportunity to win me back, to prove that he was not like the perverts at Roxy's, but how could I distinguish between the two anymore? No men were good in my eyes. Did perverts cry and beg for the ones they love? Did they feel just as we feel? He jumped in front of my car startling me as my headlights cast a spotlight on him. I was emotionally paralyzed as my high beams reflected off of his eyes and shot bolts of electricity into my soul.

He mouthed my name over and over, his two pointy front teeth looking like fangs. What more could he take from me? Was he going to dig his fangs into my neck and slurp on my blood? He had already taken my heart. Why not take all bodily organs and fluids also? He resembled a werewolf as he hollered my name at the moon, the moonlight reflecting off of his fangs, his flannel shirt unbuttoned, hair sprouting from his chest and neck. How I wanted to run him over with any car and rearrange his face into an unrecognizable configuration, but he looked so pitiful, so remorseful as he walked up to my window. He was blubbering like a small child, sniffling and rubbing his eyes, pleading for another chance, but I couldn't do it. Knowing that he had sat in a place like that, swigged a couple of beers with his pals, casually sat around that disgusting whore house while the girls shamelessly showed all. That I could not accept. God could test me if he wanted, throw a deformed, diseased, poverty ridden man my way, and if I had feelings for him love could prevail, but this I could not accept. I could handle many obstacles, but exploitation and disrespect towards women was not one of them. Whatever his intentions were towards visiting those places did not matter to me, because in my heart I believed that he was morally wrong for being in a place like that.

Like out of a corny *Lifetime* Movie of the week, he kissed his palm and lovingly placed it upon my window, his hand slowly slithering down the glass, leaving behind a trail of saliva. Part of me wanted to stay and bury this nightmare, but I couldn't. As I drove away and Carl's outline became indistinct, I cried yet again, wilting in my seat like a dead rose, the petals descending to the soil below. I wished so badly that I had a mother I could talk to, or a comforting motherly substitute to soothe the soreness that lingered in my core.

I dialed the keypad on my cell phone frantically dialing my best friend, Katt. I needed her to tell me that everything was alright, hold me, hug and console me for the awful things I had seen. Despite my earsplitting cries, I heard her voice on the other end of the receiver attempt to calm me down. I hysterically cried out her name. I sounded like an escaped mental patient, fresh out of the sanitarium, my spine-tingling cries echoing. *I NEED YOU! I NEED YOU!* I kept repeating, desperately trying to capture her attention, but she was not emotionally available. I could tell by the airy sound of her voice. She was drunk. I didn't care though. I needed her so badly. I could not see the cars or the headlights in front of me. All I could see was Katt, her arms spread wide open, ready to embrace me. This was the image that I hung on to the entire way to her house. She looked like an angel to me, almost translucent, her ghostly figure illuminating a path and guiding me to her home.

I hysterically bawled the remainder of the car ride, wailing even harder as I walked into her house, but as soon as I walked in I knew that I had made a mistake. Katt was not alone. There was a man with her, the one half of the human race I did not wish to see. He introduced himself as Steve, actually sung his name as he strummed at his guitar. It looked like a thin layer of snowfall had fallen upon her living room coffee table, the white powder not really snow but cocaine arranged into two neat white lines. Both her and Steve looked disoriented, their pupils dilated, their noses pink as a baby kitten. She seemed more annoyed than concerned with me, because all she could say was *"calm down."* I could not relax though. My body had gone into shock, been through a war. I needed to be reassured that the world was not a sick place, that my boyfriend was not a pervert.

I managed to lighten up for a moment as I took a seat and lit up a Kool Menthol cigarette. I had quit smoking, but the stress was too severe. The smoke soothed my nerves as I exhaled the mint smoke, blowing it out though my nostrils. Steve gently strummed the guitar, mellow musical tones easing my sorrow.

I began to tearfully recount my twisted tale, spilling out every terrible detail, but I noticed that she remained indifferent as I poured out my heart. I assumed that the coke was numbing her senses as she rolled her eyes and slowly folded her hands under her chin. She was so condescending as she started to speak to me, her demeaning words rolling off of her tongue, piercing my heart yet again. She proceeded to critique how I felt about strip clubs, how "all men" go there, how at least they are not having sex with the girls or touching them, but I didn't care about that. She told me that I hated the world. I needed a man not only to be physically present, but mentally there as well. To me a man cannot only physically cheat but emotionally cheat as well. I cannot travel into Carl's mind and know what he is thinking. Carl could have mentally caressed their breasts, circled their perky areolas with the tip of his finger, nuzzled his face in between their breasts. He could have been sucking each pink nipple, licking their clitorises like a thirsty dog greedily lapping at a puddle, the mud dirtying his fuzzy face. All the men in Roxy's were dogs, hungry dogs leaping from puddle to puddle infecting each other with crabs, maggots, infectious germs. The men in there had erections like animals, their erections visible for the world to see, like a dog's penis wagging between its ass. The entire room could be mentally fucking one girl, squeezing her tits in his mind like a farmer milking the udders of a cow. **ANIMALS! ALL OF THEM! THE STRIPPERS! THE PERVERTS! CARL! KATT! STEVE!** Was anyone good anymore? I couldn't listen to her anymore, endure her patronizing lecture about how men are just like that and how I need to get with it. I wanted Steve to disappear along with his story about how strip clubs are just a tease to men and about how he has a pornographic magazine collection in his room. Quickly I rose to my feet and grabbed my keys off of the coffee table.

"I'm just going to kill myself." I calmly announced. "Katt, thank you, I love you, but I think I am just going to have to kill myself." I repeated.

I did not understand how my best friend could be so judgmental to me. Why was she reprimanding me, punishing me for thinking there is something wrong with the world? I did not judge her, even when she had done horrible things to herself, me, others. I did not lecture her on the dangers of prostitution when she sat on a stranger's face, a three hundred pound black man donning spectacles, a sexually starved fat ass, when she grinded her hips on his chunky chin and almost shattered his glasses for a measly $150.00 she used for cosmetics and body glitter. I did not criticize her for her abortion, especially after she waited three months. I listened and comforted her when I really felt like vomiting, when she filled me in on every detail of the procedure, how they had to pick out pieces of the baby's body; the legs, the arms, the head, how her baby was chopped into countless chunks, her dear sweet baby. I did not look down on her when she ran drunk and naked through Rock 'N Roll Mcdonalds in Chicago, or took off her shirt in a bar and started to dance, or punched one of my best friends in the stomach. I did not abandon her as a friend when she left me in Chicago, pregnant and with my three year old daughter. I did not turn my back on her when she was so inebriated that she fell down the stairs outside of a bar and smashed her chin and mouth on a banister. I did not leave her there.

No, I sponged off her blood with a hair scrunchie and walked her into the bar, but when I proceeded to tell her that she had too much to drink she left me stranded with no money and no car, leaving me to ride home with one of the bouncers. I did not stop being her friend. No, I rewarded her by buying her cupcakes for her birthday the following day. I saved her from her father, giving her a place to live when he beat her and gave her a black eye. She had always talked down to me, pushed me, called me selfish, a bitch, a horrible friend. I could not do it anymore.

I ran through the dim parking lot, lost, sobbing, blindly searching for my car in the darkness of the night. Why couldn't anyone hear me? I had been crying all night. Carl couldn't hear me. Katt couldn't hear me. No one could hear what I was saying. I hopped in my car and sped away, screaming at the top of my lungs, such angry frustrating screams. How dare she tell me that men just do that sort of thing. Tennis, golf, eating at nice restaurants; these were fun recreational activities men could do, not salivate at the first sight of bare naked flesh of a complete stranger.

The stale smoky air was beginning to have an effect on me as I lit a dirty cigarette butt laying on the bottom of my ashtray. I felt like all four sides of my car were closing in on me, the darkness wrapping itself around my shoulders, a cloak to represent my sadness. I screamed once more, howled at the heavens, at the lord, at anyone or anything who would listen to me. I wanted the angels to cradle me in their arms and hum lullabies, carry me upon their shoulders, run their fingers through my hair and massage my head. This void in my chest was opening up more each minute. I yearned to fill my void, satisfy it with loving words, compliments, praises from a mother, a friend, Carl, anyone that could hear me. No one answered though. No thunderous prayers from heaven to salvage my soul, no sweet melodies from the angels strumming their harps, no rings on my cell phone from friends or Carl.

As I pulled up to the parking lot, I noticed that Carl's car was missing, and as I entered our apartment I observed that he had packed his belongings and left me to mourn by myself. Exhausted, I crawled under the covers and slipped them over any head. I was too tired to cry, too tired to scream, too tired to kill myself. Laying in my bed staring at the pasty white walls I realized that I had never felt so alone. Not only because Carl was gone, but because the world was not such a nice place anymore.

I began to think about where this all originated from, my first visit to a strip club. The year was 1996. I was twenty-two years old, still trapped at Mike's house, but living with his mother while the house was being worked on. Madeline was two years old, and Katt was living at the Victorian house while the crew was working on it. I had already been having a horrible day, Mike expressing his disapproval in me through physical violence. Naively, I thought just as I had tonight that it was going to turn out to be a wonderful day full of opportunities. Katt and I were going to search for cocktail waitress jobs, and like many young naive women we had heard that strip clubs were a very lucrative means to earning this money. Ironically, dressed in a short sleeve crisp wbite blouse, I chose to epitomize innocence that day. Dressed in white, the color of purity I was going to make my entrance into the underworld. As luck would have it though I would not be entering satan's playground as a paragon of virtue.

I had disappointed Mike that day, so much so that he dragged me across the dusty basement floor. Like many competent adults I was not proficient in the area of doing laundry. I never had to do laundry as a child, a teenager, an adult, and this angered Mike. I was sitting on the floor, my legs folded over one another when he grabbed my tiny wrist with his mammoth hands and dragged me across the basement floor like a limp rag doll. My sleeves began to dig into my underarms constricting my blood flow and forming such deep cuts that I began to bleed, the blood beginning to seep through the clean white sleeve of my shirt. As he drug my fragile lifeless body further my sleeves began to tear. I should have taken the destruction of my clean white shirt as a warning, how a spotless shirt can become dirtied by outside forces too powerful to ward off. Only a few minutes before I had looked like an angel, dressed in my white wrinkle free blouse, but the evil spirits had had their amusement, my shirt now bloodied, torn and crumpled. I had no idea of how my perception of the world would change from this day on, how my mind, once pure would be sullied with the truths of the world.

I was not prepared for what my eyes would see later that day as me and Katt entered *PT's,* a strip club located in the center of Sauget. A collage of breasts covered the walls, not drooping natural breasts like mine, but artificial ballooned breasts. The hallway was dim, little lighting to spotlight the mounds of flesh, but I could still distinguish the young gentleman, donned in a tuxedo, standing behind a glass counter. I could not speak. It was as if the breasts were silencing me, their nipples pointing to the exit door, an invisible force pushing me towards the door, but it was too late. Katt, the voice for both of us, asked for two applications which he handed to us and pointed to the entrance of the club where we were to fill them out. I think I had always had the perception that strip clubs were glamorous. I could sit at home and watch *Striptease* or *Flashdance* without a problem, but in all reality this is not what they were like. Unlike the movies the aura was not jovial or festive, but sleazy. My heart was slowly sinking as I obediently sat at a stool, my head down, my eyes fixed only on the application. I felt as if I was being held captive. I wanted to run so bad, scrunch up the application into a neat little ball and toss it into the trash where it belonged. I felt like I was back in junior high, in the girls locker room after swim practice, when all the girls stripped naked, casually dressing and talking as if nothing were out of the ordinary, except for me that is. I was the only girl practically glued to her locker, struggling to cover myself with a towel and dress at the same time. No one was as shy as I. I felt like what I was seeing around me should be forbidden, not so easily accessible to dirty old men.

A cocktail waitress passed me wearing a shiny pink satin jacket, black fishnet stockings, and a g-string. Her hair was teased into a countrified style. In the corner another girl with a strikingly similar hair style, donned only a g-string and performed seductive gyrations on one man. He appeared spellbound by this woman, this seductress ensnaring him in her web, as he hypnotically gazed at her breasts. My eyes then turned towards the stage where a rail thin woman wearing glasses and platinum blonde hair down to her waist stood. She placed her bare behind on the floor, opening and closing her legs for the one old man in the audience fixated on her. I wanted to die. This was not how I imagined these places, so cold and impersonal, completely geared towards men's sick twisted fantasies with no regard for women whatsoever. I wanted so badly to turn around and run, but Katt looked so impassive to her surroundings. Were we in the same place, her and I?

The manager, his hair not stylishly feathered, and dressed in a cheap brown suit, a silk tan handkerchief stuffed into his right breast pocket nervously approached us inquiring if we were underage. Katt not having her ID made him even more nervous causing him to hurry us out of his establishment. I couldn't have been more relieved. He escorted us to the old familiar glass booth where we handed our applications to the host in the tuxedo. A brunette, wrapped in some sort of Indian sari, her long wavy hair extending to the center of her stomach stared us down with such resentment, perhaps sizing us up as competition, making me extremely uncomfortable. I could feel her wicked eyes searing into me as I exited. I had never encountered a woman with such little softness, only sin swimming through those eyeballs.

I wanted to remain impervious by the images that I saw, unaffected like my best friend, Katt, but I was too sensitive. I had never seen men or women in this way, wild animals, no emotional contact, only physical. It sickened me so, how humans could remain so impersonal, only money and nakedness to move them. I couldn't share my feelings with anyone that afternoon as we drove back to St. Louis from the East Side. I convincingly wore my cheery mask, widely smiling for my two year old and best friend. It was extremely difficult to convince them that I was in such good spirits when in all reality I wanted to vomit, throw up the sinful images wedged in my brain.

Katt said that the strip club really did not bother her. She said that it wasn't real, that it was only a fantasy for men to live out. I could not summarize the experience I had so nonchalantly. It was real to me. If that was a man's fantasy I wanted no part of them, those dirty disgusting pigs. I had been deeply disturbed that day by what I had seen. I could not understand why others did not see things the same way as I did. This day had marked the beginning of my isolation. I wish I would have had a motherly figure to lay my head upon, cry in her lap, and cry about the injustices of the world, but I did not have anyone, only my daughter who relied on me for comfort. The world was becoming a horrible place, alive with abusive and perverted men, and men and women only interested in profiting off of sex. I was having overwhelming feelings of disorientation, bewilderment, repulsion. How badly I wanted to run away with Madeline to a monastery, to a church, a temple, any building which housed God's people.

My mind then drifted to another place and time; six years later, the strip bar: Ms. Kitty's. Ms. Kitty's, a poorly constructed reproduction of an old Wild West tavern, stood on the outskirts of Washington Park. Ms. Kitty's could easily be seen off the highway, along with its neighbor; the Jewel Box, situated directly across the street. C-Mowe's, another strip bar down the block has since been closed down due to prostitution. My sister had been searching for a cocktail waitress job, but she had no idea that the job she would accept would require much more than serving drinks.

Ms. Kitty's, from a distance, looked like many of the other quickly assembled buildings in Washington Park, almost certainly put together in less than a week. Approaching the structure though, one got quite a different impression. The flat rectangular club, covered in drab gray siding, had an old western flavoring, especially with the gigantic swinging wooden doors in the center. The sign, hanging above the swinging doors, in bright red bubble lettering read Ms. Kitty's, with a lasso affixed over the letter "S". Katt and I patiently waited in the car for Sarah while she went in to inquire about the waitress position A stocky woman, her short hair plastered to the side of her head by globs of hair gel, hungrily stared us down malting us feel unwelcome. She was the bodyguard of Ms. Kitty's, patrolling the parking lot. I envisioned Sarah at any moment running out of Ms. Kitty's, her trembling hands holding together the shredded fabric of her floral dress, her dark brown hair wildly tousled, her dampened cheeks flushed, howling **RAPE** at the top of her lungs. There was no sign of Sarah though, of that naive pretty girl shoving those swinging wooden doors open.

Staring at the slimy little creeps that exited Ms. Kitty's made me sick to my stomach. They slithered out of the club like poisonous snakes, their venomous stares inducing queasiness in the base of my stomach. The butch bodyguard staring us down was making me more and more uncomfortable. I imagined her drawing her revolver out of her holster, spinning it around her index finger, and having an old fashioned western standoff. Katt and I did not exactly blend in with our surroundings, being the only two innocent and pretty girls in a predominantly crime infested neighborhood. She feared that we would steal customers away. Therefore, she wanted us as far away from Ms. Kitty's as possible.

A dark skinned woman, her skin brown as chocolate, approached us, begging for money. She had glossy black hair cropped closely to her scalp and gold caps on two of her existing front teeth that perfectly matched her chunky gold hoop earrings. She wore an outdated acid washed jean skirt and a canary yellow halter top, soiled with what looked like stains of blood. I felt sorry for the poor woman and began to reach into my pocket for a dollar bill to perhaps help buy her a meal, but the lesbian bouncer howled at her to leave, snottily informing us that she was a prostitute. I could understand why a prostitute would search for her prospective clients in the parking lot of a strip club, as the perverts would be extremely titillated at the prospect of being serviced by yet another *"whore."*

Katt, squirming in her seat like an impatient child, was becoming quite impatient. She kept pushing me to go inside and get Sarah out, but I was hesitant to visit the past. Beyond those swinging doors was not an old western saloon complete with a jolly mustached man playing his piano, and rowdy cowboys hollering at the bartender to pour them more scotch. No, that door was an entrance into a memory I struggled to forget, but I knew that it was no longer my choice. I had to rescue Sarah from making the biggest mistake of her life and salvaging her innocence. Could there have been a scrap of compassion remaining in this hardened woman's heart? I had to rescue my little sister.

I visualized Sarah as a two year old, her brown curly hair cutely framing her face, holding her Fred Flinstone bottle, gazing up into the camera with doe eyes. I then envisioned her as a five year old, a quiet preschooler, still unable to express herself verbally and becoming frustrated because of it. She kept developing before my very eyes, a nine year old and a sweet gifted viola player plucking her instrument in the Children's Symphony Orchestra, and then she was twelve, abandoned by my mother, forced to move to Indiana, alienated by her peers, brawling with the children at her school, pounding one girl's head continually into the ground on the school bus. I had to get Sarah out of there! I pleaded with the bouncer to please let me enter her club and get my sister. I explained that she was only in there to apply for a cocktail waitress job, not work as a stripper. I suppose my insistence paid off, because she finally let me go into Ms. Kitty's to rescue my sister.

I looked over at Katt with an expression of relief on my face and began to stroll over to the saloon. An older man, amazingly close in resemblance to my late Uncle Bill, sat with his arms folded in a metal folding chair. Just like Uncle Bill his bifocal glasses magnified his eyes, but detracted attention from his fluffy eyebrows; stray hairs poking every which way. It did not look as hygiene was this man's greatest asset considering the countless dark hairs poking out of both nostrils. He wore knee high length socks, navy blue stripes circling the top of each sock pulled up just under his knee and brown leather loafers scuffed at the tips. I repeated my tale of how Sarah was just supposed to fill out an application for a cocktail waitress and not stay and strip. The bouncer and him must have thought Katt and I were the dumbest most naive girls ever, hanging out in the parking lot of a strip club in Washington Park.

Uncle Bill waved his hand in front of me motioning for me to enter the club. I took a deep breath, thrusting the heavy swinging doors open and then twisting the knob to another heavier steel door behind that one. I prayed to God, hoping that Ms. Kitty's would not be as bad as PT's. I stepped inside the club, silently cursing Katt for not braving this with me. For about twenty seconds, but what seemed like an eternity, I took in my surroundings.

Ms. Kitty's was a small club, the men surprisingly close to the strippers. A thin blonde, her face blurry in my mind to this day, her blonde hair pinned up sat her behind on the cold stage and spread her legs wide open directly in front of a customer drinking his beer. He probably was not even an arm's length away from this woman, this stranger who he shared such intimate things with. He guzzled his beer, a wide grin spread across his pock marked face and took in the scenery. To be so close to a stranger's vagina shocked me, being able to see every pubic hair, every fold, every detail of someone's restricted private spot. How he did not retch on his drink baffles me, how he was able to gobble his dinner that night, probably with his wife, visualizing that vagina staring him in the eye sickened me. Another stripper, this one plump with curly red hair just past her shoulders danced on the corner stage, but at least she kept her panties on.

The atmosphere around me was too jovial, almost festive, men shouting across the room at each other, swigging their cocktails. I wanted to vanish as I asked the bartender behind the bar to find me my sister. My head was down, but I could feel all eyes on me. I could hear their thoughts, how pretty my face was, how my cheeks were well structured, how they liked my long blond hair, how my skin glowed and how my sheer red glossy lips perfectly matched my bright red Capri and tank set, how they thought I'd look naked, my legs spread wide open, giving them a lap dance, fucking them. I raised my head and stared off into space, my eyes not closed, yet blinding myself to the surroundings.

Finally my sister magically appeared from the back room buttoning up her dress, her bra completely visible to the room. As nonchalantly as I could I lowly muttered that she should not be here and that we should leave, but she seemed too entrenched in her surroundings. She was hypnotized by the lights, the music, the flattery, and I could not shake her out of the spell she was put under. She told me she'd be out in a minute, that she had to get her purse out of the back room, but my intuition told me different. I knew she'd never be out.

Katt and I waited again, this time even more intimidated from the strange bouncer giving us the evil eye. The men longingly looking our way were really starting to creep us out and starting to engage the bouncer so much that she told us we'd have to leave, to come back at 2:00 in the morning to pick up my sister. Katt and I drove away, exhausted, defeated, too weak and tired to fight the battle any longer. My sister was twenty-two years old; an adult, but what these men did not know was that my sister was still a little girl inside, a mere child lost and confused, seduced by money, sex, compliments used in return for sexual favors. These men did not care to know about how difficult a childhood my sister had, that she could not talk until the age of five, that my mother treated her like she was stupid, how mean the children at school were to her, how my mother abandoned her, how she wished so badly to have a mother figure. No, all these men saw my little sister as was a pussy, and for that I wanted to kick their ass.

Katt and I silently drove home to the safety of St. Louis, away from Ms. Kitty's and Washington Park. I tried to take my mind off of Sarah, took an exhilarating run for an hour while Katt went to see a boyfriend, went to eat at Steak 'N Shake with Katt while we tried to make humor out of the bad situation. Pulling up into Ms. Kitty's in total darkness was so much more frightening than in the daytime. We sat in the car, complete silence surrounding us except for the booming vibrations emanating from the club. The car was our bubble, protecting us from the prostitutes, the strippers, the gunmen waiting to kidnap, rape, and then shoot us in the head. We could not believe how inconsiderate Sarah was being, making us wait in what she knew was a terrible area in the parking lot of one of the seediest strip clubs in Illinois.

Stripper after stripper exited Ms. Kitty's escorted by the butch bouncer. The strippers looked so worn as they were walked to their car. Unlike my experience before I did not find these woman attractive in the least bit. They were so countrified, so unhealthy looking probably due to their heavy drug use. We excitedly held our breath as each girl walked out, but then exhaled disgruntled as we saw that each girl was not Sarah, but then we saw her. She had a wide smile plastered across her face as she ran out to the car, hopped in the back seat and told us to drive because she ran off with all of her earnings, not giving a cut to the manager. All she had earned was $35.00, and the manager was supposed to get a cut of that! I had never witnessed Katt drive so fast as she screeched out of the parking lot, her tires creating clouds of smoke as we sped away.

Katt was furious with Sarah, expressing how she thoughtlessly endangered us while only thinking about herself. I was not angry. I more so felt sorry for her. She didn't understand the consequences of her actions. Sarah was not sophisticated or worldly. She had been sheltered by my father, discarded like an old pair of shoes by my mother, and manipulated by the men in her life. She did not always vocalize anger but held it deep inside. She did not comprehend the severity of the situation, how she could have been sexually assaulted or worse raped. Most likely the caliber of people in Ms. Kitty's would not have been as caring to rescue a damsel in distress, her cries audible in the near distance. Sarah did not consider that Katt or I could have been raped, robbed, or shot, but she did not purposely intend to wish us harm.

In no way was Sarah malicious or spiteful, just inexperienced. Like a foolish adolescent that becomes unmanageable, Sarah was also experimenting with her newfound independence. For once she was away from our parents. My father could not smother her, and my mother could not dictate how she wants her to live her life. She could finally taste the freedom and lick away the restraints put upon her. The problem was that she was overindulging in the delicacies of life, gorging herself with the sweetest temptations that life could offer. She was being gluttonous, yearning the extravagances that life has to offer yet not willing to offer anything of substantial value back to the world.

Whether we wanted to hear or not, Sarah recounted the evening's events back to us. She told us how some of the men in the bar gushed at her, how big her nipples were, and how others were more quiet even relating how one stripper had been shot in the head in the parking lot the previous year. Lap dances were given in the back room, a dark gloomy dungeon complete with its own separate stalls and booths. One couple had been engaging in sexual intercourse. Sarah had known because she heard the moans, the heavy breathing, and the hot sticky bodies humping and grinding each other. About six different men had gotten lap dances from Sarah, three of them trying to stick their fingers or penis in her vagina. She sat on one man's lap, a meek scrawny creep wearing tinted lenses and danced on his lap as be mistook her highly spiced gyrations for an invitation to finger her. Repetitively, she was forced to grab his hands and put them back behind his back. Other men were not as physically disgusting, but mentally deranged all the same. Sarah boasted about one extremely attractive New Yorker with sandy blonde hair and baby blue eyes. While Sarah gave him a lap dance he blabbed nonstop about his home state and casually tried to slip his penis into her panties. Again, she coolly grabbed his hands and placed them at his side. How desperate would someone have to be to enter a strip bar by oneself and fuck one of the strippers in the back room? Sarah had said this man was very attractive, probably able to pick up any girl he wanted, but instead he'd risk catching a communicable disease and engaging in impersonal sexual contact. I did not understand the ways of these men!

OVER ON THE EAST SIDE

CHAPTER 30

As Carl stepped out of the car, the familiar setting made his heart sink.

"Good old Brooklyn." Carl sarcastically uttered to himself. Brooklyn, Illinois was a town infected by poverty, a town which most of these men would never even think about entering if it were not for the plentiful strip club district. The majority of the residents in Brooklyn were African American, and many of them were poverty- stricken. Old abandoned apartment buildings could be found on every street, the windows boarded up and graffiti scribbled on every square inch.. Many of these beautiful long-standing buildings had been destroyed by fire. Underprivileged souls living on the streets wandered the city begging for money. Carl could not believe that he had returned to this slum. Tuesday continually placed an emphasis on Carl's background, insinuating that he would never live up to her precious standards, that he was white trash. Maybe Tuesday was right this entire time. Look where he had found himself, in Brooklyn, Illinois, one of the trashiest towns in America, in the strip club district, of all places. An older African American gentleman, perhaps sixty, with a knit stocking upon his head, roamed the parking lot with a spray bottle in one hand and a rag in the other. He was hoping to earn some side cash by washing windows. Out of the corner of Carl's eye, he could see that the man was going to approach him at any moment.

"Hey man, how you doing today?"
the homeless man asked reaching for Carl's hand in an attempt to shake it.

"Alright man."
"Listen, I was wondering if you could help me out.
I'm from Jackson, Mississippi, and my car broke down. I need to make enough money to catch the bus out of town. Any way you can help me out, a dollar, two dollars, five. All I need to do is earn enough to get back to my home."

Carl obviously could sense that this man concocted the entire story. His leathery wrinkled hands jittered as he continued to create the tale. The vagrant continued to babble, but his voice grew quieter as Carl's guilty conscience grew louder. His mind was consumed by an enormous amount of guilt at the moment, and the last thing he needed was a drifter begging him for a few measly dollars. Irritated,

Carl pulled out his leather wallet and pulled out a five dollar bill, placing it into the beggar's hand.

"Thank you man. I appreciate it." He gratefully said eagerly walking over to the windshield.

"No, man. You're alright. Just go on."

"Thank you. Thank you."

The man tiptoed in reverse grinning, his open mouth displaying a rotted set of teeth, and changing direction as soon as he caught sight of another gullible victim.

Carl stood in the center of the parking lot studying the countless strip clubs that surrounded him. Several small wooden shacks with signs reading *"Massage Parlor"* were scattered across the parking lot from the strip clubs, and an adult book store was situated across the street. If Tuesday only knew what he was doing, she would simply die. For a brief moment he contemplated getting back in the car and just sitting there staring out of the window while his buddies were in the club, but he would never hear the end of it. He reached into his jean pocket for his box of cigarettes, pulled out one of the cancer sticks and stuck the tip to the bottom of his lip as he performed mouth acrobatics with the it. He did not display the same degree of enthusiasm as the other men in the parking lot who eagerly bustled to the various club entrances. His visions differed from the other men in the parking lot who only imagined naked women and nothing else. All he could see was Tuesday sobbing, her face buried in her hands. He looked up at the neon lights that read **"DREAMGIRLS"** that bathed his face in a reddish glow. They began to blur together causing Carl to squint his eyes. He could have sworn that the letters were changing into the word **"PERVERT"**, but he quickly shook his head from side to side causing him to jolt back into reality. Why did Tuesday have such a hold over him? Tuesday's voice echoed incessantly. He could hear her pleading with him not to go into the club, her voice quivering, the agony in her voice more evident than he had ever heard before.

Ironically, Carl caught sight of a church steeple with a cross affixed at the top looming in the near distance. The steeple looked like an entryway to the vault of heaven, and as Carl stared harder at the house of worship the bells began to chime. The pinkish skies at that moment appeared incensed, the golden fireballs shooting in all directions against the tangerine colored swirls. They looked like scoops of orange sherbet ice cream suspended in the heavens. The eerie tolling of the church bell chimed louder and louder, causing the shacks among him to quake. Slightly further into the distance were several dilapidated trailer homes. A large group of teenagers congregated in front of one trailer home barely visible behind the tall blades of grass that had not been maintained in years. Despite the distance, their rumbling voices and crude laughter boomed. Rusty tricycles, toy trucks, and soiled diapers were scattered among the front yard. How these people could live in this environment baffled Carl, but they did not inhabit these poverty ridden streets by choice. The inhabitants of Brooklyn were a product of unfortunate circumstances. Carl and the others were here by choice.

James took one last drag from the joint which was now a tiny roach and tossed it into his ashtray. He squeezed his portly body out of the car and wobbled over to Carl who looked miserable and as if he was deep in thought. James had resented Carl ever since him and Tuesday got together. Carl just was not the same as he used to be. James had never met Tuesday, therefore he had no conception of how attractive or intelligent she was, but it did not matter. He could not comprehend how one woman could possess the power to ensnare a man in her web of entanglement. To him Tuesday represented the most lethal spider in existence, a gigantic fuzzy tarantula who preyed on innocent little insects spewing her venomous poison.

"You going to stand here all day buddy?" James asked, slapping Carl on the back and practically knocking the wind out of him.

James's flabby arms jiggled as he brought them back to his side. Lately, James had been expanding to an almost nauseating size. In many places his skin hung loosely off of his body dangling if he moved even ever so slightly.

"I guarantee that the view in there is way better than the view out here." James chuckled.

Carl, jolted out of his trance by the swift slap on his back lost the cigarette sticking to the tip of his lips. It descended to the ground and into a puddle causing grimy rainwater sprinkles to splash onto his spotless white sneakers.

"You know what. I'm not feeling all that well." Carl

mumbled rubbing his stomach in a circular motion to indicate that he was nauseous. I think I'm going to stay in the car and lay down."

"Come on. Don't be a pussy man. You'll be fine once we get inside." James anxiously stated, irritated that Carl was putting a hamper on the excitement of the evening.

James's manhood began to stiffen and was already tingling. Like a drug addict he needed to feed his addiction, and fast. Carl remained stationary, his thumbs nervously twiddling, his head down, and his eyes locked on the cigarette butt drowning in the filthy puddle of water below. For a brief moment he could have sworn that Tuesday's reflection was staring up at him from within the dirty puddle of muddy water.

"Is this about you not feeling well, or is this about your old lady having some sort of sick hold over you?

"I told you boss, I feel like shit. Something didn't agree with me."

"Bullshit. Her pussy is not that good is it? Or is it laced with gold, cause if it is, you are going to have to let me have some of that." James disgustingly chuckled.

Carl's stomach churned. No one, not even his boss was going to disrespect his girl or him like that. Carl charged for James, his muscular forearm clenching as he made a fist directed for James's pudgy cheek. James, not even the least bit fazed, clutched Carl's wrist and began to twist it until Carl could squirm no longer.

"Carl, Carl. Poor kid. You are pussy whipped. I guess you can find your own way home. Call your old lady. Maybe she'll pick up your sorry ass! She might be wondering why she has to pick you up in Brooklyn though, in front of Foxy Tails. You know, I didn't come here after a hard week of work to deal with some pussy who can't look at pussy because his old lady won't let him." He cruelly mimicked in a feminine voice. "Don't be ungrateful Carl. This is supposed to be a treat for my boys, a gesture of appreciation. You boys work hard all week, and I reward you. Don't you see what an ass you're being. If I had a boss that cool I'd be thanking my lucky stars, not trying to kick his ass! The only reason I am even keeping your sorry ass around is because you are the hardest worker I've got. If it wasn't for that I would make your ass walk home. For the entire year you have gone out with Tuesday I have kept quiet. You blew me and the boys off plenty of times, and I said nothing. I'm married for Gods sake, and I still party, have my fun on the side.

OVER ON THE EAST SIDE

Barb doesn't have to know, and no one needs to tell her. Sure it's nice having someone to come home to every night, a main dish to enjoy, but sometimes you need a little something on the side. You are starting to worry me. None of these boys out here are as devoted to their women as you are. Doesn't that tell you that something is not right? Seriously, Carl, are you a faggot, cause I don't need no faggots working for me."

"James, why don't you chill out! I'll go in there." Carl hollered, infuriated that Carl would accuse him of being a homosexual. Carl was extremely homophobic, and did not appreciate James's accusations."

"Just give me a minute."

"Well, me and the other guys are ready to have some fun. When you are ready to join the rest of the group let me know."

"Alright, alright I'm coming."

James, Donny, and Chris walked ahead in the direction of Foxy Tails while Carl lagged behind. Each of Tuesday's suspicions, every one of her insecurities, all of her accusations were going to be proven true as soon as he entered Foxy Tails. Carl realized that this would devastate Tuesday. Tuesday's obsession with strippers had been gnawing away at her mind, her soul, her sanity. She hadn't been herself in a while. Her fixation had been eating away at her heart for a while now. Her central core, once healthy, spongy, and pink was almost eroded, a black lung, oozing of phlegm. Tuesday had abandoned this relationship a long time ago. She was still present physically, but emotionally she had nothing left to give. Her heart was dead. Carl was exhausted of proving his devotion to her. If she was going to assume that he was an immoral pig, then dammit, he was going to be one.

The exterior of Foxy Tails was the most tasteless display of decor ever beheld with its bright pink aluminum siding and colorful strand of Christmas lights draped around the top of the building. What separated Foxy's from the other strip clubs and continued to boost its popularity was the eye-catching sign. Affixed over the front entrance were blinding bright neon pink lettering which read Foxy Tails. A cartoon character reaching lengths of at least ten feet tall of a creature half fox/half woman stood directly above the light. The top portion of the caricature displayed an exaggerated depiction of a curvaceous nude woman with a fiery red mane and ridiculously enormous breasts with a pair of fox ears on top of her head. The bottom half looked as if it were covered in orange matted down fur. It was the legs and rear appendage of a fox with a striped bushy tail and a frosted white tip. There were no windows in Foxy Tails. No light could be shed upon this dungeon of immortality. No sunshine to purify and warm the souls of these heartless monsters that preyed on women's vulnerability. Therefore, Foxy Tails would be shrouded in darkness, only the wicked shadows visible, gyrating seductively to the thumping of the melody.

James swung open the front door and motioned with an anxious wave of his hand that it was time for Carl to hustle. A husky man in a tuxedo and blonde crew cut heavily slicked down with gel stood behind the door checking id's. After checking id's he handed out fliers with two colossal breasts advertising the drink specials of the evening. As Carl entered the club, the memories flooded back. He did not care to be back at Foxy Tails. He told himself that he would never return, but here he was, back in the abysmal purgatory of lost souls. A thick haze of smoke concealed the club, creating a bleary film. The dancers, their imperfections hidden by the misty smoke film, looked like shadowy figures, deceptive goddesses of perfection. The lights were dimmed making any defects that these girls possessed barely detectable.

Carl immediately walked over to the bar, looking like a child guilty of some misdeed. He stuffed both of his hands deep into his jean pockets and carried his head down, paying careful attention not to look up at the stage. The guilt ate away at him like never before. He imagined his eyeballs exploding, the whites of his eyes frying like an egg as soon as he looked up at the dancers. Every ethical principle he ever insisted on having would disintegrate as soon as he laid his eyes on the naked flesh swarming around him. As his watch ticked and time progressed at Foxy Tails his morality was slowly corroding. He was destined to become just like James, a depthless corrupt human being, incapable of treating women with the precious amount of respect which they deserved.

Carl ordered a beer, swigging the intoxicating drink rapidly in order to muffle Tuesday's cries thundering in his head. The chilled neck of the bottle felt wonderful and refreshing as he pressed it against his clammy forehead. He ordered beer after beer until the room began to swirl and the floor beneath him plummeted. He staggered over to

OVER ON THE EAST SIDE

James and the other boys who were congregated around a circular wooden table hooting and hollering. A platinum blonde, completely nude, was sprawled out on the table. Her head leaned back, her golden mane tumbling down to the matted down carpet beneath her. She spread her legs wide open revealing her smooth spot of intimacy, and invoking gasps of ecstasy from the men gathered around the table. Her mammoth breasts, looking like they had been injected with helium, lay perfectly still not jiggling a bit as she squirmed onto her side and her stomach. James peeled dollar after dollar from his thick roll of bills and stuffed each bill into her lacy black garter strapped around her thigh. He grazed her silky tan thigh with his fingertip each time he gave her a dollar, and she did not protest a bit. James considered these women to be his property, playthings that he could treat however he wished, and unfortunately these women indulged him in his repulsive behavior. This was the one place where James felt accepted for who he was. He did not grasp the concept that these women were only interested in him for his money. They would act fascinated as he told them his tales, but in reality they were unconcerned, conjuring up in their greedy minds how they could extract more money out of the pathetic chump. For an entire weekend, a year before, James had been missing in action. His friends found James's car in the parking lot of the strip club district. Everyone thought that James had been killed, stuffed in a garbage bag and tossed into a dump in East St. Louis, but of course this wasn't the state of affairs which had taken place. James had been in Foxy Tails for two entire days, so engrossed in the dancers that he lost track of time. The strippers showered attention on him that he had been craving, that he assumed he could find nowhere else.

Carl plunked himself down on a bar stool, three tables behind where James and the other men were congregated. James caught sight of Carl insulating himself from the lewdness amongst him, and waved his hand motioning for Carl to join the rest of the group. Carl's reclusive tactics were serving as a shield, a protective bubble, so that in his mind he would not have to be held accountable for his actions. Physically, he was present in the club, but mentally his mind was elsewhere. Out of the corner of his eye he saw James's pale freckled fleshy arm motion for him to join the group again, but Carl pretended not to notice. He focused his eyes on a big screen television in the corner of the room broadcasting a local baseball game. He secretly hoped that James would leave him alone and not pressure him to partake in the festivities of the evening. All he wanted to do was go home and snuggle up to Tuesday. As he swigged his beer, the room swirled around him and the people whizzed by causing him to almost fall off of his stool. James dashed over, grabbing Carl forcefully by the elbow and propping him back up onto the stool

"Easy boy. If you don't watch it, we'll all get kicked out of here."

"I'm soooorry. I'm so sooooorry." Carl incoherently slurred as he regained his footing and plopped back onto the stool.

"Boy, you are going to have to get a hold of yourself. Instead of having fun you are sulking over here in the corner thinking about how bad your old lady is going to whip your ass. You gotta get a hold of yourself. Think of tonight as your one night of freedom. I know that things aren't going well between you and Tuesday."

"You don't know what you are talking about. We couldn't be better." Carl defensively retorted.

"Carl, I wasn't born yesterday. I could be your father, remember. Do you really think that you and Tuesday are going to be together forever?"

Carl stood perfectly still, propped against the stool, his arms folded, silently sulking like a spoiled toddler.

"Carl, realistically. You are a young guy. You need to consider your options. You haven't been with that many women in the first place. You get some steady pussy and you want to marry the girl. You and Tuesday are having problems that just won't go away. Do you think it will get better? Do you think this is love? If this is supposed to be love, then why are you so damn unhappy Carl? You could be having fun with the rest of us. Why do you think I just don't limit myself to one female? I'm not going to live my life bored by the same pussy. There are so many beautiful women around you. Breathe it in. Enjoy it. These women are here for you to have a good time, to practically service any desire or need you have. Here, I want you to meet a friend of mine."

James began to waddle over to the rear of the club, and Carl was left with no choice but to follow him like a feeble little puppy dog. James directed Carl over to the darkest section of the club, in the back, cluttered with cocktail tables.

OVER ON THE EAST SIDE

A chocolate brown love goddess enticingly walked over to James, massaging her elegantly shaped fingers topped with fire red fingernails throughout his pumpkin colored tresses and enfolding her arms around James to treat him with a soft warm hug.

"Jimmy, I'm so glad to see you tonight!" the stripper excitedly gushed.

"Candy, I'd like you to meet my good friend and business associate, Carl. Carl, this is Candy, my favorite girl."

Candy licked her glossed Burgundy lips provocatively, her eyes focused on Carl's manhood. Her skin, the shade of a sweet chocolate confection glistened with golden body glitter and body paint. Carl had never seen skin so soft, fresh bathed skin soaked in body oils and moisturizing lotions, skin as creamy as a batch of milk chocolate pudding. The golden sparkles looked like small specks of cinnamon sticking to a sweet creamy chocolate covered cherry. Her glossy raven black mane, polished with coconut oils and herbal conditioners cascaded past her shoulders and adorably curled up at the ends. She was dressed in a glitzy black leather outfit, the shorts barely extending past her buttocks. It looked like she was wrapped in black licorice, the snug fitting outfit clinging tightly to her every curve. Her cleavage gushed forth from her top looking like two chocolate bonbons ready to be nibbled on at any moment.

James unfolded her hand and slipped two crisp hundred dollar bills in the center of her palm. He folded her hand back up and wrapped his flabby arms around Candy's waist, moving her chunky gold hoop earring to the side and whispering into her ear.

"Tonight, I want you and one of your delicious friends to take care of me and my boy. Alright?" James asked caressing her plump buttocks with his stubby fingers.

"Sure, Jimmy. Anything for my favorite customer. I'll be right back." She said grinning

Carl was too absorbed with his present problems and Tuesday to notice that Jimmy was propositioning Cindy for sexual favors, to gratify him and James in any so way which they wished. He plunked into a chair, nearly missing the seat cushion, and began to snooze off.

"Carl!" James shouted, shaking Carl's shoulder roughly. "Why the hell are you going to sleep?" James rudely pulled a cocktail waitress wearing a pink satin jacket, black fishnet stockings, and a g-string as she walked by.

Her tray topped with several glasses full of alcohol, balanced on the palm of her hand almost toppled over.

"Hey watch it!" the girl annoyingly hollered, not realizing that she was screaming at their best customer until she turned around "Oh, Jimmy, I'm sorry. I thought you were someone else. "That's alright hon, Get me a Tequila with a twist of lime right away!" James demanded. The waitress rolled her eyes and headed immediately for the bar knowing that she better comply to his wishes, for he was the most regular customer in that hellhole.

"I did not know that I was going to have to babysit tonight. You are going to have fun whether you like it or not. I do not care if I have to pour drink after drink down your throat. You are going to get wasted, fuck around, and basically have the best time you ever had!"

"Nooo....I can't do that. I need to go home to Tuuuuuuesssday, pllleeeease. She will be soooo worried about me." Carl incoherently slurred, his muddled speech difficult to comprehend.

"Fuck Tuesday, Carl. Stop being a pussy for God sakes."

The waitress strutted back over to their table, her shiny patent leather pink heels clacking and removed the crystal glass of Tequila from her tray handing it to James. James handed the waitress a crisp twenty dollar bill, patting her behind and whispering into her ear to keep the change. She rolled her eyes again, fed up that this sicko thought he owned her and the other girls. He dipped his asphalt stained fingers into the Tequila, grabbed the fluorescent green lime by the rind and squeezed the lime juice into the intoxicating beverage, the lemony drops splashing as they added a sour flavor that would stimulate Carl's dulled senses.

"Here, drink this. It'll wake you up." James demanded shoving the glass of Tequila directly under his nose so that the invigorating aroma roused him and cleared his nasal passage. Carl's expression soured, his lips furrowing and eyes scrunching up, but he inhaled the entire glass of Tequila in one swig.

"Get me another one." Carl ordered, slamming the glass on the table.

"That's my boy. Now we're ready to have some fun."

Carl gulped down six more glasses of the intoxicating

concoction in addition to the eight previous beers he had already started drinking just two hours prior. The alcohol gave him the courage to take a good look around the chamber of sinful pleasures. The room orbited around him, the nude bodies encircling him in a claustrophobic tunnel. Hoots and hollers emanated from the bar area causing Carl to glance. The men recited a chant, *"Take it off, take it off."* To where a new stripper, probably eighteen years old, reluctantly shed her shirt, revealing her bare naked breasts garnished by enormous blushing pink nipples. They looked like two gigantic vanilla scoops of ice cream topped with cherry sauce.

"*Damn, you have some big nipples*!" the men screamed distastefully, slamming their hands on the bar counter, their faces blushing brightly due to their contagious laughter. The girl held her head down, ashamed that God had gifted her with such plentiful areolas.

Carl's eyes drifted to another corner of the room to a stripper performing a lap dance. A petite muscular brunette, her hair feathered, rocked back and forth swiveling her hips. She simulated the act of sex so perfectly that from a distance it looked like they were fucking. Several times her breasts practically brushed the man's face, teasing him mercilessly. From the expression on his face one could tell that he only wished to take one of her nipples into his mouth and flick it with his tongue. It was obvious that this man had not had not fucked in years unless he had to pay for the services. The silvery strobe light reflected off of his shiny bald head, except for the few remaining strands combed over. His flannel red and white shirt and dark blue denim Levis hung loosely over his skeletal figure. His frosty blue eyes remained glued to the dancer's silicone injected breasts.

Carl's eyes then floated to the main stage. Candy and another dancer, Ginger began to dance together, rubbing their brilliantly sparkling bodies against each other. Their breasts touched, their nipples becoming erect, exciting and invoking cheers from the men in the crowd. The oils on their bodies trickled down the center of their chests, the droplets of perspiration looking like warmed maple syrup. Ginger then unclipped the plastic fastener on the side of her g-string. Her deep purple panties descended to the floor, revealing her bare buttocks and genatalia as she excitedly spun her hips to the throbbing of the melody. Candy sat herself on the edge of the stage opening and closing her chocolatey legs while men took turns placing dollar bills into her g-string. Ginger crept down to her hands and knees and crawled over to where Candy was sitting opening her legs while other men scrambled to have a closer look. There was a silver plated pole placed in the center of the milky white linoleum stage. Ginger stood up and grabbed a hold of the pole. She slithered down the slippery pole like a slimy serpent contorting her body in positions that even the prince of darkness would gasp at, Candy sneaked up behind Ginger and began to hump her backside, placing her arms around Ginger's plentiful chest and squeezing her ballooned breasts.

Each and every man in Foxy Tails scrambled to the stage to feast their eyes on the sizzling lesbian tryst taking place. If the girls masqueraded as lesbians, they were guaranteed to triple their earnings in one evening, each girl earning at least one thousand dollars. One year ago when Carl would go these places, he never witnessed such immortality. Before this night he remained oblivious to the perversion brewing in the underworld.

Every Friday evening Foxy Tails promoted live nude showers. This special feature attracted massive crowds, making Friday night the busiest of the week. A light mist of water began to trickle from the built in shower heads above them, the light downpour simulating a rain shower. The showery sprinkle saturated their creamy bronzed skin, the wetness creating a slick surface for the girls to squirm on the linoleum beneath them. Ginger flung her dampened cherry mane, the color of red pepper, over her shoulder, the droplets adhered to her fiery strands flinging through the air and splashing the men in the audience. Ginger and Candy immersed themselves wholeheartedly in the artificial rain flurry, savagely scrubbing each other's bodies with a sponge that their manager tossed onto the stage. As they took turns squeezing the sponge, a trail of soapy suds dribbled forth, creating a frothy creamed lather with which they could massage into each other's damp flesh. A scoop of the foamy fluff clung to the tip of one of Ginger's nipples looking like a spurt of whipped cream topping a scoop of butterscotch.

James bulldozed his way through the cluster of men congregated near the front of the stage and flashed the girls a hundred dollar bill, waving the bill in the air like a streamer. Ginger strutted in his direction, her ruby red heels the only article remaining on her body. Ginger knelt down on her hands and knees like an obedient puppy dog while her master, James, patted and stroked her soapy back, his fingers squeaking as they brushed against her slick flesh. She erotically opened her plum stained lips while James slipped the hundred dollar bill between them. Ginger turned around and crawled off of the stage, the hundred dollar bill still sticking to her lips, and wagging her plump buns while the men cheered. They waved their hands in the air, clapping, their thunderous applause echoing, the vibrations shaking the shoddy building, causing it to quake. The steam emitted from the showers cleared and the lights once again dimmed as the stage was cleared for the next dancer. A young boy on the staff, also dressed in a tuxedo, mopped the excess water off of the stage while another staff member wiped it down with a large fluffy towel.

James excitedly ran up to Carl, panting, while a few of the other regulars patted James on the backside. This was the way they expressed their gratitude, commending him for influencing Ginger to crawl away, her buttocks pointed high in the air feeding and fulfilling their appetite for sleaziness.

"Did you see that?" James breathlessly panted.

"Yey. How could I have possibly missed it?'

"Good point. You should have come up there. These girls don't show you that stuff for free, you know. Do you really think that the hot lesbo action would have taken place if we didn't support them?"

"Nope." Carl said shaking his head.

James's voice began to blend in with the other voices and music of the club. Carl would never be able to explain this to Tuesday. If she found out it would be over. He remembered their conversation wherein Tuesday told him that she'd only break up with him due to two conditions; the first being him committing the act of adultery and the other, him going to a strip club. She was already envious enough, and this would simply kill her, would fry her heart until it melted like a dab of butter smeared in a frying pan. There was no salvaging his spirit. He had disrespected her, crushed his promise to only lay his eyes upon her naked flesh and no one elses. His eyes were the windows to his soul, once clear and unsoiled, but now they were tarnished, caked with filth which could never be cleansed. His eyes were reflective instruments, compasses of truth to direct

Tuesday to Foxy Tails. When Tuesday would stare into his muddied brown eyes, she would catch sight of the truth, make out the ghostly figures dancing in his pupils. She would feel her skin begin to moisten as she felt the sprinkles from the nude shower soak into her skin. She would be able to sniff the bitter stench of the Tequila and lime which Carl gulped down all evening. She would see the crisp green dollar bills being place into g-string after g-string. Tuesday always had a sixth sense about situations. Tuesday would know, and Carl knew he would lose her.

Candy strolled over to James, her drenched hair miraculously dried, and makeup applied perfectly. She whispered in James's ear and led him over to a dark corner compounded by the smoky haze that made both of them barely detectable. James wagged his finger implying for Carl to join them. Carl knew that him and Tuesday would be over anyway, so he joined Candy and James at their table. James reclined his head back and unzipped his pants, pulling his manhood out. Candy began to stroke his shaft, squeezing his penis tightly every so often to invoke moans of pleasure. She then motioned for Carl to sit in the chair next to James. Carl hesitantly stood still for what seemed like an eternity, his hands folded up into his pockets.

"Come on Carl. Have a seat. You are here to enjoy yourself, remember." James said.

"Sweetheart, sit down, let Candy make you feel good." Candy soothingly whispered into Carl's ear giving Carl goosebumps as her hot breath warmed his neck.

Carl reluctantly complied, sitting down in the chair across from James. Candy unzipped his pants zipper, since he was not going to attempt to make the first move himself. She felt for his manhood and pulled it out, beginning to squeeze the head of his penis softly. Carl could feel his inhibitions dissolve as he too reclined his head back. He shut his eyes and drifted off into a divine paradise, shutting out any memories of Tuesday, only to enjoy the pleasurable sensations swirling throughout his genitals.

"Does that feel good baby?" Candy erotically cooed

"Oh yey." Carl moaned, losing himself in the moment of bliss

"Then do you want the job finished?" Candy asked, her eyebrows raising as she propositioned him. Carl's head swiftly raised up, every pleasant sensation dissipating. It was terrible enough that he was betraying Tuesday by entering the strip club, and now he had shown a complete lack of inhibition by having another women fondle his most intimate of parts. Sexual intercourse was a completely different story though. This was an act of adultery that could never be taken back.

"I have someone in the back who wants to take care of you." Candy whispered into Carl's ear, her sizzling breath melting his eardrum and sending tingles throughout his spine.

"Uh, uh...I can't. I have a girlfriend...." Carl blurted out in an attempt to redeem himself.

"She won't mind. She wants you to be happy, doesn't she?" Candy cooed as she brushed her hand over Carl's thigh.

Carl couldn't dispute such profound logic, especially coming from Candy.

"Come on, Carl. Don't be rude. Let the girls take care of you. You've already started. Why not finish?"

For what seemed like an eternity, Carl sat back in the chair, burying his face into his hands, and contemplating whether he could betray Tuesday so heartlessly. Their relationship was already suffering, but as James clearly stated, he had already started, so why not finish. As soon as Tuesday discovered that James had even entered Foxy Tails, she would be through. Tuesday was his world, his special angel that he cherished like no other before, but his voyage into the bottomless pit of iniquity would cause her to flutter away, to flap her angelic wings as speedily as possible and soar away from the flaming abyss back into the heavens.

Carl lifted his head up and saw Ginger standing directly over him. She invitingly held out her hand in an attempt to whisk Carl off into the back room. Ginger's hair and makeup was also somehow miraculously dried and reapplied. Ginger was easily the most striking dancer at Foxy Tails. Carl's eyes rested on her perfect pedicure, her cherry apple red toenails sticking out from underneath her sandal straps. Her shoes almost looked like the glass slippers in the beloved fairytale, Cinderella. The three inch heels were constructed of a sturdy translucent plastic material which resembled glass, and interwoven between the sandal straps were colorful beads of an assortment of colors. His eyes moved up her bronzed muscular legs but rested on the muscles in her well defined calves. They looked like bars of soap placed in each calf. Her eggplant colored bikini clung tightly to her silicone induced balloons, and a row of sparkling sequins was embedded along the hem of her bikini top and bikini bottoms.

Ginger's name was tattooed on the upper right portion of her back just to the right of her shoulder blade. The tattoo was in Old English navy blue lettering, and a long red rose with a curved green stem was positioned directly below her name. Her swollen breasts poured forth from out of her bikini top, only leaving the sight of her nipples to Carl's imagination. Her skin was glazed with perfumed moisturizers and glistening body lotions that made her flesh twinkle, but her hair had to be her greatest asset. Spirals, the color of hot cayenne pepper, hung loosely over her shoulders. Her fiery red hair, as spicy as salsa, is what attracted many of her customers, but Carl was captivated by her eyes. They were the deepest shade of aqua that Carl had ever laid his eyes on, a deeper blue than any lake or body of fresh salt water. Her pupils looked like dolphins swimming through the high seas, their fins flipping wildly as they darted from side to side. She invitingly held out her hand, but Carl remained frozen. Carl was unaware that James had slipped Candy and Ginger at least five hundred dollars between the both of them to satisfy him and Carl in any so which way they desired.

"Come on hon. Follow me." Ginger teasingly cooed in a husky voice as she placed her silky hand onto Carl and pulled him up out of his seat. Her bubble gum pink nails dug into Carl's flesh as he pretended to protest, but his judgment at this point was severely clouded. He wobbled back and forth, hardly able to balance himself or stand upright.

"I can't. I can't. I have a girlfriend. Someone I love more than anybody." he mumbled, his whisper beginning to taper off as she again forcefully clenched his wrist and pulled him out of his chair. The room began to spin as he stumbled to the floor. James leaped out of his seat and rushed over to Carl who was at this point was hunched over, his head placed in between his legs. Carl kept uttering gibberish which no one could understand. James forcefully placed his jiggly arms under Carl's armpits and lifted him back onto the chair. The room continued to whirl around him, the naked strippers circling him, their bouncing breasts smothering him and muffling his pleas for forgiveness.

"You need to calm down, Carl." James gruffly scolded, placing his hand on Carl's shoulders and shaking them. "I didn't buy you those drinks so we'd get kicked out of here. If you are falling down stupid drunk, do you think that they'll let you stay? Straighten your shit out. I got you drunk so you'd loosen up a little, but if you can't handle your alcohol like a man, then you are going to have to find you own way home."

"I donnnn...tttt give a shit you fat fuck. I dooonn't waaant to be here anywayyyss. I'm leeeeaving." Carl burbled as he rose from his seat and regained his footing.

"You are not going anywhere." James sternly ordered as he forcefully placed his palm onto Carl's chest and pushed him into the chair. "You are going to sit down, shut up, and enjoy yourself, because if you don't, I promise you, I will tell Tuesday everything. Do you understand me?"

Carl defiantly glared into James's eyes for what seemed like infinity. Carl had never gazed into eyes so cold, eyes so dark that they sent cool chills throughout your spine.

"Maaan. It's cool. I'llll stay. Just don't tell Tuesday...Please."

"Man, I promise. I won't say a thing to your old lady as long as you behave. I am a man of my word. Now go with the fine lady. Let her show you a good time. No one has to know. This is our little secret. Alright." James pleasantly responded, his tone of voice completely changed as he patted Carl on the back.

Once again Ginger grasped Carl's wrist and pulled him out of his seat. The room twirled as Ginger dragged Carl across the dance floor onto the flashing multihued colored squares. Carl turned around and caught sight of James's face. It was a blur, but he could still discern a broad grin lightening up his otherwise pale freckled face. James applauded as a gesture of congratulations. He wanted an accomplice to aid him in his naughty conquests and alleviate his guilty conscience, and now he had found one.

Ginger held onto Carl's wrist for dear life, her hand so tightly wound around Carl's wrist that a numbness began to circulate beginning at his wrist and ending at his fingertips. The deadness in his hand began to travel throughout his forearms, into his upper arms, his shoulders, his back, and began to creep into his heart. Without Tuesday he would feel lifeless. She did not know yet, but in the event that she did discover the truth, Carl was going to prepare himself for the way he was going to feel. Small balls of fire erupted onto the stage as a curvy blonde bombshell galloped across the stage. Topless, the curvaceous fair haired beauty straddled the silver pole and twirled her cowboy hat over her hand, throwing it directly at Carl. Carl caught the felt cow print hat and placed it onto his head as people on the dance floor were bumping and grinding and slapped Carl's hand in high five gestures.

They finally came to a poorly painted black door with globs of paint splattered onto the wall. Ginger thrust open the door with her thigh and dragged Carl through the narrow passageway bathed in a warm reddish glow. When they reached the end of the corridor they made a swift right turn into a room filled with black and red booths and shabby circular wooden tables. This room was also bathed in a warm reddish glow, but a few shades darker than the hallway, making many of the illegal activities taking place in the room barely detectable. Carl could hear the heavy breathing, the breathless panting, the sinful moaning, but his eyes could not penetrate the wickedness. His eyes could not soak in the various strangers having sex or the old men fooling around with women young enough to be their daughters. Gently, but implying dominance, Ginger pushed Carl into a black leather booth with the tips of her glossy acrylic nails. She dominantly stood over his body, her legs straddled over his. Carl did not object, It was a little late for that. His eyes were glazed over due to the incredible amount of alcohol he had just consumed and rubbing them did not make his surroundings any clearer. The shallow breathing and moans of a couple in the corner was becoming blatantly obvious. Carl could hear the sexual juices sticking to their legs as they humped. He never knew that people fucked in these places. Ultimately, he was in a whore house, being serviced by a prostitute, and there was nothing he could do. He was helpless, a drunk slovenly piece of trash about to commit adultery. He heard the couple softly climax in unison, and then quickly get up. Two naked goblins darted past him, cackling as they put their clothing back on. Carl rubbed his eyes again as his eyes attempted to adjust to the light.

Ginger unclasped her bikini top and began to rub Carl's face with the cups. She massaged his lips, his pinkish cheeks, and then his clammy forehead.

    "I want you to pretend that these are my breasts." Ginger

huskily whispered into Carl's ear. Her milky white breasts were not the same color as the remainder of her golden tanned body. They bounced off of her chest like two frisky kittens as she plunked herself onto Carl's lap.

"Have you ever had a lap dance, Carl?"

"Uhhh. No Ne ne never." Carl nervously stammered.

"Why not?" she questioned as she moved up and down on his lap simulating the act of sexual intercourse.

"Be be because. I never felt the need to."

"Well. You have the need tonight. Don't you Carl?." Ginger asked, running her pink cotton candy nails through his jet black curls.

Carl did not wish to clarify his reason for going into the back room with Ginger. He had an intelligent beautiful woman at home, someone who possessed other talents than using her body, but as his manhood became harder, he could not deny that he was becoming strangely aroused.

"You need to relax, Carl." Ginger cooed fiddling with Carl's polo shirt collar. "You are too uptight. Relax and enjoy my dance, because it is only going to get better."

Ginger moved up and down to the pulsating beats of the music, her breasts jiggling like two gelatin molds. Her breasts teased Carl as they grazed his chin as she bounced.

"Are you hungry Carl?" she sensuously asked.

Carl remained silent for he did not know what to say when a stranger asked him such a question.

"Carl, don't be shy. We are going to be getting to know each other real well in just a minute." Ginger crammed her scrumptious breast into Carl's mouth. Carl's instincts and tingling in intimate places prompted him to begin to suckle on her stiff nipple, nourishing himself with the filthy nutrients that her bloated mammary provided. He slurped at her nipple as if he was a famished doe pumping a quart of milk out of an overly inflated udder.

"You like that?"

Carl nodded his head.

"I knew you would." Ginger whispered into his ear, melting his good senses. Ginger unzipped Carl's jean zipper, reached for his penis, and pulled it out of the slit of his flannel boxers. She moved the panel of her bikini bottoms, which covered her crotch, to the side and slipped Carl's manhood into her whiskerless mound. Carl gasped as she began to rock back and fourth. She lusciously arched her back swaying to the thumping flow of the music, sticking out her breasts out as an inviting gesture to Carl to nibble on them. Carl once again nursed from her succulent edibles. He looked like a gluttonous infant gulping down a bottle of formula. She performed twists and twirls and gyrations that Carl had never experienced. At one point she so forcefully grinded her hips into Carls that he lurched back almost falling out of the booth. Ironically, they never kissed. Not once did their tongues entwine. Forcefully, Carl bumped his hips into hers, the prickles in his shaft becoming more pronounced as he heartlessly humped her like an untamed dog. Carl began to moan, his shrill howls sounding like a wounded wolf, and then it was over. A moment of uncomfortable silence ensued, and Ginger immediately rose, her slimy thighs sticking to Carl as she got up.

Carl had never felt so unfulfilled and disgusting. Every object in the dungeon of indignity became telescopically minimized. It was as if Carl was looking into a dark narrow tunnel. Ginger's curvaceous body stretched.like a clump of silly puddy or a clown in the fun house mirror.

"Hey. Come here." Carl uttered, tugging at Ginger's forearm, but Ginger completely ignored him. She slipped her bikini top over her shoulders and began to walk towards a small door which led to the dressing room built into the back wall.

"Ginger." He called out again rising from his seat and stuffing his dangling manhood back into his boxers.

"It's over. Our time is up. Go back to the club. Jimmy is waiting for you."

"What do you mean it's over? We just fucked each other. That's what you do when you fuck guys. You just pretend like it never happened, then move on to the next one!"

"Listen Biff!"

"My name isn't Biff. It's Carl!"

"Alright then, Carl. We had our fun. It's over. Just let it go."

"What do you mean let it go? You liked me. You brought me back here to have sex with me. You were incredibly sexually attracted to me. Right?"

OVER ON THE EAST SIDE

Ginger began to cackle, her raspy laugh sounding like a witch. She reached for a gold Zippo laying on the back of the booth and lit up a cigarette. Carl took a good look at Ginger. He was beginning to sober up by this point, and Ginger just was not looking as incredible as she had appeared an hour earlier. Her silky ginger tresses that had magically captivated him earlier that evening were not what they appeared to be. Instead of being glossy and lustrous, the supposed "ginger" mane was closer to the shade of a rotten pumpkin. Her loose flowing tendrils were in reality tightly curled, the texture being extremely frizzy. Her vivid aqua doe eyes were not blue at all, but closer to a drab gray and squinty. Ginger looked to be about fifty years old, but actually was thirty-one. She was a crack addict and by feeding her habit, she aged extremely poorly. Crow's feet lined the corners of her eyes and creases surrounded her thin lips. She was not exactly curvaceous, but almost emaciated, a skeletal figure. Her hollowed out cheeks darkened her face and caused her eyes to sink into the back of her head. Ginger did have breast implants, but gravity was starting to take effect. She looked absolutely ridiculous with two plentiful cantaloupes dangling off to the side of her scrawny rib cage. Carl stepped back, almost frightened. Could his goggle vision have been that deceiving?

"Sexually attracted to you. Biff, where are you?"

"It's Carl, and what do you mean, where am I?"

"I mean where the fuck do you think you are? You are not at home with your girlfriend."

"What do you mean, what the fuck am I talking about. Do I need to repeat myself? Your great friend out there gave me fifty dollars to fuck the shit out of you. Now you want to cuddle, have pillow talk, have a special moment. I'm sorry, but Jimmy didn't pay me enough for that. Do you know how many guys I fuck a night? If I had to sit and talk to them after each fuckin, I'd never make any money. You are no different from all the rest. You might pretend to be, but you are not. If you were, you wouldn't be in this place, and you certainly wouldn't have fucked me, no matter how much your friend paid me. I got you off. Be happy. Go home to your girlfriend like you should have done in the first place. Go cry on her shoulder." Ginger wickedly smiled, displaying an entire set of rotted stinking teeth.

Carl stood, dumbfounded, disgusted that he fucked this crack whore and second that his supposed friend and boss James would pay a stripper to have sex with him when he damn well knew he had a girlfriend at home.

Ginger circled around and reentered the dressing room, shaking her head in disbelief.

"These guys are going to have to start paying me for pillow talk!" Carl heard Ginger holler to the other girls behind the door.

Carl plopped himself back onto the bench and buried his head into the palms of his hands.

"Why, why?" he repeatedly uttered to himself, tugging at the ends of his tar black ringlets.

Carl quietly sobbed, his pitiful cries drowning out the moans of the couples in the neighboring booths. From this moment on he would begin to mourn the death of his and Tuesday's partnership. Their bond was now broken. Carl began to visualize Tuesday's face when hearing the news. He could see her icy green eyes, her frozen features, her vacant stare, her pursed up lips sealed shut. He imagined telling her the news.

"Tuesday, I have to tell you something. You know that night that I was out all night. Well, I wasn't really working. I went to Foxy Tails, this strip club, and fucked some stripper named Ginger in the back room. What else could I do? My boss made me do it, especially after getting the hand job from the stripper named Candy."

There was no salvaging the relationship, and Carl knew it. He plowed his fingernails into a crusty blister on his forearm until blood trickled forth from the festering boil. Oddly, the bubbling eruption was located on the chest of his Christ tattoo. As the blood trickled down Christ's chest Carl looked up to the ceiling, his eyes rolling back in his head.

"Please, God Forgive me. I never meant to disrespect you."
Carl wailed, his hands folded together, pleading and praying for absolution of his dirty deed. *"I love Tuesday with all my heart. I was drunk, didn't know what I was doing. Those whores don't mean nothing to me. Tuesday is my life. I was barely conscious. You can't hold that against me.*

Carl picked up a glass bottle of beer laying on the side of the booth and hurled it against the wall, the alcoholic brew splashing and shards of glass smashing against the wall. Carl stumbled to his feet and staggered through the long dark hallway, slamming the swinging door open with his fist. The music drowned out his vicious punching and kicking the door. Carl unsteadily walked across the dance floor, shoving his way through the crowd ogling the dancers on the stage until he saw the darkness before him, the hollow cavity of wickedness where he had misplaced his morality for the time being. Carl submerged himself into the sinister space of shadowy spirits. Through the smog, Carl could barely distinguish where his boss had retreated to, but it was not long before he could make out James's portly silhouette reclining back in one of the old tattered recliner chairs. Between James's crotch lay Candy's head snugly nestled, bobbing up and down to the pulse of the music.

"James!" Carl hollered, startling James.
James massive head lurched forward, his fudge colored eyes almost spiraling out of his eye sockets.

"What the fuck do you think you are doing? Can't you see I'm busy here boy?"
Candy's head rose from between James's blubbery pale freckled inner thighs. She wiped away at her slimy collagen injected lips with the back of her hand.

"James. Get the fuck up. I want out of here. Do you understand me?"

Carl screamed, his arms flailing wildly and his eyeballs darting from side to side. "Come on. We need to get out of here. I need to get home to Tuesday now. I mean it." he stomped his feet upon the ground like a child.
James's pink cheeks faded and a pasty ashen color replaced it.

"Boy. You better back up. You're here to enjoy yourself remember."
Candy rose up to her feet and placed her hand upon Carl's shoulder.

"Sit down. Relax baby."
Carl violently shrugged her off as if she was the most vile infectious disease.

"Don't touch me you fucking whore."
James struggled to rise from out of his chair.

"Boy. Don't talk to the ladies like that. They work for a living just like you do."

"What the luck are you talking about? Fucking and blowing guys' dicks is working for a living. You are the most pathetic guy I have ever met. You see, I have you all figured out.

You were jealous that I had a great girl, that I was happy. You see I don't have to pay for sex James. I can get it whenever I want, unlike some people. You purposely wanted to ruin me and Tuesday, because you are miserable, because you are not happy with your relationship. You see, I am not a pervert like you. I don't have to look at all sorts of naked women to satisfy me. I had one woman, naked or clothed, who was the most beautiful woman I ever laid my eyes on, and you fucked it up. You think these women like you for you. The only reason they give you the time of day is because you shell out the big bucks. If you had nothing, they'd treat you as if you had the plague. Now let's go. You got me into this. Now get me out of it."

"Now just wait a minute." James retorted, pulling up his pants as they began to creep down his behind. "Stop blaming other people for what you did wrong. What did you do? You went into a strip bar. Big fucking deal! Why don't you try to be a man for once. Look at Donny. Look at Chris. Do you see them freaking out. No, they take it like a man, because they realize that this is what every man is supposed to do. Don't be a pussy for God's sake. You are just in a strip bar like every other man in this planet. That girl of yours has some kind of unreal control over you."

"No, James. I just didn't go into a strip bar. I just didn't sit here twiddling my thumbs keeping to myself. I fucked a stripper. I fucked Ginger, because you paid her to. You got me shit ass drunk and paid that nasty bitch to fuck me in the back room. I don't need to pay people to fuck me James. I can get pussy anytime I want, unlike some fat fuck I know. Get that through your fat ass head!"

"You need to relax boy. There's no need for name calling. Go outside. Get some fresh air. Go jack off boy. Just leave me the fuck alone so I can get back to business." He irritatingly hollered, putting his arm around Candy's shoulder and pulling her towards him.

"Fuck you!" Carl screamed, shoving James into the wall.

"Stop it!" Candy screamed.

"Oh, so you want to fight, huh. Do you really think that is smart? Look at me and look at you. I am twice your size boy. Be smart Carl. Use your head for once. I'm just looking out for you. I don't want you to get hurt now."

"I don't fucking care. I don't care if I fucking die right now you disgusting piece of shit."

"Baby, calm down." Candy squealed.

OVER ON THE EAST SIDE

"Shut up!" Carl screamed pushing Candy out of the way.

"Alright. You want to show me how much of a man you are. Then let's do it the right way. Let's take it outside."

A crowd began to gather around James and Carl.

"Fuck you, you piece of shit!" Carl screamed lunging towards James with outstretched hands. He reached for James' doughy neck, dripping with flabby folds of lard. He dug his fingernails into James's blubbery throat, placing a tremendous amount of pressure on his artery. James began to retch, his face turning into the shade of cranberry sauce. He looked like a turkey gobbling to and fro, his folds of fat jiggling.

"How does this feel, huh you fat piece of shit! Now I have the power. I bet you'll think twice about playing with my life now, huh Jimmyboy. You might control these women with your money and you might control Chris and Donny, but you don't control me. You never did and you never will. I'm more of a man than that."

Carl felt like he was on a power trip, but soon the walls started closing in, the room started spinning, and a cloak of darkness surrounded him, and Carl fell to the floor with a loud thump

CHAPTER 31

I drifted into a blissful sleep only to be tainted by a tart taste of reality. In my dream I believed i had met the man of my dreams. He was everything a woman would desire and a man would envy. He possessed good looks, charm, and not to mention dressed impeccably. After all the years of endless soul searching I believed that I had met my true soul mate. The relationship reached near perfection status, but only after we exchanged vows did I truly realize what a horrible mistake I had made. In my dream it was as if I was looking into my past, but trapped in it because of the degree of abusiveness I suffered. I could not distinguish between the past and the present. Time exists as a circular continuum, and I cannot escape. The abuse began with little comments here and there. Every morning would begin with a belittling session robbing me of any shred of self worth that I possessed. He would call me ugly, fat, worthless, a whore, but the most frequent criticism came in the form of putting down my breasts. They were too saggy, not large enough, not the right shape, uneven, pretty much every rotten thing which could be said about a breast. We could not leave the house without him ogling at other women and praising their breasts. He'd interrogate me as to why I could not resemble those symbols of perfection. I'd reply that these girls were not real at all. They were fabricated plastic like creatures. I'd question him as to why he would marry a "real" woman such as myself compared to the Pamela Anderson type he placed on a pedestal. His explanation to this was that a "real" woman was someone who could clean, cook, and pop out children. These other varieties of women were objects of lust and the kind he wanted to have sex with. At this point I felt like the most undesirable woman to ever exist.

Soon after the physical abuse began. He'd beat me for hours and show me no mercy. He screamed and his voice reached curdling proportions begging me to get a boob job so he would not have to hide me away in the house, away from his friends and anyone of great importance to him. At times I became a bruised and bleeding blubbering piece of flesh strewn out over the cold tile of my bathroom floor. I no longer resembled myself, but instead resembled an ogre of such tragic proportions. I awakened in and out of consciousness, slowly lifting my head off the blood stained cold tile only to hear the moaning of my husband and other women having sex in our bed. One woman even had the nerve to use the bathroom nude while I lay on the floor bruised, battered, shivering, and shaking, crying blood stained tears of repulsion. Continually he cheated on me bringing home a different woman each night. He brought home quite an assortment ranging from strippers to prostitutes to young girls he met at bars, but there was one attribute which all these women had in common, and this was that they all had large breasts. At times I would consider having breast surgery to tranquilize his obsession, but not having the surgery was the only sort of control I could have over him. By not fulfilling this one request I was standing up for myself.

I could not fathom as to why I stayed with someone so abusive, such a beast. I only reason I could conjure up is that all the emotional and physical abuse drove me to complete insanity. I alienated myself and believed myself to be the hideous ungrateful degenerate he perceived me to be. In my mind I was now the foul creation he had brought into being. I could not compare to the airbrushed beauties, which laid in the countless Playboys and Hustlers, which occupied our house. If I threatened to leave he said he would kill me, and there was not doubt in my mind that he would.

The day I discovered he had terminal cancer brought me a mixture of relief and sadness. I was comforted by the fact that the torment would cease, but I had become quite accustomed to this pattern of abuse. I became an obedient slave taking care of his every whim. It was on his deathbed that he made one final request. I prayed that he would beg for forgiveness. Would my evil husband fill my last memory of him with peace? Instead though he asked me to get a boob job, and if I did not he would haunt me for the remainder of my life. I had made his life miserable, because for eight years he had to stare at two hideous unsightly mounds of flesh. He exclaimed that from the heavens he wanted to peer at two delightfully shaped melons. He specifically uttered that if I did not fulfill this final request, that wicked consequences would follow. There was no doubt in my mind that this man with such an overpowering, evil demeanor, who filled me with such wicked fright, could haunt me forever more.

Two years passed since his death. He would not leave me alone. He continues to have the same amount of control of me in death as in life, Every time I stand in my garden I can see his reflection in our bedroom window. I can hear his shrill whispering voice continue to insult me as I walk from the darkness of one room to another. At night I can still hear my pleas and cries for help echo from the bathroom. Images of big breasted women envelop me wherever I go, reminding me of what I lack. I realize that I have to fulfill his last dying wish and that if I do not my life will continue to be haunted by his presence. No longer can I live my life as a normal person. So many times I wish for a kind hearted savior to rescue me from these fiery depths of hell. I try to do everything in my power to absolve myself of him. A ghost specialist and priest come to my home to attempt to rid me of this evil spirit, but he continues to persist. I wander the streets trying to put his soul to rest until I am an elderly woman no longer able to stand upright, but supporting herself with a cane. My saggy breasts drag across the floor as I walk, my dark brown wrinkled nipples inverted. The only image I can see is my husband, cackling like a fiend, teasing me mercilessly. I cannot tolerate it any longer. I march over to the nearest plastic surgery doctor and demand that he inject my breasts with a ton of helium. He reluctantly obliges, but without much prodding he stabs at my breast with a foot long needle. He pumps at the needle filling my breast until it lifts up from off of the floor and floats. I look into the mirror at my wrinkled face, gray hair, and sagging skin. Then I look at my breasts, two lovely symbols of perfection, a representation of youth, I look into the mirror and grin, breathe in a sigh of relief that I am able to recapture youth once again, but my glee is short lived for the air in my breasts begin to fizzle out until they look like two long sausages dangling from a meat hook. My husband begins to reappear through the reflection of the glass, cackling away like a maniac.

"You will never have nice big breasts honey." He mockingly coos *I hobble towards the corner of the room and fold up into a ball sobbing.*

And then I wake up.

OVER ON THE EAST SIDE

CHAPTER 32

I am not quite sure when exactly my and Carl's relationship began to deteriorate. When I evoke past memories of the commencement of our partnership, a warm tingly sensation washes throughout my insides. Carl's warmth used to satisfy my soul like a steaming hot cup of apple cider sprinkled with cinnamon specks. When we were together no one could invade our personal universe. We were encircled by a bubble that not even the sharpest needle could pop. I pledged my own personal promise to him that I would be the one girl never to hurt him, and he did so to me. Throughout all of the disappointment and heartache that life hurled our way, we had finally found a safe place, a speck of innocence in one another which could aid us in our expression of love. Carl's nativity was at one time adorable. He was like an overgrown child not familiar in the ways of discretion. If he slipped and blurted out an insensitive remark, I would dismiss it. At the time I would be shocked and appalled, but I would overlook it.

Over time though all of the tactless remarks began to whittle away at my heart. Every inconsiderate comment hammered away at my spirit, until my once sturdy boulder collapsed into a pile of crumbled pebbles, and as the blustery winds carried the pebbles into the atmosphere, my compassion evaporated until it was nonexistent. This man that I had once adored, this companion of mine who I shared my most intimate of secrets was slowly becoming my rival. My chilled spirit tortured him until he too had no empathy for me. Our long forgotten love had vanished as if it had never existed. Where at one time I once had thrived through our love for each other, I now flourished through our hatred for one another. My frosty center remained detached. I no longer had a conscience. I could never bring myself to do it, but if I committed adultery I do not believe I would feel remorseful. The prospect of Carl's death caused me to feel nothing except maybe relief. I could have easily slipped the rope around his neck, pulled the cord until the bulging blood vessels in his neck constricted, and continued to throttle until the poor soul gurgled and spit up foul bloody phlegm. I could have pressed the cold barrel of a revolver against his sweaty forehead, dug it into his skull and pulled the trigger. I simply did not care. I do not know how I had graduated to this level, how at one time I would have died for Carl, but now I would have gladly sacrificed his life for my own. I wanted to feel again, needed to experience the sensations that love triggers. I yearned for my heart to soften like a golden dab of margarine melting in a liquid puddle of maple syrup in the center of a hotcake, but it only iced up. We never had a chance. Two damaged people could not miraculously heal themselves and commit to a perfect union of two souls. We heaped on an unreasonable amount of responsibility onto one another. We tried to be each others savior, but failed miserably.

We became a mirror image of each person who had failed us in one way or another, because of our unfair expectations. Every day became worse than the day before. Even if there was no physical violence or verbal abuse, it was torture to constantly churn out perverted images of my boyfriend and the strippers.

My reflection harshly bounced off of me as I critically stared into the oval mirror above my caramel colored oak dresser dabbed with swirls of dark chocolate wood. I was going to need some work, to be made over so that the opposite sex found me absolutely irresistible, so sizzling that they could not refuse my advances to accompany them to a hotel room. Dearest James was going to be my first victim. The hatred I felt for that man was so intense that to me he was not classified as a human being, He was not even a warm blooded mammal capable of instilling some goodness in this filthy crooked world. To me he was a soiled gorilla moping in a monkey cage, munching on a mushy banana and scratching and picking out muddy clumps ensnared in his furry behind. At least animals had some couth about themselves. They possessed maternal instincts and protected their young ones or their comrades in their contrived tribal clan. Animals could learn to be loving, display affection to their owners or the people who regularly presented themselves in their sad humble lives. Kittens and puppies could nuzzle their sweet fuzzy faces into their protector's lap, scrunch their triangular pinkish noses and pounce on the shin of an owner after they lapped at a warm bowl of milk. They bathe in the simplicity of their surroundings and treasure their masters for relieving their simple struggle of finding food and water. James only simulated warmth and affection in an attempt to attain what he would always desire; pussy. He did not care who or what it came from. Any assorted size or shape would do. James had surpassed any hope of ever respecting women. Even the holy union of matrimony did not deter him from dipping into the muddy swamp of iniquity. He submerged himself so deeply in this foul marsh, this quicksand like substance that he could not rise up from the barrier that entrapped him.

To objectify women was to exist as James, to dissect them until they are a rickety skeleton peeled of all soft tender skin. Pare away their ripe bouncing breasts, their smooth stomachs, their plump buttocks, until they exist as absolutely nothing, what he intended for them to be. Their skeletal silhouettes haunt James crying out for understanding, pleading with him to recognize them for their minds, but he chuckles. His mother didn't have a mind, his wife didn't have a mind. No woman possesses a mind. Therefore he could tinker around as he wished, amuse himself with a woman's predicament of having an addiction or living at a poverty ridden level, a woman so downhearted that she has to resort to shedding her clothes for the satisfaction of some lonely perverts jacking off under a cocktail table. Because of James's ignorance toward the opposite sex, I would show total disregard towards him.

The value of his life was about as insignificant as a bread crumb. If it was not for James my beloved boyfriend would not have been tempted to enter Foxy Tails, would never have been pushed to fuck some stripper that he didn't know or give a shit about. James felt so insecure about himself and so empty inside concerning his relationship with his wife that he had to wreak havoc on other people's lives, a couple who at least seemed happy to a certain extent. Carl and I were happy at one time. We were extremely sexually attracted to each other, and our sex life was phenomenal. James could sense this, and he wasn't about to have it. He could not comprehend how a man could love a woman like Carl at one time loved me. He was envious, and therefore would do anything to destroy what little happiness remained. I was not only going to murder James, but I was going to torture him little by little, make the last moments of his life incredibly uncomfortable so unpleasant that he would be begging to die.

CHAPTER 33

I met Mike on a warm breezy evening at Pop's, a twenty-four hour bar in East St. Louis sandwiched between PT's and Penthouse Club. Ironically only about twenty minutes before I had laid my eyes on Mike, I spotted an extremely handsome guy named Ryan with dark brown hair, tanned skin, and movie star looks. We didn't hit it off so well, and he left for the evening. Ryan was so stunning in fact that I could not imagine liking anyone else that evening, that is until I laid my eyes on Mike Teasdale. Mike was not as traditionally handsome as Rob, but he retained a quality which I could not describe. We had made eye contact earlier, and through this unspoken gesture, I could feel an electric current wash over me and travel from one of us to the other. I called my best friend, Katt, over and told her to tell him that I liked him. While she went up to him I nervously put my head down, fearful of rejection once again, but when she walked over with a smile on her face, I knew that she had good news. My heart was thumping so loudly that I could not even hear my shoes click against the sticky beer stained floor as I made my way towards him. The chemistry was apparent instantly, but since the beginning I could sense that he enjoyed toying with girls' emotions. He showed me a tattoo shaped like a cross on his stomach, and from that day on I loved tattoos on a guys stomach. He would dismiss himself every so often, and once I even caught him eyeing me as I talked to a guy I knew that worked in my building. We exchanged numbers that evening, but unfortunately I made the fatal error of my adoration for him obviously apparent. I expressed my concern of him not calling me back which he did not find very attractive.

The next day when I woke up, I was practically in hysterics, curled up in a ball in the corner of my room, staring at the phone, and preparing myself for the inevitable, the tragedy that trailed me whenever I met someone who I genuinely liked. This was different though. It was as I lacked control. I craved to see him and touch him so badly that I could taste it. I frantically circled my apartment several times, driving my sister absolutely crazy. She reassured me that he would call, but I was hesitant to believe her. So many times in my life men had made me promises and broken them. I could bear it no longer. I ran up to my sister and announced that I had to go see a psychic at this very moment. I thumbed through the Yellow Pages for a reasonable Psychic and found one on the opposite side of town for $50.00. I called her up to see if she was there, and she directed me to her house. Relief was the only word I could use to describe how I felt. Foolishly, I felt that I would receive the answer I was looking for from a psychic. She was going to reveal to me if Mike was going to call.

My sister and I drove clear on the other side of town to see this woman, and of course while I was seeing her Mike called me at home, and that was the last time he called me. A few years later I ran into him at *Pops* where upon he asked me to come over to his house. I drove to his house, and I pounded on the front door until the frosty winter winds chilled my exposed skin. My fingers felt like ten congealed Popsicle sticks. I continued to rap at the door. I looked down at my now bluish frigid fingers and clenched my fists, stuffing them in the soft warm cotton lining of my coat pockets. My fingers were so deadened that I could not feel the cottony fluff brush against the pads of my fingertips. The crisp arctic wind chilled my crimson cheeks, my anesthetized jowls so numb that they felt as if they were injected with a pound of novocaine. My skinned knuckles determinedly tapped at the solid pine door. A steady stream began to trickle fourth from the flaky section of my knuckle, the padded skin in that area slowly thinning as I stubbornly knocked. I pressed my flushed face against the front window, peeking in between the blinds to search for any small sign of life, even a miniscule microorganism to humor me in my time of desperation. He was not going to humiliate me like this. I cautiously hobbled down the stone steps covered with ice giving them an almost glassy appearance. A rusted yellow toy construction truck, perhaps his sons, was sprawled out at the bottom of the steps.

My ebony leather flats stepped over the frozen grass blades, making crunching sounds. I retreated to the rear of the house and sluggishly stepped up the back steps to the kitchen door. An outdated lime colored paisley drapery hung over the rectangular smoggy window destroying any hope I had to sneak a glance at this contrived idol I worshipped. I do not know what I expected to accomplish or what foolhardy resolution I hoped to result from persisting to knock on his door. I twisted the brass doorknob hoping that this was the magical portal to guide me to my cheerful destiny, but it would not budge. Perhaps Mike was sleeping soundly in his bedroom, snoring so powerfully that he could not hear the heavy pounding at his door.

Maybe he would bury his face in his hands and sob when he awoke at daybreak to find me no where in his bed. Or perhaps in a worse case scenario he was awake the entire time, covering his ears with the palm of his hands, praying that I would lose hope and finally leave. I did not want to cease this mission that I so anxiously had driven out of my way to. As the sun rose up, like a scoop of orange sherbet suspended in the heavens, I turned around and headed back down the steps, dejected and blue. How this cruel twist of fate had destroyed me. I shivered as I reluctantly treaded back to the car, my head held down, my teeth persistently chattering.

An image of Mike strolling in slow motion, dressed in his navy blue mechanic uniform with his name label directly over his right breast, washed through my mind. No body was as cool and contained as him. He was suave, smoother than any man I had ever laid my eyes on. I had thought that we had a connection, or maybe I just misunderstood his signals. I interpreted our connection as something more, I suppose. When we stared into each others eyes it was as if we were having eye sex. I knew deep down that I did not fabricate these feelings that we had for each other. He just obviously did not want to let me into his heart perhaps due to a preoccupation with another.

I dug in my cluttered purse for my car keys, my desensitized fingers barely able to grab a hold of my key chain. I stuck the metal plated key in the door lock and slumped myself down into my now chilled gray seat. This could not be happening, This was not reality. Right now I was sleeping under his covers, his arms ensnarled around my naked chest, and I had finally found my place. I slipped my key into the ignition and placed my frozen foot on the gas pedal, not knowing where I was driving to. I wouldn't be surprised if my toes turned into icicles by now.

I found myself in the parking lot of a Wal-Mart. I got out of the car and walked into the Super Center, conscious that these Sunday morning folks simply dressed, and probably on their way to church or breakfast were confusingly eyeing me in my sparkling black dress and heaving cleavage, but I ignored them. I was on a mission to win the heart of another. I purchased a pad of notebook paper with an apricot colored cover, a box of letter size envelopes, and a dark purple gel pen. I gaily almost skipped back to my car, confident that my plan was sure to work, that Mike would be so delighted with my note that he would almost immediately give me a call and admit to his wrongs. I began to scribble on the inside front cover to eject all the liquid globs first, as I planned my great thesis on winning Mike over. The letter went like this:

Dear Mike:

> *I have already relinquished any amount of pride I had formerly retained just by writing this letter, but it is something I have to do. I do not know if you were at home when I knocked on your door, somewhere else, sleeping, or if you were purposely avoiding me, but that is not relevant. I know you think that I have issues, and we do not agree on many things, and for that I cannot offer you a solution. I also realize that it bothers you that my best friend dislikes you, but I do not care about that. I think you are a good person despite what she thinks. Yes, I could have said something, stood up for you in some way, but I didn't want to get into it. She was drunk and she gets very mean, so please do not hold that against, me. All I know is that I have feelings for you and by so candidly revealing myself, I hope you can at least have the common courtesy to at least let me know how you feel, no matter how badly. My phone number is (555) 555-5555. See you around someday. (Maybe)*
> *Tuesday Jones*

I reread the letter at least a dozen times, scratching out the language I felt too presumptuous. Finally, when the revision was complete, I rewrote it, folded it up into thirds, and stuffed it into an envelope, licking the gummed adhesive cautiously so as not to saturate the seal with my saliva. I scrawled **To Mike** on the envelope. I dreamily drove back to his house conjuring up foolish images of Mike calling me on the phone and apologizing for blowing me off. He'd then ask me out on a date, and I'd playfully hesitate, but finally accept. We'd have a wonderful first date and eventually become boyfriend and girlfriend, get married and have more children and a puppy dog. I turned down the radio and discreetly pulled up to his house, tiptoeing up to the mailbox and slipping my letter on the top of the other mail. Idolizing Mike as I did I was unusually inquisitive toward any aspect of his life and therefore decided to pry a bit. I pulled out the other letters piled on the bottom of his mailbox and studied them. The top letter was a utility bill addressed to Mike Teasdale. I held the utility bill between the palms of my hands, realizing that this might be the closest I'd ever get to Mike Teasdale ever again.

I slipped the bill back into the mailbox and headed home, instantly retreating to my bedroom where I slipped in my favorite CD by Snead O' Connor into my boom box and plopped into bed. *The song Nothing Compares To You* came on, and as the melodious lyrics filled my room, the tears began to flow down my now thawed cheeks. This song captured my sentiment towards Mike like no other. Sure, I could meet plenty of other men, but they'd all remind me of Mike . Noone compared to Mike, but unfortunately he did not share the same passion as I towards us, because Mike never responded to my letter. He was not as spellbound of I as I was of him. He probably tore open that letter, scoffed, and crumpled it up, tossing it into the garbage can. I believe he was uncomfortable with the idea of someone glorifying his image as much as I did. I treated him like a celebrity. I wish to God I had never laid my eyes upon him for I believe he was the one that destroyed me. To this day I cannot extinguish the flame I held for Mike. Mike's heart was chilled, as cold as that wintry day that I pitifully waited at his doorstep, hoping for a chance to be implanted in his memory. He did not care how intelligent I was or what wonderful assets I could contribute to a relationship. Like all of the other men in my life the only thing he cared about was getting laid. Would I ever be valued as a human being and not a piece of ass? I yearned for the old time traditions, when women were respected by men, when things were taken slower. Men used to hold the door open for women. Now they let it slam in the woman's face. How times had changed and I despised it.

OVER ON THE EAST SIDE

CHAPTER 34

It was 5:30 a.m. The piercing buzz of the alarm clock startled me out of my grogginess. I scooted closer to Carl and warmly nuzzled up to him. For one year, since the day he moved in I never had to sleep with my electric blanket. His body exuded warmth, making me anticipate the evenings when I could nestle up to him, but at this moment in time it felt peculiarly different. For all of my life I had been searching for that one individual who could reciprocate my gestures of affection. I misinterpreted men taking advantage of me sexually as an expression of love, which was extremely naive on my part. These men sensed that they could stomp all over me, because I exuded nativity and had a tendency to be too trustworthy. At bedtime I would burrow my head against his brawny chest and listen to the energetic thumping of his heart. I would playfully nudge my nose into his collarbone sniffing the fragrant scent of *Latitude/Longitude* by *Nautica* which he had sprayed on after his shower. The sweet smelling aroma rejuvenated my senses making me want to unite with him as one entity and never detach. His tender infantile gibberish was endearing, because I knew that he solely interacted with me like this. The wedge of my heart that had been severed off so brutally had regenerated and for that I could truly express gratitude. He represented the compassionate savior that I had been in pursuit of my entire life. For once there was a man who actually flaunted his sensitivity, and was not ashamed to let everyone know it. This is what made him exceptional, and this is why I loved him.

When I was a small girl my favorite fairy tale was *Snow White*. There was a record that I owned with all of the *Snow White* tracks which was my most beloved possession. All day I'd sit sheltered in my room, listening to the record and humming the melodious tunes. Her tone of voice was so sweet sounding, and it transported me into a world where there was no sorrow. My favorite song on the album was *Someday My Prince Will Come*. I lingered about my room expecting that my own personal Prince Charming would sweep me off my feet. Before bedtime I would doll up like my much loved fairy princess and amuse my father by pretending that he was Prince Charming and pecking him on the cheek. It was my ambition to be a *Snow White* actress when I entered adulthood. I breathed, ate, and slept *Snow White*. My mentality at that time was pure, and I always envisioned at what moment I would encounter Prince Charming. I never searched in the right places or in the right people. I continued to try to fill the missing void within myself by finding happiness in others, and these were always men drained of any feeling who did not desire to be pestered by my neediness, but Carl was distinctive from the others. I had finally found my Prince Charming.

This particular morning when I stretched my arm around his chest, there was no warmth radiating from within. His skin felt frosty, and he remained indifferent to my outpouring of affection. It was as if I was embracing a bitter cool snow man that would never liquefy. He was immune to the rays of sunshine that I secreted. He dazedly staggered out from under the soft comfy comforter and pressed the off button on the alarm. His first stop every morning was the bathroom where he would relieve himself, but on this morning he hurriedly dressed and retreated to the living room where he immediately smoked his first cigarette of the day.

I cautiously tiptoed into the living room sensing that he was in an irritable mood.

"So are you going to work out with me after work?" I guardedly asked.

"I don't care. Just go by yourself?"

"Why would you say that? Why are you acting like you are mad at me? I thought we were fine last night."

"I just want my girlfriend back. You never spend time with me. It's always your work or your kids with all of their dance classes. What is that about anyway, dance class?" he mocked, sarcastically chuckling. "If you are not lugging your kids around then you are running or writing your damn book. What about me? What about Carl?" he eerily referred to himself in third person.

"What do you want me to do? If you wanted a servant than you need someone who doesn't work, or you need to support their ass! Work takes up ten hours out of my day. I don't have time for anything else. I'm exhausted Carl. I wake up with dark bags under my eyes. All I do is work and try my hardest to please everyone, but it is never good enough for you. What do you want me to do? Quit my job, but devote my entire life to serving you. Sure, I'll do that if the bills and rent get paid, but I can't rely on your cheap ass to come up with that. Maybe you'd rather that I sit on my ass all day and eat multiple bags of Doritoes like Shannon the whale"

OVER ON THE EAST SIDE

"Why does it always come back to her? This is not about her. I didn't care about the fat bitch, and I certainly didn't care if I spent time with her, but you I care about. You are my girlfriend, but it doesn't feel like it."

I felt debilitated from all of the incessant conflict which we engaged in. My hands were quivering due to the hostile banter that Carl inflicted upon me, but I managed to make it to the bathroom where I could prepare for my run. I squirted a dime sized dollop of sunscreen on my palm and smeared the creamy emollient on my chin, cheeks, and nose in a circular motion. I had laser surgery for my Rosacea only three days before, making my cheeks bulge and my appearance distorted. I was all bruised and had vivid Scarlet splotches, and the faded freckles directly to the corner of my eye were temporarily darkened and enlarged, some of the specks resembling moles instead of adorable tiny cinnamon flecks. I was dashing around the bathroom like a lunatic, preoccupied by the objective of being punctual to work at least one day when I looked up and saw Carl looking as if he was permanently rooted in the doorway of the washroom. He was staring me down like a barbarous cannibal who just sniffed raw bloodstained meat.

"Can I help you?" I harshly asked.

"You know, if you don't keep giving me bootie like you did last night, then I'll have to get it somewhere else."

"How can you even say that? I would never say that to you no matter how angry I was at you."

"Well, I mean it doesn't even seem like you like me anymore. You are twenty-eight years old. You are supposed to be in your prime!"

"Carl! It was one night. I was tired. I can't help it when I fall asleep. The concept that you would even think about cheating on me because I didn't have sex with you last night is sick. Just go do some little hoar you find in a bar asshole!" I hysterically squealed, hurling the door in his face. Carl propelled the door open with all the propulsion he could muster and pressed his face against mine. Our noses rubbed against each other as he harshly hollered in my face.

"Don't you ever disrespect me by talking to me like that. Do you understand?"

A mist of salivation spewed out onto my face as he reprimanded me.

He regained composure of himself gradually backing into the hallway.

"I don't even know why I get all crazy over you. Look at you. You're not even pretty. You are ugly, and you have a mullet!"

He lifted a lively porcelain vase off of the living room coffee table. It was dotted with adorable little red and black ladybugs, my favorite insect, that my daughter gave me as a gift for Mothers Day. He hurled it at the wall, my most beloved possession shattering into millions of shards. I began to snivel like a spoiled infant who craved to suckle at her mother's breast. I turned around to catch a reflection of myself in the polished metal surface which stood over the sink. He was absolutely correct. I was a monstrous eyesore. How could I of ever even thought that I was attractive? My face looked misshapen, an odd-looking rendition of its traditional self'. I resembled a rotten flawed potato with its distorted shape, gashes, and thistly spuds. But unlike a potato, I could not pare away at the outer rind to unveil a refreshed sleek finish. My unlit pellet sized eyes were a drab shade of brown. It seemed as if someone mixed together a batch of brownie batter and spooned out two heap fulls and tossed them into my eye sockets. My hair stuck out in directions, short little uneven strands sticking straight up as if I was Alfalfa. It did look like a mullet. I might as well of been on an episode of "Cops" in the back yard of my trailer with my wife beater shirt, mullet, and cigarette in one hand and beer in the other. Despite the self mutilation I imposed upon myself, I somehow succeeded to halt my whimpering and conjure up the motivation and strength to jog. I trotted out of the door at a steady pace feeling the cool invigorating air renew my former state of tranquility until I caught a glimmer of Carl standing in front of his driver's side door, his arms folded.

"Hey aren't you even going to say goodbye?" he asked.
There was no possible way that I could acknowledge his presence after all of the cold-blooded insults he flailed at me. I whisked right past him snobbishly twisting my head and not uttering an acknowledgment.

"Fine, bitch! I'll be gone by the time you get back!"

His impending threats pricked at my heart hatching severe puncture wounds. His desperate cries to regain dominance diminished in intensity though as his figure dwindled into the distance. At last I felt liberated! I could not stomach the mistreatment any longer, but he had not admitted defeat yet. His 1987 Honda aggressively screeched into the parking lot I was running by. He hurled out of the car like an uncultivated barbarian and marched over to me in a frenzy. I giggled nervously as I do whenever I encounter tension which enraged him even more. He was holding a blistering hot cup of coffee from the gas station across the street.

"You are going to talk to me bitch." He hollered getting right in my face.

"I have nothing to say to you. I want you out of my house tonight! As soon as I get back I want you gone." I hollered trotting in reverse.

"I'm not going anywhere." He charged towards me. "You make my blood boil. God, I can't stand you." He screamed heaving his coffee cup into the breezy spring air.

I flinched back, assuming he was going to toss the coffee at me. The coffee splattered, several blistering sprinkles splashing off of my cheek, but most of the sizzling hot cup of liquid dribbled down the sidewalk

"Yes you are leaving tonight. What part of this don't you understand. It's over! You have never been so mean to me, not ever. I can't take that kind of treatment, Carl. I'm not some dog or one of your white trash bitches that you fucked. I don't deserve it. I'm serious. You better be out of my house by the time I get back, or I'll call the cops this time. I mean it!"

I turned around and continued to dash down the street congested with traffic.

"Come back here bitch!"

I could not turn back. He had persecuted me for something so trivial, and made me feel as if I was nothing. No matter how little I thought of myself there was no way I would continue on this sequence of cruelty, but he still wouldn't let it die. He swerved his car into the parking lot in front of Woody's, a billow of smoky exhaust sputtering out of the tail pipe.

"Come here and talk to me." He ordered in a gentler tone.

"I can't Carl. God, just let it die. You fucked up! Maybe you should have learned hew to treat me better while you had the chance. Remember when we first went out. You said how bad you treated Shannon, because you didn't like her. You were so nice to me, but now it seems like you treat me now the same way you treated Shannon then. It scares me. I think that you loved her just like you loved me, and now the same thing is happening again. You can't treat me like that Carl."

"I know baby. I just get in my bad moods in the morning. You know that. You just have to ignore me. I'll get out of it. See that cop car over there. He's been watching us the whole time. Now come over here and give me a kiss and act like everything is alright, or he'll bust me and take me to jail."

"I can't do that. I hate you right now."

"Come on baby. Just kiss me and then we'll talk about it tonight."

He lightly grasped my wrist and pulled me towards him, planting a moist squishy kiss upon my lips. I felt as if I was being orally raped, forced to conceal the truth for the benefit of another. I loved him so much, but at the same time his behavior repulsed me.

"I'll talk to you tonight baby girl." he said blowing me a kiss.

"Yey, I'll talk to you tonight."

His tires squealed, creating a hazy puff of smoke as he drove away. I felt so immobilized, but I had to run. I did not want to, but somehow my long strides carried me down the road. As the bottom of my front foot made contact with the beginning of the next block, the police car pulled up behind me.

I realized that I had to stop even though I wanted more than anything to escape. I peered into the car and observed that the cop appeared kind and gentle.

"Are you alright?" the police officer asked in a concerned manner.

"Yey, I'm alright."

"Are you sure?"

"Yey, I'm sure." I continued to persist, sniffling and patting away at the teardrops that would not cease.

My insistence that everything was peaches and cream was not very persuasive, due to the perpetual stream of dampness that dribbled down my cheek.

"I'm just asking, because we got some calls. If you ever need anything we are right across the street."

"Thank you." I gratefully replied knowing inside that I would never call them for help.

CHAPTER 35

"So, do you want to do it?" Carl asked as his fingertips gingerly stroked the center of my back.

I could feel myself drifting in and out of consciousness as I accidentally nodded off.

"Tuesday! What the hell are you going to sleep for? Your boyfriend needs some lovin'!" He hollered, rousing me from my peaceful slumber.

"Huh?" I confusingly questioned. "Carl, please I am so tired. My sex drive is like nonexistent at this moment.

"Fine, good night." he unfeelingly replied as he turned over clutching a hold of the floral olive comforter and creating a barrier between him and myself.

At the moment I was too exhausted to be perturbed concerning his outburst. Usually I craved his warm embrace at nighttime, but any sparkle that I formerly possessed was lacking. He contrived an artificial detachment that was excessive, but he didn't see it in this way. He interpreted my rejection of his advances as an insult to his pride instead of construing my refusal in the light of reality that I was just plain fatigued. I reached over to cuddle with him as I always did, but his frosty skin sent shivers down my spine causing me to pull away. My eyes began to shut and I could feel myself retreating into a dream world full of harmony. I decided to cherish this serene moment for I knew as soon as I awoke in the morning the bickering would begin, but my dreams were not sweetened with a syrupy flavor that night.

In my dream I dreamed of a most eerie and grotesque creature not familiar with the concept of restrainment. This creature of course was no other than myself. In this dream I circled my dining room cackling like a demon. My body was contorted into an odd pretzel shape and I was hunched over resembling the character, Quasi Moto from the childrens' fairy tale. I terrified everyone circled around me, including my sister, Sarah, and my daughter, Madeline. I had no control over my behavior, and the image of my sister and daughter shivering with terror did not impede me in any way. There was a spark of recognition that gushed through my brain cells causing me to realize that my madness was an oddity compared to the sanity which encompassed me, but nothing could be done. I was a freak of nature infected by an outside force which permeated my brain.

Suddenly, the focus of my dream changes into a sexual tone, and I am overcome with an urge to gratify myself. I wildly wave my hands in the air signaling my audience that it is time to watch, taking special attention to my sister. I sit in the center of the room, my legs straddled, completely naked, while I fondle my breasts and finger myself to orgasm. Somehow my uncontrollable urge to relieve myself by reaching climax symbolized the unrest in me and the only way to pacify my pangs of madness was to do something insane. In my dream I am very much disgusted with myself, especially the last portion where I masturbate to full climax in front of my sister. Sarah was disillusioned with what I had done. She was so mortified to be related to such a peculiar troll as myself. I am interrupted with a glimmer of reality causing me to shudder in complete repulsion at the incestuous overtones which inhabit my vision. Suddenly I am hooting and hollering, running around in circles pecking like a rooster while the others distance themselves in revulsion until I collapse. I lay upon the cold cement ground dead to the world detached from all prior illogical notions. From my death I am able to scrounge up an inner peace within myself. There is nothing to terminate the turmoil which swims within me except for eternal and blissful sleep. Never would I have imagined that a surrounding cloud of blackness could saturate me with such tranquility.

Surprisingly, I woke up in a cheerful mood despite the nightmarish imagery which gushed through the tributary of my mind the evening before. I turned over and gazed indulgently at my sweet love. His face looked so beautiful, so sculpted, so perfected. His cheekbones were placed so perfect, so proportional. He was American Indian with his thick black hair and tan skin tinged with a crimson tint, the color similar to the smoldering rays reflected from a sunset. I could have stroked and touched him forever. I removed my shirt and pants and pressed my naked body against his. We hugged and I could feel the warmth, the safety, and all was right again with the world until his eyes flew open and he lapsed into a conscious state. He coldly turned over tugging the blanket away from me, leaving me shivering, cold, and exposed.

"Carl, why are you acting so funny. It seems like you are being cold again." I said, snuggling up against his muscular back and arms, saturating his shoulder with warm, moist kisses.

"Honestly, how do you expect me to act, Tuesday? Your sex drive is nonexistent! How do you think that makes me feel? I bet you didn't say that when you fucked Mike like that? What about when you had two dicks stuck up inside you. I bet you didn't say that then? Did you?"

The salty crescent shaped tears began to roll down my cheeks as I pleaded with him to stop. "Carl, why do you have to bring that up? You know I didn't love Mike, and I didn't even like the threesome. Please, don't you know that I love you. Doesn't that mean anything. I was just tired, Carl. You don't understand how tired I get, Here, let me make it up to you."

I reached in between the slit of his boxers and pulled out his penis rhythmically stroking his shaft until I could detect moans of contentment slither out from the crack of his lips.

"See how much I love you and am attracted to you." I cooed in an almost sickeningly sugary voice. I sweetly kissed each perfectly chiseled cheek of his and gently stroked them, sticking my forefingers in between his lips so he could greedily slurp at my fingertips. His hands began to paw at my breasts, his moistened fingertips tweaking my stiff camel colored nipples. His tongue hungrily lapped at my nipples, his tongue flicking in and out of his mouth like a snake, Passionately, he pulled me on top of his tan strapping bare body and thrust his stiff manhood between my legs. We both moaned in ecstasy as our sweaty skin dripping with perspiration slapped against each other. He mounted me on top of him so I sat perfectly upright.

"I want you to ride me baby" He breathlessly requested.

Obediently, I complied as he wished and rocked back and forth like a stallion arching my back and seductively sticking out my breasts, silently inviting him to nibble on my delicate rigid nipples. We both moaned cries of rapture, our intimate spots tingling until an overwhelming wave ruptured throughout our insides, and we climaxed in perfect unison. We lay there naked and panting awestruck from how amazing the sex was, kissing and slobbering over each other like two wild untamed animals. We nuzzled against each other, my fingertips slithering over the hairy patch of his chest. I loved him so much, and no matter how hard he attempted to deny our attraction, I knew that I could always win.

I laid on top of him in perfect silence, our sticky wet bodies sodden with sweat. I looked down at his beautiful face admiring his beauty. He looked like an ancient clay sculpture, baked in an oven with his deep red tan and glazed shell due to his clammy skin caked with perspiration. He was disturbingly twitching his right eye looking so wounded and vulnerable. I had never pitied him more than at that exact moment.

"What are you thinking about?" I asked encircling my arms around his chest and embracing him tightly to chase away any wicked demons that were infecting his mind.

"Something bad."

"Nothing can be that bad. Believe me. I do not judge anyone. Nothing will shock me."

"I can't tell you. If I do, you'll think I'm crazy."

"Carl, just tell me. You are beginning to make me curious."

He deeply inhaled hesitant to reveal his thought to me. "Alright, I was thinking about killing you."

My heart plummeted far beneath my chest in result to his confession. I was quite uncomfortable laying on top of Carl, but I gulped in fear, too petrified to reposition myself.

"Carl, you don't mean that. Don't say something like that."

"If I can't have you, then nobody else can. Just remember that." He reminded me, cooly pushing my body off of his. He rose up from off the bed, coughing and stumbling to the bathroom as I watched his behind wiggle as he walked. When he walked out of the bathroom he was ready to argue again.

"You know, you and Mike belong together. You had two kids with the man. You guys need to get married or something, for real!" Carl ranted, his pitch becoming more shrill and elevated as he continued. "Do you know what I see when we fuck? Do you?" Carl asked as he snatched me by the wrist, wringing it like a sopping wet washcloth that needs to have all of the moisture squeezed out of it.

"No, no. I don't. Please, stop. You're hurting me. I didn't do anything. You can't take it personally, you can't[["

"What do you mean I can't take it personally! When I see you and Mike and that other guy all taking their turn with you, you can't tell me that I can't take it personally. You had to have liked it. You had to. There is something you are not telling me. You are a liar like all of the others. You damn women have hurt me my entire life."

"Don't put me in the same category as those other girls. I never hurt you. I might get mad at you, but that's it. I have always helped you."

"You have used me like all those other bitches out there. You are not special honey, by no means."

"How have I used you? If anything you have used me."

"You know you really do need to go back to Mikie. He spoiled you so bad. You want a little bitch who will do everything for you. Well, I'm not the answer to your problems. You can't be a lazy bitch around me, you can't. I already had one of those. I can't have another one!"

"Carl, why do you do that? Why do you always bring her up? I am not Shannon! I am not Brandy] I am net whomever else you fucked. I'm not trash. Get that through your head. I have helped you so much!"

"Why do you always throw that in my face. That's the Jew in you. You think that if you do something for somebody you can hold it over their head for their entire life. Well, sorry honey. You were the sucker. You can't blame it on me."

"Get out of my house! I don't want you here!" I shouted, lunging at him full force.

Carl, enraged at my attempt to defend my honor and my territory hurled me onto the bed, twisting my body into a contorted pretzel shape. He threw his body onto mine, pinning me down so I could not rise. I felt so frail and vulnerable, but I could not let him know that. I defiantly glared up at him, my eyes shining with an air of arrogance that he had never seen before.

"You think you can try to fight me, huh? You can't fight me no matter how hard you try. You think your pussy is laced with gold, don't you? Do you think that your pussy is the best out there? I'm a good looking guy. I can find better than yours! I can at least find one that doesn't hang down to your knees. You loose bitch! I bet I could stick my fist up there!"

Carl tore at my belt buckle, unfastening my zipper and sadistically pulling my jeans off. He then tugged at my underwear, tugging at them until they slashed into my privates. My privates were exposed. He then ripped my shirt open, the copper colored buttons springing off of the wall and making a clinking sound as they bounced off of the floor. I howled in horror not able to vocalize my desire for him to stop in words, only grunts. He then wedged his tongue into my mouth, viciously thrashing it around, his teeth tearing into my tongue.

"How does it feel to almost get raped, huh?"

I could not cry out loud or howl or express the terror that brewed within me. I just laid perfectly still and mute, too petrified to move an inch.

"Why do you do that? Why do you make me turn into a crazy animal? I don't know what you do to me, but the thought of losing you makes me go insane."

"But, I didn't do anything to you to make you think that you were losing me."

"You didn't want to have sex with me. You pushed me away. All of you women push me away. What is it about Carl? Why does everyone leave Carl?" He said referring to himself in third person again. His eyes began to water giving his eyes a glassy appearance. He sat down on the edge of the bed and placed his head into his lap and his hands over his head.

"I'm not going to leave you. You know that. I love you. I would never hurt you." I soothingly said, my body cautiously creeping closer to his. I laid my head down upon his shoulder, but he shrugged it off as if I was contaminated.

"I can't do this. I can't. The fighting is getting to be much. You are driving me mad. Can't you tell?"

"I didn't do anything though. You take things too personally. I don't treat you that bad. I'm sorry. I have a fucked up mind, but so do you. You are just as nutty as I am. We can work on it. There is nothing that we have done to each other that is so terrible. We can overcome it. We can."

"You just don't know, do you?"

"I just don't know what?"

"Never mind, Tuesday, never mind."

"What is that suppose to mean? Is there something that you should tell me?"

"No. Don't worry about it." Carl meekly replied avoiding eye contact.

"You are starting to make me curious. You need to tell me what you did. You are starting to worry me."

"You just don't know when to let it rest, do you? I said let it go. You need to listen to me."

"All right. That is fine, Carl. If you do not want to tell me, then I'm going to go."

"Where are you going"

"Why do you care? You probably cheated on me or went to a strip club. I knew that you were bad."

I knew it." *I began* to scream, my voice curdling and elevating in pitch as I became more irate."

"What if I did? You don't care about me anyway. All you bitches are the same. You are all nasty. You use what's between your legs to control men, and we let you do it. Well, you are not going to do it to me. You are not!"

He charged towards the closet tossing his clothes to the floor until they made a massive pile in the center of the bedroom floor.

"That's it Carl. Run away from your problems. Pack your basket and run away. Go back to your mommy and daddy where you belong! How can you even call yourself a grownup? You are still a little kid. You think you can make it on your own. You think that without me life will be good. Well, it won't. You know you'll miss me."

"Life will be sweet. No one nagging me. No one telling me what to do. No annoying kids bugging the hell out of me. I just want to leave this state. Pack up and leave this state and never turn back. Then I'll never have to see you, my friends, my family, my kid, that fat bitch. Hell, I don't even care if I live in my car. Just to get away from your bitchy ass."

He tossed his clothes into his laundry basket, ripping the hangers off and thrashing them against the wall.

"I'm going. When you decide to grow up, then maybe we'll talk sensibly!"

I slipped on my sneakers and picked up my car keys off of the table, scampering out of the door like a mad woman, slamming the front door behind me. I could hear the front door creek open as I speedily bounded up the stairs.

"Tuesday, Come back here. You better come back if you know what's good for you!"

I couldn't go back. I didn't deserve to be with someone who didn't appreciate me no matter how desperately I yearned to be with him. I could hear the echoing thumps of his footsteps stride up the stairwell which made me sprint that much more quickly. The front door flew open making *a* swishing sound.

"Tuesday, Come back here. I want to talk to you."

"No, I have to go."

"That's alright. I already fucked some bitch anyway."

I stopped dead in my tracks. His confession pricked at my heart like no sensation I ever had felt before.

"It sounded like he said that he fucked some bitch, but he couldn't have said that. *"No, he didn't, he didn't, he didn't"* I recited to myself repeatedly attempting to reassure myself that my whole world was not about to crumble at my very feet. I slowly spun my head around and noticed that Carl was no longer standing there. I unhurriedly marched towards the door and opened it only to find him standing directly behind it.

"What did you just say?" I breathlessly questioned, my heart deafeningly thumping in my chest.

"I said that I already fucked some bitch."

"No, you didn't. You are bluffing again. Please say you didn't do that. Please!"

"Sorry, I did. You didn't think I could get anybody, did you? Well, I did."

"Why? I would never do that to you? I was always loyal to you. So, I'm a little fucked up in the head, but I would never hurt you like that. Who was it? Who did you cheat on me with?"

"Why does it matter Tuesday? Why do you care?"

"I knew it! You are bluffing! If you actually fucked someone else, you could've at least told me her name."

"It was some stripper at a strip club, alright"

"A stripper?" I questioned, my throat beginning to form a lump and tightening up at the very thought of my boyfriend having sex with the one symbol which I truly despised.

"Now I know that you are lying. Please, say you are lying.

Please. If you are trying to hurt me, it's working. You can stop now. I know you wouldn't do that to me. I know it. You don't even go to those places anymore." I wailed, tears streaming down my cheeks.

"You don't even know me. Ask my friends. Ask my boss, James. Ask anyone. We go there all of the time. We go to them all. PT's, Diamond Cabaret, Dreamgirls, Ms. Kitty's, the Jewelbox. When you thought I was working or seeing my friends, I wasn't. You were the sucker, not me."

"Carl, why? You said that you didn't like those places. Why did you lie? Why? Why? Why" I collapsed to the floor curling up into a spherical shape to shield me from the daggers that were gouging out my insides. A door squeaked open and a neighbor poked her head between the frame and the door.

"Is everything alright out there?" the neighbor asked in a concerned matter.

"It's fine maam. Just having a little lovers spat. You know how those are."

The woman nervously smirked and quickly shut the door behind her.

"Tuesday, get up. You are starting to make a scene. They are going to call the cops if you don't quit it. Come on, at least come downstairs in the house where we are able to talk about this sensibly."

"Sensibly? Sensibly? My tears of sorrow began to transform into tears of laughter as I illogically cackled. "Can you please reveal to me what is sensible about going into strip bars every day, especially while you have a completely faithful girlfriend at home, and fucking a stripper god knows where with god knows what. You could have AIDS Carl. You probably gave me AIDS. What is it that they have that I don't? Huh? Tell me that. I want to know, because it feels like I have been competing with strippers since the beginning of this relationship. Is it their big fake boobs bouncing around, their sexy dancing, their high shiny heels, their smooth flat stomachs, their round tight asses, their shaved pussies? What?" I irrationally screamed, beginning to become hysterical.

"Baby, they don't have anything that you don't. I swear." He attempted to appease my anxieties by flattering me. "You are what is hot, not them. I only went there, because it was a bar."

"Then how do you justify fucking one of them, Carl? Is that what happens at a bar? Things get so out of control that you have to have sex there? Couldn't you have had sex somewhere else besides a strip club with someone else? Why did you have to hurt me like this?"

"I didn't mean to, baby. I was drunk. I swear that I don't like that stuff. My friends from work. They just don't go anywhere normal, and my boss will fuck with me too bad if I don't go with him and the guys after work. They'll call me a faggot and stuff. I can't afford to lose my job. Things just got out of control. I hardly even remember. I didn't even like the bitch. She didn't turn me on like you."

"Turn you on like me. So, she turned you on a little huh? Explain how you had sex with her. Did you like it like when you have sex with me? Did you get off Carl? Did you get off with her like you get off with me?"

Carl stood there in silence looking pitiful and very remorseful with his head turned downward.

"Carl, I am talking to you! Answer me before I fucking go crazy. Answer me! I smacked at his forehead with full force causing him to trip over his own feet and tumble to the floor.

Carl slowly raised his head up squinting his eyes as if he was fearful that I was going to strike at him again. I found it odd that this man who always made me feel meek and defenseless was turning the tables and acting like he was the abused battered victim. It was so ironic that this coward who confessed that he cheated on me expected me to have sympathy for him. Carl placed his head upon his knees and frantically scratched at his scalp covered with thick black hair. His muffled cries of remorse echoed throughout the hallway, prompting me to console him. I squatted down next to him and on impulse I attempted to comfort him. I ran my fingers through his glossy dark strands and placed my arms around his broad muscular shoulders, fondly embracing him.

"I never meant to hurt you." He murmured quietly. "1 just love you so much, and I am so scared of losing you."

"Then why did you have to tell me?" Why didn't you just hide it from me like any normal guy would do? I need to know why you volunteered this information so freely without putting up a struggle."

Carl uncomfortably shrugged his shoulders slightly. "I don't know. You know I can't tell a lie. I always tell on myself. It was eating away at me Tuesday. Every time I made love to you I felt terrible."

"Gee thanks. Don't forget to remove that foot from your mouth."

"No, I didn't mean it that way. I love making love to you, but I have a big conscience, and I have felt like such a piece of shit since I did that whore. I guess I figured that you would find out sooner or later from someone else, and I didn't want that to happen. I wanted everything to be out in the open. I have a big heart, you know."

"If you had a big heart you wouldn't have hurt me like that Carl. All I ever did was love you. Yey, sometimes I get crazy, but I am only human. Whatever I have done to you, it doesn't possibly even come close to matching this. I don't deserve this. This is torture. You know that I already thought about you looking at strippers, but at least before I could console myself by realizing it was the past. It's no longer the past. Imagining you looking at these women who have no respect for themselves kills me Carl."

"But, I didn't look at them that way baby girl." He patted my shoulder, but I flung his hand away swiftly.

"Don't even try to make me feel better. You are not the one to make me feel better. You are the one who did this to me. You had sex with these girls that I despise more that anyone or anything.

"I feel like I have been going out with a stranger for over a year now. I wasted an entire year of my life with your scummy ass. I know I had my doubts, but I thought I was creating them with my *"crazy"* mind. I basically thought I had a nice guy. Why couldn't you have just been honest with me?"

My former sense of calm rapidly deteriorated and I crumpled to the floor weeping a tear soaked trail of betrayal. I never quite envisioned that he would do this to me, but it was happening.

"Don't cry baby. I am so sorry. Please, I want you know that it never meant anything to me. I was drunk and can barely remember it."

"Bullshit, Carl. I know you are lying now. You never black out when you are drunk."

"You don't know how drunk I got. Eight Yeigermeister shots in a row. That can fuck you up. You are what I think about every single second of the day. You are what I think about from the time I wake up until the time I go to bed. I can't get you out of my mind, and you know that Tuesday!"

"If that was the case, then you wouldn't need to go to those places Carl."

"You don't understand. The guys would've thought I was a puss. I told them that I didn't want to go, but they made me."

"How do they make you, Carl? You are your own person. No one can make you do anything you don't want to do, especially you! My naked body should be enough to keep you happy. You don't see me running to *Boxers and Briefs*, that male strip club, every day after work, do you? I don't need to do that, because I love you, and even if I didn't know you, I still wouldn't need to do that. I guess men are just more visual that women though. Women are attracted to the mind while guys like tits and ass."

"Baby, you know those places were just ordinary bars to me. A naked woman could stand right in front of me, and it wouldn't even turn me on. I have to love the woman. Your body turns me on more that anything, because I love you. I practically walk around with a woody all day thinking about you. Now those bitches could never do that for me." Somehow his sincere attempt to apologize did not rekindle the soothing response from me that I showered upon him beforehand.

"Carl!" I hysterically interrupted him. "Do you hear yourself? Do you hear what you are saying? You are totally contradicting yourself here. First of all, you told me that you didn't like those places and didn't need to go those places. I thought you didn't go there anymore. What a fool I am. Looking at naked women is a stab in the back, but fucking them. That is low Carl. How could you even think about fucking that trash when you have a good girl at home? Your guilt trip is not going to work this time, Carl. We are not going to grieve about this together. I am the victim here, not you. At ordinary bars you don't fuck the employees. It's not a regular bar. I need you to leave. I want you to pack up your stuff and get the fuck out of here."

"Baby, don't do that. Don't throw away a year of your life over something so stupid."

"I'm glad that you think it is stupid. Of course you think it is stupid. Silly me. My fiance' is a big pervert everybody." I began to raise my voice. "He might as well be a peeping tom, but wait a minute. He's not, because somehow in society today, you can walk into a bar and look at naked women with their consent and it's totally acceptable. How stupid of me. My boyfriend stuck his dick into a stripper, or she might as well have been a prostitute because she probably accepted money for it. How long ago did you have sex with this woman, Carl?"

"Come on, you don't need to know that. Why do you want to hurt yourself more?"

"Tell me. I need to know. When and who?"

"Why, are you going to try to kick her ass or something?" Carl snickered callously.

"No dumbass. That is the least you could do for how badly you have hurt me. Answer my question, when and with who?"

"You don't know her anyway Tuesday."

"If you don't tell me, I swear Carl, I'll take your picture with me, go up there by myself and ask every stripper in there if they've fucked you."

"You're talking crazy. What is the point of that? It's not going to settle anything."

"No, it's not, but I'll feel a whole lot better when I shoot that bitch in the head!"

"You know, Tuesday. You are not even making sense."

"Why are you defending her? Why do you care if I kill her? Do you have feelings for her or something?

"No, of course not, but you are a good girl. Why would you want to screw up your life over me? I'm not worth it Tuesday. No guy is."

"You are right. Carl, I can't do this. You are making me into a crazy woman. It was hard enough being with you before, but I thought that there would be a light somewhere at the end of the tunnel."

I knew that if I forgave Carl and decided to remain with him that there would never be light at the end of the tunnel. There would only be darkness. If I stayed with him I would be blind to the light. Morning would exist as night. The afternoon would exist as night. The evening would exist as night. I would mistake golden sweltering sun rays for cool white glimmering moon beams. Images raced through my mind of what I would be like if I remained with Carl. I could visualize myself as an older woman, my face weathered and crinkled, crow's feet shadowing the corners of my eyes, my formerly supple pink lips lined with creases, shrunken, and faded to an abrasive peach shade. My thick flaxen mane painted with shimmering golden highlights would have changed into a frizzy drab heap of fluff splashed with specks of wiry gray strands. Most importantly though would be the soulless reflection emitted fourth from my eyes. The cheery emerald flecks surrounding my pupils that once flickered so merrily would vanish to leave bleak black cavities filled with a wintry mix of sludge. The bubbly liquid which used to course through my veins would have solidified making any movement of mine exaggeratedly sluggish. I was not proud of who I was about to become if I spent my entire life with Carl. Our union would have to cease soon or my fountain of youth was sure to dry out shortly.

"The only way that I will ever see the light is to end it. I cannot happily be with you knowing what you have done with me."

"At least you know. At least I didn't lie. I could have lied like all of the other guys, but I didn't. What do I get for telling the truth? I guess shit."

I stared at this man before me in disbelief. "Carl, how admirable of you to admit that you slept with a stripper in a strip bar of all places. You are such a great guy! Don't you see. It could never possibly work now. You have violated our code of trust. We agreed not to cheat on each other. You made the promise to me, first of all that you would never enter a strip bar again, and second of all that you would never cheat on me. I'm sorry, but there are no second chances when it comes to cheating. What if I would have slept with someone? How tolerant would you have been?"

"I would have killed the cocksucker and then probably kill you next."

"How could you even say that when you so plainly did the same exact thing to me. That's sort of a double standard, isn't it?"

I proceeded down the narrow stairwell, bewildered, my mind ensnarled with painful images churning incessantly.

"What was I even thinking by hugging and comforting you? You don't deserve a hug. I should cut your dick off for what you did to me. You really have to go before I do something I might regret."

I opened the front door and retreated to the bathroom. I could hear him scuttle directly behind me, the clomping of his heavy work boots echoing. Shutting the door behind me, I leaned against it taking a deep breath. All I wanted to do was drift away to an idyllic castle in the sky and leap from cloud to cloud never to plummet back to earth. My hands reached into the medicine cabinet scouring for the Tylenol P.M. I unscrewed the cap, pouring a dozen of the oval turquoise pills into the palm of my hand. I popped pill after pill into my mouth, gulping down a mouthful of water from a small plastic medicine cup and swallowing each pill. I laid the back of my head against the shower stall and began to feel the effects of the medicine take effect putting me into a tranquilized state.

"Tuesday! Tuesday!" Carl rapped at the door disrupting my session of relaxation. "Open the door. We need to talk about this."

"There's nothing to talk about. Please, go. You've already

done enough damage. Please, you need to go." I began to mumble, my speech becoming slurred due to the Tylenol P.M.

"Tuesday, I can't go to mom's and dad's. The trailer park won't let me live there. No one is supposed to live there besides them."

His desperate attempt to have me spun around his fingertip was wearing thin. I was not going to be manipulated any longer by him. He had to be delirious to expect me to bear any kind of tolerance towards his behavior.

"Poor baby." I hollered back to him. "That's not my concern, is it? I don't give a fuck if you sleep in your car or out on the street. After what you did to me, I cannot care about you as a human being, because you are not human to me anymore. You are a pig, and I am so disgusted to even look at you let alone share the rest of my life with you. You fucked up Carl. Maybe it felt good at the time, but you fucked up with the one girl who really loved and cared about you. I hope it was worth it. Maybe you should go back to your little strip club and be her boyfriend, because you are single once again."

I staggered to the door struggling to turn the shiny silver doorknob, finally opening it and incoherently garbling gibberish that neither of us could understand.

...."Whaaaaa... Wha do you want youuuu per, per, prevert?"

"You know, you are never going to find anyone else as good to you as I was Tuesday. No one would be desperate enough to put up with your shit and your obnoxious kids. For one thing you are crazy, for another you need to learn how to clean yourself properly, your breath stinks, you look like a clown with your makeup on, you don't know how to fuck. Nope, you are nothing special, for sure."

"Carl, it's not my number one goal in my life to find a man. Before you I had no one. I did it all by myself. I can do it again all by myself. You're not as big a catch as you think anyway. Now if you don't mind I'm going to lay down.

You need to be gone by the time I wake up." I coolly commanded trying to relay to him the impression that I was a stony hearted female not concerned with his insults or predicament in the least bit.

I staggered into the bedroom, content that the Tylenol was muting the painfully tender images that Carl placed into my head. The exhaustion that I felt was so pleasurable. The only image that I envisioned was my head hitting the silky-smooth feathery pillow and drifting into an eternal slumber. I never wanted to awaken from the self-inflicted state of unconsciousness that I was about to lapse into. I was two feet away from my inviting sanctuary, my bed. I dived head first into my pool of paradise only to feel him violently tug at the back of my hair. My head jerked back making my neck feel like it was going to snap into two pieces. He dragged me by clutching onto the ends of my glossy sun-drenched mane, hurling me onto the startlingly cold tile of the bathroom floor. I attempted to get back on my feet preoccupied only with the thought of returning to my warm cozy bed, but I couldn't even stand upright. I resembled a newborn pony frosted with a creamy slime substance from its mother struggling to stand upon its hooves, but instead wobbling upon its long scrawny legs. I began to crawl towards the bedroom, my knees chilled from the freezing tile beneath me, but again a rude interruption spoiled the prospect of my ever entering into a dreamlike trance.

"Carl, pllleasssse ..... I juuust want to go to beeed." I incoherently mumbled.

"Fuck you bitch!" he hollered shrilly shocking me out of my zombie like daze. "You are not going anywhere. Nobody talks to me like that. Do you understand me? No one, not even you, is going to make Carl feel like an idiot. You have no say in the matter whether I live here or not. If I leave it is my decision, not yours!"

I looked up at him, wide eyed, my eyeballs almost popping out of their sockets.

"God, I just want to kill you right now. I want to smash your head against that wall and crack it right open you worthless little slut."

"Carl, why are you so mad at me? You are the one that cheated on me. You hurt me. Can't you understand that it is too painful to have you around after you would do something like that to me? I'm not doing it to be a bitch. I just love you so much, and the thought of you hurting me like that kills me. I am the one who really cares about you. If I was like all of the other girls I wouldn't give a shit less about what you do to me."

A succession of crystal clear droplets spilled fourth from the corners of my eyes staining my cheeks with a damp trail of liquid. My cheeks glistened due to the remainder of teardrops that randomly affixed themselves in their place.

"You know Tuesday. You are the most selfish person I have ever met and a liar to top it off. It is not about how I have hurt you. It is about your right to exercise total control over me. Your ego is hurt, that's all. I will be so glad to be rid of you. I don't know what I was even thinking by wanting to marry you. What a joke."

"Carl, am I going to have to continue to listen to you put me down. If you want to hurt me, just hurt me already. If you want to kill me, just kill me, Just please put me out of my misery. At this point, I do not care what you do. I am no longer scared of what you are capable of."

"Kill you? I wouldn't waste my time on killing your ass. Why go to jail over some stupid girl? Why should I kill you when I can spend the rest of my life making your life hell. Death is too easy an option. I want to make you suffer."

"You are talking crazy again. You have no reason to make my life hell. You hurt me. Remember?"

"No, Tuesday. You hurt me just like all of the others have hurt me."

He grabbed a hold of my shirt collar viciously yanking at it and forcing me to stand upright. He thrust me forward into the mirror head first smearing my face against the cool silver plated reflective glass.

"I want you to take a good look at yourself. You look at yourself and tell me whether you are worthy of my love for you. You think I'm some kind of desperate loser, don't you. DON'T YOU?" he piercingly shouted repeatedly tugging at my head.

I yearned so badly to beg for him to stop, but I was paralyzed with fear. I knew that the safest bet was to keep quiet. I did not want to do anything more to enrage him. My mouth was smashed against the mirror causing it to resemble a pair of goldfish lips puffed out of proportion. I literally felt like a goldfish pressing its face against a fishbowl and craving a life void of water, fins, fish food and swimming. How badly I wished to be free at that moment. The red veins lining the inner surface of my lips were engorged giving my mouth a blood stained appearance. He finally pulled my head back gifting me with a moment to rise up from underneath the water and take in a fresh breath. I stared upward at the drab pasty popcorn ceiling. Never before had I taken the time to notice how dreadfully obnoxious popcorn ceilings were. It looked as if someone stood beneath the ceiling immediately after they painted and tossed up a bowl full of popcorn, one kernel at a time. Soon after my significant reflection on popcorn ceilings did I notice enormous brown flakes resembling wood chips slowly descending towards me. They were speckled with cherry red and grassy green flecks and were tumbling in from the cracks of the ceiling.

"Look, Carl. Fish food. Fish food is falling." I hazily mumbled enraging him even more.

"What the hell are you talking about. Fish food. You have gone insane. Are you going to listen to me, or am I going to have to slap the shit out of you?"

A glimmer of reality washed over me and I realized that I was hallucinating which caused me to retreat back into the real world.

"Tuesday, I want you to get serious now. You are beginning to piss off Carl even more, and at this point that is hard to do. Now, take a look at yourself in that mirror."

My head at that moment felt like a bowling ball. I could not have even lifted it up if I tried. Instead my head just sort of swayed from side to side, drool dribbling fourth from the corners of my lip and trickling down my chin.

"You disgusting little cunt. You're drooling like a damn dog. Can't you control yourself?" "Billlly...I am just sooooo sleepy. Please, let me go to beeeed."

`"I am not letting you go anywhere until you listen to me." He sternly ordered grabbing a washcloth out of the closet and harshly dabbing at the droplets of drool that dangled from my chin.

"Look in the damn mirror girl. I want you to take a good look at yourself."

He again thrust me into the mirror, this time my nose smacking the symbol of physical echoes before me. He forcefully held my head against it, causing me to feel as if I was underwater once again. My fins were uncontrollably flipping and my tail wildly smacked sideways, but I was eerily immobile. More flakes of fish food floated past me, but I could not open my mouth to gobble them up. The frosty floor beneath me began to crumble and transform into colorful rocks of all different shapes and sizes. They were red and blue and green and purple. Some of the stones were shiny, and some were rough. Many of them sparkled. They looked like diamonds, emeralds, opals, garnets, sapphires laying there beneath my feet and illuminating my aquarium with a comforting multihued glow. Bubbles glided beneath me, above me, and on all sides. I wanted to be encapsulated by one of the bubbles and soar up to the surface where I could inhale in a breath of refreshing untainted air. My deep breathing fleetingly stained the mirror with splotches of smoggy nostril and lip marks, but quickly the images dissolved as he jerked my head backwards once again.

"You know. I once thought that I was lucky that you went out with me. Hell, I was surprised that you even looked my way, but the more I get to know you the uglier you become." Carl sneered.

He released me from his firm grasp, and I disintegrated to the floor, a pile of ashes. His belittling remarks whipped away at me like a strong gust of wind scattering the insults throughout the atmosphere. I felt somewhat inebriated from the ingredients in the Tylenol P.M. My mind was submerged far below the waters therefore I was not able to make a clear distinction on whether Carl's remarks were in fact genuine or a figment of my imagination. The overwhelming groggy feeling kept forcing my eyes to shut which seemed to enrage Carl even further. Between my unconscious spells and attentive moments I could catch a glimpse of Carl standing over me, wildly flailing his arms and flapping his mouth. A buzzing sound circulated throughout my ears causing me to suffer hallucinations and swat away at bumblebees. I perceived his barking at me as a faint yelping. His face no longer looked familiar to me, but instead an inflamed twisted caricature of itself. Carl's face remained deeply flushed looking as if someone powdered his face with an entire compact of rouge. A steady stream of sizzling hot steam spurted fourth from within his eardrums making a shrill whistling sound as it whizzed out. Each time I reverted from a dreamlike state into a state of wakefulness, my bleary eyes focused only to see Carl commandingly standing above me, his arms sternly crossed, and his sour expression conveying disappointment.

I could feel my body being pulled beneath the undercurrent, the rolling whitecaps ambushing me as the salty sea water coursed into my lungs. I sputtered the foul flavored liquid, the foamy current finally leading me to the shore where I could relax on the damp sandy soil. I was lounging on the sand, the lush tropical sun basking my face in warmth and toasting the peach freckles across the bridge of my nose into a warm toasted chestnut shade. Suddenly a shadow floated in front of me, obstructing the heavenly rays which baked my skin.

"Tuesday, Tuesday!" Carl screamed kicking me in the round pudgy paunch of my stomach. "You better listen to me you lazy bitch! I take it as an insult when you fall asleep while I am talking."

I rolled up into a tight little ball in order to thwart off any more excruciating blows to my belly, but that only encouraged him more so. I could feel my stomach begin to swell and tighten up in response to the lacerations as his boots slashed at my tender skin. His steel toed work boots kept stomping on my abdomen, the cold tip of his boot digging into my gut. All I could do was pray, secretly beg the lord to make him stop, and finally he did. I looked like a puddle strewn out on the floor. I didn't care that my cheek was pressed against the cold tile or that my stomach was chafed and incredibly sore. I just drifted off, drifted to a pleasant world where no one or nothing could hurt me.

OVER ON THE EAST SIDE

Last night I had a dream, a nightmarish vision that left me most unsettled. I was in a strip club, and there were strippers everywhere. They were standing on stage performing a choreographed dance. They snapped their fingers in unison, swinging from side to side as their fingers clicked together. For some odd reason the girls were wearing bras, but they were not wearing panties. They spun and spun like the ballerina ceaselessly twirling in her trinket box, and I cried and cried as they persisted to perform naughty acts, as they bent over and paraded their genatalia to the room. The audience sat, captivated by their dance, almost hypnotized by the gentle swaying of their bodies as they rocked from side to side. My crying turned into anger, a deep seeded resentment towards the girls and Carl. I reached into my pocket and stumbled upon a wadded up bundle of panties. I began to toss them onto stage, yelling *"Cover up!"* at the top of my lungs, but nobody heard me. The girls ignored my never ending cries, my desperate shrieking not rousing a single soul out of their deeply hypnotic trance.

Why did my worst fears have to haunt me while I sleep? Was it enough that I spent every waking moment of the day envisaging Carl drink in the nakedness of Roxy's? Why couldn't I dream of vibrant rainbows, mythical unicorns, chocolate waterfalls, jellybean trails? I was emotionally drained, tired of the naked girls dancing in my head. I was a prisoner to these places, held captive by my imagination. If only I could wake up one morning and realize that this was all a dream, that Carl never went into Roxy's, that I never saw those girls spread their legs or spank their ass. Then I could go on, but for now I was held hostage by my mind's eye, drowned in a pool of filthy images that I could not wash away.

God I'm so disgusted with this world. How can I embrace this culture and be proud of this world I live in when such atrocities are happening at this very moment, when as a mother I have not been honored by their father or this court system, when as a girlfriend I have been beaten, when as a woman I have been disrespected, when as a person I have been jabbed at repeatedly, enduring blows that I should've never had to put up with in the first place, and who has been responsible for all my grief, standing behind the curtain ready to pull it down at any moment? Men! That's who; those filthy, perverted, sex starved maniacs.

Should I jump for joy, thank the lucky stars for my blessings when men are raping innocent women, murdering little girls, stuffing dollar bills down g-strings, getting a lap dance by some stranger, or crouched over on the toilet jacking off at some airbrushed bimbo spreading her legs in Hustler. Oh yes, let me celebrate. Why don't I pat men on the back for profiting off of women, using motherly attributes such as breasts or curvy hips to entice testosterone driven young men. We think that the battle has been won, that women are now thought of as equal to men in this society. Yes, we can vote, we can work, we can wear pants, but women's rights are sadly an illusion. Do we think that we are actually respected when millions of men are leering at stark naked women, drooling over them like pieces of meat? Those women are our daughters, our sisters, our aunts, our mothers, our girlfriends, our wives. Those women are people, and should be thought of as people, not a slab of prime rib, glazed and juicy, ready to bite into, and no one stops it, especially the people who have the power to stop it. We are a man driven society, brainwashed by airbrushing, unrealistic beauty standards, stereotyping. When are we as women going to take a step forward and express our frustration with how society is being run? Will anyone have the courage to stand up for what they believe in, and will it even make a difference?

OVER ON THE EAST SIDE

CHAPTER 37

I was never taught to love. Therefore I do not know how to love. The only two people I can love are my children. I love them unconditionally. When I wrap my arms around them I can squeeze so tight, take in the aroma of their sweet scented hair, as pleasant as fresh baked ginger snaps. I cuddle these innocent beings, embrace them with all my heart, enfold my arms around them whispering "*I love you.*" I never learned to love a man, a creature poisoned by temptation. How could I love a being so easily entertained by the sight of mere flesh? Their minds are so vacant, easily amused by a meager slap or tickle. Men are tarnished, mottled slabs of flesh weighed down by their imperfections. Every man has hurt me, but what I hate to admit is that it is not all their fault. I was not innocent. Yes, I was a child when the damage began, but I am still a sinner.

Every time a man hurt me a chunk of my heart crumbled, and now I have none. I lost my heart, my essence, my individuality, myself. I am an empty carcass wandering these dirty streets, searching for something I'll never find. Each time I was fucked, fingered, felt up, I lost a piece of my heart. I was being used, but my nativity surpassed my intellect. I was tossed to the side, constantly fed the message that I'm not good enough, and I let them do it! I let those disgusting sailors jab my insides until they were raw, ruthlessly poke me so I felt no pleasure, tweak at my nipples until they were sore, and what did I receive in return for sacrificing my body, giving them a piece of myself that I'd never get back. Nothing! Perhaps I was trying to prove to myself that I was desirable, and if that was the propose of it all, then I exceeded my wildest expectations. I was trying to fill that void within myself, quiet those discouraging voices, the voices that holler *"You're not good enough!" "You're ugly!"* The voices only got louder though, intensified with every poke, every prick, every tweak, until I can no longer shut them out.

Carl was the one man that did not abandon me, at least physically, but emotionally he did. He lost me long before he left on that rainy spring day. He had told me that the strip clubs had become a part of me, and in one sense he was right. They did become a part of me, became ingrained in my conscience until I could see nothing else, until I was blinded by the dancing girls twirling round and round their poles. After Carl my world was black and white. People could no longer be a little good and a little bad. People were either good or they were bad, and unfortunately Carl fell into the bad. He never understood how painful it was, how with one word, one scent, one song I could be transported back into Roxy's absorbing the sheer nakedness of it all Most men would be tickled pink by my thoughts, but I wasn't. In my dreams I'd always find myself in the same place, tiptoeing through the club, my soles sinking into the matted brown carpet, standing behind that one girl, the one with the flowing blonde tresses cascading down her back. Her skin is so pale, white as vanilla. She exudes this raw sexuality which captivates everyone in the room, especially one man who stands before her. She is illuminated by the light, the reddish hue which bathes her body in a warm glow. I am aghast to her display of nakedness, her bare behind, her back, her thighs, and then I begin to scream, but in my thoughts my screams are silent. My screams have turned into tears, into trails of salty water droplets.

Last night I read an article which trivialized strip clubs, said it's a guy thing, said lap dances are no big deal. I don't understand! How could a naked woman slithering around on your boyfriend be no big deal? How could your boyfriend staring at vaginas, asses, tits not arouse some hint of suspicion. Cheating can be performed in many ways, originates through a pathway in the mind, until the narrow trail expands into a full blown thought. Cheating is just not physical to me but mental.

CHAPTER 38

I am not quite sure what prompted me to pose nude on a balmy damp day in August. Perhaps it was to waken the deadened part of my spirit, or maybe it was just a desperate cry for attention. I've ceaselessly explored the motivation behind what led me to this decision, but I am still at a loss. The only genuine emotions I can equate to this experience were a feeling of importance and excitement, two emotions I had not felt for a very long time. I'd always yearned to be a sultry sex symbol, and this was allowing me to act out a long awaited fantasy. Since I was a small girl I longed to be something special. The other children at school could not look past my stringy hair, red polyester bellbottom pants, or repulsive scent of urine floating through the air as I walked by. I was never popular, and this always made me wonder if I lacked some sort of magical power that the other children had. I was never a cheerleader, a homecoming queen, a pom pom girl. I never belonged to a group, and that is why I think I am jealous of strippers and the stereotypes we hold regarding their profession. I've cast aside the stigma regarding their safety, risk of sexual disease, the drugs, the objectification. I've forgotten that many of them have no family, and if they do they keep their profession a carefully guarded secret.

Others tell me I am blinded by a lie, the unrealistic imagery which inhabits my mind. In my mind's eye they are big busted blondes, mysterious creatures with incredible curves, sex sirens with supple flesh and hot red lipstick. Even when confronting them in person I was blinded by the darkness which engulfed me leaving me with hopelessness once again. I felt inadequate as a woman, almost asexual, as if my saggy breasts, flabby stomach, and jiggly buttocks lacked sex appeal. They must possess something which I don't have, drink some magical elixir each night to draw hoards of men in and empty their pockets. I wanted to feel powerful, like the strippers that control the room with their gyrations. I wanted to feel special. If somehow I could conquer my fear of nudity I thought I could be cured. If I posed naked then maybe I could empathize with the strippers that shed their clothing every night.

There is and there will always be a part of me that thirsts for flattery from others. I never had self confidence instilled within me.

Therefore, I scrounged up whatever admiring comments I could and tried to build up my self esteem based on those, but we all know that that approach is useless. We build self esteem from within, and other people buttering me up with flattering remarks sadly will never work. I suppose I thought that posing for an artist would alleviate me of all my ails, medicate me beyond my wildest hopes, place me on the same level plane as strippers, models, actresses. I could now be described as a nude model, my expressions and poses so brilliantly captured on camera that artists and fans would be clamoring to catch sight of my exhibits in art galleries around the world.

I wholeheartedly dove into my latest diversion, surfing website after website. I was searching for tasteful presentations of the female nude form, but most everything I came across was pornographic. I had to be extremely careful in my search, considering that a nude woman vulgarly presented could transform me into a blubbering puddle of flesh. I couldn't relate to the women in these offensive photographs, their legs spread wide open for the world to see, their eyes void of any emotion. Granted, sexuality is a vital component of being not only female, but human, however big breasted androids, their crotch displayed for the world was not a sensitive approach in my opinion. I was so tired of women being recognized solely for their sexual appeal. It wasn't fair that strippers were portrayed to be these stunning wondrous beings while girls like me were depicted as average uninteresting women. The *GIRLS ! GIRLS ! GIRLS!* neon lettering over Roxy's said it all; that the women dancing inside were extraordinarily rare creatures possessing mystery and appeal that we regular women in the real world fail to give off. I was dizzy with envy. Why did society's obsession with the naked woman have to be so dirty? If the women inside these clubs were dirty, then what would stop a man from thinking that my body is dirty, or even more terrible, my daughters' body.

I was so exhausted, tired of fooling myself. I was not going to find a naked woman anywhere, her fresh face and bashful stance conveying only innocence. That is until I unexpectedly ran across Ken Mierzwa's photographs. In Ken's biography it stated that he had photographed over two hundred women, and whether clothed or nude these women were tastefully portrayed. The conventional stereotypes concerning beauty did not apply to Ken's pictures. Some of the women were muscular, others had short hair or were small breasted, and one woman was even bald. These women didn't have that glazed like expression in their eyes, their tongues wagging, or their legs spread open. They were not all replicas of each other, bubbly well endowed bimbos with ridiculously massive teased hairdos. Each woman expressed herself differently, silently sending the message that each woman is unique. One woman communicated timidity as she stood, her arms crossed over her breasts. Another woman suggested playfulness as she held her hand over her wide grin and giggled. Another woman, confidently smiling, exuded strength as she held her arms up and clenched her muscular arms.

I could barely contain my glee as my eyes darted from picture to picture. Not only were these women absolutely amazing, but the photographer that captured them so candidly was a widely admired and respected man who had a long list of credentials. Ken Mierzwa was not only a photographer, but a photo journalist. His work had been in over thirty exhibits, and some of his photos had even been published. This man was not only a photographer, but an artist. He actually cared about his work and his subjects and was not some greedy pathetic pervert behind a camera only looking to exploit women.

If I could capture the attention of a world renowned photographer, then I had to be special and just maybe a pinch of that magical pixie dust had been sprinkled upon me. We corresponded by e-mail, his gentle words feeding me with encouragement and hope. I felt a strong emotional connection, one very different from Carl and mine. I almost felt as if I was in love with this stranger. Carl never offered me that emotional stimulation I had hungered for. He didn't find me interesting. He found me crazy. Ken didn't find me to be ridiculously bizarre in the least bit though. He thought that I was an intriguing woman and the fact that I faced my demons by going into Roxy's fascinating. He actually said that confronting my fear in this way was courageous. I had never thought of it this way. I had always thought I was abnormal and uptight, that Roxy's was no big deal, and I should just get with the program. I had never thought that what I had done was heroic.

Ken and I discussed the topic of public nudity often. He assured me that the site would be free of onlookers and very private. Ken was starting to open me up, bring out the creative aspect of my personality. Most importantly though Ken was beginning to make me realize that nudity could be wholesome depending on the context and circumstances of the situation. For example, a nudist colony could be an enjoyable and clean experience free of the stigma that accompanies it in society today. I was finally beginning to realize that the naked body was not dirty. After all we are born into this world naked.

I spent hours envisaging how Ken would look. Would he be dark haired and tan, his eyes as green as a kitten. I surfed the interact, hoping for just a glimpse of Ken, but I found nothing. Feeling like a giddy school girl, I shopped for a special outfit, finally settling on a brown and pink print dress which hugged my curves tightly. I was cautious about revealing my excitement of the shoot to Carl. He was going along with it, anything to get my mind off of the strip clubs.

The day of the shoot butterflies fluttered in my Stomach. I was going to meet Ken in a *Starbucks* on the comer of Skinker and Delmar. I was looking for an intellectual type dressed in black with a big black camera bag. Walking into Starbucks I spotted Ken immediately and was greeted instantly with a warm hand shake. Ken was a middle aged man, his lean build evident as his bony elbows dropped to his side. His friendly face lit up immediately as he introduced himself to Carl and me. I tried to hide my anxiety concerning the shoot and faze out the rumbling of my stomach as I sat down.

Ken pulled out a leather bound photo album filled with pictures of his proudest accomplishments. His portfolio soothed my nerves and settled down my stomach instantly. These women were not tall and lanky fashion models but real woman with real bodies communicating all sorts of emotions. I flipped upon one page though which greatly disturbed me. During our phone conversation, Ken had discussed one of his subjects, Miranda, a former stripper whom he photographed in Ohio. He was very impressed with Miranda, a strong confident woman who had taken control of her life and triumphed over the strip club, its patrons, and managers. In fact she had become a dominatrix, proudly stating that now she had the control. I also found Miranda to be fascinating, but of course my insecurities took precedence over reality. Her photographs were in vivid color, the greens and reds and blues practically soaking through the picture. Her breasts were full and plump, not saggy and limp like mine, and her smile; it appeared as if she was snickering at me, expressing amusement that someone like me would want to pose nude. I didn't understand how I could look at picture after picture of nude women and only be bothered by one just because of her former profession. I remarked to Ken that the picture of Miranda bothered me which elicited sighs and head shaking out of Carl.

Carl and I followed Ken by car to the site, twenty peaceful acres of wooded area and fisherman ponds. Ken thought it was beneficial for his subjects to be one with nature, to blend in with their surroundings. We walked over a bridge into a well hidden area void of trees but abundant with grass. I could tell he was trying to make Carl and I comfortable, educating us about the area and his experiences as a photographer. I almost felt like it was a normal Friday afternoon hiking in the wilderness with friends. We all talked, each of us contributing our viewpoint on nudity and how we felt about it. When it was time to take off my clothes and reveal myself though, I became terrified. Ken was very gentle, softly reassuring me that everything would be fine. He told me to close my eyes and take in my surroundings, open my senses to the smells and sounds around me. I was not use to this, but I soaked in the sound of the birds chirping and the smell of dew in the air. Being a humid August day my skin soaked in the moisture. I could feel the mosquitoes crawl on my ankle and neck and nibble until I succumbed to the irritating prickling sensation and scratched.

He told me to count to twenty and then abandon all inhibitions. I closed my eyes and counted dragging on each number as long as I could finally getting to the number twenty. Ken stood holding his camera, looking almost pained. I could bear it no longer. I peeled my dress and panties off, stepped out of my shoes and stood, completely naked. Ken held the camera and began to snap away as I heavily breathed in and out. My feet sunk into the mud, causing the cold sludge to settle in between my toes. The gentle breeze on my skin felt amazing. I felt like Mother Nature held me in her broad arms at that moment and was cradling me. Blades of overgrown grass tickled my calves. The skies above were dreary, a dull shade of gray, and tiny water droplets fell from the sky cooling off my hot sticky skin. Ken kept snapping at times asking questions or talking about certain topics to invoke different emotions. At one point he even began to talk about an experience he had while at a strip club in Eureka and how one of the strippers was so good at what she did which brought about feelings of anger within me, but I believe this was exactly what he was trying to do; summon up different emotions so that interesting expressions could be captured on camera. Therefore he tried to manipulate his subjects, emotionally sculpting them by evoking certain emotions. This is why he is an artist. A little later in the shoot I began to describe what had happened between my sister and I as a child and how my parents stormed into the room. He snapped away as tears began to well up, blurring my vision for only a moment. Physically, I was lost as how to express myself. I have always been an awkward girl unable to gracefully move my body. I never danced only expressing myself by writing. Ken worked with me at certain times telling me to lift my leg or hold my arms up and stretch, but he didn't seem to be concerned with my lack of motion.

To Ken it was trivial to him if I smiled or frowned or held my arms to my sides. To Ken it was essential to capture a person's emotions by their eyes. The eyes are the windows to the soul, express every emotion; sadness, happiness, anger. Naked women were not tools of exploitation to him, but pieces of art he could sculpt from a comfortable distance by craftily drawing out emotions through conversation. Therefore his photographs could be interpreted in many ways. One of his subjects could not be encapsulated in a moment but many moments.

I felt like a breathtaking statuette as he continued to take pictures. At the beginning of the session I was a shapeless glob of clay but as Ken finished up the session I felt like a beautifully sculpted masterpiece. I never imagined that I'd feel so comfortable in my own skin with all my stretch marks and cellulite exposed. My shield has bore battle wounds from labor, abuse, weight gain, weight loss, and now my secrets were out in the open, magnified by daylight. I was baring myself to the world, practicing raw honesty at its finest. Unlike Roxy's there was no darkness to camouflage my flaws, no smoky air to shroud my body, no glittery lotion to coat my ordinarily drab skin. I actually felt beautiful. I stood straight and proud, any arms folded over my breasts to obscure them while Ken clicked away. I truly did not want it to end, but as with all good things the curtain closed.

I got dressed, and we all walked back to the car. Carl got into the car first while Ken and I said our goodbyes and I thanked him for my awakening. Ken thanked me, and informed me that if the opportunity arose he'd like to work with me again, because it was hard to find a pretty face. Carl and Ken shook hands, and Ken let Carl know how special of a person I was. I was on a natural high, my face aglow, a permanent smile affixed. I could not wait to see the pictures. Someone important actually thought I was pretty and special! Would I look like one of those centerfold girls in *Playboy*, bronzed, big-busted, and beautiful?

CHAPTER 39

I received my pictures from Ken today in the mail. It seemed like forever. I wish I could say that I was pleased with how I looked, but I cannot. Ken is a wonderful photographer, but unfortunately his subject was an obnoxiously ugly troll. I looked worn. My breasts hung limply; my stomach was pudgy; my nose was pointy. My freckled skin looked tired and old. I was nowhere near the smoldering centerfold I imagined myself to be. I looked angry, disappointed with how life had treated me. In several pictures my head turned downwards expressing solemnity. In other pictures I held my arms back and giggled, the lush green grass my backdrop. In one picture I held a cigarette and comfortably laughed. My body was not proportionate as that stripper, Miranda. I was not sexy. The pictures shouted this loud and clear. If I had known how dreadful I would have turned out, I never would have taken them. My feet looked like paddles attached to my legs. I did not look like a woman. No, I looked like a duck, a feathered foul with its large behind, waist, and skinny legs. How could I have felt sexual? I was an asexual being, genderless, an androgynous creature in this spicy scintillating society. Where was that pretty girl, the one with the smile that flung her hair and cocked her head in the mirror? Where was that girl? Where was the girl that all those sailors told she's beautiful? That girl was certainly not in the pictures. That girl never existed. My beauty was an illusion, a fib I told myself. I was living a lie. I had created a tale, one about a girl who could only rely on her beauty to fill her with happiness, but now she would have to rewrite that tale. The pictures did not lie.

September 13th, 2004

Ken,

Thank you for both of the e-mails and the pictures. I appreciate your letting me know the comments and your thoughts. It made me feel better. I really enjoyed the whole experience. It gave me a high. I wrote a little about what I felt and am attaching it. When reading it I hope you are not offended by it. It is not about your work. It is about how I feel about myself. I also went into detail comparing myself to Miranda. I am sure she is a really nice person and a sweet girl. Again, this is about the hatred i feel for myself. Thanks again and l hope to hear from you soon. I really do enjoy your feedback. Thank you.

Tuesday

So many emotions came rushing back as I looked at my pictures. At first glimpse I almost felt ashamed, that same childhood self consciousness creeping in, that lack of self confidence I fought so hard to conceal. As I stared at them longer though I realized that I bore not as close a resemblance to the hideous ogre which I make myself out to be. Sure, that unwelcome monstrous goblin still lurked in the darkest recesses of my mind pointing out my pointy nose, shapeless breasts, and round chubby stomach paunch, but I annoyingly shooed him away. In fact feeling so confident I decided to travel back into one of Ken Mierzwa's websites and take in some of his work. I loved how he had magically purged me of my fears, cleansed my insides of all the dirty sewage that had accumulated over the years, how he could make nudity seem all so innocent.

As a child I was taught that the naked body was evil, a secret which at all times must be buried underneath ones clothes. Nudity, in any foam, induced such anger in my parents. From the age of a small child, they spoon fed me the message that my body was shameful, not only in their words but their actions. My dad stomped off on a tirade when at age four I confessed that I showed my private spot and Jason Burger showed me his, or when at the age of seven my mother and father stormed into our bedroom like warriors ready for combat at the sight of seeing my sister and I experiment like all small children do. I was absolutely terrified, petrified that I could be pregnant or have A.I.D.S. at the age of seven. The lack of communication within our household was heart breaking. I did not understand why sexuality induced such rage within my mother and father, why they never talked about anything sexual but my father hid his Playboy in his sock and underwear drawer. The nude body was shameful, something to be hidden and tossed away among one's underwear and socks.

I journeyed through some of Ken's model portfolios admiring his work and how brave his models had been, but then my mouse moved upon Miranda. I was feeling fearless so I entered her

293

portfolio, and then my heart sank. She did not look worn as some strippers did. I imagined Carl in a strip club, how he would be staring at this beautiful masterpiece dancing. I looked at Miranda's face, her fiery red hair, her milky white skin lightly freckled, her cherry colored lip stick. Despite her situation, she amazingly had retained a youthful innocence, an inviting childlike quality. I loved the center picture where she playfully smiled, a coil of hair hanging in one eye. The picture stared back at me perfectly still, yet I could feel the wind blowing her scarlet tresses and hear her lively laughter. I then flipped back to my pictures. The goblin savagely cackled as I critiqued my body and face. My breasts hung limply, unlike Miranda's full lush perky ones. I looked so worn and haunted by my past. My eyes were hollow, vacuous sockets residing in my skull, not emitting an ounce of warmth. I was not sexy like Miranda. I was a joke with my pudgy stomach, saggy breasts and ghoulish eyes.

I ran to the living room, dramatically throwing myself onto the couch and buried my face into the pillow. I cried and cried, letting out every pang of jealousy, anger, and hurt. I wailed, my chest actually physically aching by now, the tenderness worsening as I continued to cry. The painful twinges traveled from the center of my stomach gradually moving to my heart. Carl had broken my heart yet again, not directly this time, but his words continued to haunt me.

I yearned to be back in the fields on the afternoon of my photo shoot, how fresh and alive I felt. I wanted to feel the same sensations I had felt that day, innocent as a child yet powerful. Being nude had awakened me, slurred my senses. For once I actually paid attention to my surroundings, how sweet the birds sounded chirping, how the grass was green as emeralds, how the mud felt wet and slippery sandwiched between my toes. I was one with the earth, the dirt, the trees, the water. For weeks prior to the shoot I had felt like someone who is in love, so energetic and full of life. For once in my life I felt important, being the subject of a wonderful and well established artist and photographer. Through a perfect stranger I was able to rediscover myself and my greatest passion, writing. He had made me feel as if on that afternoon I was the only woman in the world, but as every great love affair ends, so did this mind set. For now I am not the only woman in the world.

OVER ON THE EAST SIDE

Sadly, I do not even amount to one complete woman.

September 14, 2004

Tuesday,

Thanks for the comments. I'm so happy that the experience itself was so good for you after that...well only you have control over that. The only real problem is that you 're still comparing yourself to others. There are how many billion people on earth? Pick any trait, some are "better" or "'worse" than us. Let me use a running metaphor: some are always faster, some are always slower: We may be able to move up a few places through training and discipline, but we will never be first. There is only one world record holder. The record will be broken someday, so we can only be ourselves.

*As for Miranda: those breasts cost her several thousand dollars. Yep, a good enhancement job, but an artificial one. I've also seen her with no makeup and in ratty clothes and to be honest, you've got a better face (and your eyes are fine, seriously). In Miranda's case, the relevant quote is on her website. I don 't recall the exact words, but something about attitude is everything. You know, she's right. If l may defend her for a moment. The girl grew up in a trailer park with white trash parents, long since divorced. She stripped to work her way through college which took her nine years. She taught herself to write, and now she's been published several times. Read the item called "**that pretty girl Mandy** " in her fiction section, which uses my photos. You'll see what she survived. I assume the story is a composite of the experiences of several people, but it's at least partially true. I recognize two of the characters from that day in May. What matters is that she rose above it all, and has just opened her own space in Akron. Against all odds, she took control of her life, took it back from the strip club managers and the patrons, from everybody. She's a self made woman. The biggest difference between the two of you is her confidence. Oh, I'm sure she has her down days, she just doesn't let on, doesn't let it stop her for long.*

Are you going to take control of your own life? You're at least trying. It's never easy, but over time you can do it, if you want to badly enough. Just never stop evolving. Do stop comparing, please.

You are unique. You can get better, we all can; but the comparison point, the baseline, is what you are now, not what anyone else is. If you decide you want help, you can always come out here. We can walk around naked at the hot springs with dozen of other people of all shapes and sizes, secure (mostly) in their bodies. I don't know why]'m making the offer, must think you're worth it. If you are ready I can show you other things that will make nudity no big deal, but that's a much riskier course.

If any of this is confusing it's because there are four people over here right now and things are a bit noisy and chaotic. I'll think about it some more, read your words again; well written words by the way, better than last time, so you've already grown since then. Forgive me if I've been aggressive on anything, 1 had to confront a few issues myself last night, and I'm still sorting through some of that, but I know you understand I'm trying to help. Comments? Reactions?

Ken

I thumbed through some of our old emails before the photo shoot:

August 3, 2004

Tuesday,

Of course I'd like to work with you. You'll get past the shyness quickly enough once we start, I can help with that. In fact, beiing aware of it, conscious of it, can sometimes result in some powerful photos.

I grew up in Chicago, so I have a pretty good idea of Midwestern attitudes; especially after moving to California, where most residents have an open attitude toward the body, more like that typical of Western Europe. Here, the body is just the body...beautiful, unique, functional, sometimes used for erotic purposes, but usually separate from that. The difference is that many people here recognize that nudity and eroticism are overlapping but different things, and they do not confuse the two. Thus, it is easier to create art for purely aesthetic purposes.

OVER ON THE EAST SIDE

I have no illusions about Missouri. Even St. Louis is more conservative than Chicago. Once I worked with a nude model at Elephant Rocks, and we were both conscious that in that location, any encounter with the public could lead to a major hassle. Still, intelligent and open minded people will rise above their surroundings, test limits, widen their experience. It sounds like you are trying to do that. The fact that you've written about this offers an opportunity for true artistic collaboration, something I encourage. I'm honored that you've chosen to offer me the opportunity to participate in your explorations.

I'll call a little later so we can discuss this some more. For now, I'll just say that I'll do everything in my power to make this a positive experience for you. I understand, more than you could know, how important it can be to take these steps.

By the way, you're correct about the potential for a feeling of freedom and liberation. There can be a feeling of hyperawareness, feeling every breeze on the skin, feeling the warmth of the sun, and so much more. I'm not sure how to explain, but soon enough, you'll have more words of your own for it.

August 4, 2004

Tuesday,

Yes, I know what you mean. Just a few months ago an opportunity came along to explore it visually. One of my models....she goes by Miranda, although that's not her real name...brought me into the strip club where she worked her way through college, and we were allowed to do photos inside. We got the red carpet treatment, the manager appeared hours earlier than usual, turned up all the lights for us, even got into a few of the photos.

It was an education for me. I've seen a lot, but for a while we shot right inside the locker room, dancers getting dressed or undressed right next to us, and we talked to them. Yes, they do have lives, sometimes they do have children. One woman was working on a masters degree in engineering, and this paid better than the alternatives for part time work. But I saw the other end of th4e *spectrum, too; the once beautiful meth freak who had worked a 12 hour shift, made $2, and had to beg cab fare to get home. She was last seen wandering in endless circles in the parking lot. Miranda is a survivor of all this, and she's written about her experiences, published a few of them. She's remarkably comfortable about her body, her dealings with men, life in general, but I think she's had to work through a lot of things to get there. There's a set of photos of her on my web page, I've only met her in person once but the images say a lot.*

We see the exploitation issue in other places too, including MuseCube. I'm not even talking about the handful of creeps and weirdos preying on underage girls; there's a subtle pressure to do pseudo glamour body shots, and a lot of it is by what we call GWCs, or guys with cameras (as distinguished from real photographers). Unfortunately, they'll sell a camera to anyone with a credit card. Most are pursuing their lust, not art, and it's pretty obvious in the results.

I could spend another few thousand words on the elements of society which contribute to this warped view of beauty. What's important though, is that you understand there is an alternative, a way to empower yourself a way all those others in metro east will never understand. I'd love to hear more of your thoughts on this, either in e-mails or while we shoot. I'll try to call again so we can work out the schedule details...still plenty of time.

Ken

August 4, 2004

Tuesday

Let's concentrate on you then, on the present, and not on the past. I photograph people who I find to be interesting. Just by the fact that you try to understand yourself that you write about these ideas, that you seek personal growth; makes you an interesting person. That is all I can ask of anyone. Be yourself, and I have no doubt that I can create good images of which you are an important part. Thanks for sharing your thoughts and feelings.

OVER ON THE EAST SIDE

Ken

August 10, 2004

Tuesday,

I'd love to see your writing. Thank you for offering. I've been doing a little...for lack of a better term, I'll call it research. Mostly it's been reading and a little web browsing, for example I looked up the clubs in Brooklyn and glanced quickly at their web sites. I've also asked my friend in Ohio a few questions, the answers were a little different than I would have expected. Finally, last night I went with a local female friend to the club in Eureka, admittedly pretty tame and exceptionally clean by the standards of these things, Except for the Ohio photos, it's the first time I'd been in one of these places in over a long time, since adolescence, basically. This was the first time I ever watched the customers; mostly a nondescript lot, a few young guys in tee shirts and jeans, a couple of obvious businessmen on the road. Mostly what I saw was lonely men. I saw men who don't get any meaningful feminine attention anyplace else. Some might be trapped in marriages which died long ago, others might just have no luck meeting people. Some of them looked at me with envy just because I sat next to the only woman in the place who didn't work there. We ended the evening talking to two of the dancers. They have curious eyes, some like what they do, others are going through the motions; all remain a little detached, of necessity I'm sure. They don't get too close to the customers, they might take it the wrong way.

Again, this is an atypical club, owned by an artist, maybe it's not representative. In any case I don't know what it means yet, just not enough data, but I'm beginning to see the framework. Maybe your writing will add another piece to the puzzle.] look forward to seeing it.

Even I can't believe this is drawing so much effort. You're onto something, though; this has far reaching cultural implications, and now I want to understand.

Ken

August 25, 2004

Tuesday,

Here are a few of the digital photos; remember usually my B&W work is stronger; but it will be at least tomorrow or Friday til I am done processing everything.

I did enjoy working with you, in some ways more so than with the experienced models in Kansas City the next day. Mostly they are fashion models, nice enough girls, but for them it's a job, more so about the clothing than about themselves. I have no illusions about it; they are all pestering me for images because shooting with a California photographer will look good on the resume of a Kansas City model. That's all there is though, at least with five of the seven from that day.

With you, I had a chance to explore the hidden corners of human nature. The emotion was real not some learned and practiced expression turned on and off at will. If you choose to go that route, the poses, the expressions will come. They are merely manifestations of the person. Right now, you express yourself through writing. It is possible to learn to let those same emotions express themselves through the physical body, as any good ballet dancer will attest. You just need to learn to trust yourself, to be who you are, to let it out. I could have provoked some of those things, but you were already taking a big step, I was hesitant to risk scaring you. It will happen when the time is right.

How are you feeling about the whole experience, with a few days to think about it? It sounds like you're doing OK, but I'm curious because a lot can race through the mind in the hours after a shoot.

Ken

September 25, 2004

Tuesday,

Last night I brought a few proof sheets to a local party, mostly photos of a few people from last weekend. One of the sheets was a collection of end-of-roll frames from half a dozen different shoots, and there were about four frames from our shoot there. A lot more people than I expected wanted to look at photos. Had some interesting reactions, thought I'd share.

Of course they all looked at the photos of people they knew, the people who were elsewhere in the same room. But of the others, there were comments on two: It's not surprising people would notice a girl in black latex and a gas mask. But two people in particular singled out the photos of you. One young woman asked about the expressions, noted the presence of emotion and was curious about the story behind it. One guy, probably in his late-2Os, really raved about them, specifically called you "beautiful". He was very much in demand among the various young women at the party, so not a bad person to have as a long-distance fan...very much the sensitive guy type.

There were a lot of general "these are nice" comments too, but as I'm sure you know relatively few people articulate detailed reactions. Still, the fact that two people did go into detail about their thoughts is unusual.

Ken

February 17, 2005

Tuesday,

Last weekend in San Francisco was an interesting contrast, three very different people.

My first shoot was with an experienced art model who it turns out is a corporate project manager by day. While she is very comfortable with her (less than flawless) body, does mostly nude work etc., she leads a bit of a dual life. Her art activities might be misunderstood at the office, might get in the way of promotions even in liberal California, and she's an ambitious young lady. So she uses a trade name, a pseudonym; she researches the legalities, only will do nudes in places where she cannot get arrested for it (even though what codes exist in the Bay Area are very rarely enforced). While I found her to be very bright, her constant looking over the shoulder;

don't want anybody to find out attitude got in the way of really good images. She was good, but could be better if she'd relax a little. She couldn't quite let go, almost but not quite. Part of it though was that she's a lot like me, cautious most of the time and able to cut loose only under the right circumstances. As you will see in a minute, I do better with a different personality type, one different from my own.

First though, an interlude. The core reason for the drive down was to attend a friiends gallery opening, her first ever. I leave her anonymous because it 's another dual life thing; she's a nationally famous professional dominatrix, gets paid $200/hour to do consensual but often painful or humiliating things to men. In that role, she 's a femme fatale, in provocative leather or pvd, confident, sadistic. She can turn it on and off at will. Saturday night though, she was not so sure of herself in a room full of better known artists. Google her dome name, you'll get hundreds or thousands of hits. Do the same with her real name, she's nobody, the only thing that comes up is a couple of 5k race results. We're getting set to photograph her later this spring, and she spent 10 minutes apologizing to me the other night because she doesn't think she 's ready to do nudity, just can't handle it. One of the smarter and more assertive women I know, but pushing 35 and while within the "attractive " body range, at 5 "7" and 140 lbs she's not anorexic, so the insecurities come out. So...it can happen to anyone, even those you'd least expect it

The next day I photographed one of the least inhibited women I've ever met. She came alone, no chaperone, got stoned before we started, and was out of her clothes in minutes, and then in and out of them the rest of the afternoon. Gradually l learned that she was an exotic dancer in Prague at the age of l 6, and she's only 27 now. We didn't have time to go over her stories, and she was so unpredictable she had trouble completing a paragraph anyway. For four hours, she was a lot of fun to be with. After a week she would have driven me half mad. All that matters though is that I have so many good photos it's hard to pick. What makes a spectacular model is not always what might be conducive to a responsible life.

Ken

OVER ON THE EAST SIDE

CHAPTER 40

There only seemed to be one resolution, and that was to rid this town of all the perverts. It was imperative that I formulate some sort of strategy. No, it wasn't realistic to believe that I could absolve this city of the perversion which brews within. The only solution which I could foresee was to frighten these perverts and make them recognize that by frequenting the strip clubs they were jeopardizing their survival.

I deemed one man accountable for the destruction of my relationship, and he would have to suffer. In order to triumphantly achieve the resolution which I so desperately desired, I would have to masquerade as the entity which I truly despised. My initial intent was to camouflage myself as a stripper, but due to careful consideration I determined this ploy to be hazardous. First and foremost, being so bashful and modest I did not realistically envision myself as persuading the audience and my victim that I genuinely was a stripper. Secondly, by impersonating these fraudulent women I detested, I would be contradicting my values. The ultimate and most significant argument was that by being eyed and ogled so intimately, I was a prime suspect for whatever wrongdoing I was about to execute. To strip I would be jeopardizing any concept of moral decency I treasured. There had to be a better solution.

An investigation of immense proportions would have to be conducted on my victim. I would have to dissect his background and attempt to intellectualize why a human being would require such perversion in his life. I am not asserting that I could embrace this depraved degenerate's life style. I could never sympathize with an individual who constructed his entire character around such an objectionable scene. Instead by delving into his pornographic mentality, I could design a most humiliating conclusion to his miserable life.

Carl only revealed to me a few sparse truths about his boss, James, but I had done my research and this is what I found out: James, a forty five year old man, ran with the Harley Davidson set. You could classify him as grotesquely overweight, weighing in at over three hundred fifty pounds, and reaching a stature of 5"10. He appeared unkempt and unshaven, donning a lengthy red beard speckled with gray droplets which extended past his chest. He sported antiquated acid washed jeans adorned with an enormous brass belt buckle, snug jet black T-shirts emblazoned with the Harley Davidson motif and a tattered rawhide leather vest decorated with colorful buttons displaying brash distasteful phrases. His gut bulged out from over his trousers exposing his doughy stomach brimming with belly hair.

I was startled to discover that he had been wedded to an extremely attractive woman named Barb. Barb was forty three years old, tall and slender, with a fashionable feather cut that she preferred to pin up. She regularly colored her hair a warm ash blonde shade tinged with pale lemon color highlights. Her style of dress could be categorized as high society, including impeccable name brand suits in exquisite shades and textures, priced exorbitantly. Her only imperfection was her slightly hardened appearance possibly brought about by her frequent alcohol binges.

She was the mother of two grown sons, Donny, age twenty seven, and Chris, age twenty four. Barb had initially entered motherhood with admirable intentions, but as her boys developed, she forgot to be a role model for two impressionable teenagers.

Chris had always been the quiet and composed brother. He was opposed to Donny's personal convictions and condemned him for his treatment and ill manipulation of the opposite sex. Donny was labeled as to what many would refer to as a *"player"*. While Chris remained faithful to one girl for an extensive period of time, Donny would date several. What Chris was blind to though was Donny's heart. Donny might of capitalized on the fragility of women, but by no means were his intentions dishonorable. He should not of been held accountable for how he treated women since he didn't have a decent father figure. Donny was taught by James that women were toys, not people. Bobby had a big heart, but he hadn't really discovered it yet.

Chris had remained with the same girl, Luna, for over seven years, but after the repetitive emotional abuse and being taken advantage of, not even Chris could remain loyal. Each and every payday Luna would snatch Chris's check, leaving him with nothing. She made him feel as if he should feel privileged to be graced with her presence.

Ultimately, he could not endure Luna's abuse and greed which had left him indebted to countless creditors and not to mention her behind was horrible. When Luna would peel away the outer layers of her attire and expose her behind, Chris had to do everything conceivable to keep himself from regurgitating his supper, for the surprise which awaited him was enough to invoke squeamishness in even the most valiant. Luna possessed an extremely flabby behind, decorated with an immeasurable amount of indentations. The cottage cheese impressions began directly beneath her back and extended to the region immediately above her thighs. This was no incident of conventional cellulite, but instead a grotesque exaggeration not even the most insane could visualize. Chris mastered techniques for blocking out these unpleasant images, but in reality, he sincerely adored and paid homage to Luna, and an ass bejeweled by an infinite quantity of pock marks was and never would be an authentic excuse for the abrupt termination of their union. Even the most feeble in times of desperation can stumble upon strength. Chris never even conceived of being intimate with another female, but in his heart he could sense that she was not the special one.

Before he was married Bobby was never faced with a predicament such as his brothers. He would distance himself from a girl as soon as feelings were involved. He built a barrier between the girls. This way he didn't get hurt.

Every Friday and Saturday night Donny went to Woody's, a miniscule nightclub sanwiched between two auto dealerships. Despite Woody's size, it always managed to attract a tremendous crowd. For Donny there was a broad diversity of women to choose from, but the majority of these girls were far from refined and lacked manners. These were definitely not the class of women you'd eagerly introduce to your mother. On the dance floor these girls would contort their body in all sorts of seductive stances, gyrating provocatively to the throbs and pulses of the music. Donny could effortlessly differentiate between the girls who were guaranteed to give him a piece and the girls who had respect for themselves. He did not even attempt to date girls with substance. Donny adamantly refused to embroil his dating life with a girl who possessed the potential to tug at his heartstrings. The familiar routine of fucking them and forgetting was easier. This built up his ego. Many of Donny's friends were envious of his smoothness with the ladies, but they only cared to look at the superficial aspect. They could not perceive the bleakness in his eyes due to the bareness of his soul.

It was not unusual for Donny to persuade a girl to accompany him to the rear parking lot, behind the dumpster, where he could have his way with her. Donny strategized his flawless Friday night ritual without a glitch in the game plan. Every Friday night Donny confidently made his entrance into Woody's giving out high fives as if they were candy. His arrogance made the ladies swarm to him, and it was not rare that a confrontation to win his affections between two gifts would develop. Donny was not selective in the choices he made. Generally, he would choose a girl wearing snug-fitting skirts, a low cut shirt displaying an ample amount of cleavage, and a vacant look in her eyes which complimented an expressionless face. The girl, displaying such ecstasy, was anxious to please Donny, and created a mythical fantasy that she would be his exclusively. To appease his desires they'd accompany him on a harmless stroll ending up behind the dumpster. Shoving rancid fast food wrappers and crushed beer cans out of the way, he'd tear off her clothes ferociously letting tatters descend to the ground. He'd brutally pound away at them, mauling their breasts and behind, panting heavily, until he released his seeds of passion. Both of them perspiring, their hair laden of perspiration, they would return to Woody's where Donny would behave casually as if they didn't even fuck. The girl would always surrender, too heartbroken to challenge him in front of his friends, and would leave Woody's in a trance, bewildered that she was such an imbecile. Unconsciously, Donny was copying his stepfather's chauvinistic behavior.

Chris was ten and Donny was thirteen when a shadow of darkness was cast over these impressionable youth. Barb had been introduced to James through her older brother, Marc. Marc worked with James across the river in Illinois and presumed James to be an upstanding man, worthy of his sister's affections. James never exposed his perverse fixation of frequenting strip bars to Marc, for Marc was a church man, religiously attending church every Sunday, and preaching his gospel to the other men in his construction crew.

OVER ON THE EAST SIDE

Ironically it was at church that Barb was introduced to James.

James could not capture much interest from the opposite sex. In fact, the majority of women introduced to him were repulsed, but not Barb. Barb did not see him as the fat greasy biker that he really was. Instead she indulged in a foolish self-deception where he was brawny, handsome, and charming, a present day Prince Charming. To be adored by a woman whom he did not have to pay for services mystified him, and for a brief period he incorrectly assumed that he could adapt to the normalcy of a traditional relationship. For dates they would dine at quaint little restaurants and then proceed to a movie, usually a light romantic comedy, obviously Barb's preference. Initially, James was pleasantly surprised that such a refined wholesome woman would find him intriguing. Barb represented a refreshing alternative to the disreputable woman James generally gravitated towards, but it was not long before the relationship drifted into a severe stage of boredom. Barb did not realize that the monotony would provoke James to pursue other perverted opportunities. To Barb James was a devoted and adorable soft, downy teddy bear. Even in the bedroom James did not reveal his smutty side. The only position they ever engaged in was missionary. The lights dimmed to a level which would make almost any object discernable. Barb would remove his pants obediently while James would robatically thrust his penis into her. She never could see the loathsome look in his eyes when they engaged in sex, but if she could she would have scrambled away squealing in alarm for the act of sex depleted any trace of compassion which engrossed his insides. His chestnut brown eyes flecked with dashes of cinnamon shaded specs would mutate into a dusky shade of ebony black.

His mind was besieged by a deranged preoccupation that all women were destructive. Every woman in his life with the exception of Barb had bruised his tender ego. James was rejected by an infinite number of women, not one who could reciprocate his affections. A small number of girls flirted with the notion of dating James, but each and every one of these girls bore a significant defect. Mary Krueger, his first admirer, possessed the loveliest porcelain complexion many would be envious of, if it was not for the stubble which graced her chin and the area under her nose. Unfortunately, back in the seventies, there was no such procedure known as laser hair removal, so Mary had to endure the provoking banter from the school bullys. The only boy Mary neglected to poke fun at Mary's five o'clock shadow was James. He basically kept to himself anyways. He really had no room to make fun of Mary since he was teased more than her.

Since a very young age, James was held back by his obesity. While the other children played tag and swung on the monkey bars, James would perch himself against the wall, focusing intensely on his comic books.

"Fat boy, blubberbut, jewboy", was just a smattering of cruel names they'd unrelentlessly cast at him. It was difficult to conceal his heritage, because his parents were practicing orthodox Jews. James was not to depart from his house without wearing a yamaca upon his head. Not one child who attended his grammar school was Jewish, so they could not comprehend as to why James would wear- such absurd headgear.

James's parents, Sylvia and Ernie had preferred to send James to a premier private orthodox school, but their meager income could not cover the costly tuition. Therefore, they had to put aside their solid convictions and send James to a school where he was encircled by basically only Christians, Catholics, and Penacostols.

While the other children scurried to the vibrations of the lunch bell and scrambled for a spot in the hot lunch line, James would silently engulf his kosher brown bag lunch. Sylvia and Emie exclusively purchased their edibles from the kosher corner markets, kosher butchers, bakeries, and dells. Every scrap of food that entered their household was marked by the letter "k", and a hearty portion was marked by the phrase, "pareve". The letter "k" obviously meant kosher, and pareve meant that the product could be mixed with meat or milk. Unfortunately, James was not permitted to consume a mixture of meat and milk products. He was also a virgin to all pork products, never devouring mouth watering sausage links or patties and bacon sodden in grease. The kosher pizza he'd nibble on coated with crunchy green peppers appeared inferior to the restaurant pizzas laden with sausage. All meats had to be entirely devoid of blood and blessed by a rabbi. The dishes were separated according to if they were meat dishes or milk dishes, and each and every piece of silverware, bowl, plate, and glass had to be submerged in scalding hot water and then a prayer would have to be recited to cleanse the dishes of their sacrilegious grime.

On Friday nights when most families gobbled down cheese burgers and shakes at *Steak N Shake*, James lay on his bed skimming over his comic books. From sundown Friday night to sundown Saturday night it was the holy Sabbath. James and his family could not utilize the electricity, watch television, or drive their vehicle. The only place they'd visit on Friday night or Saturday morning was synagogue. They'd painstakingly make the two mile trek through the frigid cold, blankets of powdery snow, cloudbursts resulting in pools of rainwater so deep one could practically bathe. There was never a pardon from paying homage to God.

James despised every aspect of the Jewish faith but one. In the Jewish religion once a month orthodox women are required to purify themselves after their menstruation cycle is completed. During their period they are prohibited from partaking in sexual intercourse and to keep temptation at arm's length from either side, the couple is restricted from sleeping in the same bed until she is finished with her period. After her period ends, the woman must go to a migva. This is a house which contains cleansing baths to purge these women from the filth which compiles in their system during the duration of their blood stained cycle. The woman will then enter the purification area stripped bare and immerse herself in the mildly warm frothy water. A woman, usually possessing more seniority over them will position herself in front of the exposed and recite a prayer to alleviate the restrictions they had to pursue due to the vital juices which stream from the rupture which bears youth. After this ritual is complete, the woman is at liberty to resume relations with her husband.

Every month, without deliberation, Sylvia would trudge over to 2401 Maple, Migvah de Israel, to regenerate herself. Ernie slaved six days a week and over seventy hours at the Welsh Baby Carriage Factory, so Sylvia had to haul along James to these monthly affairs. Migvah de Israel resembled any other ordinary brick building on the block, but upon entering this holy habitat one could differentiate how distinct it really was. James would curl up on the frumpy overstuffed recliner and pour over the countless cartoons contained in his comic books. He did not grasp the concept of why he sat in the same mango orange shaded chair once a month. After the first half hour when the comic books would forfeit their appeal, James would sit spellbound staring at the lose strings of hot orange yarn resembling stringy strands of pulp suspended from the cushion. Ms. Rabinawitz, the supervisor of the migvah, loved to lavish all of her affections on James.

"Those adorable chipmunk cheeks" she'd say as she squeezed a pinch full of his fleshy skin zealously.

James despised the senile old woman for calling attention to his resemblance to a chipmunk, but he overlooked his discomfort every time she crammed her home made delicacies in his face. He especially liked her mandel bread rolled in chocolate chips, savory raisins, and pecan halves.

One drizzly rain soaked afternoon Ms. Rabinawitz was nowhere to be found. James, quite accustomed to scarfing down mandel bread on these humdrum occasions, nibbled on his fingertips until every trace of fingernail was destroyed. James had already skimmed over every cartoon bubble and illustration of his comic book. The secret door which was so cleverly arranged between the two mahogany stained bookshelves appeared a very inviting option to the monotony which occupied these familiar afternoons.

"What could lay beyond the secret door?" James reflected to himself. Could there be pastel rainbows, twinkling pots of gold, and emerald colored leprechauns waiting beyond to greet James behind the drab gray door?

At a snaillike pace James proceeded toward the mystery which lay before him. He knew that his actions were forbidden, but these dreary afternoons were proving unbearingly painful. James would inquisitively ask his mother what was behind the door, but she warned him not to ask such questions *for curiosity pesters the soul, causes humans to behave as animals. What occurs beyond that door is not meant for such infantile eyes. What one may witness behind the door may appear sinful, but remember it is the only defense in reclaiming the cleanliness God originally gifted his children with."* She would say and James would promise.

Sylvia's request and James promise echoed unceasingly as he made his way towards the forbidden door. James placed his pudgy stumps on the frigid iron door knob taking much care not to stir up suspicion. Placing his squinty brown eye between the molding and the door, James could not refrain from centralizing all of his focus on the unclothed women surrendering their chastity to gratify God. At any moment James calculated his eyeballs rupturing due to the spectacle he was beholding.

"If God unearths my freakish secret may he strike me dead." he uttered to himself.

For now he could bathe in the tranquility and lull of this moment forever more. Whenever the children at school tormented him or his parents irritated him James could divert into a mystical vision of unclad goddesses appeasing his colossal cravings. This was the first time James had ever seen bare flesh. In the past his imagination would stir with desire at the mere display of an ankle or a forearm, but never like this. Never before could he experience the tingling sensation which engulfed his testicles. Spread out before him lay a mouth watering buffet of nude orthodox Jewish women in all reality attempting to salvage their dignity. His polluted interpretation was so artificial. Instead of relishing in the spiritualism, he converted the migvah and what it stood for into a filthy whore house entrusted with muck.

His eyes darted rapidly from one woman to the other not caring to distinguish that these women existed as separate beings. He scrutinized each woman from the top of their head to the tips of their toes, taking special care not to slobber when his eyeballs rested on their personal parts. His most passionate obsession was a plump firm breast. He salivated when he visualized sucking on a supple pink nipple or caressing a velvety buttock cheek. The majority of the women who cleansed themselves at the migvah were mature, but James did not discriminate against anyone. James embraced all varieties of women, as long as they were naked. They could be chubby, elderly, gangly, or unattractive. There was no conventional set of rules and regulations to abide by when it came to his eccentric fixation with nude women. It enticed him even more that these women did not suspect that they were being observed. If they discovered that James, an eleven year old boy, was holding surveillance sessions at their beloved migvah, Sylvia and Emie would be prohibited from mingling with the congregation for all eternity.

The entire month until the momentous day, James would envisage the exhilarating prospect. James could not contain his enthusiasm for all but one day out of the month, and on that day James would remain composed, calm, and blissful. Sylvia could almost detect a brilliant glow oozing from every minute opening which covered his expansive stature. She attempted to speculate as to why James would behave so bizarrely on the days when she attended migvah, but her saintly perspective caused her never to suspect such naughty behavior from her own offspring. In former days the walk to the migvah presented a time when Sylvia could converse with James about school, other children, and the Jewish laws, but lately James remained abnormally uncommunicative. The only expression which Sylvia could discern was the faraway look in his eyes creating images which no eleven year old boy or rather no human being, man or woman, should ever conceive of. If James would of belonged to a family who did not shun the sexual nature of the human race, he might of developed a more healthy outlook towards women, but he felt obligated to keep this quality of himself a secret. His parents would never understand this obsession with nudity.

"No one must think like me." James thought to himself. *"All I can imagine are tits and ass. I don't even read comic books anymore. How could a stupid book with cartoon characters keep me interested compared to the beauty of a naked woman?* When the other kids at school talked about the latest movie they saw or shopping at their favorite store, he didn't understand. It all seemed so childlike and trivial to him. Nothing captured his interest anymore. He didn't even want to go to school anymore, unless of course he could peek in the girls locker room at changing time, but those girls had nothing compared to what he stared at once a month. To James those were real women and noone could take his imagination away.

That fateful day had arrived again. James pounced out of bed like a tiger hounding its prey. The sun streamed through the gaps of the window, the brilliant sun streaks thawing the frostiness of the room bathing the room in toasty warm tranquility. James selected his favorite outfit from his closet, the cream colored corduroy slacks and a silk burgundy top and polished his coffee colored loafers until they twinkled. He sauntered out into the kitchen, the sweet aroma of eggs and french toast sizzling in the frying pan.

OVER ON THE EAST SIDE

Sylvia suspiciously eyed James quizzically speculating as to why he was so energized only one day a month, but there was no indication that her son was developing into a peeping tom. James was not about to reveal the truth, about the magnificent unclothed women smeared in baby oil rubbing themselves all over his chunky self. These were the only dreams he had anymore. Before he would dream and marvel about comic book heroes, but these juvenile imaginings were exchanged for stark naked women well lubricated with glistening oils, their lustrous figures glossy and radiant, only existing to cater to his every whim.

As he thought about these women, he could feel his face altering into a smoldering shade of crimson. He could not disclose to his mother why he did not feel like a boy anymore. A boy would not preoccupy himself with such a sinful fixation. A boy would not shiver, his testicles tingling and prickling over the mere twinkling of a nude woman. A boy would not crave to perform naughty acts on women incessantly and without a reprieve in sight. James thought that these actions were representative of an authentic man. He had no concept that his abnormal preoccupation was detrimental to his development. Surely any boy that age is fascinated by the opposite sex, but when the interest turns into obsession, this is an indication that this boy is entering into a hazardous cycle of exploitation. He will never view women as equals, only as bodies. It was distressing that James view on life and love was so impersonal. If women were only bodies to him how could he ever sense his heart fill with adoration and compassion. That could turn into a lonesome existence, but James was not pondering over the future. All he could concentrate on were the naked women swirling through his every brainwave. Sylvia had no conception of what her son was thinking about. She still treated him like a baby.

Unlike James, Silvia was growing tiresome of her monthly visits to the migvah. She did not take pleasure in having to strip off her clothes in front of other individuals. It made her feel vulnerable, but she felt as if it was an obligation she had to abide by or she would suffer. Existing as an orthodox Jew resulted in Sylvia materializing into a very superstitious woman. If she did not respect all of the conventional rules of the Jewish religion she was petrified that misfortune would ensue.

She recalled a bible story she read from the Old Testament where Sara was advised not to turn around or she'd turn into a pillar of salt. Surely Sara's inquisitiveness got the better of her and as predicted she turned into a mammoth salt pillar which shortly thereafter disintegrated due to a wind storm. The salt crystals scattered over the sandy wasteland leaving no indication that she ever existed. Sylvia was confident that her life would burst into flames if she did not stick to her stringent religious convictions. She was never so fanatical though until she met Ernie. In fact Sylvia was not born Jewish, but Ernie influenced her to convert to Judaism. It was a humiliating troth that Ernie and Sylvia never divulged to anyone, not even James. If anyone ever discovered this scandalous revelation, both Sylvia and Ernie would be prohibited from participating in synagogue. In order to satisfy the others suspicions about her being an authentic Jew, Sylvia colored her sandy blonde hair a dark chestnut brown to resemble her fellow friends in the congregation. The only motivation which hurled her fool force was her adulation for Ernie. She glorified him as no other woman ever did, therefore compelling him to make an exception. She hated being an orthodox Jew, but in order to stay with Ernie she had to abide. Therefore she would have to maintain this fictitious charade to secure the affections of her husband. Not one of the rituals she hated more than the migvah. Sylvia found having to stoop to a level where you are required to bow in front of someone more authoritative sexist, but everything about being orthodox was chauvinist. All she desired was to resume relations with her husband without having to undergo the same trials and tribulations each and every month.

At temple during services the women always sat upstairs on the tiny balcony while the men sat on the spacious floor downstairs. When services were complete the men of the congregation would swig down countess bottles of grape wine and assemble into a circle performing the hava nagila. They danced boisterously, their faces transforming into a vivid shade of ruby red until they could no longer remain standing erect. Sylvia and the other women were just spectators from above, remaining composed and undeterred by the tumultuous festivities beneath them.

James had no concept of how much his mother detested her monthly migvah engagements, but this was not his concern. He also found following the traditions of Orthodox Judaism challenging but he found himself extremely appreciative that his mother remained so passionate when it came to following the traditions of the migvah. James was grateful that Ms. Rabinawitz had vanished. She could no longer scrutinize his every action.

Upon entering the migvah Sylvia and James separated, Sylvia retreating to the changing room and James wobbling over to the familiar mango orange recliner. James had calculated that waiting approximately five minutes before he began his spying session an ideal time. He sauntered over to the secret door squeezing his head between the narrow crevice he allowed himself. His tongue was saturated with beads of dribble. His eyes meandered to one lady in particular who retained fair porcelain skin and an absolute radiance. His hand gradually crawled down to his testicles his hand moving back and forth repeatedly while he wheezed breathlessly. His eyeballs began to focus on her dainty feet with her impeccably polished pink toenails and inched up her flawlessly formed legs to her succulent thighs finally to rest on her most personal part prettified by a bountiful abundance of ginger tresses. Her firm supple behind enticed him, but his time was limited so he graduated onto her belly, so smooth, and ornamented with such an appealing belly button. Her breasts captivated him, the two fleshy mounds festooned with two stiff, petite rosy pink nipples he desired to nibble on ferociously. Her graceful swan like neck appeared so dainty holding her sweet face so elegantly. Her lilac stained heart shaped lips recited a Hebrew prayer while she immersed herself into the lukewarm bubbly bath. Upon exiting the pool of heavenly bliss the supervisor supplied her with a burgundy towel, a similar shade to the shirt James was wearing. He aspired to be that towel so badly so that he could smear himself all over her drenched silky flesh. Her emerald green eyes remained somber while she completed her tribute to God, and James squinty brown eyes for the first time altered into an ebony black, the brown nonexistent while he fondled himself and squeezed out the gooey pasty white fluid. His breath remained shallow, sweat droplets sticking to his forehead moistening his carrot colored hair significantly.

At a snails pace he toddled over to the washroom where he dampened a washcloth. James placed the fresh, cool cloth on his forehead wiping away the perspiration and erasing away any indication that he pleasured himself. He sat himself on the toilet seat quivering anxiously hoping that his act did not stir up any suspicion. He tried to contain himself swiftly, for his mother was about to return at any moment.

As James predicted, a few brief moments later Sylvia's scrawny knuckles thumped at the door causing thunderous vibrations. James rapidly fastened his silver brass belt buckle and dabbed the washcloth over his dampened brow one last time. Sylvia desired to know why she had to drag James out of the restroom every time her migvah session was complete. She was already exasperated from these monthly ordeals, and she was in no frame of mind to linger at this house that she so truly despised. James nonchalantly unlocked the door attempting to remain unperturbed by the suspicious circumstances of the situation.

"I'm all ready mama. Let's go." James said casually.

"James, you are soaking wet. Are you running a fever." Sylvia knelt over to touch his forehead.

"You don't feel as if you're running a fever" she replied her eyes gradually creeping down to the noticeable circular damp stain positioned directly underneath his belt clasp.

James fixated his gaze onto hers and hesitantly offered a feeble explanation as to why his pants were sodden in that one spot.

"Oh, I was pressed up against the sink and the water sprayed me. It'll be dry in no time though."

Sylvia recognized that James wasn't telling the truth. Her motherly intuition told her different. He remained so withdrawn and distant. He no longer was interested in any of the activities that had captured his former interest. Sylvia, almost unable to contain her enthusiasm had leaped upon an advertisement in the newspaper for a comic book convention, but James remained dispassionate concerning the diversion he formerly treasured. Deep within her heart Sylvia knew that James was entering a perilous world complete of indulgence and temptation. Sylvia projected with utmost certainty that James metamorphosis would come hence as soon as he entered adolescence, but she did not anticipate losing her only son to a higher power which she could not manipulate.

Unfortunately, Ernie offered no comfort. He was too engrossed in being an orthodox Jew to take a genuine interest into what his son was emerging as, so Sylvia had to bear the unpleasantness of the circumstances and delve into an environment she had absolutely no preparation for. Basically she would have to shadow her son every moment of every waking hour no matter how sickened she would find herself. This was her only born, her baby, and she could not let that formerly jovial and gregarious boy always filled with hilarity and warmth vanish.

On the way back from the migvah Sylvia attempted to put her arm around James, but he apprehensively flinched back signaling Sylvia that she was not invited to lavish any physical affections on him whatsoever. James felt extremely awkward around Sylvia considering the fact that he had unintentionally glimpsed her while she was bathing at the migvah. He tried to relate to his mother, but his perception of her was dirtied. She was no longer a mother to him, but a woman identical to all the other grubby sluts out there. From now on he would mistake any fondness she would try to bestow upon him as sexual. Sylvia stretched out her arm trying to place it through his, but James hastily positioned his portly hands in his coat pockets. All he could think about was his mother naked.

Visualizing sucking on his mother's breast as a pacifier sickened him. How could she of wedged those elongated floppy milk jugs in his face. Imagining himself gurgling, creamy milk beads sloshing off of his jowls made him feel as if he was going to regurgitate. He puckered his lips in a sour expression and tried to lick the bitter remnants away.

As soon as they returned home James as expected retreated to his room and Sylvia began rinsing the meats off for supper. The stillness began to prove unnerving for Sylvia. Usually she could hear James stir about in his room thumping into the furnishings or toys which congested his room, but there was not one echo coming from that corner of the house. She deliberated repeatedly whether she should tap at his door to reassure herself that James was out of harms way. A peculiar hunch persisted to slither into her mind causing her imagination to concoct some fanatical hallucinations. Hurriedly, she dashed to his door, but remembered to act with discretion so she rapped lightly several times calmly calling his name.

Sylvia could not distinguish one audible noise from behind that door so she retreated to the end of the corridor and sprinted forward with all the potency she could muster up smashing into the locked door causing several wooden slivers to plummet to the floor. Her eyes fearfully scurried from one corner of the room to the other, but James had gone astray. A chilled breeze blew upon her chestnut mane causing her to focus on the window which was halfway open.

James, so irritated with his mother, had astonishingly squeezed himself out of his window and slithered down the gutter pipe. He scuttled as speedily as his stout flabby legs would permit him, oblivious to where his journey would take him. Not more that a few minutes later he began to wheeze frenziedly sniveling like an infant whose diaper was sodden with urine. He plunged into the soggy mud - covered lawn bewildered as to how he even got there, but it was too late to return. How would he justify his running off without am excuse to his mother.

About a mile away there were several stores and restaurants where James could browse and find something to snack on while he formulated a plan. He just hoped he could walk that far without crumpling up and collapsing to the ground. Miraculously, an hour later James found himself looking onto his destination. He had never performed such a grueling task, and for what? He could not even recollect why he had gone astray. His mother was not so horrendous, but still she was a woman, and women to him existed as insignificant filthy rubbish. If his father was at home he would not of dare disrespected him for fear that his behind would have ended up encrusted with gory blood splattered welts as last time.

James wandered down the picturesque avenue crammed full of an assortment of specialty stores, but his eyes rested on one shop in particular adorned by a sizeable hot pink neon sign which read **"BOOKSTORE"** in capital letters. The windows were tinted a murky shade of black, so it was difficult to perceive what mystery lay beyond those windows. His inquisitiveness was beginning to inflict great suffering upon him. He treaded softly toward the entrance opening the door bit by bit as to not ignite upheaval from the other patrons browsing through the aisles.

James could not help but to inspect what kind of merchandise this store sold. He could not believe where his voyage had transported him. How fortunate could he have been? Magazine covers exhibiting nude woman were flaunted in every imaginable space of the shop. There was quite an expansive assortment ranging from the more traditional publications such as *Playboy* to *Hustler* to the more raunchy such as *High Society*. Other magazines specialized in freakish or grotesque fetishes. There was *Large and Lovely* displaying overweight women, *Younguns*, a revolting publication parading adolescent school girls in pigtails, *Hermaphrodite Heaven*, a monthly periodical presenting hermaphrodites, and *Bushy Babes*.

James walked to the rear shelf of the shop glimpsing at the magnificence which encircled him. James mounted himself onto a flimsy wooden circular footstool fearful that it would shatter beneath him due to the pressure he placed upon it. He stretched his chunky, stunted fingers out reaching for the magazine entitled *Beaver Weekly* and flipped it open. He stroked the glossy cover tenderly placing a dramatically poignant kiss onto the cover model. He licked his salty fingers in order to flick through the pages faster opening his polluted "bible" to page 49. Ms. Georgia 1978 looked as if she was plucked fresh off the plantation. James cautiously tilted his head to the side to admire her heavenly curvaceous body resting alongside a withered bale of hay. Her fiery scarlet mane was tied into an adorable pair of braids fastened by two olive checkered ribbons, Although she was nude she gave the impression of being so angelic resting in her cherubic pose. Her tan shimmering skin appeared so silky, its iridescence inspiring in him divine sensations. Her plentiful globular breasts were festooned with the sweetest pair of velvety stiff pink nipples. His tongue flitted in and out of his mouth eagerly in anticipation, envisioning lapping at each swollen fleshy mound of delight. Her legs were spread wide open revealing an almost completely shaven patch bejeweled by a slender trail of ginger fuzz arranged in a decorative triangular pattern. Her glittery plump lips pouted so invitingly causing any salivating man or boy who dared to glance at her to become ensnared in her web of seduction. His mental obsession was beginning to make him feel physically ill. Hiding such a significant secret was causing him severe migraines and heartburn. The guilt was compiling in his system ultimately waiting to detonate if he did not alleviate a portion of the strain. Suddenly James recognized that the new life he was leading was unethical and dishonest. He was not only damaging others, but impairing himself as well. To him, it was acceptable to live with his dirty little secret from day to day, but to have others discover that he was not who he appeared to be filled him with a panicky feeling. If someone who knew of James was asked to depict an illustration of who James existed to be, they'd almost certainly state that he was a quiet and subdued boy, incredibly considerate of others feelings, and very intellectual. They would never speculate that James was a shady pervert who pleasured himself by spying on nude women who did not wish to be ogled at.

James then walked further to the rear of the shop and was led to into a dim narrow hallway. At the end of the passageway laid a drab gray door flaking of paint chips. Placed above the door was a vivid pink neon sign marked *"PRIVATE."* Chuck slowly turned the knob and opened the door. Positioned on each side of James were five plastic booths marked with blue and black scrawl, and on the side of each booth was a glass hole. James placed his face against the glass hole. He squeezed his ample behind in the uncomfortable plastic booth. Hesitantly, he placed his youthful freckled face against the plate of circular glass.

James obediently placed the quarter in a tiny slit just large enough to fit the quarter into and placed his face back against the glass hole slightly misting the window with his deep shallow breathing. The darkness of the room behind the glass vanished and a shadowy outline gradually materialized as the room brightened. This ethereal silhouette shrouded in mystery began to swivel seductively as a recognizable striptease tune blared through the speakers. James, mesmerized, looked intently at this strikingly exotic Asian woman with gleaming stick straight black hair past her buttocks. The chintzy light bulb above her flickered causing James to squint so he would not neglect one moment of her performance. She energetically gyrated, being careful not to make eye contact with James. This was what James found so thrilling about the experience. It stimulated James when these girls did not detect him spying on them. Without their consent, it was as if he was being especially naughty. Although this show before him was completely fabricated and artificial, James could imagine that she was oblivious to the truth that he was watching her. The naked Asian woman then sat herself on a metallic silver chair in the middle of the room and began to spread open her petite, muscular legs, but a shadow of dimness abruptly fell on the room. James heatedly sprung out of the cubicle breathlessly. James frantically shuffled through his pants pockets trying to locate a quarter, but there was none to be found.

There was a man sitting in the booth next to him, a freakishly small man in fact, his elfin face pasted with facial hair. The man withdrew a quarter from his shirt pocket and callously dangled it in front of James.

"Exactly what will you do for this quarter?" the man mockingly inquired. James remained perplexed as to what the man wanted. The man stood up and reached his freakishly miniature hands down to his pants button slowly unfastening it and began to undo his zipper. He playfully stared into James's eyes and reaching behind the zipper began to fondle himself.

"I think you know what I want." The man cooed in an obvious manner. James still didn't know what the man wanted.

The man slowly inched closer towards James almost touching him. James could feel his hot foul breath on his neck and began to hobble in reverse towards the door. The man slammed James into the wall. Forcefully he cupped his hand around James neck beginning to strangle him. The man released his grasp from James's pudgy rolls of flab and cackled as James buckled down to the floor, wheezing painfully and clutching his tender neck and began to cry. James realized that he was not going to triumph. The man had prevailed long before James was alert to what was about to arise. James surrendered what small amount of dignity he held dear and submissively relinquished to the man's wishes.

The man placed his hand on James's carroty colored curls and shoved his head down to the front of his blue faded denims. He flipped James pumpkin tinted ringlets and patted the crowning of his head rewardingly. The man rummaged above his head for a light switch and flicked it off while James hesitantly performed his obligation. James's queasiness was beginning to supercede his performance, and the could sense how reluctant James was to finish his responsibility.

"Listen, you little runt, you better finish me off or I'll tell your mom what you've been doing." the irritably advised as he rammed James's head into the wall behind him. James could foretell that his life was to abruptly enter its last stages if he did not provide the man with the kind of gratification that he reckoned he warranted. James could begin to feel himself suffocate as his throbbing throat constricted. He struggled with every ounce of strength he could muster up not to shed a tear, but compromising his sexuality proved too heartbreaking to tolerate. The salty wet droplets persistently gushed forth bleeding through the cracks of his parched lips which stung immensely.

At last the man moaned cries of sickening satisfaction signaling James that his chore was complete. Viciously, the man yanked at James's head and thrust him at the wall treating him as if he was no more than a soiled mud-splattered swine.
"Thanks kid. I really needed that, and with those last words the man walked out the back door and vanished.

James, in a squatting stance, held his face in his hands softly sniveling. He slowly collected himself and trudged towards the exit door feebly pushing it open, momentarily glimpsing at the rumpled up magazine in the corner. He swiftly snatched the glossy periodical, its cover graced with a nude flaxen haired big busted woman and tightly wound the periodical into a thin cylinder, squeezing it into his pocket. He stumbled down the steps, placing his hands over his eyes to shield himself from the sweltering golden sun above. He wiped at his lips unceasingly attempting to rinse the foul putrid flavor away, but it would not evaporate. This day would never vanish from his memory. He would recollect every last waking minute of his existence of what he had done. From this moment on he would not consider himself as a purely heterosexual man. A heterosexual man does not give a blow job to a tiny, hairy, sordid man in an adult bookstore and peepshow shop. No matter how vigorously he tried to bathe these images out of his mind, the stain would forever bleed. He could persist to reiterate his fondness for women, but he knew the truth. Walking home he observed the cheery innocent faces of passerby's, and yearned so desperately to retain their childish nativity. It was likely that these people did not bear the weight of the world upon their shoulders as he did. He felt emotionally battered, his heart bruised and bleeding profusely. He wanted nothing more than to head back in the direction of that smutty store, point a gun in the direction of that man and blow his brains out all over his filthy shop. He longed to make the man taste the vulnerability that he felt, but the vengeance he hungered for did not appear likely. He found being intimidated by the man unnerving. Before James could flirt with the prospect of engaging in the adult lifestyle, but now he was beginning to realize that every action had a consequence. It was no longer all amusement and entertainment, but instead a hazardous hobby that could obliterate anyone who converged in its path. James did not want to disrupt the routine that he had become so accustomed to, therefore he could not be so susceptible to the wrongdoing of others. He would never place faith in another living soul as long as he was cognizant of his actions.

Meanwhile Sylvia remained at the kitchen table for over two hours twiddling her thumbs and stewing in a mixed brew of seething madness, uneasiness, and unadulterated apprehension. She contemplated probing the neighborhood and questioning neighbors, but she did not foresee herself as salvaging James this way. Therefore she believed that remaining at the house was the most sensible decision.

At first when she discovered that James had been missing, she truly believed that she would go stark raving mad in the short span of time before he returned, but shortly thereafter she came to her senses. *"He probably just went to a friends house to look at comic books."* She wishfully thought to herself. She was not knowledgeable to the other putrid ingredients that were being added to his soiled mixture. She would never suspect that James had already caught a glimpse of half of her friends naked, or that he had become a devoted connoisseur of pornography, or that he was performing oral sex on perverted dwarflike psychopaths in adult bookstores and peepshow shops. If she had any realization whatsoever of the destruction that was beginning to impede on his defenses, then she surely would of sprinted down the streets of their town thunderously bellowing out his name. She truly cared about her son and was attentive to his needs. She nursed him when he was ill, smeared away his tears of shame, and educated James in the philosophies of Judaism, but her attempt to make her son into a well rounded individual was crumbling away before her very eyes. She had no concept of how to resuscitate the purity he once so faithfully retained.

Unexpectedly, she could hear someone frantically jiggling at the front door knob. She prayed that at any moment she would catch a glimpse of the chubby cheeks dappled with sun speckles which she loved to tweak, the auburn tinged ringlets she tenderly stroked, and the warm chestnut brown eyes which reflected a level of intelligence no other sixteen year old could approximate. She animatedly scurried to the front door forcefully heaving it open and howling cries of relief as her eyes focused in on her beloved son's features.

"Oh, my God. James, I thought something happened to you." she blubbered as she dramatically clutched him close to her bosom.

Sylvia, winded at this point from sheer exhaustion grasped ahold of his fiery red ringlets and warmly stroked his full freckled cheeks. When she fixated her eyes on his she detected a ripeness never present before. He displayed an unfamiliar expression which she could not quite identify. It was as if this brief journey of his aged him into an elderly vegetable like man, his skin rough and leather like, his face furrowed with creases and sun spots.

"James, James!" She alarmingly rattled him trying to revive him out of his surreal state.

"Listen, mom. I'm awfully tired. I think I'm going to go to bed."

"What? I was so worried.

"You wouldn't be if you knew what I did." He indistinctly uttered to himself as he ascended up the stairway.

Sylvia distinctly heard what James had said but she lightheartedly chose to dismiss it as just another theatrical expression of adolescent rebellion on his part. She was determined to bathe herself in the blissful moment with or without his companionship. Meanwhile James dissected every repelling attribute of his decomposing diseased face in the bathroom mirror. James weakly removed his clothing and crawled into the shower stall rotating the knob until the rainfall which drizzled from the showerhead above scorched his aching inflamed flesh. He sadistically scoured himself with a coarse loofa scrub, attempting to expunge the sludge that feasted on his remains. He feverishly massaged his hands together breeding a bubbly swelling mass of froth. Lathering the foamy creation, he buttered himself attempting to melt away his dismal recollection of the afternoon. He soaped his copper colored coils which adorned his scalp, shredding away at several sections with the intention of muffling the indignity that was imposed upon him. If the physical pain could supercede the twinges of the emotional mauling he harbored, then perhaps he could be rewarded with a glimmer of serenity.

He hypnotically watched as the flood of rain water spiraled down the drain, and revolving the knob into the off position he clomped out of the shower stall seizing a lush green towel garlanded with delicate pink flower petals which appeared as if it was blossoming. Hurriedly he changed into his fluffy terry cloth robe and grabbed his toothbrush and toothpaste out of the medicine cabinet. Brutally he polished his teeth with the jagged bristles of his toothbrush trying to replace the curdling vinegary flavor lodged in his tongue with a fresh mint taste. He fumbled around the medicine cabinet for the goblet of peppermint flavored mouthwash and took a few swigs of the tangy potion. He gulped down the elixir and gargled repeatedly until he extinguished the bacteria which persistently lingered on his tongue, gums, and teeth. He could still smell the overwhelming stench that clung to Chuck's dirtied flesh, and attempted to purge his airway of the foulness that implanted itself in his nostrils. He rubbed his nose raw with a washcloth chafing it severely until droplets of blood leisurely trickled downward.

He nearly vomited as he glimpsed his likeness in the reflective instrument of truth. His eyes appeared sunken, submerged in a substantial covering of lard. His chin converged into his neckline dangling limply not unlike a chicken noose. It seemed as if he gulped a gust of air and did not puff out considering the roundness of his cheeks. The splash of freckles, shaped like a butterfly, that spattered the bridge of his nose and cheeks, once so endearing currently proved obnoxious, and his mop of uncontrolled crimson curls caused him to bear a resemblance to a jester. The jester extracted laugher from his audience awarding his spectators with unadulterated amusement. He could not depend on his exterior to captivate the audience, but instead relied on his charm and wittiness. James would never enchant his fellow classmates by flaunting his outer shell, and unfortunately he was losing contact with his inner spirit as well. He obtained an opportunity to gain his peer's respect, but allowed this prospect to slip through his plump portly fingers. The probability of him developing into a mentally healthy and wholesome man was steadily fluttering away.

It was time to profess his appreciation for women. Yes, he depleted the bodily fluid out of a male organ, but he was forced to do so. There was not one aspect about a male that aroused James. Women's bodies were pleasurable to the eye with their delicate curves and their silky skin. Men's bodies on the other hand bore a remarkable resemblance to an unkempt bushy primate. Masculinity lacked sex appeal, and James found men to be incredibly dull.

James reached into his pants pocket for the crinkled pore magazine and spread it out onto his sapphire blue comforter. He eagerly bounced onto the snugly bedspread and began absorbedly flipping the pages. This magazine entitled *"Screw"* was a good deal more raunchy than the other periodicals which he had been privileged enough to preview. This publication featured numerous sexual acts being simulated opposed to the standard centerfold girl. One spread displayed two women replicating the act of oral sex on each other.
    "Girls on girls are so much sexier than guys on guys." James thought to himself. James's outlook on lesbian sex was a viewpoint that many chauvinistic men share. Homosexual men are assaulted each and every day. They are perceived as perverts, and their lifestyle as sinful. Lesbians, on the other hand are applauded for their way of life. Many men develop a distorted depiction of gay women, fantasizing that all lesbian women are towering golden-haired beauties. In all actuality the majority of these women are obese dumpy masculine women with short spiked haircuts, but society continues to portray these falsehoods as authentic in order to kindle a deceptive portrayal which men can aspire to romanticize.

He leisurely flicked the remaining pages paying careful attention not to tear the few pieces that were oddly wedged together. On several pages, it appeared that there was some sort of gummy residue which some degenerate in one of the cubicles sprayed on, but James preferred to disregard this unsanitary attribute and resumed leafing through the sticky pages. The one layout which mesmerized him consisted of a buxom redhead, her hair teased and hair sprayed amorously gazing into the camera lens. A whitish milky fluid was squirted on her chest, and her full pouty lips were invitingly spread open. James envisaged that this cheap woman was seducing only him. In his imagination the scarlet haired vixen seductively straddled James passionately stroking his flesh and heatedly humping him until they concurrently climaxed. Their shrill shattering yelps of contentment piercingly echoed through their bedroom awakening the neighbors below.

Unexpectedly, the swift vigorous pounding at the bathroom door disconnected his brain circuits from generating additional injurious and exaggerated notions. He distinctly requested from his mother that she not infringe on his privacy. Since he was a small boy his eccentric appetite for seclusion persisted to remain distinct contrasted to the other children his age.

From the instant that James unlocked the door, Sylvia sensed his confusion and disarray. She startlingly jolted backwards when she stared at the upheaval in James's eyes. They resembled two blazing volcanoes, the gold flecks of his iris igniting with fury and his dusky sable pupils constricting and deadened like the gritty ashes that deposit themselves at the depths of the volcanic eruption. His dampened tousled tresses were teeming with several gnarled tangles, and his richly rosy cheeks made him appear feverish, and when James ran right past her and out the door Sylvia knew that her little boy wasn't the same James he was a few months ago.

CHAPTER 41

Main Street was breathtaking at night. For years it had been the cornerstone of the community. Therefore when Chuck's adult shop and the adult theater found its way onto Main Street, the distinguished citizens of the town were enraged, but it was out of their jurisdiction to exercise their authority. The only consolation offered to the residents of the town was that these adult themed businesses were tucked away towards the back alley of Main Street, not easily visible to tourists and children. Chinese lanterns, in an assortment of pastel shades were strung between the antique lamp posts bathing James's freckled face in a warm bluish glow. His feet were beginning to ache due to the cobblestone streets beneath him, which created an awkward surface for James to keep his footing, but his determination drove him to finish his journey.

At last, he could recognize the scarlet flickering bulbs in the distance reading *"Adult Marquee"*. Perspiration implanted itself between the crevices of his clammy palms, causing him to frantically rub his hands together. The drumming of his heart became louder as he neared the theater, the steady thumping in his chest creating a backup beat for James to make his entrance. The flashy lights began to blur together, obscuring his vision, but James quickly gained control of his senses, reclaiming the courage which he had stumbled upon in adult book store. Brightly lit posters of the featured picture of the evening were tacked up behind glass displays. This evening's film was entitled *"Pizza Party."* In the poster three large busted platinum blondes stood behind a pizza delivery man. The women had expressions of ecstasy pasted onto their face, their glistening tongues protuding and erotically wagging. The pizza man reveled in his fortuity, bearing a mixed expression of euphoria and satisfaction, as the women massaged their polished fingernails into his ebony gnarled tresses.

James's manhood began to prickle in response to the provocative pester, causing him to swiftly scurry to the ticket window. A dumpy looking man in his twenties unexcitedty sat in the booth. He switched from twiddling his thumbs to stroking his thick cocoa colored mustache. His cold gray eyes remained unresponsive as James approached the ticket window. The man extensively studied James's youthful ring-shaped face, his nose and cheeks splashed with an array of bright orange freckles assembled into an unusual butterfly pattern.

"How old are you?" the ticket vender crudely asked, his arms folded on top of each other to convey *an* impression of authority.

"I am eighteen, of course. I would like one ticket for "Pizza Party" please." James impatiently emphasized, his throat beginning to crackle under the pressure.

"Listen kid. I don't think I can do that for you. Read this sign." The man curtly requested, his stubby finger scattered with several stray hairs pointing to the small square sign painted in white with bold red letters directly above his head. The overbearing print read "No minors allowed. You must be eighteen to enter the premises."

"Uh, uh..." James nervously stammered, his throat constricting due to the chilled glaze the man placed upon him.

"What, kid you can't read. Is that it? Are you that young?" the man cruelly chuckled.

James, one to definitely buckle under excessive pressure, reached his quivering hand into his pocket pulling out a laminated business card which he had found earlier in the evening. He silently presented it to the man, slipping it under the window, and observed how his frosty expression warmed at the sight of the card. An instant impression of recognition washed over the man's pock marked face, dotted with pink inflamed pustules which looked like they were about to rupture at any moment.

"That will be two dollars."
James was so appreciative at that very moment that he reached into his pocket for a twenty dollar bill, *casually* slipping it beneath the opening of the window.

Paul sarcastically grinned, rolling his murky gray eyes as he turned his head. It was not difficult for Paul to predict which of these youthful boys suffered an unhealthy preoccupation with sex. Ironically, pornography did not hold great appeal for Paul. The theater was a family business he had inherited from his father. When his father was a young man he owned a shop filled with machines where if you slipped a quarter in the slot, a movie would appear of various nude women. As time progressed, Paul's father decided to make his business that much more profitable and opened the "XXX" theater. Paul was not infatuated with sex or these girls in any way. To him the theater was just business. Therefore he expressed great amusement in the shady characters who frequented his establishment.

James mightily opened the front entrance, his newfound air of confidence visibly apparent to the others in the theater. The soles of his shoes sunk into the spongy padded carpeting beneath him. James had never viewed such a garish spectacle. The decorative theme of the theater was terribly tasteless, with the blinding blood red shag carpeting, and the gaudy golden chandeliers that dangled from the ceiling. A wooden door stained with a reddish maple syrup tint that read *"Gentleman"* was sandwiched in the corner opposite the refreshment stand. James felt the urge to use the restroom facility. His portly fingers lightly grazed over the varnished surface of the door, gently prodding it open. As he gazed upon the wall, a sensation of giddiness overwhelmed him. Arranged on the wall were thousands of pornographic photographs cut out and decoratively assembled into a collage. An assortment of nude women positioned in sinful poses were pasted onto each and every last crevice of the wall, including over the toilets, the sinks, and on the ceiling. James delicately swept his fingertips over the pictures glazed over with a glossy finish.

He caressed their breasts, their buttocks, their most intimate of places, becoming so immersed in his special moment with these objects of his affection that he did not even notice the creaking of the door. It was Paul who entered, but as soon as he witnessed James in his hypnotic state, Paul made his presence barely detectable. He was embarrassed for the boy, so inappropriately enchanted by the mere peek of exposed flesh. James circled the room, his eyes never straying from the divine imagery before him. He began to smear his face over the colorful photographs, placing dripping wet kisses over the centerfold girls saturating their images with a trail of saliva. Paul stood there, his face buried in his palms, shaking his face from side to side in disbelief. He could not endure this pathetic display of distasteful behavior any longer. He was used to perverts coming into his movie theater, but this happened to be a little excessive.

James fumbled around in his pocket for his monogrammed

handkerchief and dabbed at the drool swimming in the fleshy pockets of the corners of his mouth. He hurriedly scurried past Paul and out the door, averting eye contact. James did not turn around to acknowledge Paul. He only waved his hand in the air as recognition that he heard and wobbled over to the refreshment counter to ogle the candy, popcorn, and drinks.

In the meantime Paul leisurely stepped towards the wall to explore the smudges and spit that had been left by his new young friend. Paul gasped as he moved closer to these provocative pornographic images. Almost every photograph was covered in fingerprints, lip smudges, and saliva. Amazingly, James did not happen to neglect one of the women. Paul's eyes darted from the African American goddess with the creamy chocolate skin to the Asian beauty with her shiny coal black hair and golden skin to the freckly pale redheaded girl. James lavished his attention on a broad range of women smothering their naked bodies with kisses. Paul was beginning to realize that this young man who entered his theater harbored an unhealthy obsession with female nudity and that he was contributing to this boy's sickness by allowing him into his theater, but his hands were tied. Paul pitied the poor boy, fearing that his twisted fixation could lead to violence and rape in the future, but he pocketed these unsettling premonitions in the back of his mind for the safety of his family. If he only discovered how that strange little man had orally raped him earlier that afternoon, Paul would have been outraged. If there was one behavior which he did not condone, it had to be child molestation, but even if Paul found out, again, his mouth would have to stay sealed for his and his family's well being.

James struggled to squat and pressed his freckled pug nose and chubby jowls, smudging the front window of the glass counter. He breathed in the heavenly aroma of the sweetly salted popcorn and carefully gazed over the plentiful assortment of candy. There were gummy drops rolled in sugar, chocolate mint patties, peanut butter brittle, chocolate caramel bars crammed with peanuts, and dark chocolate drops dusted by blinding white snow sprinkles. Every one of these sweet delicacies looked so delicious, teasing James with their endless chocolate layers and sugary fillings.

"Can I help you Sir?" a lanky fiery haired young woman with pale freckled skin and crimson wiry glasses asked.

Sixteen year old James was stunned that he was being

formally addressed by the title of Sir, but he decided not to challenge her poor judgment any further.

"Yes, I know what I would like." He replied, lowering his voice one octave in an attempt to impress the naive girl behind the counter. "1 would like a box of those gummy drops, a box of Snowcaps, the large tub of cheese buttered popcorn, and a large Coke with a squirt of cherry"

"Alright Sir. You said you wanted a box of gummy drops, a box of Snowcaps, a large tub of cheese buttered popcorn, and a large Coke with a squirt of cherry. Will that be all?

"Yes maam." He said, his eyes resting on her blossoming breasts and her hardened nipples poking through her blouse.

The girl uncomfortably looked down at her chest sensing that this man before her was staring at her chest. She felt violated, but working at an "XXX" rated theater had its disadvantages.

"All right" the woman hesitantly answered. "That will be $4.00."

James pulled out the bundle of cash from out of his pocket and thumbed through the large assortment of bills, finally handing the woman a $5.00 bill. He gently caressed her hand as she handed him his change. James was beginning to discover a newfound confidence deep within him, but what he did not realize was how inappropriate he was acting.

"Can I have your name?" James inquired confidently winking his right eye.

"No. You can't have my name, but I can loan it to you." The woman teasingly replied.

James blushed, his cheeks turning the color of bubble gum. His rich red freckles faded away as the color washed over his forehead, cheeks, and chin.

"My name is Katt. I'm Irish of course. You probably could tell with my red hair and freckles. I can't even tan. I try every summer, but I just burn. I wind up blistering really bad, Are you Irish?"

"No."

"Oh, I thought you were since you have red hair and freckles also."

"Nope. I'm not. I'm not quite sure how I got red hair."

"Yey." Samantha uncomfortably paused. "Hey, that's an interesting birthmark on your nose. It sort of looks like a butterfly."

"I hate it. Everyone at school has always teased me about it."

"You can't listen to those kids. That butterfly makes you unique. Don't ever let anyone bring you down. For instance, I hate working at this theater. These old perverts are always coming in here harassing me and staring. I know that I'm not pretty, but they don't care. It makes me feel so cheap, but I try not to let it get me down. I only work here, because Paul is a good friend of mine and I need the money. So, why are you in a place like this anyway?"

Suddenly, James felt ashamed. This genuine wholesome girl before him had been deceived by his youth and innocent appearance. She held no comprehension of how perverted he really existed to be.

"Uh, I'm just killing time, I guess. This is the only movie theater that was open."

"Well, I guess that is as good a reason as any."

Samantha reached under the counter and handed him the box of gum drops and Snowcaps. She then walked over to the popcorn machine, shoveling out the popcorn with a large metal scooping spoon. She held the bucket under the butter dispenser, showering the freshly popped kernels with a golden stream of liquid butter and finished by sprinkling it with large flakes of powdered cheese.

"Alright, James. I think that is it."

"I still need my Coke."

"Oh my. I am so sorry. I really am. How 'bout I offer you something free?"

James found her apologetic demeanor endearing. No one in his life had ever been so accommodating to his requests. He felt so guilty for peeping at her breasts like all of the other perverts, but no matter how well he could maintain the phony charade, he could not conceal the truth to himself. He was and always would be a pervert.

"No, that's quite alright. Thank you anyway."

Samantha quickly scuffled over to the soda fountain, grabbing a large paper cup and filled it to the rim. She then squirted a dash of cherry flavoring onto the top, the bubbles fizzing as the cherry flavor sunk to the bottom.

"Well, I guess that is it. Enjoy the show...."

"Listen, would you like to join me for the movie. There is no way I can finish this food all by myself."

"Oh, I'm sorry, James. I would really like to, but I'm still on the clock for another two hours. Thanks, though. Maybe I'll see you again sometime."

"Yey," James disappointedly agreed, attempting to conceal his frustration. He would always be the sort of guy that girls could talk to, but not be intimate with. Samantha was just like all of the others. She pretended to appreciate James for who he really was, but underneath it all she found him disgusting just as all of the other girls did. He no longer was embarrassed about visually fondling her breasts, for she was a tramp like all of the other girls, a dirty little whore whom he only wished to see naked and could have his way with.

James crammed the two boxes of candy into his pants pocket and grabbed the popcorn tub and cup of Coke off of the counter, arrogantly twisting in the direction of the door of the theater. He proceeded to sail right past the usher collecting the tickets for the evening show.

"Ticket please, Sir." The usher requested, dressed in an elegant black suit and bow tie.

"Oh, sorry." James absentmindedly answered, shuffling thorough his pants pocket for the ticket. "Here you go."

"Enjoy the show, Sir."

"Thank you."

The usher opened the threshold to the theater for James. If James had thought that the lobby was flashy, he had been mistaken for the actual theater was far more extravagant. The tin roof ceiling was ornately detailed. Cherubic carvings of eighteenth century angelic figures were carved into the border of the ceiling and statuettes of Greek goddesses stood on pedestals in every corner. Sculptures of richly assorted bowls of fruit stood on various other platforms, and a massive crystal chandelier was suspended from a golden chain in the center of the ceiling. The cushy seats were upholstered in the richest shade of royal red velvet, and the white marble floor twinkled as the light from the chandelier reflected off it.

James found a seat in the center of the theater. He wanted to remain as inconspicuous as possible and maintain a safe distance from the other patrons of the theater. He slumped into the seat nonchalantly looking over at the other people around him. Surprisingly, most of the other people were men. There were only two other women in the theater, and they were with a man. Many of the men looked older and creepy with their unkempt fluffy hair, glasses, ridiculously bushy mustasche, and bulky coats. It was as if they were also in disguise, camouflaging themselves so as to not be recognized by others and to keep suspicion to a minimum. James reached his hand into the popcorn, shuffling the dried kernels to the side and reaching for the perfectly glazed moist ones. He laid each piece of popcorn onto the tip of his tongue, pressing it against the roof of his mouth until each buttery morsel dissolved, and then drowned the remaining scraps with a swish of the cherry coke.

James wished to be isolated during his first experience at an "XXX" rated theater, but it did not look like this was going to happen. An awkwardly thin gentleman with a curled mushcthasce, thick black glasses, hook nose, and plaid shirt sat directly next to James.

"Hi." The man shyly said.

"Hi." James answered in an irritated tone.

"So, you don't mind if I sit by you, do you?"

James, concealing how aggravated he was, offered the man with the reply that he
was hoping for.

"No, not at all. Feel free to sit here."

"Thank you. Listen," the man softly whispered, inching his head closer to James.   "Have you ever been in a place like this before?"

"No, I haven't."

"I wish I could say the same.. I'm sort of embarrassed, actually. I have a wife and two kids, but they don't know that I'm here. They never know that I come here. If my wife knew, she'd divorce me. Yep, yep, she definitely would. She doesn't understand how exciting it can be. She thinks it's trashy. She doesn't want to listen to the truth. I've tried to get a sitter for the kids and take her with me, but she won't go. Oh, well. It's not my fault right?" the man questioned nervously.

"No, no. Not at all." James reassuringly offered, not knowing quite what to say to the man.

"Thanks. So, I've been a little rude, talking nonstop and not finding out what your name is."

"James. My name is James."

"James, that's a neat name. My name is Rick. It's nice to

meet you." He said, offering out his hand to shake as a courteous gesture.

James, stirring his hand in the popcorn tub, lifted his greasy hand out, and reached for Rick's hand. Rick squeezed James's hand tightly, the oily buttered juices seeping into the cracks of his palm and between his knuckles.

"It's nice to meet you too. Listen, I don't think I can eat all of this food by myself. Would you like some?"

"Oh, no. Thank you though. I just can't eat during these flicks. It's hard to eat and watch people having sex at the same time."

"Yey, I suppose so." James ashamedly replied

The lights from the crystal bulbs in the chandeliers dimmed, covering the theater in a blanket of darkness. The chattering and chewing of food momentarily paused swaddling the theater with a brief moment of silence. James lounged back in the velvety chair, the butterflies in his stomach excitedly fluttering.

Gradually the screen brightened and the sound of birds chirping billowed out from the surrounding speakers. A middle class suburban house materialized, painted a shade of forest green. A small orange two door hatchback with a pizza delivery sign up top pulled up in front of the perfectly manicured emerald green lawn, the lush strands of grass glistening with moistened drops of dew. The delivery man, dressed in a navy blue shirt, emblazoned with a picture of a pizza and a baseball cap swung open the door of his car and grabbed the pizza out of the passenger seat. He cheerfully strolled up to the door, whistling while he rang the doorbell A glamorous blonde bombshell opened the door, draped in a slinky red negligee.

"Hello." The pizza man startlingly greeted, thunderstruck by the woman's beauty and flimsy lace camisole.

"Hello." The woman responded, her baby blue eyes and thick black eyelashes fluttered flirtatiously while she licked her cherry red lips.

"That will be $5.50 for the pizza maam."

"Al right. Let me go get my wallet."

The woman seductively twisted her body around, her shiny patent leather red heels clicking as they touched the twinkling white marble floor. Her feathered flaxen tresses bounced off of her lightly tanned shoulders as she walked over to the cherry wood hallway table and reached for her leather coin purse. Slowly, she bent over for her coin purse, her lacy camisole rising, revealing her rounded plump buttocks. The pizza man began to cough, astonished that this vixen wore no panties.

"Oh no. You know what." The woman said, jiggling her empty coin purse. "This is very embarrassing, but I don't have any money. My husband must have taken it to work. Can I offer you something else perhaps." The woman offered, licking her pearly white teeth, and running her glossy red nails through her golden mane.

"Yey....What do you exactly have in mind?" the man asked, curious and tempted by her proposition.

"Follow me,"
They both walked through a long hallway and into a master bedroom. The bedroom was painted a rich buttery shade of cream and accented by various paintings of blossoming gardens. Flourishing plants stood in every corner of the room, and a silky black bedspread covered the king size bed. A light sprinkle could be heard echoing from the shower in the bathroom.

"Is your husband in the shower?"

"My husband?" the woman softly chuckled. "No. My friend, Tawny is in the shower. I was just about to jump in there with her when you rang the door bell. Tawny and I are really tired, and we are going to need some help washing each other. If you don't mind, I'd really like for you to take a shower with us and help out."

"Yey. Sure." The man, wide eyed exclaimed eagerly, his tongue hungrily wagging.

The woman opened the door. The steam from the shower clouded the bathroom veiling it in a shadowy haze. An outline of a curvy nude woman scrubbing herself behind the glass shower stall began to materialize through the mist. The woman grasped the pizza man's hand and led him to the shower stall, reaching for the silver handle and opening the entryway to a heavenly shower of naked flesh. Tawny tilted her head back, her buttery beige waves tumbling down her bronzed soaking wet back. The camera inched closer to the front of her body, moving in to her dripping wet breasts. Her breasts were not tanned but instead a delicate creamy shade of white, perfectly framing her erect pink nipples. She began to knead her doughy mounds, pinching her nipples with her glossy pink nails, a faint pink, the color of bubble gum. She wrung her washcloth

Rachel Gunn

*under the scorching waterfall, squeezing the spongy rag over each
breast. The trickle of water dribbled down her chest, the tear shaped
drops of condensation sticking to her perfectly shaped mounds of
delight. The drops of water then oozed into her naval, finally
seeping into her orifice of pleasurable sensations. Tawny,
disoriented by the rhythmic patter of the artificial cloudbursts and
the soothing warmth, was oblivious to the two blurred figures
behind the glass door. The woman tossed the spaghetti straps of her
negligee off of her shoulders, causing the silky dress to slide to the
floor. She stepped into the shower, her sweet fatty buns jiggling as
she stepped behind Tawny and circled her arms around her waist.
She began nibbling on Tawny's neck, stroking her slick polished
nails over her naval. Tawny moaned, arching her neck back in
appreciation as the woman began to fondle her breasts. Tawny
turned her body and faced the woman who began to nuzzle her face
in between her breasts. Her fuzzy pink tongue greedily lapped at her
nipples and her cherry red nails dug into Tawny's behind, squeezing
a spongy handful of flesh. The pizza man stood spellbound,
hypnotized by the two unclad goddesses before him. He began to
unzip his pants, reaching for his stiff manhood and shamelessly
stroke it. The girls began to dance, twirling their hips and
massaging their breasts while their buttocks friskily bounced.
Tawny wedged her wet tongue into the woman's mouth, the two
tongues becoming a twisted alliance of ecstasy. They hungrily
slurped, their whimpering cries of fulfillment echoing as they
slapped each others behinds. The stinging red welts represented a
battle wound inflicted by their deep hunger for a sexual
gratification which could only be satisfied by the same sex. The
pizza man was only an accessory to accompany the leading ladies.*

James sat spellbound by the cinematography before him. He was a
sixteen year old boy, definitely oversexed, and most importantly
perverted. As an older man he would drop pencils under the table at
libraries just so he could look under the women's skirts. He
frequented porn movies and strip clubs every night. James was a
pig, and I was going to do something about it!

OVER ON THE EAST SIDE

CHAPTER 42

I sat in my car waiting for James to exit the club. I should have expected that he'd spend a couple of hours in the dungeon of foul misbehaving, but not four hours. I deliberated whether I should actually stay in the car and wait until he comes out, go into the club and approach him, or abandon the entire plan, my squealing tires emitting a thick haze of smoke to shroud the parking lot in a vaporous smog. I tapped my pearly pink fingernails against the cream colored dashboard, hoping that the decision would magically appear in my head at any moment. I was exhausted of waiting in my run down hunk of scrap metal. I glanced down at my silver watch, the ticking faintly audible, and saw that it was already 12:15 a.m. in the morning. I had gotten here at 8:00 p.m., expecting that he'd leave at 10:00 p.m. I was hoping that I didn't miss him, but I couldn't have. First of all, his car was still in the parking lot, and secondly his ballooned figure, flaming red ringlets, reddish freckled skin, and obnoxious leatherwear was hard to miss.

"Shit, come on you pervert. How long can you stare at naked women, you fucking freak!" I irritatingly shouted, slamming my head against the steering wheel and resting it there for a minute. Just as I lifted my head and lost all hope, James appeared, wobbling down the front stairway of *Foxy Tails*. He reached into his front jeans pocket for his set of car keys, jiggling them as he limped out of breath to his snowy white Oldsmobile,

For weeks I had been planning this, but as it became real and I saw my enemy in the flesh, I began to get nervous. My heart would not stop beating, my fingers became numb, and my stomach began to do somersaults, but I had to gain control of my anxiousness and my bodily reactions. I was not going to let James prevail. In fact I was going to try to do everything in my power to punish that miserable slovenly sinner for destroying my life. Exuding a phony sense of confidence, I got out of my car and seductively strolled over to James, clearly intoxicated, and fidgeting with his car keys, trying to find the right one to open his door.

"Can I help you there?" it looks like you are having some difficulty." I politely pointed out, the trembling in my voice barely evident.

"Why? Are you a cop?" he suspiciously questioned, his eyes scrunching as he looked me up and down.

"No. I am not a cop. A little paranoid?" I huskily asked, walking towards him and grabbing the keys out of his freckled pale pudgy hands.

"Hey, what do you think you are doing?" James incoherently slurred, trying to grab the keys out of my palm.

"Now, now. Do you really think you are sober enough to drive? You are stumbling, slurring, you can't even find the right key to open your door. Your eyes are glassy. Why don't you let me take you home?"

James almost collapsed to the ground as he leaned his inflated frame against the chilled metal body of his Oldsmobile, pondered my offer for what seemed like the end of time. He scrutinized me from the tips of my black riding boots to the top of my sunny golden mane. His fat pink tongue hungrily lapped at his plump bottom lip as he looked me over and pondered my offer. I definitely was not portraying myself as the likeness of innocence that evening. Lustfully, his glazed blackened eyes dissected me, beginning at my brilliantly polished black leather boots, ending just below my knee. His eyes wandered up my enticing fishnet stockings, to my short sable black skirt, and contentedly rested on my bare naval. My ebony belly baring shirt, emblazoned with glittery silver rhinestones pressed into the silky fabric, was cut daringly low to reveal my ample cleavage, cleverly pushed up by a lacy push up bra, The golden shimmer lotion I had applied earlier that evening reflected off of my heaving bosom, the honey colored sparkles causing James to visualize my breasts nude and in all their glorious splendor. Finally, his eyes moved up from my chest to my glossy red lips, as shiny as a freshly licked lollypop.

"I guess I can do that." James cunningly grinned, his wide smirk revealing that he assumed he was going to have his way with me.

For a moment I became infuriated. How could this repulsive beast so easily assume that he was going to get lucky, but then I quelled myself by realizing that my plan was going exactly as I had hoped for. Yes, it sickened me that this contaminated swine was so smug, but I had to be convincing and not let my repulsion for him interfere.

"You've made the right decision....Your name?"

"James, my name is James."

"It is nice to meet you, James." I graciously offered, extending my hand out as a polite gesture. James grasped a hold of my comparatively small hand and lifted it up to his watering mouth. He puckered his pink fleshy lips and tenderly placed a kiss on the top of my hand, leaving a film of drool. This filthy dumpling shaped man physically lavishing his affections on me made me want to retch, but again I continued with my performance and controlled myself.

"And what is your name, my lovely lady?"

"My name is Kendall." I sputtered off the top of my lips.

"Kendall, what a beautiful name. A beautiful name for a beautiful lady." He complimented raising his bushy orange eyebrows.

"Why, thank you." I pleasantly acknowledged."

"Well, where is your car pretty lady?" James curiously asked, scanning the parking lot for my vehicle.

At that moment, my stomach sunk. I was trying to convey an air of sophistication, an experienced working woman, well seasoned in the area of sensual indulgence. I did not know though how I was going to convince James of this when he had a look at my tarnished 1977 Plymouth Duster. Realistically, I did not expect to carry the charade so far without him suspecting a thing. Oh well. He probably could care less what my car looked like. All the sucker wanted was sex anyway. He liked me. He was horny, and that was all that counted.

"Over this way." I speedily strutted towards my car, avoiding looking at his face while I jiggled the keys into the car lock.

He did not seem phased in the least bit though as I stepped into my car and unlocked the passenger door. James knelt down and squeezed his tubby body into the tawny leather seat. I placed my key into the ignition and turned the key. The car began to snort out cloudy puffs of smoke, chugging as roughly as a freight train, I cautiously pressed on the gas, my boots causing my legs to sweat as never before, and made my way out of the parking lot.

"So, James. I was thinking, since it is early, would you like to go to a hotel room? I cleverly propositioned, turning to face him, and studying his face for any expression of excitement. His neck began to twinge as he shook his head up and down.

"Sure, the night is still young. I am up for that. What hotel did you have in mind?"

"I was thinking about Motel 76 on Highway 255. Their rates are pretty reasonable, and they charge by the hour."

"That sounds just fine." He cooed, squeezing a mound full of flesh on my thigh.

I drove down the country road about a mile and a half, golden wheat fields and plentiful stalks of corn on either side of us. I finally pulled into the rear of Motel 76. I glanced over at James, his sooty eyes fixated on my breasts.

"Would you mind getting the room, James? It's safer that way."

"Sure, no problem, baby." James agreed, eagerly springing out of the door, and running faster than I ever saw a stocky man run.

I rested my forehead on the steering wheel, considering just driving away and never looking back, but then I began to think. I began to envision nude women enticing Carl with their inflated breasts and smooth creamy skin. Then I began to imagine Ginger straddling Carl, her overblown breasts smacking Carl's chiseled cheek bones, his tongue flicking at her stiff rigid nipples. Yes, I was going to go through with my plan. James was at fault for the destruction of my life. By ridding this earth of such impurity, I was doing this earth of such impurity, I was doing this world a favor. Who knows how far James would carry his charade as he became older and bolder. Would he rape women, molest pure innocent children, murder for the thrill of it? Yes, I was performing a service. James wobbled to the car, the room key in one hand, and waving his other hand, motioning for me to follow him to the room. Slowly, I got out of the car, pulling my skirt down as it dangerously hiked up my thigh.

"Room number seven, baby. My lucky number." James jovially announced dangling a fluorescent yellow plastic key chain in the shape of the number seven.
How short lived his ecstasy was about to become. For a brief moment I almost pitied the man. He thought he was going to undergo an adventure full of pleasure and delight, not death, but how mistaken he was.

"Stop feeling sorry for him, Remember what he did to you, If it was not for that fat piece of shit you and Carl would still be together and happy. He wouldn't of cheated on you or gone to the strip clubs. It is all James's fault." I told myself.

Suddenly, my pity converted to maniacal glee, and laughter

began to wash over me.

"What are you laughing at?" James foolishly grinned.

"Oh, nothing." I coughed, trying to conceal my beam of delight.

For a brief moment it appeared as if had a twinkling of sudden insight swaying him to escape as quickly as he could, but his eyes, black as licorice, fixated on my glistening chest, made him bury all doubts.

"Ladies first." He smoothly uttered, clearing the path so I could walk in front of him.

I could feel his dark eyes, as black as embers pierce into my behind. I knew that he was picturing my soft fattened ass exposed as his vacuous sockets penetrated my rounded rear. How badly I wanted to regurgitate my breakfast from that morning. I could picture my fluffy scrambled eggs, blackened greasy bacon, and buttered toast gushing out like a raging rapid. I walked up to the unvarnished pine door with a gold plated number seven affixed to the center with a slender rusty nail and turned around to see exactly where James was.

"I'm coming. I'm coming." He breathlessly panted, his forehead and carrot colored curls saturated with beads of moisture as he wobbled over to the door.

He jiggled the key in the lock, turning it to the right. The door squeaked as he pushed it open and fumbled to find the light switch, grazing his hairy hand over the yellow walls tinged by cigarette smoke. As he turned the light on, the overhead light bulb flickered, making an electric buzzing sound. Cautiously, I studied the room, making sure that I could finish what I was coming here for in the first place. This was the most depressing motel room I had ever laid my eyes on. "The chipped walls, strewn with scribble, was the color of runny egg yolk. The shaggy charcoal carpeting was covered with globs of mashed bubble gum and soda stains. Two plum colored tweed cheaply made chairs with metal legs were situated at the each side of the front picture window. A queen size bed with a Native American quilt in shades of turquoise and orange sat in the center of the room. The drapes matched the bedspread. A cherry oak nightstand table was placed at each side of the bed, and on top of each table was a frumpy outdated lamp with a clay base and a mammoth lampshade. On the nightstand to the right of the bed sat a mustard yellow rotary phone and a bible with a black leather cover and a golden inscription reading *New Testament* carved into the center. A shiny golden tassel laid wedged in between the water damaged pages. I walked into the bathroom, bare, white, no color splashed anywhere, not even a shower curtain. A large greasy cockroach waved its antennas and scurried across the cold tile floor into a crack beneath the baseboard. Spots of greenish mildew were sprinkled on the shower tile stinking up the room with an offensive odor.

"So, how long did you get the room for anyway?" I casually asked, hoping that he had gotten it for an entire night. I did not want the police finding the body an hour after I left.

"I got it for one night. An hour is not enough time to spend spanking your ass." He distastefully snorted as he smacked my behind.

I uncomfortably moved back as he wrapped his sunburned, peeling arms around my waist.

"You need to wait for the good stuff." I huskily cooed, pressing my index finger into the center of his fleshy chest and gently pushing him away, batting my eyes. He wrapped his hand around his throat and began tugging at his disheveled pumpkin colored strands of chest hair peeking out of his jet black T-shirt. He took off his shirt much to my dismay.

His sweaty stomach looked like a sticky batch of cinnamon rolls, but not so sweet and tasty. I deserved an Oscar for this performance. Even if I was a desperate greedy crack whore, I could still not reciprocate his enthusiasm. My intentions though were not so simple. I did not thirst for material possessions, precious stones, cash, luxury cars. No, I hungered for the sweet taste of revenge, for my appetite to be satiated. My gluttonous fascination with inflicting such suffering onto another human being was not of my character at all. I was always such a sweet sensitive woman. I could not even kill a spider, because I could never grasp the concept of extinguishing the life out of any living being, no matter how insignificant. In a twinkling from the time I grab the tissue and smash the poor insect, that vermin is terrified and forced to confront his unforeseen demise. I always valued life, but concerning James it was a completely different story. James was not human to me. I did not even hold him in as high regard as a spider. To me, James was the devil disguised beneath layers and mounds of dripping flesh and lard I have wept for the death of children, mothers, fathers, grandparents, but I would never weep for a man such as this. I wanted so badly to shut my eyes and be transported to a picturesque meadow full of fresh vegetation, trees brimming with juicy vegetables, and succulent stalks planted in muddy watered patches. I couldn't escape though. It was too late. I couldn't turn back now.

As he unbuttoned his jeans I unconsciously began to scrunch my nose as if I had been slurping on a sour lemon.

"Is there something wrong?" he asked, oblivious to my repulsion for him.

"No. No. Nothing at all." I unconfidently stammered.

"Then why don't you come a little closet. Don't be shy babe."

"Quick. Think of something you idiot. Anything so you don't have to touch this disgusting beast." I uttered to myself.

"You know James. You can keep your boxers on. I'll take care of those myself. Why don't you just take your jeans off, lie down on the bed and relax."

"All right. I can handle that." James replied, pleasantly surprised that I was going to initiate his disrobing.

James unclasped his clunky brass belt buckle, unsnapped his silver pants button and unzipped his zipper. His heavy faded denims collapsed to the ground like a ten pound sack of potatoes. His doughy white legs were coated in a layer of curly, thick orange matted down fur, as orange as a bowl of glazed candied yams. The frayed elastic waistband encircling the top of his paisley faded boxers severely cut into his stomach. He plopped himself onto the bed looking like a giant beached well smacking its fins against the sand and blasting out a jet of water from its blow hole. He laid flat on the bed, his sweaty plump body looking like a glazed butterball turkey.

"I'm ready, baby. Come here to daddy and perform your magic." He arrogantly ordered.

"Now hold on. I need to put this on you first." I said, my voice fluttering.

James lifted his head off of the pillow, his massive head making a deep indentation in the flat feather pillow. I pulled a black blindfold out of my pocket and began to walk towards him.

"Woah. What do you think you are doing?"

"Just relax. Hasn't the girl ever been in charge, James?"

"Yey. Plenty of times." James improbably boasted, his voice cracking.

"Then you should be used to this, not acting like a scared little boy."

"I'm not acting like a scared little boy. You just caught me off guard. That's all." James shrugged, lifting his head off of the bed.

"It's alright. You don't have to be scared. Why be scared about something that is going to feel good. Right?" I logically reasoned as I leaned over James's head and placed the blindfold around his clammy forehead. I was praying that the string on the blindfold would not tear apart as it stretched around his enormous head, made even greater in size by his puffy pumpkin colored curls. I could see the white elastic band begin to emerge through the black fabric string, but besides the extensive stretching the band did not tear.

I climbed on top of this huge sea mammal, straddling him as I reached under my black garter for my set of silver handcuffs.

"Oooh, you're a kinky one, huh girl?" James cooed, hearing the handcuffs and key jingle as I lifted them.

"Yey. I told you you'd like this. Now lift your arms up so I can handcuff you to the bed."

"But I want to be able to touch you." He disappointedly moaned like a child, mauling my breasts like a filthy rat scraping at a wall.

"Be patient." I sternly ordered, secretly shuddering, and removing his mammoth hands from my bosom. There will be enough time for that. Right now, just let me be in control." I huskily uttered.

As I continued to play the part, pretending that I was an experienced, sexy, and confident prostitute, I found myself beginning to derive joy from the misery which I was about to inflict upon another. I felt like I did when I was a child, masquerading as a fairy princess or movie star. Despite the fact that I was impersonating a prostitute, it almost felt glamorous, and it certainly felt powerful.

As I straddled James, I could feel his manhood stiffen. To

make my deception plausible I began to rock back and fourth.

"Now behave like a good little boy and place your hands between that bed post behind you."

James obediently complied and anxiously squeezed his chunky wrists between the iron bed post. I could sense that he was beginning to take pleasure from this sick twisted game. He began to wriggle beneath me like a slimy worm squirming through a bed of mud.

"Why don't you take off my pants, baby? And then take off your clothes. I'm ready to get down to business."

"You need to shut your mouth and let me do my job!" I commandingly yelled, slipping the handcuffs around his bulky waists and clasping them shut.

"Now, stay still. I'll be back in a minute." I casually ordered swinging my leg back over his body and stepping onto the filthy matted carpeting.

"Where are you going?" James helplessly hollered, the pitch of his voice becoming shrill as I stepped to the other side of the room. The tips of my shiny black heels sunk into the carpeting as I tiptoed to the torn leather chair with my black leather trench coat laying on top of it. I reached into the inside pocket and grabbed my shiny black handgun, miniature enough and stylishly shaped to be branded a feminine item of weaponry. I held it up to the light, turning it over and examining the heavy gloss finish. It glistened, the polished surface sleek. It almost slipped out of my hand, the slippery surface resembling a twist of black licorice or a jet black burnished jelly bean.

"You are starting to make me uneasy baby." James said. "Now bring your pretty little self over here, I might not be able to use my hands, but I can sure use my mouth." He disgustingly chuckled, flicking his tongue in and out of his mouth. Even from the other side of the room I could spot a thick coating of white thrash frosting the tip of his tongue.

My stomach began to do somersaults imagining James bathing my breasts with his puffy slime covered tongue.

"I thought I told you not to talk."

"Listen, I can't afford to play this game anymore. You're charging me by the hour, and this is your way of getting more money out of me. I just want to fuck. That's all. If you want to be the dominant one you are more than welcome, but let's just fuck already." He irritatingly hollered, his face beginning to mutate into the shade of a red pepper.

I clenched that gun tightly, using every ounce of self control I could muster not to fire at that very moment. No, that would not be as satisfying. I wanted to torment him, intimidate him like no other woman ever, demean him just as he had always degraded women. I wanted to savor this sin I was performing forever, to have this iniquity eradicate Carl's adultery. This was my secret revenge. I was retaliating in honor of women, a small morsel of victory we could claim as our own. I only hoped that God could forgive me, overlook this annihilation as an act of insanity for intentionally scraping out my soul. I knew that God could deliver frightening repercussions, hurl me into a fiery abyss covered in hot coals, but I did not care. At this moment the thought of spending the remainder of eternity being scalded by the sinful blazes, my skin blistering, bloody boils and infected pustules oozing out gooey pus did not perturb me. The satisfaction that would accompany this massacre would befriend me, create an immune layer that could not be affected by the flames dancing about me.

"Well, are you going to come over and fuck me or what?" he asked, his blushing cheeks puffing out like a chipmunks and steam beginning to whistle out of his reddened ears like a tea kettle.

"There's nothing I hate more than a tease, a fucking cock tease to get me all in a tizzy and then just bail. It's not right. I am warning you. If you don't take care of me like you promised, you will regret it, just like that other whore that didn't live up to what she promised."

"And what happened to that other whore, James?" I asked, half curious, and half humoring him at the same time.

"What do you think I did? I fucking cut up that bitch, stuffed her in a bag, and threw her on the other side of the river in a fucking waste dump. I threw her right next to a stolen ATM machine. No one ever found out who did it, and nobody ever will. Her body was too badly mutilated just as yours will be if you don't come over here and do your duty."

"Oh, really, my duty. How do you even expect to cut me up into little pieces when you're handcuffed to the bed you dumb ass?" I smugly retorted.

"Do you think these flimsy pieces of shit can hold a man

like me down? Nothing will bold me down baby" he violently screamed yanking at the handcuffs, the new formed scratches on his wrists beginning to bleed. He squiggled and contorted his body into all different positions, lifting his backside into the air and slamming it against the bed.

"Unfortunately, I do not think you are going to be so lucky this time. You see, I am different from that girl that you cut up into little pieces, or any girl for that matter of fact that you have come into contact with." I confidently said as I began to stroll towards the bed. "I am different from the strippers you look at every day, the hookers that you bring into sleazy motel rooms like this dump, and your painfully stupid wife."

"What are you talking about? You are a whore. You're a fucking hooker. Yon get naked and fuck complete strangers."

"James, I'd shut up now if I were you. You don't want to put yourself in a worse position than you are already in."

James who was almost hyperventilating by this point, could sense that my voice was getting closer as I neared the bed. I climbed on top of him again, and almost giggled as he sighed in relief.

"So daddy convinced you that you need to do the right thing, huh baby?" he uttered, rhythmically gyrating his hips."

"Oh yeah." I fraudulently moaned. "I'm doing the right thing alright." I said, pressing the chilled head of the revolver against the center of his sticky freckled forehead.

"What the fuck!" James hysterically screamed, his heart visibly thumping through his chest."

I was surprised that I could see his heart thumping through the layers of flab. His breasts were larger than mine, but sagged more.

"You see, James, I am not who you think I am."

"You are a cop, aren't you. Shit. You're a fucking cop. Listen, we can forget that this ever happened. I have a pretty wad of cash in my left pants pocket. Just grab that and forget that this little incident ever happened. And forget about what I said about cutting up that hooker and throwing her in that dump. I'm all talk. You need to realize that about me. I couldn't hurt a flea. I'm just a big teddy beat-."

"Uhhhhh...."I sighed in boredom. "Are you done talking yet? You wish I was a cop James. You know it's refreshing to see you try to talk your way out of this one. That's all you do, huh

James, talk, talk, talk. You try to talk people out of things. You try to talk people into things. For once, why don't you just try to shut up and see how things work out for you."

James laid there, motionless as a stone, the lump on his throat the only part of him constricting.

"You mess up people's lives James. Just because you are a sick fuck you try to make everyone else just like you, but not everyone is just like you. Carl was not like
you, but yon wouldn't stop. You tried so hard to corrupt him until you won."

"Carl, how do you know Carl?." he confusingly asked.

"Carl was my boyfriend, you dumb fuck. We were happy at one time until he told me what you made him do."

"What are you talking about?"

"Don't play stupid. If it wasn't for you Carl never would have gone into *Foxy Tails*. He would of never fucked that nasty skank, Ginger."

"Yon think that I made Carl do that. Oh, no. You have it totally turned around. He is the sicko. He actually made me go into those places. Darling, I know you are upset, but please, don't let your love for that boy blind you into seeing what he really is."

"Don't fucking lie to me you fat ass coward!" I cried, pressing the gun more firmly into his forehead. I could feel his skull beneath the cold barrel of the revolver.

"Honey. I'm not. You have to believe me. Do you know how badly you would feel if you murdered an innocent man? You need to learn the facts. I would never intentionally hurt someone like the way that you me hurting right now."

"You are so pathetic." I wailed, sobbing harder, warm teardrops splashing off of his overblown belly. "Does it feel good? Does it feel good, James? I want you to know that this is how you made me feel. This is how you make every girl feel. Women are not toys created solely for your amusement, James. Women are real people with fucking feelings, emotions, a brain. Women actually think, James. They weren't just created to get naked and dance for you. Women can do other things besides fuck, James. I can do so many things, but the one thing that I cannot do is forgive. You have filled my heart with. such hate that I don't want to forgive. Because of you I see the world as a totally dirty place. There is not one man that I will ever trust again because of you. I will never be able to have a boyfriend, get married, have more kids, and it is all your fault. You don't realize the amount of hate I walk around with every day. There is so much hate in my heart that I am surprised that I haven't had a heart attack. Because of you my kids have a crazy spiteful mom now. Carl was the love of my life. When I met Carl I thought that I had finally met someone worth waiting for. He was so faithful, until he started working with you. Yey, he told me the stories of how you took him to the strip clubs every day, and yes, it broke my heart, but I could live with it knowing that it was in the past. When he told me that he began to work for you again, my heart sank. You don't know the amount of fear I walked around with every day. Because of you, I am more insecure than ever. Every day I prayed that Carl would not succumb to you. I prayed that he would be strong enough to stand up to you, but just as I had feared, he wasn't."

"Hon, you need to calm down, before you do something that you regret. You need to put that gun down."

"Shut up. You need to stop telling me what to do, like you are somebody. You are a fat piece of shit that can't get anybody. That's why you go to strip clubs. That's why you pay hookers to have sex with you, because no body in their right mind would have sex with such a disgusting pig. How does it feel, James? How does it feel to be as vulnerable as those naked girls that you watch dance every day. Do you think that they actually enjoy taking their clothes off?. Do you think that they actually enjoy dancing around in those uncomfortable heels until their legs are black and blue. They don't. They do it for their kids, their husbands, their boyfriends, their families, college, drugs, alcohol. They have to be so fucked up when they do that so they don't remember, and all pigs like you do is take advantage of the situation. You don't look at women like they are human beings. You treat them like pieces of meat, and your wife. You are such a coward that when your wife calls you in those places you have to run outside to talk to her. What's that about? You are the most pathetic piece of shit I have ever seen.

The queasiness in my stomach persisted as I bent down. James prematurely moaned, his heavy breathing causing his stomach flab to jiggle. I looked up at his huge stomach, the small piece of cottony lint trapped in his belly button, the crimson belly hair, his chubby jowls, his unkempt beard. I looked straight into those beady black eyes of his and licked my lips, licked that plum brandy color right off my lips. Then I reached in my pocket for my rubber gloves and razor blade and closed my eyes, pretended that I was anyplace but here. I wrapped my fist around his dick and sliced, the razor cutting his penis in half like a piece of sausage. I held it in my hand and didn't know what to do next, so I tossed it against the wall.

It was not as effortless as I imagined, severing this bodily organ of such great importance. I bit and gnawed like a famished coyote, blood splattering everywhere. James desperately screamed, such petrified screams that brought me sweet pleasure. His sickening cries were as sharp as the sounds of a violin, his melodious squeals similar to a sow being butchered. Not one ounce of mercy was stored in my heart, no warmness to thaw the frigid nucleus within me. The stinging induced such blood curdling howls, like a pair of fingernails   screeching   along   a   chalk   board.

At last I was free. The opportunities were limitless. Symphonies played, daffodils bloomed, robins twittered. At last all was right with the world. This bittersweet revenge enlivened me, throttled me back to the world of the living, provided me with such power. 1 loved with how one swipe of a razor blade I dominated man. No longer could James degrade women, undress them with his beady black eyes. No, the tingling would vanish. His penis no longer was an instrument to guide him to the east side. His penis laid in the corner, curled up like a dead worm. Yes, his penis, that overbearing phallus men use to claim dominance was gone, withering away more and more each moment until it dissolved, existed only as a remnant of the past used to inflict harm on others. I walked over to it while James hollered for help, for someone to rescue him before the penis could no longer be attached. It lay as limp as a wet noodle or   a   filthy   larvae   ingesting   scraps   of   moldy   food.
"You   fuckin   cock   suckin   slut!"   James   yelled.

I pulled the masking tape out of my bag and tore off a piece, smacking it on James's mouth. Perhaps that would teach him to shut up. I pulled up a chair and sat down taking great delight in his incoherent garble. His face turned as red as a cherry tomato, looking like it would explode at any moment. He looked at me like a helpless child, squeezing out tears he had not set free for years, since that strange little man forced him to fornicate. He was no longer a man, that testosterone filled sexist pig he took great pride in.

OVER ON THE EAST SIDE

He was equal to the women he demeaned for so long, left with a gaping hole just like us, a cavity we are forced to fill with men's grimy juices. Now he could spread his legs open for all the world to see, have dirty little men look into his diseased crotch to provoke all sorts of perverted fantasies.

Each moment he squirmed I was more content than the last. Was I insane to take such pleasure in another one's suffering? No, I'd call it a passionate need for revenge caused by the insensitivity of another. No matter how badly he hurt at this moment I hurt ten times worse when Carl fucked Ginger. If it wasn't for James Carl never would have gone into *Roxy's*, lusted for those naked women, fucked that slut Ginger. James had to suffer. These were the consequences he took for his actions. The world would be better off with one less pervert anyway.

James thrashed side to side like a wild animal as I continued to smile and stare. How outlandish would this sound to someone on the outside, that I chopped off a man's penis because he took my boyfriend to a strip club and made him cheat on me. His eyes silently implored me to spare his life, to show some mercy, but I couldn't. For a brief moment his beseeching eyes overcame me, and I actually felt compassion, but soon that passed. I don't think there was a speck of kindness left in me. I had become cold, no feeling for the people that associated with those places. I imagine he felt like an animal, perhaps a pig about to be butchered. I could sense the life slowly draining out of him as he sat there bleeding to death. It was like he was a sieve, his existence gradually draining. To at one time be so animated, to intimidate others with your forceful loud-mouthed demeanor, to cause such heartache in another's soul. No, his time was to end on this earth. Like the sun that sets in the west, a beetle struggling for its life in a sink basin, its legs frantically twiddling. This was now James.

I reached in my bag for my carving knife, the same exact one I used to carve my children's pumpkin last year, the identical knife I used to slice out crooked teeth, slit eyes, and a square nose, the same knife that I used to dig up pumpkin seeds and pulp for pumpkin pie. This knife was familiar only with innocence, with a children's holiday of dress up and sweet treats, but tonight this knife would be dirtied, would make contact with the slime of this earth, an undesirable individual created from sullied sperm.

I lightly pressed the knife against James's flesh, the blade barely touching his sticky flesh. He uncomfortably squirmed, wriggling like a drowned cockroach in a shallow puddle. James softly grunted, his high pitched squeals maddening me so that I pressed the blade harder until it broke the skin. I was going to brand this swine, like *Hester Prynne* in the *Scarlet Letter* forced to bear the letter "*A*" upon her breast. James was going to carry this emblem with him into infinity. I began to cut, the knife smoothly cutting into his flesh like a butterball turkey. He kicked, only forcing me to cut harder the letter **P**, then the letter **I**, then the letter **G**. Drops of blood trickled to the surface causing him to cry.

"Oh, James. Don't worry. Only a little longer." I calmly reassured him.

James wildly flailed his legs until I could take it no longer. Unsettling imagery of James and Carl slamming their car doors in the parking lot of the strip club, walking to the door, entering, staring at the appetizing flesh encircling them, receiving hand jobs, lap dances, fucking Ginger in the back room. I could endure it no longer! I plunged the knife directly into his heart, over and over, until he was still, until all was silent, until his eyeballs rolled into the back of his head. I stabbed at his frosty soul, destroyed him like he had destroyed me, and then as soon as I knew it he was gone. I stepped back to examine my work.

"Pure sickening." I disgustingly uttered.

How had I gotten like this? How had I turned into this monster, this murderer? I suppose it could be worse. I was doing this world a favor; ridding it of the undesirable scum that roamed the earth. Perhaps I was a hero, a crusader for the feminist movement. Who knew what James was capable of. He was the type of scum bag to rape or even kill a woman. Maybe I had saved lives.

I walked over to the bloody battered penis lying in the comer of the room and carefully picked it up, dangling it from my thumb and index finger. I then pried open James's mouth and placed the penis into it.

"Now who's the cock sucker pig?." I quietly uttered.

Like a holiday ham holding the candied apple in its mouth. This is what James looked like.

OVER ON THE EAST SIDE

CHAPTER 43

Serial killers are not born that way. They are created. Society and its expectations have molded me. I would not say I am a narcissist. Narcissists cannot empathize with any human being. I can identify with most humans, but I will not apologize for my lack of compassion concerning perverts. They say that the victims of serial killers are symbols, special, or the chosen one. James was not the chosen one. He carved his own destiny, crossed my path, meddled with what fate had in store for me. Should I express regret for what I have done? If I had murdered an innocent child or woman than perhaps I'd ask for forgiveness, but that is an area I'd never even think about exploring. Women and children exude innocence, but all that James exuded was perversion. He was apiece of shit, and as he sits slumped in his chair, his penis chopped off and stuffed into his mouth and the word *"pig"* carved into his stomach, he is still a piece of shit. For his entire lifetime James had been exploiting women, relentlessly objectifying them and influencing others to treat women just as he had. For once I had objectified James, used him for self gratification, made him feel helpless, how a woman usually feels in this mixed up society we live in.

Like a ballerina which eternally twirls in its jewel box the stripper danced in my head. Her **DDD** globulin" breasts are motionless as she twists her sparkly self round and round the pole. She is the ballerina perpetually trapped on a pole she cannot break away from. All is silent except for the song, the sweet melody she spins to. The music plays and the men bow, bow to the ballerina, their heroine. Her golden curly tresses cascade down her back as she moves to the music.

Jealousy has destroyed me, burnt my soul to a crisp, forced my heart to condemn others based upon their actions. No one understands how I can hate so, how the green eyed monster has interfered with my sense of morality. Unlike other serial killers I did not hold grandiose expectations that I was going to be some sort of twisted celebrity. I would not kill for a selfish reason such as that. The only force which drove me to kill was hate. Each slice, each stab, each inscription had been made out of the disgust and hatred swimming throughout my soul. As I stabbed at James the girl danced through my mind, twisted and spun, gyrated, slid down the pole. As I cut all of Carl's dirty little secrets that manifested themselves swirl through my mind making me dizzy.

Why Carl? Why did you have to be so insensitive? Why did you let me into your world, a land where men frolic in their perverse fantasies and think of women as objects, where women are like rides, "hop on and I'll give you a lap dance ". Women are used solely for their amusement. I did nothing to you. I was not familiar with your world, thought the world was only sprinkled with sugar and spice, not toxins and the corruption you told me about. I reside in your memories now. It is like I am stuck in quicksand, in a swamp of your soiled secrets, and the only way I can get out is to attack the vermin which inhabit it. You thought you were doing me a favor by spilling your secrets, but you didn't, because the girl keeps dancing Carl. The ballerina spins while the men worship her; pray to her breasts, her buttocks, her smooth flat stomach. They lay back while she brings joy to their lives, fills their empty meaningless lives with hope. And now all it takes is a flash of skin, a reminder, a crude remark to hurl me back into your swamp where I sink deeper and deeper each day. I don't know who you are, who you ever were. You lied to me! You lied to me making me so angry that I hated you, and now I've tortured myself tortured myself and others so I can drain that slush .filled marsh until no memories are left.

CHAPTER 44

It's 5:00 a.m., that time of the morning when the sun begins to rise, the wonderful oranges and yellows combine creating a breathtaking golden masterpiece. I don't feel different. My lack of emotion frightens me and amazes me, forces me to wonder how human I really am. I wouldn't dare compare myself to these monsters out there that dice their victims into little pieces, squeeze them into jars, and then store them in their refrigerator. These killers serve no purpose. They only kill for their own enjoyment. I am ridding the earth of scum, preventing future rapes, molestations, and possibly murders. I should be praised, not punished, but society will never see it that way. This same society that allows eighteen year old girls to strip but will not allow them to drink. The same society that will allow an eighteen year old to die and fight for their country but not drink. The same society that in certain states allows prostitution. The same society that worships *Pam Anderson* and big breasted women. This same society will prosecute me, would probably put me to death for what I did - ridding the earth of scum. Yes, I am full aware of the fact that I will most definitely either die for my sins or rot away in jail my entire life. I do not care though. Fry me, poke me, hang me. Do whatever you need to extinguish my existence, because all hope is lost.

CHAPTER 45

Hmmm, those two look good. I was in the mood for two good old country boys. These two were definitely rednecks with their big truck tires on their 4 x 4 Dodge pick up truck, the confederate flag hanging on their antenna. It was hard not to hear the Charlie Daniels song blaring from their loud speakers. They almost skipped to their car their wide grins radiating extreme giddiness. I could hear them bragging to each other about which one had tits shoved in their face more and how much money they wasted. I take back my description of rednecks. These two were white trash!

I drove up to their truck, my heart thumping so loudly I could barely hear myself offer to take them back to a hotel. Upon closer examination I noticed that these two country bumpkins looked strangely familiar, and then it hit me. Bumpkin #1 and bumpkin #2 were no other than Carl's cousins from Richwood, Jeremiah and Jeffrey. Jeremiah and Jeffrey, though sharing a remarkable resemblance, were not brothers. They were cousins, Jeremiah being the son of Aunt Irene and Uncle Buck, and Jeffrey being the son of the late Aunt Frye and Uncle Buck. Aunt Faye had not been old at all, dropped dead of a brain aneurism at the tender age of sixty. Carl told me that she had been a very mean lady, beating her sons with a shoe in the head until they bled. I just couldn't imagine her that way though. The only night I had seen her was the night she died, a frail old woman with cotton candy hair sleeping for all eternity. Uncle Buck was devastated, for at least a year until he found a new wife to live in his double wide and take care of his grand kids.

Jeremiah and Jeffrey were not bad looking at all. They both wore tight blue Levis, cowboy boots, and wife beater shirts. Jeremiah looked a bit like *Matthew Mconugey* with his sandy blonde hair and strong jaw line. Freckles dotted his nose and cheeks highlighting his warm brown eyes. Jeffrey was the town slut, his handsome face slightly worn from all the methamphetamines he'd done in the past ten years. I was surprised Jeffrey was even out in public considering he was schizophrenic and had been known not to leave his trailer for eight month periods. He slept with the bible under his mattress every night to ward off the devil. Jeffrey was married to his high school sweetheart, Missy, a once beautiful brunette who had gained weight and aged over the years. This of course caused Jeffrey to stray. The last time I had seen him he was with an eighteen year old crack whore with spiked blonde hair. Jeffrey had three kids, all adorable while Jeremiah only had one, a spunky six year old named Thomas. I knew practically everything about their lives, but they didn't even seem to recognize me. I was sure that my plan would backfire, but they were so drunk they probably could not recognize even their own children.

As I stopped in front of their truck Jeremiah stuck his fingers in his mouth and catcalled me. *"Perfect!"* I thought to myself. Just the opportunity I was looking for.

"You boys had fun in there, huh?" I yelled.

"Oh, yey!" They screamed in unison, giggling as they said it.

"How'd you boys like to go to my hotel room, have a little more fun?"

Jeremiah and Jeffrey both turned silent at my proposition, their laughter fading as I waited for an answer.

"I'm flat broke." Jeremiah answered. "Spent all my money in there." He said pointing to *the Palace.*

I could see Jeffrey shuffling around his pockets, pulling out crumpled one dollar bills.

"It looks like your friend over there has some money. Anyways I'm not looking for money tonight. I'm just looking for a good time."

"I don't know." Jeremiah hesitantly replied. "I've had so many lap dances tonight, I don't think I can handle anymore.

"But did they finish the job?"

Jeremiah grinned, his eyes lighting up at my proposition. "Let me get this straight a girl as good looking as you are if you don't mind me saying wants to take us to her hotel room free of charge and flick our brains out."

"Yey. Is that so hard to believe?"

"How do we not know you're some crazy bitch or something and we end up with our dicks cut off like that one guy they found dead in the hotel room? That was my cousin's boss, you know."

"I'm not psycho. Your dicks aren't going to end up being chopped off. I promise."

Jeremiah and Jeffrey looked at each other and then back to me excitedly shaking their heads in unison.

"So where you stayin' at?" Jeremiah asked as he opened the door to his truck.

"I'm at the Economy Lodge down there off Vandalia, but why don't you guys ride with me. I'll take you guys back to your truck when we're done. I, I, I just don't want to see you drive drunk is all." I stammered.

"I guess. I just don't want to leave my truck here. Who knows who could take
it?" he quietly uttered eying an older black gentleman walking to his car.

"Just hop in before the cops come by."
Jeffrey and Jeremiah locked up their car. Jeffrey hopped into the back seat and Jeremiah hopped into the front, lighting up a Marlboro Red as soon as he closed the door.

"You don't mind if I smoke?" Jeremiah asked looking down at the bare flesh showing on my legs.

"No. Feel free. Your friend looks tired." I said eyeing my rearview mirror and seeing Jeffrey slumped over in the back seat.

Jeremiah chuckled, blowing out his cigarette smoke. "Yey. He was quite a busy boy over at the Palace.

"Oh yey? I hesitantly asked.

Lank of discretion seemed to be a trend in most conversations lately. These blabbering idiots is what got me into trouble in the first place. Each time a man opens his mouth and says something idiotic, my body prepares it self. Like the fight n' flight syndrome my body has learned to defend itself. I can feel the muscles in my chest tighten whenever these men rattle on about tits mad pussy and ass. My heart begins to constrict, and then the tears start flowing and usually do not end for hours, but this time it had to be different. I had to convey self confidence, a care free attitude, I had to pretend that I was one of those girls, a money hungry slut not affected by visual images of naked flesh.

"Yey. I have never seen so many bitches fightin' over one guy. They all wanted to do a lap dance on him. I was mad. Finally, one of the bitches walked over to me and hopped on my lap. That greedy bitch took all my money, but it was worth it. She rode me hard. Stuck her big titties right in my face. Before I knew it that bitch had all my money." He chuckled.

"How much?" I asked trying to act like it didn't bother me in the least bit.

"At least three hundred, my entire work check this week"

"Three hundred dollars and she didn't even fuck you."

"Tried to slip it in, but the dirty bitch wouldn't let me."

"Don't they have a back room for that or something?"

"Yey, but not at the Palace. At Puss'N Boots or Ms. Kitty's they do, even Roxy's I think. At least Roxy's has those showers though. That's hot. That's why I can't go to those places all the time. I'm just not rich enough. Daddy don't make enough money, but the bitch was hot." He chucked again, placing his rough calloused hand on my knee and rubbing it in a circular motion.

I felt like gagging and vomiting on his lap, but I couldn't. I felt like saying, *are you that desperate for pussy that you have to pay some chick, waste your whole paycheck on a stripper instead of buying food for your son. Find a real girl!*, I felt like saying.

'Yey, sometimes they'll jack you off if no body's lookin, but there were a bunch of pigs around."

"Yon mean cops?"

"Yey. Those guys get it all. They get to work and get favors for nothing."

"What do you mean?"

"I mean the pigs get lap dances for free, sometimes even fucked so the places don't get shut down."

"Are you serious?" the disgust in my voice difficult to hide at this point.

"Yey. It's fucked up, huh?"

It was a little more than fucked up. This country was disgusting! The police have power. With their influence they could shut these placed down, but instead they're getting fondled and fucked by these girls. I tried to just keep any eyes on the road, but I wanted to cry so badly. Why did I have to have so much heart? Why couldn't I just blow stuff off like everybody else? I felt like the darkness was going to swallow me whole, nibble on my flesh until I consisted of only bones, a carcass with flaps of skin dangling off my dainty frame.

"Hey, do you mind if we stop at a gas station. I need a drink."

"No..I managed to spit out. I could use something too."

I pulled up to a Quik Mart, and Jeremiah hopped out to buy some liquor. I turned on the radio, turning the dial to and finally settling on a classic rock station I thought these hoosiers would like. Jeffrey was snoring by now, dead to the world. He looked so innocent and peaceful, his hands folded under his head. He had no idea what was about to happen. For a moment, a tinge of compassion washed over me, but as soon as Jeremiah bounced out of the store, that stupid grin plastered on his freckled face, I forgot why I felt sorry for them.

Jeremiah held a 40 wrapped in a paper bag in one hand, a bottle of Goldschlager Cinnamon Schnaps in the other hand and a six pack of Budweiser under his elbow.

"This makes great shots if you down it with beer." Jeremiah said handing me the bottle of Cinnamon Schnaps. I held the brownish colored concoction in front of me observing the floating golden flakes. It reminded me of one of those snow globes I shook up as a kid.

"That's real 24 karat gold." He said raising his eyebrows like I was supposed to be impressed.

"Wow." I enthusiastically said, trying to sound convincing.

"Have a drink." He offered, opening a can of beer.

"I....I shouldn't. I have to drive." I stuttered.

I couldn't afford to get pulled over, especially since they were looking for me. I needed to have a clear head upon my shoulders, but it did sound tempting, something to calm my nerves. I pressed the bottle to my lips and gulped down the spicy brew. As I swallowed the peppery drink, it felt like my insides liquefied. He handed me the can of beer, but I waved my hand in refusal as I gasped for air. I swigged down another drink, this time the pungent liquid dripping from the corners of my mouth as I sloppily guzzled.

"All right. I think I'm done." I declared, handing the bottle back to Jeremiah.

"You like it, huh?" he asked, that stupid smirk spread across his chapped lips again.

"Yey. Not bad." I smiled, almost forgetting that I was not here to have fun but to instead inflict misery on others.

"Good. You need to loosen up anyways gift." He said squeezing my shoulder. Goosebumps traveled up and down my spine. It felt so nice to be touched as he began to massage my shoulders and neck. I dropped my head forward as he kneaded my skin like a batch of dough.

"You're soooo tense girl." He whispered in my ear.

Jeremiah's tongue began to nibble at my earlobe, his warm tongue inducing chills in me. It felt so good to be touched and kissed by a man, no matter how disgusting he was. I closed my eyes and began to imagine how wonderful it would feel to have sex. His hand began to stroke my left breast causing me to jerk backwards.

"Stop it." I blurted out.

Taken aback Jeremiah immediately retracted his hand from my breast and jerked his head back to take a good look at me. His eyes traveled up and down my legs to my ridiculously overblown DDD breasts and finally back to my face.

"You don't look like the kind of girl to say no. I mean we're going to be doing everything that two people can possibly do together and you're telling me to stop. Why'd you even get those things if you don't want guys touching them?"

God, I wanted to chop this guy's penis off right now, but I couldn't. Control yourself. Control is the key, I repeated to myself. This was not how I had planned this night at all. I was supposed to remain detached from any victims, not succumb to their sexual cravings. Yes, I was aroused, but I was not going to let a small detail like that get in the way. I was not some hormone driven teenager easily affected by a cute boy. My needs would be fulfilled shortly - in the hotel room. Yes, I was to be the biggest tease of them all, better than any stripper in the Palace. I was going to torment these country bumpkins. They wouldn't only have blue balls for the evening. No, they'd suffer for all eternity, wherever they were destined to spend their endless days, either mingling with the devil or humming with the angels. Forever their dicks would tingle, that irritating almost painful prickling. The rustling in the back seat interrupted my train of thought. Jeffrey rubbed his blood shot eyes like a little boy and pressed his face against the window.

"Where the fuck are we?" Jeffrey asked.

"Just relax Jeff. We'll be there in a minute." Jeremiah impatiently answered. "Come on. You know where we're going. Drive." Jeremiah ordered.

At this point I not only wanted to chop off Jeremiah's penis, but stuff it in his mouth. Maybe that'd finally shut him up. I had to play a part though. They thought I was a whore. That's what I was supposed to be. I couldn't blame them. I was taking them to a hotel, misleading them into believing they were going to get the fuck of their lives. I put on my phoniest smile, turned the key in the ignition and drove. I could sense Jeremiah staring at me, searching my face for an inkling of an expression.

"You know. You look familiar to me, like I've seen you before somewhere....Did you go out with a buddy of mine maybe?"

My heart tightened, and for a moment I could not breathe. If he remembered that I was Carl's girlfriend, my plan would be destroyed. He didn't strike me as an overly observant guy, but the fact that he thought he recognized me was beginning to scare me. "....No. I don't think so."

"Then where have I seen you before? Oh, my God. I know."

My heart plummeted. What if he recognized me from the family reunion? My entire strategy was about to unravel.

"You look just like that girl on that show. You could be her twin."

I finally felt movement in my chest as my heart finally fluttered again.

"It doesn't matterrr." He slurred while he took a sip out of his forty. The paper bag rustled as he set it back in his lap. 'You look like a movie star. That's all that counts."

He was beginning to make me feel guilty. Why was he trying to boost my ego by saying that I look like a movie star? His over excessive sweet talk was flattering, but I did not want it to interfere with my plan. Anyways I doubt he was being genuine. I imagine his glowing praise was used only for his benefit, to get what be wanted. Isn't that what all men did anyways, lied to get what they wanted. At least that's what men always did to me, disguised themselves as sincere upright individuals only to abandon me as soon as they got in my pants. There was a full moon out tonight. It almost looked like a block of cheese suspended in the sky, preferably muenster with the two tones of yellow.

"So, A pretty gift like yourself has to turn tricks, huh? Must be rough."

"Play the part, play the part!" I repeated to myself.

"Oh, it's not so bad. A lot of the guys are just lonely and need someone to talk to."

"Really?" Jeremiah replied, sounding surprised. "I wouldn't pay no girl just to talk. If I'm paying her she better be doing something for me." He chuckled, guzzling on his forty like a famished whine.

What a pig! Any compassion I held for this man was quickly vanishing. Every
time he opened his mouth he was making my job that much easier.

"Do you do this a lot?" I asked.

"Mhhh, a couple of times. Not too often though. I usually don't have much trouble getting some. Pussy is everywhere."

I cringed in revulsion. Why did men insist on using the word pussy? It was so demeaning, identifying women by their genitalia. What were we, walking, talking hairy wet vaginas just wandering around searching for an available man to fuck us. I certainly would not want to be referred to as a pussy, especially my daughters, two wonderful creative beings able to offer so much more to the world than gyrating poles and straddling dirty old men. Tits and ass. That's all men thought about anymore, especially hoosiers like Jeffrey and Jeremiah.

Jeremiah placed his hand on my leg and squeezed it. I remained silent. No matter how hard I tried I could not play the part of a whore. I might have looked like one with my mini, low cut shirt and boots, but inside I still remained that strong willed feminist, crying out to be recognized as more than a pair of hooters and tight buns. I never understood how a woman could tolerate being objectified by a man. What part of their conscience could be missing as they spread their legs to appease some dirty old pervert? I'd feel like a caged animal at the zoo being gawked at by such animals.

"Why so quiet?" he asked rubbing my earlobe with his fingertips. "You not having second thoughts, are ya?"

'No! No, no, no. I'm just concentrating on the road." I confidently reassured
him.

"Alright, just making sure. You just don't look like the kinda girl that would do something like this. Most hookers are missing teeth or haven't taken a bath in like a week. I'd think that maybe you'd work for one of those fancy escort services, not in some parking lot in Brooklyn."

"Everyone has to make a living. Unfortunately some of us have to take our clothes off to do it."

"You make it sound like it's a chore. The girls at the Palace looked like they were havin' plenty of fun, the way they rode us.

Think, they get to dance and act sexy for their job. If I was as woman, I'd be a whore in a second."

My blood boiled. How badly I wanted to hurt him. How could he think that these girls were actually having fun? Didn't he know it was all fake, a male generated fantasy used to deceive men into thinking that women really act like whores. I wanted to chop off his penis and stuff it into his mouth. Men without heart did not deserve a penis, therefore castration of my two friends here was the solution.

Actually the technical term "penis" before Freud meant removal of the testicles, not removal of the penis, but why be so technical, balls and penis the same thing, right? At least they're in the same general area. Cutting off their penis might have advantages.

It did years ago as animals became domesticated. Castrating bulls created workable oxen. Several societies even self-castrated for Jesus until 1970. Maybe I was doing this for Jesus. Perhaps Jesus would reward me in the afterlife. Castration is used to treat prostrate cancer. I could be curing them of a cancerous infection in the future. Infant boys are circumcised, and they have no say in the matter. Infant circumcision has been called foreskin amputation by force. I'd much rather do it to two filthy grown men than an adorable innocent baby. Circumcision has always been used like a treatment. In the Victorian age it was believed to discourage masturbation and alleviate masculine promiscuity. It began as a Jewish tradition therefore I was just sticking to a long held ritual. Why not start a trend in circumcision on grown men? It has been practiced on women for thousands of years. There continues to exist female genital mutilation in Africa. They falsely believe that it controls women's sex drive and calms their personality. What a sexist society! Men are the ones that need to control their sex drive. How often do we hear about a man getting raped? Why is it cool for a man to be promiscuous but slutty for a female? How many male strip clubs are there compared to female? Why is pornography centered towards the male audience with their cheesy story lines and unmelodious soundtracks? Men are the ones that would benefit from having a calming personality.

Their testosterone induced brawls are much more frequent that estrogen induced clashes. As recent as the nineteenth century women were circumcised to relieve hysteria and insanity. How many women have we deprived of a normal life because men's surplus of testosterone caused them to mistake mood swings for insanity. Men have always lacked the passion, the zest for life that we females cherish. Perhaps without testosterone men would realize what it feels like to be a woman. They could finally see the world through our eyes. Finally they'd be sensitive, emotional, not use raunchy sex clubs as a substitute for a genuine loving relationship. Maybe Jeremiah and Jeffrey would turn gay, get a tough abusive boyfriend, get pulverized to a bloody pulp and finally realize how it feels to be victimized by men.

The technical term for a castrated male is a Eunuch. They are actually recognized as a third sex. In the early centuries of the Roman Empire, Eunuchs were used as sex toys for men. How sweet would it be to witness Jeremiah and Jeffrey fondled and mistreated by a barrage of men. In Europe in the sixteenth to nineteenth centuries Eunuchs were recognized for their angelic voices. I am sure that Jeffrey and Jeremiah will be singing with the angels as well, their once booming voices now so melodious, so syrupy sweet and delightful.

"I prefer that you don't call me a whore. Working girl is a much nicer term." I snottily replied.

"Fine Ms. Attitude. It's all the same to me. Whatever you call it, working girl, hooker, prostitute, lady of the evening, call gift, slut, whore, skank, whatever floats your boat."

It was to my benefit if I restrained myself from engaging in feminist chatter with a sexist pig. I didn't want to piss him off and then not finish what I had come out for this evening. I just plastered a false smile on my face and drove, drove into the evil shadows that lurk in the darkness of the night. No titties, no ass, no pussy where they were going, only souls, fulfilled meaningful souls not preoccupied with such shallow trivial behavior. The spirits were probably already watching, setting aside two spots for their latest guests. The ghosts were peeping through the clouds, closely inspecting who their new companions were about to be.

The parking lot was sparsely populated much to my satisfaction. The motel was almost deserted, especially our side. There could not have been more than one car parked across from us. I don't believe that the Knights Inn in East St. Louis was a frequently visited establishment. The motel was just basically depressing with its darkly painted walls and deep mahogany furnishings. Our room was painted a deep plum. Instead of pictures the Knights Inn opted to decorate the walls with paintings of palaces with turrets, draw bridges, knights on horses, matronly royals, dragons breathing out tawny flames. The thick velvet drapery blocked out all sunshine, the rich burgundy color casting a reddish shade on the room. I absorbed in my surroundings, breathing in the gloom that the room radiated. I couldn't imagine a family vacationing here. The only people or acts I could visualize in this dump were crude sex acts, prostitutes, slayings. This hotel wreaked of evil.

Jeremiah and Jeffrey didn't take in their surroundings, failed to inhale the lemony disinfectant streaming from the bathroom or the majestic paintings spread onto the walls. The two incredibly dense idiots propped themselves on the bed with their elbows and laid back sort of spreading open their legs.

"Wanna Fuck?" Jeremiah asked, his stormy eyes shifting from my buttocks to my breasts. I almost choked, surprised at how brazen he was being.

"Well...That's what I'm here for. Both of you at the same time?" I asked.

"Don't care. We've fucked a couple of girls together. We're not shy."

Either Jeremiah was a bald-faced liar or completely shameless when it came to matters in the bedroom. My stomach rumbled caused by my gluttonous appetite to supersede their expectations. I needed their erogenous zones to experience a rebirth, for them to become so thunderstruck that they break into convulsions. I yearned for them to crumble to the floor, transform into shivering piles of flesh. I longed for them to only be aroused by my naked flesh, by my touch, not those trampy strippers at the Palace.

"Alright. We need some music." I nervously stuttered, attempting to stall. The stereo equipment in the Knight's Inn was not up to date, but it would suffice. I imagine these stereo systems they equipped in each room were wonderful, but in 2004 they were quite archaic. I found the turntables amazingly quaint, but completely useless. I pressed the rectangular fluorescent orange power button and was instantly bombarded with an overwhelmingly loud Spanish station. I quickly diddled with the turn knob and settled on a top forty station popular in St. Louis. Fortunately a dance mix was playing this evening. The overpowering beat began to soften my inhibitions, the passionate climax giving me courage to strip my clothes, shed my second skin with reckless abandonment.

Jeremiah handed me the bottle of cinnamon schaps while Jeffrey handed me a chilled can of beer. I knew what they were planning to do. They thought they were going to get me drunk, force fiery liquors down my throat until I was so inebriated that I would do anything, suck their dicks, ride them like a wild stallion, let them fuck me up the ass. I was to be their sex toy, their live breathing blow up doll which they could twist and turn and manipulate into all sorts of positions. I was a bottomless hole to them, a flea pit which they could poke anytime they wanted. What they failed to comprehend was that they were going to by my sex toys, my slaves, my submissive partners. I was going to use them for what I needed and then poof, they'd magically disappear, I'd wave my wand, and they'd vanish.

The crescendo enlivened me, awakened my senses. From this moment on I smelled sex, saw sex, heard sex, tasted sex. I was the ideal embodiment of sex. I stripped off my skirt and my shirt. I was now exposed, left to be gawked at in my lacy black crotchless panties, bra, boots, and garter. My rigid nipples poked out from the holes cut out of my bra, revealing that I was thirsty, eager to be quenched by nature's juices. I began to dance as I sipped any schnaps, savoring the spicy nectar as I moved my body fluidly like the wind. I wagged my behind like a friendly puppy dog desperate for attention. I strutted over to Jeremiah and exchanged heated kisses, the stench of cinnamon and ale wafted through my nostrils. I then gently brushed my lips against Jeffreys almost melting his tongue with my fervent kisses. My plum brandy lipstick was smeared across their faces making them look like two mischievous youngsters guilty of getting into their mom's makeup kit. For a moment this image of them made me picture them as two rambunctious but impressionable boys, their scrawny but lithe bodies poured into their baggy stone washed overalls, their sun kissed curls dangling in their eyes. For a split second I sympathized with them, pitied their child within, felt for them as only a mother could.

Jeremiah and Jeffrey morphed into one being as I moved from one to the other spoiling them with bitter sweet kisses, my juicy kisses leaving a plan brandy trail from their necks to their stomach. I bent over giving them the signal that I wanted to be spanked. They took turns savagely slapping my ass, the stinging hand prints beginning to form into welts. They spit out obscenities, calling me dirty bitch, worthless whore, sexy slut, whatever came to their minds as their rough hands mauled and squeezed my ass. I knelt upon the bed, almost wheezing from all the stimulation and unclasped my bra. My swollen breasts poured fourth from out of my bra, the perfectly rounded melons balancing upon my chest. Both Jeremiah and Jeffrey dived into my breasts rubbing their stubbly faces against my vanilla scented skin. My skin burned but strangely tingled as they licked at my luscious breasts, ever so often straying to any nipples. Their hot breath warmed my skin as their kisses moved from my neck to my chest to my back.

I moved onto Jeremiah's lap and began to rock back and forth. I closed my eyes, but I could feel him eagerly unzip his pants and pull out his cock. He plunged his manhood into my moist pussy. I slithered and squirmed on his dick as he rammed it into me. He looked to be delirious as his eyes rolled back into his head, the pupils receding further each moment. I roughly rammed myself into him, putting all any aggression and anger into the moment. What would Carl think now if he saw two guys fucking me at the same time. *See, Carl I could be as slutty as any of those strippers.* Carl always said that if he caught me fucking anybody else he'd shove a broomstick up my cunt. Here I was now, taking pleasure in my selfish desires, using men as pieces of meat, exactly how they've used us for thousands of years, and Carl couldn't do shit. I moved onto Jeffrey, gasping as he thrust his fat cock into one. He whimpered like a wounded coyote as I dug my fingernails into his tattooed back, and then the images appeared; images of Ginger writhing on Carl, squirming on his lap like an impatient child, her large breasts brushing against his cheek; images of delicious blondes and exotic Asians straddling poles, their breasts rhythmically bouncing to the music. These were the images I struggled with, the images that got me into trouble, the images that made me lose my boyfriend, best friend, work friends. I was a tortured soul, forced to bear the weight of the world upon my tiny shoulders. I wiggled about on Jeffrey's lap like I imagined Ginger would, her back arched, her breasts protruding forward.

Jeremiah, envious of the extra attention I was paying to his cousin tightly squeezed my arms and forcefully pulled me off of Jeffrey, flipping me over and placing me on my hands and knees so that I was in doggie position. He entered me from behind, slamming his pelvis into me. I yelped like a stray dog, partly from pain and partly from pleasure as he jabbed his manhood into me. I suddenly felt feverish, and a sweet ripple washed over my body like a tide which ebbs in the night. My heart rate quickened, muscles tightened, and I could feel the blood rush to my clitoris, making it swell like a balloon. Our sticky flesh melted into one as I released euphoric moans.

We all remained frozen for a minute, the stagnant air making it almost impossible to breathe in a gulp of fresh air. I sat perfectly frozen, still as a statue, too terrified to make a movement. I suddenly felt nauseated, repulsed by my own actions. I had climaxed, reached the pinnacle of the evening and to top things off, my buzz was gone. I shut out their voices urging me to continue, their groping hands all over my naked body, their sticky lips kissing my stomach, my thighs, my breasts. I thought I could control how I felt. I thought I would feel this strong sense of empowerment, but instead I only felt sleazy. I felt ashamed, like that naive seven year old that pulled her little sister into the bedroom or that fifteen year old teenager spotted with hickeys. Why couldn't I be like those girls, spread my legs for nasty old men and not think twice. They remained detached, but I couldn't.

I could remember my last New Years Eve, another tear filled New Years Eve void of celebration. No joyous revelry to bring in the New Year. No noise makers, confetti, sloppy kisses, or hugs. There was only anger, resentment towards the world, and jealousy, that same green eyed monster that intrudes with my sanity. That night the green eyed monster was persistent, ready to snarl at the world with its sharp pointy fangs. I tried to hide him, bury him so deeply that he'd never find his way out, but he was adamant.

We're not supposed to judge others. Only God is given the authority to condemn for we are his children, and he is the father. We are taught to forgive our brothers and sisters, but I cannot. I silently attack, spew out insults in my head. The hatred in me practically bubbles, foams out at the mouth, but I hold my lips together. I tried to be good that night, but I couldn't. Anything at all could bring me back to that night at Roxy's, a flash of skin, a conversation, a stripper herself. This stripper was clothed, but it did not matter for she symbolized all that I came to despise. I had to impose the distance, stay far away. I couldn't face this girl, a girl that takes her clothes off for a living, a girl that profits by sheer exploitation. I persuaded myself not to look into her eyes. I was scared that her story would be revealed, that by staring into those soiled pools she'd expose me to her life. I couldn't bear to see those naked girls again, watch them strut down the stage, swirl round their poles, spread their legs for those nasty perverts. I didn't want to be pulled into those black holes of hers, for I'd never find my way out, but they were like magnets, pulling me in until I could no longer deny her presence. It was unfair that she was so happy, merrily skipping, her bounce annoyingly cheerful, wrapping her gangly arms around her boyfriend, showering him with kisses while I sat brokenhearted. I sat at the bar, physically by Carl's side, but mentally far far away enviously watching her. How could she be so happy while I was so miserable? She was the reason for my pain. She was the enemy.

I scowled at Carl every time she'd walk by. How dare she walk by shaking that little ass for the whinos that sit at the bar. It's enough that she gets all that attention at work, nasty perverts drooling over her body.

Just her presence infuriated me, transported me back to a place I had no desire of revisiting. While friends broke the news of engagements, while other couples laughed and kissed, I mourned. I grieved over the eventual passing of our relationship, how deep inside I knew that we had ended. Physically we were only inches apart, but emotionally we were a lifetime apart. I had grown to hate him. I hated him for how he had hurt me, for how he mad made me feel less than a woman. At one time it was just Carl and me, but no longer.

I looked at Jeremiah and then turned to look at Jeffrey and back at Jeremiah again. I glared at Jeremiah's hairy freckled forearms, the black panther identical to Carl's tattooed on his right upper arm, his tight white tank top, and his bony calloused hands he used to stroke his shaft while he waited for me to satisfy him. I then fixed my stare on Jeffrey, on his lean muscular legs, his smooth flat stomach and muscular pectorals. Unlike Jeremiah Jeffrey was hairless. His face was so handsome, almost a pretty boy with his piercing blue eyes and square jaw line. He also had that same black panther tattoo identical to Carl and Jeremiah. I remember Carl mentioning that he and a group of guys went to get the tattoos, proudly calling themselves the Wu Tang Clan. I just wasn't aware that Jeffrey and Jeremiah had been part of that gang. It was sort of a shame to have to kill two well-built country boys with sex appeal. At what point did I lose my heart? When did I forget how to forgive? When did I lose my conscious?

"Girl! What are you doing? Come on! We're not paying you to sit here!" Jeremiah hollered

I hated that tone of voice, how he used that chauvinistic tone to get what he wanted. I wanted to attack, but my nerves were frazzled. I never really had planned anything out. Their dicks looked like two slimy maggots, two disgusting greasy larvae scuttling through the trash. I remembered that women's article I read on the internet about self defense that said to always aim for the groin, knees, neck, or eyes. I had to distract them though. *Yes, distraction is the key*, I thought to myself.

I dived forward planting a warm wet kiss upon Jeffrey's lips. Our tongues melted together, like chocolate warmed in a pants pocket, gooey chocolate kisses. Jeremiah came from behind and tenderly kissed my shoulders and back. It was as if they were silently rivaling for my attention. I grabbed Jeremiah's cock from behind and cupped my hand around it, moving my hand up and down, faster and faster.

"That's it baby." Jeremiah contentedly moaned.

I reached into my garter for the straight razor blade and quickly pulled it out discreetly switching hands for a moment so that the hand doing all the work now held the straight razor. Up and down, up and down; I kept moving his hand over his penis, so scared to slice. They were absolutely clueless to the straight razor tucked in between my thumb and index finger. I couldn't keep going though. I wasn't going to give them that satisfaction. I was the one in power. I had gotten off, not them. My fingers were slippery, but I managed to gain control of the blade. I jabbed the blade into the lower end of his penis and sliced. I was shocked to see that despite how effortlessly I had sliced that a moment later the penis lay in the palm of my hand, and then the screaming began. At first Jeremiah was in shock, just staring at that hollow space between his legs, that hollow cavity we, as women, are forced to live with.

"Oh my God! You crazy bitch. My dick! My dick! My fucking dick!" he screamed clutching what was left of his precious jewels.

It was as if with his screams he was creating a musical composition, like he was singing in an opera with that falsetto voice. How ironic that they use to use castrated males to sing in the church choir when women were not allowed to sing, and now here was Jeremiah repeating history. He was reaching soprano, alto ranges, feminine squeals he would never dream of reaching if he still possessed a penis.

Jeffrey was taking a calmer more dazed approach as he drunkenly staggered around the room trying to find his pants and mumbling she's a nutty bitch over and over. I didn't know what to do. Jeremiah was sitting on the bed weeping, his heartrending howls stirring up chills within me, and Jeffrey was clumsily staggering round the room trying to find his pants, a shirt, any article of clothing that would cover his dearly beloved penis. I picked up the chair sitting beside me, held it high above my arms and swung it directly at Jeffrey's head, the impact of the hit knocking him out immediately. There Jeffrey lay, sprawled across the floor like a peacefully sleeping child, unconscious and unaware of the fate which lay before him. Jeremiah continued to cry, cupping his hands together and praying to the lord for a savior. The prayers rolled off his lips as he rocked back and forth.

"No ones coming to save you Jeremiah." I uttered as I walked over to where he sat.

"Please, God! Someone! Help me! Please, give me my dick. They can still save it! Please!" He begged, choking on his own tears.

"You might as well stop your crying." I annoyingly answered "I'm not giving it back." I said dangling the bloody phallus like a piece of bait in front of his face. "You need to learn how to use it properly. Maybe then I'll give it back."

"What the fuck are you talking about?" he struggled to spit

out in between his tearful sobs.

"I'm talking about you and the lousy attitude you have when it comes to women. You could have avoided all this if you'd only keep those silly hormones of yours under control. You just had to go to the Palace, didn't you. What is it about strip clubs that guys like, huh? I once talked to this guy that said it doesn't matter, the point is that they're naked. It's like you don't care if they're good looking or trashy. All you care about is that they are naked. Do you like that they spread their legs open, their big breasts bouncing, their ass shaking. I want to know what it is!" I said raising my voice as I continued to ramble. "I've lost everything because of guys like you. Was it worth it? Was it worth one night of trashy whores stuffing their tits in your face?

By this point in time it felt like I was screaming at Carl. Jeremiah's features twisted, his freckles faded, his eyebrows thickened. It looked like Carl but a ridiculously exaggerated cartoon version, and my judgment at this point was becoming so distorted, partly due to the alcohol, and partly to the sheer excitement of it all that I didn't know who was who.

"Did you enjoy it, huh? Fucking that slut Ginger? Was it worth losing me, lusting after strange tits and ass?"

"What are you talking about? I don't know any Giiiinger!" he screamed, his eyes fixated on the dead fish I swung from my fingertips.

God, how badly I wanted to die. Every minute we are living we are in all reality dying. Every new year brings in a fresh liver spot, a wrinkle, a gray hair until we are a shriveled up rendition of our formerly youthful self. We breathe in the contaminated air which pollutes our lungs, get baked by the sun's rays until we are burnt, drink in the contaminates causing infections. We revert back to our infancy, a time when we were helpless, completely dependent on our care givers, but who would look after me? I imagined myself sitting in a nursing home, being spoon fed tapioca pudding, having my diapers changed, or maybe some sick nursing assistant would rape me, take advantage of me in the bathtub. Perhaps if I had something I could aspire to, the promise of paradise, then I would look forward to growing older. Jeremiah was dying anyway just like the rest of us. I was only advancing the process much more rapidly.

His crying stirred up absolutely no emotion in me. In fact it only annoyed me, grated on my nerves like a colicky infant. Jeremiah was hunched over, a blubbering puddle pleading with me to salvage his manhood. I had come too far to just give him back his penis and be on my way. Why give him a chance to experience happiness again when I have lost my chance to feel genuine contentment in this lifetime? Men have been known to have their penises chopped off and then profited from it, used the agonizing experience to become famous, use women, star in porn movies. There was no way I was going to let these perverts take advantage of what had happened to them. I had to do something quickly

I walked over to where he lay weeping and began to raise my leg, kicking him in the crotch again and again, so many times that my feet went numb, over and over so that he lay crouched over, his hands guarding the mangled bleeding depression. I kicked and kicked, just like Carl had kicked me, when he thrust his steel toed boot into my stomach, when I rolled myself into a ball to thwart off the never ending blows.

"Fucking piece of shit!" I screamed at him, spit flying from the comers of my mouth and spraying him in the face.

"Please, stop! Please. Please." Jeremiah begged, his brown eyes pleading with me, searching for a spark of compassion, a morsel of sanity, anything within me that would make it stop.

It wasn't going to stop though. That is what Jeremiah did not understand. He was my target. All my was directed at him. In my eyes Jeremiah was Carl, James, Paul Potter, every pervert I had ever known mixed together and rolled up into a hodgepodge of sordidness. Every serial killer had their target, despised one kind of being and went after that being, torturing them until they were dead. For some odd reason everyone else was immune to their hate, but that poor unlucky victim, the target of their hatred had to be killed, extinguished to quiet the voices within so that killer could experience peace for a moment, a dysfunctional harmony which in his world equated to heaven. Some killers chose children, other chose boys, some chose brunettes while others wanted blondes. Some even targeted the elderly or disabled, anyone who was more vulnerable than they were. To me this was sick. I would never put a child, a woman, an elderly person in danger. No, I was after the physically powerful race, the smut of society, men responsible for keeping strip clubs open, porn thriving, rape acceptable. Since when were these kind of men vital to humanity? To me these men were litter, the trash which needed to be cleaned from this dysfunctional society. Through the hatred, peace would prevail. Jeremiah tilted back his head as he sobbed, the tears streaming down the side of his face and wetting his curls.

"*I* give up. I give up. Lord, if I'm meant to be, then save me. Please. I pray to the lord." He mumbled.

"The lord is not going to save you. Why would the lord save someone like you? Do you go to church? The only time you even pray to God is when you think your life is in danger. You don't care about God. Do you think God can really help you? Do you think God is listening to some pervert that wastes all his money at a tittie bar?

Jeremiah wouldn't look at me. His head was still tilted back, his adam's apple throbbing. I raised my arm, the one holding the straight blade and swung it at Jeremiah's neck, slicing his adam's apple open. Blood spurted out as I released the blade. He dropped his head forward and fell back to the floor with a heavy clomp. I circled his corpse to assess the damage. He resembled one of those realistic looking wax figures they have at museums. His blood stained tank top was pulled up around his chest, and his hands were still cupped over his testicles. I couldn't even look at his neck, the jugular vein split in half, the puddle of dried up blood under his head. His eyes were still open, giving the illusion that he was still alive, but he was still, resting for all eternity. I couldn't hate the man now. How could I? He was only a shell, the casing which once housed a very sick man, a perverted twisted scum bag, but no longer. I knew I could breathe easier realizing that this planet was rid of one more piece of shit pervert, but there was still one to go. I walked over to Jeffrey, laying peacefully and scrutinized him carefully for about a minute, and I realized I couldn't do it. Was I really this monster who killed people? Who was I?

I walked over to the bed, grabbed my clothes and ran out of that hotel room, ran and ran and ran until I couldn't run anymore, and then it hit me. I was going to get caught anyways. Why not burn down the strip club?

CHAPTER 46

Later that night:

I sat back on a tree stump and watched the flickering flames dance excitedly. Through the smoky haze of the blaze an ethereal silhouette straddled its legs around the silver plated pole and twirled into the ground. The nakedness, dirty indulgences, and temptations buried itself in the cavernous firestorm. The ghostly image put to death my obsessions, my jealousy, my fixation with all I deemed evil in this world. Her lovely golden mane sizzled in the fires, blackening until the crispy singed strands broke off and descended into the hellhole. I softly laughed. I did not care how crazy they thought I was. I knew that I was doing the right thing. These girls, these messengers of voyeurism basking in the wicked rays danced with the devil in life and now their ghostly images would waltz with the devil straight into their graves, into Satan's fiery pit of glory.

At last I felt free, not bound by the restrictions I imposed upon myself. Along with Roxy's the memories would be reduced to ashes, expunged from my mind. My memories would now be fuel for the devil, a playground of memoirs for satan to amuse himself. The cracked leather booths reeking of cheap aftershave, the flimsy wooden tables, the sharp sound of asses being smacked, the echoing harmonies, the sadistic laughter and applause; all of these would vanish. I'm sure that some sick fuck will have bigger and better plans for building a new one, but for now I was satisfied.

I did not know where I was going. If I had to I'd drive forever, drive away from the demons that inhabited my mind for so long. I slowly stood up and walked to the car, the melody of *Tuesdays Gone With the Wind* echoing through my mind. Through the smoke, I became an indistinguishable shape, blending in with the trees swaying in the wind. The sirens from the city could be heard sadly wailing as I hummed my song *Tuesdays Gone With the Wind.*

> Train roll on, on down the line.
> Won't you please take me far away?
> Now I feel the wind blow outside my door.
> Means I'm leaving my woman behind.
> Tuesday's Gone With the Wind.

OVER ON THE EAST SIDE

My woman's gone with the wind.
And I don't know where I'm going
I just want to be left alone.
Well, when this train ends I'll try again.
But I'm leaving my woman at home.
Tuesday's gone with the wind.
Tuesday's gone with the wind.
Tuesday's gone with the wind.
My woman's gone with the wind.
Train roll on many miles from my home,
See, I'm riding my blues away.
Tuesday, you see, she had to be free.
But somehow I've got to carry on.
And from that moment on I was free!